GOOD TOWN

MARY LOUISE WELLS

To my father's sister, my Brooklyn aunt,
Doris Mary Wells O'Hara
"a keen intellect with a chic urbane appearance"

Preface

When my mother was seventy-three years old in 2001, she wrote a memoir of her time growing up in Guttstadt, East Prussia—a centuries-old German territory. She came of age during the rise of Nazism and World War II and their aftermath. The stories were of my grandparents, aunts, uncles, and, of course, my own mother. Many of the relatives I had met, but others I knew only from their black-and-white photographs. Those old photos hung framed in our foyer arrayed next to a woodcut of the historic crest of Guttstadt. It was a family memorial—with love and no judgment.

I often thought that one day I would write a coming-of-age novel based on my mother's memoir, but decades later when I finally started on the book, I learned something that changed its direction. I discovered that my grandfather, who once had been a local leader in the Zentrum Party and an opponent of Nazism, eventually became the Nazi government's local agricultural leader, the Ortsbauernführer. So many questions came to mind. Why would an educated, kind, and deeply religious man—one who had actively opposed Hitler—capitulate and become a cog in the wheel of the Reich? How would he live with himself and his choice? How would he feel as his Jewish neighbors and business partners were sent to their deaths? How would a child respond to learning one thing in church and in the home and living another reality as she walked the streets of her town? What would it be like to lose brothers and sons to a war you didn't believe in? And what would a family feel as their lives fell apart never to be the same again?

Maps

These maps are not intended to bemoan the loss of German territory or culture, but simply to show locations in the book and the changed geography over time.

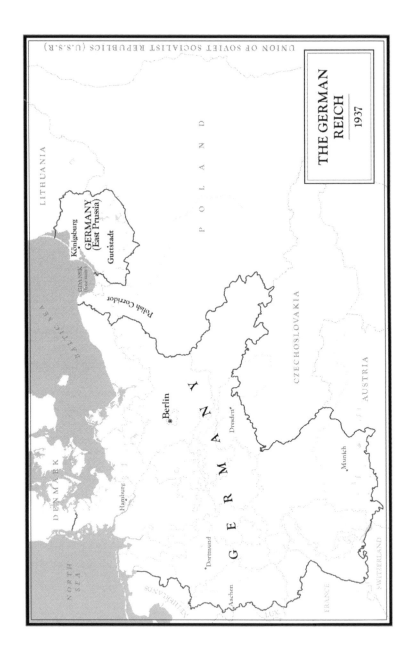

THE GERMAN
REICH
1937

UNION OF SOVIET SOCIALIST REPUBLICS (U.S.S.R.)

LITHUANIA

POLAND

GERMANY
(East Prussia)

Königsberg

Gutristadt

GDANSK
(free state)

Polish Corridor

BALTIC SEA

DENMARK

NORTH
SEA

CZECHOSLOVAKIA

AUSTRIA

Berlin

Dresden

Munich

Hamburg

Dortmund

Aachen

NETHERLANDS

BEL.

LUX.

FRANCE

SWITZERLAND

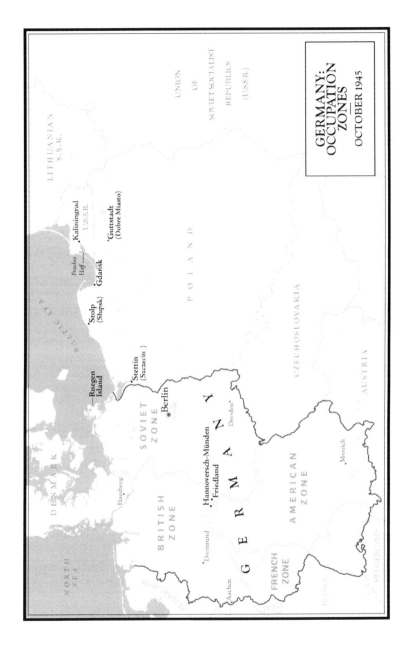

GERMANY:
OCCUPATION
ZONES
—
OCTOBER 1945

Chapter One

Margarete

She always said yes. Even if the question wasn't about a trip to town, Margarete answered yes. She was the agreeable child.

But an errand to Guttstadt with her father offered excitement away from the daily life of school, church, and chores. Albert also jumped at the chance—though he was a boy and three years older, so his trips were more interesting and profitable. Their father would take Albert to his business meetings, which sometimes ended with an hour of gentlemanly, low-stakes card playing, and he would let Albert keep the winnings.

When Albert arrived home, he would open his palm and show Margarete, who smiled in anticipation at what the pennies might bring one day. She alone knew that he tucked them away in an old sugar tin behind a beam in the barn. There the money was safe from their three bullying big brothers and three annoying baby sisters. Over time the pennies would grow into reichsmarks, and Albert said he would share the riches with her.

That day, the horses' hooves clopped against the hardened ground, providing the rhythm to nature's orchestra where rustling crops accompanied songbirds. If they had lived in a city, they would drive an automobile and miss the sounds of summer. Instead, they traveled their usual way by horse and carriage.

Margarete looked at her father, who sat with the posture of a former cavalryman and guided the horses with subtle changes of his hands. Simple signals from master to beast navigated the gleaming black landau down the road. Josef rarely used his voice to communicate directions, and he never laid a whip on them. This was true for every animal under his care, though horses were his pride and joy.

A matched pair, Sonne and Mond were appropriately named as their velvety brown hides reflected the shine of the heavens, day or night. Both wore the single elk antler of a Trakehner brand on their left haunch. The giant animals strode ahead of the carriage as if they knew their place in their owner's world and their owner's place in the world around him.

Before a train could be seen, the grinding rumble of metal began to muffle all other noise. As the carriage neared blocked railroad tracks, Josef brought the horses to a halt while a passenger train passed by. Soldiers peered out of the train windows, studying a region they had only seen on a map. An officer stood outside the final car smoking a cigarette, and he acknowledged Josef and Margarete with a polite nod.

When the train passed, Herr Radau trotted out of his barn on the other side of the tracks. The Radau family scraped by farming their small parcel and operating the railroad gates. In their house, a telegraph machine alerted them to oncoming trains. Herr Radau waved at the carriage.

"*Guten Tag*, Herr Haupt."

"Guten Tag," Josef answered, tipping his hat.

Herr Radau pressed down on the short end of the long white beam blocking the road and raised it until it was perpendicular to the tracks. When he moved to the other side's beam, Josef commented, "It seems the gates are always closed lately."

"It's easier these days to keep them down." Herr Radau went about his work for a moment before he stole a glance at Josef. "The *Wehrmacht* is busy."

At Herr Radau's mention of the military, Margarete looked at her father for a response. Herr Radau was the sort of man who saw things going on around him that caused him to question. Josef Haupt was the sort of man privy to the answers.

"Indeed," was all Josef offered in reply.

With that answer in Margarete's mind, her eyes drifted down the long line of railroad tracks to the west. The military came from that direction, but all she saw was farmland and hills that looked like the Haupt estate. Somewhere beyond, the tracks led to Berlin and the rest of Germany. She wondered if she might ever see it. On the radio, Adolf Hitler said East Prussia would be reunified with the rest of Germany and the German Empire would be one again.

Margarete wasn't interested in the other side of the tracks toward the east. She knew what lay there—just more East Prussia until the border with Poland. Farther on, the Union of Soviet Socialist Republics began. No one Margarete knew referred to that country by its chosen name. It remained enemy Russia.

After the carriage crossed the tracks and they were far enough from Herr Radau's earshot, Margarete asked the man's question herself. "Papa, why are there so many soldiers here?"

Josef kept his eyes fixed on the road ahead. "Security, of course. East Prussia is isolated, and we have an enemy on our doorstep. It's precautionary."

Margarete silently accepted the good reason, though she always wanted more answers. They were still a kilometer away from town. No one could hear, so now was the time.

"Will there be a war?"

Margarete studied her father as she waited for an answer. While not in his Sunday best, he wore a finely tailored suit and freshly steamed and shaped hat for the venture into town. He kept his head shaved close as the older men and younger boys always did. Margarete's mother said it was because young boys were always dirty and older men lost their hair. The lack of hair made Josef's eyes even more prominent. Margarete believed everything those deep-set, dark eyes told her, though she knew they rarely told her everything.

Josef's attention remained ahead as he considered a response to his nine-year-old daughter's precocious questions. Worrying she might be scolded for speaking as she did, Margarete fidgeted with one of the light brown braids that hung down her back. She didn't know what was going on in the world, but she was aware things were different from when she was little.

Josef turned and met her gaze. "I'm impressed by your questions. You also know to ask only when we're alone, but you shouldn't worry. Germany and Poland have a peace treaty, and Russia is far away."

Margarete nodded, knowing that was all the information she would receive because they were nearing town.

The giant red bell tower of Guttstadt's Gothic *Domkirche* appeared in the distance, rising thirty stories into the sky. Built when the town was still governed by the Teutonic Knights, the ornate basilica matched the red brick of the medieval walls that once had encircled the town. One of the wall's giant towers remained, and storks had nested there for centuries, caring for their young and guarding the town. Beyond the walls, the Alle River divided into the *Grosse Alle* and the *Kleine Alle* before it rejoined itself, protecting much of Guttstadt between its waters. The *Dom* was the town's magnificent centerpiece. There were other churches for the Lutherans and the Eastern Orthodox and a synagogue for the Jews, but the Catholic church was the pride of the community and a symbol for Guttstadt. Everyone Margarete knew agreed the town lived up to its name. It was indeed a good town.

As they passed by the Dom, more people came into view.

Guttstadt was a small burg with a few thousand citizens. Hardly Berlin, yet to Margarete, it was a city, while the closest real city, Allenstein, felt like a metropolis. Margarete's mother, Dorothea, would take the train there for her finer shopping that no seamstress or merchant in Guttstadt could sew or sell.

As her father parked the carriage in front of Kunigk's Inn, the normal clatter of horses, wagons, and conversations surrounded them, but Margarete focused on her job. She hopped out of the carriage, and Josef handed her the reins to secure to the hitching post.

While Margarete's attention was squarely on tying a proper knot, she heard her father call out in a friendly voice, "Herr Katz. *Was ist los?* Why are you sweeping the street?"

Margarete looked up to see Herr Katz in the middle of the street. He was the patriarch of a family of grain merchants and other businessmen. It was an odd sight to see the distinguished man in his fine clothes with a broom in the middle of the street. The Haupt family were farmers. No matter how well-to-do or well-dressed or well-educated they were, they performed manual labor. This wasn't true of the Katz family and certainly not its most senior member.

To Margarete's eyes, the broom didn't even match Herr Katz. Aaron Katz's broom should have been new, maybe painted a shiny red. This old broomstick was broken at the top, jagged with splinters, and at its base, the straw was ragged. Josef would have told Margarete to throw it onto the kindling pile long ago.

Yet there was Herr Katz sweeping the street, which looked no dirtier than on any other day. Her father had asked a good question. Why was Herr Katz out there?

As Josef walked toward Herr Katz, the old man didn't raise his head to acknowledge him. Margarete wondered if he had become deaf because she had seen her father and Herr Katz talk many times.

"Aaron, did you break something? If the street must be swept, your grandsons should do it for you." Josef stood with one hand on his hip and gestured to the road. "This isn't your place."

Despite the personal plea, Herr Katz ignored him and kept sweeping. Margarete sensed something was wrong and scanned the sidewalks. Everyone went about their business, paying no attention to the scene. This might have been normal if it were a different set of men standing in the street, but not her father and Herr Katz. Both men had been members of the town council and were leaders in the Catholic and Jewish communities. People should have been taking notice; storekeepers might even stand in their doorways to observe the event. Instead, everyone moved purposefully along or remained inside and out of view.

Margarete searched for people noticing her father and Herr Katz and only found two men at the corner of Adolf Hitler Strasse and Dom Strasse. She didn't recognize them, except for their Gestapo uniforms—jackboots, earthen gray jodhpurs, and belted jackets. Margarete remembered when only the local police and soldiers lived in town. The police were helpful neighbors, and everyone had at least one family member in the military. Soldiers were like older brothers, giving children pats on the head and candy. The Gestapo gave disapproving scowls with one hand on their guns; no one chatted with them.

Margarete clenched the reins of the horse in terror as she watched the Gestapo step down from the curb in unison and walk across the street. She wanted to rush out, grab her father's arm, and drag him to the carriage and off to the safety of the farm. But she knew she must stay put. The situation was too dangerous.

Josef turned from Herr Katz with a nonplussed brow. Margarete realized he must not have seen the Gestapo watching him, nor did he know they were now making their way toward him. Desperate to save him, she could only stamp her feet, urging her father to hurry.

The voice of the taller officer rose from a few yards away. "Herr Haupt, may we speak with you for a moment, please?"

Josef shifted his head toward the voice, his features and

manner unchanging. "Of course," he answered as if they had asked for a cigarette.

Margarete held her breath as she watched her father switch direction and head over to the police officers. They spoke in soft voices, leaving her to wonder what was said. What had drawn the Gestapo's attention?

She considered the scene again and realized her father had spoken to a Jew. Reich propaganda discouraged it, and it was looked down upon by many, but it wasn't a crime. Margarete thought of the anti-Jewish fervor as just another part of the incoherent world she lived in.

The Church taught them to follow the Golden Rule, but Hitler railed against the Catholic Church. Regardless of what Hitler might say on the radio, the Haupts and all of their family and friends remained good Catholics. Margarete couldn't imagine her father ever treating another person poorly or ignoring an elder townsman like Herr Katz.

After all, who would the Haupts sell their grain to if not Herr Katz? Margarete was accustomed to her family being above suspicion even during these suspicious times. The Gestapo had been friendly. Maybe they were speaking to her father about nothing.

Less than a minute later, Josef turned his back to the Gestapo, and both sides walked in opposite directions. As Josef's expression remained placid, Margarete breathed deeply, filling her body with oxygen and relief. There had been nothing to worry about after all, so she expected her father to announce their first stop in town.

Instead, Josef came close to her and placed a hand on her shoulder. His strong hand warmed her arm through her summer dress. When the grip tightened, his solemn eyes searched her own.

"Margarete," whispered Josef. "I need you to walk home. The carriage and horses will be safe here. When you arrive home, you should say I had an unexpected meeting, so you came home early. You're not to tell anyone, including your mother, about Herr Katz. Don't worry. I'll tell her later."

It took a moment for Margarete to grasp the ramifications of what her father was asking. Could he be asking her to lie and, most shockingly, lie to her mother? It was completely contradictory to his character, and her mother would be irate. Dorothea Haupt could smell a lie on her children before they even said it aloud.

Margarete asked in a low voice, "Papa, what—"

"No questions. This is all you need to know. You will say nothing and finish your schoolwork. Do you hear me?"

Margarete feared the worst, despite Josef's admonition not to worry. Something bad was happening. Determined to be brave and follow her father's orders, she stood taller. "I'll do just as you say."

A small smile crept over Josef's lips. "*Danke*. Now please go home."

After a nod, Margarete walked toward home, stunned by the last few minutes. Had it really happened? She looked over her shoulder and saw the horses obediently standing where she had tied them. She twisted a little farther so she could see her father one more time.

Josef crossed the street, not hurriedly or slowly, just his usual pace. He headed in the direction of any number of places where he might shop or have an errand. Trying to accept that things were all right, she looked ahead, but doubt took hold again. With a last glance behind her, she recognized her father might also be on the shortest path to the Gestapo's headquarters.

Chapter Two

Josef

No one stopped to greet Josef or even tip their hat as he walked down the street. He shifted his eyes to the right and left, peering at the storefronts where closed doors kept patrons and storekeepers inside. The streets were empty except for danger. Everyone was still too scared by the Gestapo to venture outside.

Confident he could straighten things out, Josef kept worry at bay until he thought of Margarete. She had stared at him with the same marine blue eyes as his wife, but hers were filled with fear. She knew he was under suspicion, so he looked behind him in case she needed reassurance nothing would be done to him.

Far in the distance, he saw his oldest yet still little girl in her dress and cuffed white socks nearing the town wall. With eight children, Josef had sons and daughters of all personalities, and luckily, empathetic and dutiful Margarete had been with him that day. She walked to the safety of the farm with the Dom looming protectively over her.

As Josef turned his attention to the road ahead of him, he saw two men step out of the barbershop. Dressed in nondescript suits with small swastika pins on their lapels, they were unremarkable but for their size. They were thick and tall—as large as his eldest son Paul at nearly two meters. Though he had never laid eyes on them before, he assumed he was being followed by plainclothes Gestapo. Throughout the Reich, undercover Gestapo far outnumbered those in uniform. Secret police were best kept a secret.

Their Bavarian accents revealed they were officers from western Germany purportedly to train local police departments in Prussia. In reality, the Nazi Party was infiltrating local law enforcement. The Gestapo was under the paramilitary *Schutzstaffel*, so the SS now had eyes and ears in every town.

Despite the Gestapo trailing behind him, Josef held his head high as he approached the police station. For the town's Reich outpost, the police station was another example of Guttstadt's quaint architecture. The structures varied among combinations of mullioned windows, gables, and entries. Exposed brick often matched the Dom, or it was plastered and painted red, yellow, gray, or brown. Only the roofs matched. Covered in red tiles, each roof was angled with an exaggerated slant to ease the heavy burden of snow. There was one identifying detail that the Gestapo had added to the old police building—a foreboding iron gate now fronted it.

Outside the gate, two officers stood guard on either side. Josef attempted to make eye contact, but both men looked past him, seeming to communicate with his minders. After receiving a signal Josef couldn't see, the guards moved aside, though still at attention.

The lobby of the station was quiet as usual. There was never much crime in Guttstadt, but now the town was governed by an authoritarian state. Unless it was staged on the street for the public to see and fear, police activity went on behind closed doors. Interrogations and summary judgments weren't for public consumption.

A uniformed man stood with his back to the entrance as he filed documents in a wall of mailboxes. Josef recognized the withered hand moving papers and envelopes as belonging to someone who had worked on Josef's farm. Otto was the only son of one of Dorothea's former housemaids who was a widow. When he was younger, he had earned extra money for his mother by doing small chores for Josef. Otto could only do so much because his delicate burned skin barely covered the bones of his hand.

Josef wasn't surprised to see him in a desk job or in a Gestapo uniform. It was a decent-paying job for someone with limited education who couldn't work with his hands.

But when Otto turned to see who had walked in the door, he was surprised. He cocked his head and smiled. "Herr Haupt. Guten Tag. How are you?"

"Guten Tag to you, Otto," answered Josef, removing his hat.

He had no intention of explaining what had brought him into the Gestapo headquarters. Nor was it necessary. Within seconds, Otto saw the goons behind Josef, and he snapped to attention, saluting them with his scarred hand.

Josef turned to acknowledge the men who had followed him. They stood ramrod straight, with their chests puffed out, insisting on reverence as they accepted Otto's salute. Unimpressed with their faux militarism, Josef said nothing.

Down a hallway, a door cracked, breaking the silence. One pair of jackboots and then another stepped through the doorway. As they neared, Josef identified them by their uniforms and insignia as SS lieutenants.

His mind ran through the possible scenarios of what might happen next. He had done nothing wrong by speaking to Aaron Katz. He would explain himself without apology. He showed respect to the authorities, and only when necessary did he pay lip service to their goals.

"Guten Tag, lieutenants," he said with a slight bow of his head.

The lower-ranked second lieutenant snapped his arm up into an angled salute at such a speed that a rush of air blew the sandy blond hair on his forehead. "*Heil Hitler!*"

In unison, Otto and the other plainclothes officers copied the salute with a resounding "Heil Hitler."

The ranking officer also raised his arm, though he didn't speak. His commanding glare informed Josef he must answer the greeting.

Josef hated the silly spectacle of Nazism. Thirty years older than these men, he had lived most of his life under a monarchy. He had fought for *Kaiser* and country. At no time had German citizens said "Hail Kaiser" as if the Kaiser were Caesar Augustus himself. Yet this was an accommodation he now must make. He raised his arm, answering with a firm "Heil Hitler."

After they lowered their arms, the first lieutenant spoke with a Swabian accent. "Herr Haupt, I'm *Obersturmführer* Bernhard Pehl, and this is my comrade, *Sturmführer* Mathäus Elsner. Please follow me."

"Certainly, Obersturmführer," said Josef.

Lieutenant Pehl turned on his heel and strode down the hall. Before Josef followed, he glanced at Otto, who still stood at perfect attention. Otto shifted his eyes to meet his gaze, and Josef sensed the young man's worry for him.

With the SS henchmen's footsteps marching behind Josef, they passed the doorway that the lieutenants had exited minutes earlier. He peered into the room and saw a large desk of glossy wood surrounded by comfortable chairs with photos, maps, and distinctions on the wall. If he was going to have a conversation with the police, it was the sort of office he would expect to be ushered into.

Instead, the lieutenant led him to a spartan room farther down the hall. Nothing decorated the walls except for a lone photo of Hitler. A small table sat in the middle of the room, with one wooden chair on one side and two on the other. This was a room where you brought criminals, not recent members of the city council.

"*Bitte*, have a seat," said Lieutenant Pehl, touching the single chair.

As Josef did as he was told, he felt all eyes staring at him. He looked ahead and saw the photo of Hitler also appeared to be trained on him. He focused on the tyrant's black eyes, and a prescient memory came to mind that he had long forgotten.

Five years before, he had been at that same intersection with Aaron Katz as they had minutes before, though in 1932, Adolf Hitler Strasse was Post Strasse. Josef had stood admiring a new election poster of the Zentrum Party pasted on a building wall. There had never been a more critical election since Germany had abandoned its monarchy.

The dark poster depicted a castle with Nazis in brown shirts waving flags as they stormed the gates. A small Hitler stood in the distance. The words *"BRÜNING—DER FREIHEIT, UND ORDNUNG, LETZTES BOLLWERK, WAHRHEIT, FREIHEIT, RECHT"* covered the castle's tower. A banner waved above the castle with the words *"Wählt Zentrum, Liste 4."*

As he stared at the poster, Aaron approached him.

"Josef, shouldn't you be in your fields planting? How am I to buy and sell your harvest if it doesn't get in the ground? I'm relying on you."

Josef grinned at his business partner. "I'll get back." He pointed toward the poster. "We had a party meeting. What do you think?"

Aaron stepped toward the poster to examine it and read aloud, "Vote Center. Heinrich Brüning—the last bulwark of freedom and order. Truth, freedom, rights."

With a step backward, Aaron shook his head. "Honestly? I think it's naive with 30 percent unemployment in the cities. People don't care about freedom and civility when they can't feed their family. Hitler is promising bread for children and work for parents."

"But people see how the Nazis act. The preposterous things Hitler says. We're no longer a monarchy. People know better."

"They do?"

"We must appeal to their better angels."

"Better angels? Whose angels?" asked Aaron with a dark chuckle. "Almost every party in this election has something terrible about Jews in its platform."

"People want a scapegoat for their troubles," Josef said with a sympathetic sigh. "Jews are convenient. I'm sorry."

Aaron gave him a wistful smile; they both knew Josef was glossing over a graver situation. "Well, you Catholics will have my vote. I must go. Give my regards to Dorothea."

"And mine to Rosa," he replied with a tip of his hat.

Josef was jolted back into the present day when Pehl announced, "I'll let Lieutenant Elsner begin."

Leaning over the table, Elsner rested his clasped hands upon it. Two lines creased in his forehead between his eyes as he said, "I'm sure you know why you're here."

"Actually, I don't."

"Are you a fool?"

Josef took a moment to formulate a reply that was polite but truthful. "*Nein*, Lieutenant. I was asked by the officers to report to the headquarters, so I've complied."

"You defied Gestapo orders!" shouted Elsner. "That Jew—"

"In a moment," said Pehl, raising his hand. "We need Herr Haupt to introduce himself to us first."

Josef touched his chest and chuckled. "The Gestapo knows everyone. You may know me better than I know myself."

A moment lapsed as Pehl's lips turned up into a pursed smile. "But I'm new to the area. Do go on."

Josef swallowed as he absorbed their lie. He was sure the lieutenants had read his file, so they intended to trap him somehow. With a modulated voice, he began, "My name is Josef Haupt. I own a farm outside of town. Until last year, I sat on the city council. During the Great War, I was a sergeant in the cavalry division of the *Regiment der Gardes du Corps*, stationed in Potsdam. I fought on the Western Front in Belgium."

"An officer in the Kaiser's personal guard of select Prussians," said Pehl with approval.

Elsner glared at Josef. "Since coming to East Prussia, I think you people long for the backward days of the Kaiser."

"Why is that?" asked Josef.

"You've been cut off from the rest of Germany for so long you haven't modernized." Elsner scrunched his face as if he had eaten something sour. "You act as if the Kaiser is still on the throne and you are the chosen people of the kingdom. You have more allegiance to Prussia than to Germany."

There was some truth there, but Josef deflected. "We have a centuries-old military tradition. Many Wehrmacht officers are East Prussian."

"You're a proud veteran. Why do your children not attend Hitler Youth meetings?" asked Pehl.

Josef found a smile that he didn't feel. If they tracked his children's uneven attendance at Hitler Youth meetings, the Nazis' file on him was thorough. They knew he didn't want his children too involved in the organization, but Josef gave his usual excuse.

"Paul is too old. Franz attends when he can, but for all of my children, chores on the farm take precedence over everything but school."

"You have farmworkers. You're well-off. Why do your children need to work?" asked Pehl.

"Some of my boys will have an estate of their own one day, and the girls will be farmers' wives. Keeping the farm productive is critical for everyone. We are providing for the *Vaterland*." When the lieutenants didn't respond, he knew he had gained some ground with them. "I do need to get back to the farm. I was only in town for a quick errand. May I leave now?"

"Nein." Pehl's eyes narrowed.

Josef locked eyes with the first lieutenant, now understanding his predicament. Normally, his place in the town's society privileged him to do as he pleased, but these men didn't know him and saw him as a dissident.

Despite his concerns, he remained poised. "What else would you like to discuss?"

"Let's return the conversation to where Lieutenant Elsner started. Why did you take the side of a Jew over the Reich?"

"With all due respect, Lieutenant Pehl, I believe we have a misunderstanding. When I asked Herr Katz why he was sweeping the street, I didn't know he had been directed to do so by the police. If I had known, I wouldn't have interfered. I believe you've heard enough about me to know I don't question authority."

"Why do you care if a Jew is sweeping the street?" asked Elsner. "He's scum."

"Herr Katz's family and my family have done business for generations," he said with a shrug. "We served on the city council together. It was unusual that he was sweeping the street. If he spilled something, someone else in his family should see to it."

Pehl tapped his finger against the table as if his patience was waning. "Your family has been swindled by this Jew for generations, and yet you worry he's in the street?"

Josef raised his hands, making light of their argument. "But we have treated each other fairly. This is how Guttstadt has lived for centuries despite our differences—German, Pole, Jew, Catholic, Lutheran."

"You're a political man. You understand times have changed," said Pehl, leaning back in his chair as if he was settling into the conversation.

"I don't involve myself in politics."

"No, you don't anymore, but you did for years. You were a member of the Center Party," said Pehl.

"I was a member."

"You were even a delegate to Zentrum's executive committee," said Elsner. "And now five years after Zentrum collapsed you still haven't joined the *Führer*'s National Socialist Party. Why not?"

Pehl gave Josef a knowing smile. "Or do you call us Nazis?"

"As you know, most of the Ermland is Catholic," he deflected. "Zentrum was the Catholic party."

"Yet after five years?" Pehl pressed on. "Why do you not follow the Führer?"

It was a question to which everyone in the room knew the answer. He was a large landowner and educated, but most of all, it was because he was a devout Catholic. Only three months earlier on Palm Sunday, every German Catholic had heard the Pope's directive to resist the "mad prophet" and steadfastly practice their religion. In response, the Reich's anti-Catholic propaganda only worsened, and dissident priests were sent to prison camps.

As Josef sat stone-faced, deciding the most politic reply, Pehl smirked and announced, "Herr Haupt, you're a respected citizen in town. People look up to you, but you broke the law by questioning what that Jew was doing. Everyone saw it. There will be a punishment."

Josef froze in fear, wondering what that punishment might be. He stared at his captors, so smug and assured of their power. Both men leaned back in their chairs with their arms crossed and unsympathetic smiles plastered on their faces. They took glee in ruining his life.

Pehl motioned to the goons. "Take him to a cell."

For the first time, Josef outwardly displayed his inner fear as his hand trembled holding his hat. "What is going to happen to me, may I ask?"

"I don't quite know yet," said Pehl, looking at his watch. "I need to make arrangements."

CHAPTER THREE

JOSEF

The goons didn't handcuff Josef before they led him to the jail. He wasn't the sort to resist arrest, and if he attempted an escape, the SS simply would have shot him. Handcuffs were the mark of a society with a nod toward due process.

Though he felt eyes staring at him, Josef didn't look in the other cells. When the goons stopped at the final stall in the row, he felt some relief seeing it empty. At least he could think and not have to explain himself to a common criminal.

Josef closed his eyes as he stepped inside. The gate slammed behind him followed by the key turning in the lock. When he heard footsteps head down the hall, he attempted a deep breath, but his nostrils burned with the smell of sewage.

He opened his eyes and followed the smell to the round hole in the corner of the room. That was his toilet. Beyond the hole, there was a large wooden bench, serving both as bed and chair.

For the next five hours, Josef worried, his mind spinning through all the possible outcomes before he turned to prayer to calm his fear for his family. Why was God testing him this way? What about his wife and children? What was God's plan for them if the worst happened to him? He stood, he sat, and he even kneeled in his suit, but no answers to his questions arrived.

In the evening, a guard arrived with a tray. Josef peered through the cell bars to see a plate with two slices of bread and a tin cup of water. He was famished, but the brown bread looked a few days past stale with a fuzzy mold blooming on its crust.

"*Abendbrot*," grunted the pasty-faced guard. He opened the cell door and handed the tray to Josef. Though the guard didn't say it sarcastically, it was a joke to call the fare evening bread.

"Danke," said Josef, trying to make eye contact with the guard, whose attention was on the door as he began to close it. "Excuse me, Herr *Wachtmeister*, do you know what is going to happen to me?"

The guard raised his gaze. For a brief second, he looked Josef in the eye before returning his attention to locking the door. He whispered, "I don't know, but you should eat the bread."

The guard's simple instruction was both a favor and a warning. The guard had told him not to think the meal beneath him because there might be little food in his future. Josef's hunger vanished as he stared at the tray—not at the sight of the bread but at the nightmare of what lay ahead.

He thought of his children setting the dining room table at that very moment and asking if they should set a place for him. Dorothea might snap at them, saying, "Of course your father will come home." Did she also worry he might not?

An hour later, the bread still sat untouched on its tray. With the guard's advice in mind, he broke off an unappetizing piece. He said the same prayer of thanks to God for the bread as he would if he were at his own table.

When he heard the cellblock door open, he stopped before taking the first bite. Footsteps came striding down the hall with a fervor destined for him. He looked at the uneaten bread. The guard's warning had been a small act of kindness during an unkind time. What if the guard was offended and told the SS he was insubordinate? He slid the bread into his suit pocket and finished the water as the guard arrived.

The guard stared down the cellblock as he opened the door wide. "*Raus.*"

Stepping into the hall, Josef hoped the guard might take further pity on him. "Bitte, Herr Wachtmeister, where am I going?"

Without turning to answer, the guard kept walking and grunted one word. "*Zug.*"

The little word caused Josef to halt. Trains were transports to concentration camps, and he knew of no one yet to return. Jews vanished without any notice or explanation, never to be heard from again. Sometimes a gentile might disappear—a persecuted priest or a nun—or a troublemaker like a communist or a leftist intellectual. How could Josef be seen as one of those?

When the guard realized Josef was no longer following him, he glanced over his shoulder. "Come on."

Josef closed his eyes, thinking, yes, he had to move forward. For whatever reason, God had placed him in this situation. He must make the best of it and walk as Christ would. He would treat his captors with respect, and hopefully, they might do the same to him.

"*Ja, mein Herr.*"

Alone again in the interrogation room, Josef sat staring at his hat, which Dorothea had found for him on one of her trips to Allenstein. He fingered the hat's thick wool felt and matching ribbon. He hoped he could keep it wherever he was going. A good hat was important in sun, rain, or snow.

Moments later, the door cracked open. As Josef leapt to his feet, Pehl, Elsner, and their henchmen entered the room. He wondered if he should offer the Hitler salute, but Pehl spoke before he could. "Have a seat. This will be short."

"What is happening to me?"

"Because of your action against the Reich, a protective detention order has been issued against you."

Despite hearing the confirmation of his worst fears, Josef willed himself to keep his voice calm. "Lieutenant, I'm only a farmer. I'm not a threat to society."

Pehl crossed his arms, so sure of everything he might say or do. "You defied the Gestapo and favored a Jew over the Reich."

"But I had no intention of questioning the authorities, I simply—"

The door cracked open again, startling everyone because they all turned their heads at once. Josef was surprised to see someone he recognized. It was the SS major from Allenstein whom he had met at a city council meeting the year before. Since then, he had only seen Major Kablau from afar on the street.

Pehl, Elsner, and the goons snapped to attention, with Pehl throwing his arm up into the air. "Heil Hitler!" they said.

After Kablau returned the greeting, Elsner barked at Josef, "Stand!"

As Josef placed his hand on the seat of the chair to raise himself, Kablau held up his hand. In a voice one would use urging a guest to stay for dinner, Kablau said, "Nein. Please sit."

"Pardon me, *Sturmbannführer* Kablau," said Pehl. "I didn't know you were in town, or I would have told you about this situation at once." He puffed his chest in pride. "I have issued a protective order against this man. He publicly defied the orders of the Gestapo against a Jew. We have arranged for his transport to Sachsenhausen within the hour."

Josef forgot everything Pehl had said except the name, Sachsenhausen—a notorious labor camp for dissidents. He looked at Pehl, who seemed to be waiting for Kablau to promote him immediately.

"Excellent work, Pehl," said Kablau. "But I fear in this case there is a misunderstanding. We don't send men like Herr Haupt to Sachsenhausen."

Pehl's eyes widened in confusion as Kablau motioned to the door. "Please, let's go to an office where we can speak more comfortably."

After being left alone in the stately front office, Josef studied the framed maps of the Reich and Europe. Another portrait of Hitler stared down at him, this one warning that a trip to Sachsenhausen was still a possibility. When he looked out the windows, the view of the street and its freedom provoked a longing near a torment.

Lost in his thoughts, he almost missed Otto popping into the room with a glass of water and a plate with fresh bread and cut hard sausage. Without looking at him, Otto set the plate and glass on a coffee table and scurried out.

As Josef eyed the food and water, he saw a pair of shiny Oxford shoes step into the room. He raised his eyes to see a man in a tailored suit with a conspicuous swastika on its lapel.

Taking a step back, Josef asked in surprise, "*Bürgermeister* Renkel?"

"Good evening, Josef," said the Bürgermeister.

Dazed by Renkel's appearance and warned by his usual untrustworthy smile, Josef paused before he spoke. The mayor also operated as the local Nazi Party leader—the Ortsgruppenleiter. Kablau broke the silence when he walked in and offered them a seat. As the three men sat in the cushioned chairs, Kablau motioned to them.

"You two know each other well."

"Otto found me," said Renkel, turning to Josef.

"Otto contacted you?"

"And then I reached the major in Allenstein," said Renkel.

Kablau settled his eyes on Josef. "Occasionally, it's necessary to go around your superior officer. Pehl and Elsner are new and don't know the townsfolk well. Otto must respect you greatly to take such a risk."

Josef remained silent, thinking of the enormous debt he owed the boy.

"I thought you might be hungry," said Kablau. "I'm sorry we don't have anything more elaborate."

"Danke." Josef's voice was hesitant, wondering what sort of

signal Kablau meant with better food. Josef could feel the moldy bread in his pockets—another reminder that he was still in danger. Out of politeness, he took a bite of the fresh bread before him.

Pehl walked into the room, and Kablau's tone became more formal. "Herr Haupt, your family must be waiting for you, so I won't delay you much longer."

Relief coursed through Josef, and he cleared his throat of emotion.

"I imagine abendbrot is a nice meal at your home," Kablau continued. "You have a big family, do you not?"

Renkel answered for him. "He has eight children—four strapping boys and four sweet little girls."

"Eight?" said Kablau, somewhat impressed. "What are their ages?"

"Paul is the eldest," said Josef. "He is seventeen. Franz is sixteen. Stefan is fourteen. Albert is twelve. Margarete is nine. Sophia is seven. Katharina is five, and the youngest, Martha, was born three years ago."

"What a wonderful family. My wife and I only have twin boys. You must be very proud, but eight children are quite a responsibility. You're lucky to have such a large farm to provide for them. Is it doing well?"

"Much better than it has in years."

"You see. The Führer has made the Reich prosper." Kablau's smile widened. "And now you've grasped the error of your ways this morning."

"Indeed, I have."

"Of course, he has," said Renkel.

Josef wondered if the ultimate lesson was that no one in his family should even talk to a Jewish person in public. It seemed unavoidable in Guttstadt's tight-knit community. And how could he conduct his business with the Katz family? He peered at Renkel, wondering what his presence meant for his future.

"Good, good," said Kablau with a gratified grin. He leaned

back in his chair and spoke with a silky voice. "But now there is something you could help me with. You work with the *Reichsnährstand*, don't you?"

"Yes, the Reich's new agricultural agency," Josef said, still guessing where this was all leading. "I report my harvest."

"The Reich needs an *Ortsbauernführer* to organize and lead the farming community in the area." Kablau gestured to Renkel. "Herr Renkel believes you would make a wonderful Ortsbauernführer."

Josef sat still as he absorbed everything said and unsaid in Kablau's words. Renkel had approached him about the position before, but he had declined. Now Kablau had rescued him from Sachsenhausen because Josef was more useful to the Reich as the local Ortsbauernführer than as a prisoner toiling away until death.

Josef glanced at Pehl, who stared at Kablau with awe and respect. Pehl was the apprentice watching the master achieve things he couldn't even comprehend. This was how Pehl must look at the world if he wanted to become a major one day.

Josef reached for the glass of water, and before he drank, he asked, "Could you tell me more about what would be required of me?"

Kablau went on about the basic duties of the job—keeping track of local production, assisting farmers with problems, and reporting on the region's needs to the Reich. Josef knew it was much more than that. The Reichsnährstand allowed the Reich to insert itself into an otherwise closed community. Those farmers who pleased the Reich would benefit, while those who didn't would see their livelihoods wither away.

"So those are the primary expectations," Kablau said before he held up a finger. "Plus your choice of seed, additional labor for your fields, a few extras as you may need them."

Josef took a piece of bread and nibbled so that he had an excuse not to speak. His mind whirred, wondering if he had any choice in the matter.

"Finish eating," Kablau said with a smile.

Renkel lightly touched Josef's jacket and announced in a conciliatory voice, "I should say, if you become the Ortsbauern-führer, you don't have to join the party. As the head of the party in Guttstadt, I would like for you to join, but I understand."

Kablau leaned back in his seat. "It would be better for you, but there are some who choose to wait."

"May I have some time to consider?"

"Come by tomorrow morning at ten o'clock with your answer."

Before Josef could object, Renkel spoke up. "Tomorrow is Sunday. Our families attend the ten o'clock Mass."

Kablau shrugged. "Noon then."

Kablau rose from his seat, ending the discussion. As Josef and Renkel stood as well, a knot formed in Josef's stomach. By telling him to return to the police station, Kablau was making it clear he had two choices—assume the role of Ortsbauernführer or face punishment. Kablau had laid out Josef's dilemma. He had enormous responsibilities with such a large family and prosperous farm. Many people depended on him. He could make their lives even better or ruin them forever.

"Now it's time for you to go home. I saw your fine horses at the inn. They need feeding," said Kablau." Maybe the farm will do well enough one day that you could even buy an automobile."

"I could purchase one now, but the road to my farm is steep. It needs to be graded, which will be an additional expense."

"Ah, interesting," said Kablau. He held out his hand for a final handshake. "That may be something the Reich could help you out with."

Josef wore a tense smile as he shook the major's hand, knowing he was simultaneously being forced and bribed. He had no confidence in the bribe ever being delivered, but punishment was certain if he did not obey.

CHAPTER FOUR

JOSEF

As Josef turned from the main road to his farm, healthy fields surrounded him with the sun low in the distance, ready to fall behind the horizon. At the corner of the property, he passed the building that housed the electrical transformer providing light for his home and those of four neighbors. At 250 acres, his farm didn't match the giant estates of the blueblood *Junkers*, but it was larger than most nonetheless.

Across the hills, the light high on the flagpole beckoned him to the warmth of the Haupt family compound. Multiple large stables housed the many horses, cows, sheep, and swine, while farmworkers and two sharecropper families lived in modest houses. Smaller buildings and sheds provided shelter for work-shops, firewood, and coal. A pack of cats roamed the grounds, keeping the giant granary and other buildings rodent-free.

The Haupt house crowned the estate. Two stories high, the home had a steep cross-gabled roof with multiple dormers, and thick clay walls fortressed the family from winter. They had recently expanded the house, adding several rooms, another stair-case for the west wing, and a bathroom attached to Josef and

Dorothea's room. Dorothea employed a gardener to maintain the grounds to her vision. A flowering manicured courtyard fronted the building, while lawns and flower beds surrounded the other three sides dotted with fruit trees. Towering tree hedges flanked the compound to the east and north, providing protection against wind and blizzards.

When Josef reached the last hill, one of the many females who loved him ran to the carriage. Senta had an innate sense of good and bad, happiness and woe, and friend and foe, which she declared from her doghouse next to the flagpole. If a stranger came to the property, the Saint Bernard's booming bark would announce the visitor before he was in anyone's sight. Windows rattled if she deemed the person particularly suspicious. For her family and their friends and employees, she only gave love. Because Josef was the alpha of her pack, she adored him most of all.

As he drove the carriage to the front of the garage, her bushy tail wagged in a circle like a propeller until she sat and awaited his attention. Two farmworkers approached Josef to see to the horses and carriage. The long brick garage had four entrances, where each of the family's carriages and the big sled entered and exited. Josef would usually help with the horses while the farmworkers parked the carriage. He had good relationships with his staff, but he was in no mood for small talk that night. After a greeting, he left them to work.

Despite Josef's hellish day, Senta's innocent affection tugged at his heart, so he scratched the ruff of fur behind her droopy ears. He remembered the bread in his pockets and held a bit of crust to her.

"For you."

Senta sniffed the bread, her black nostrils moving in and out, absorbing all the foreign prison scents. She took a step back with a confused expression.

"*Ja, ja,*" Josef muttered. "I'll give it to the pigs."

After a trip to the swine house, Josef headed to his own while

Senta returned to her post by the flagpole. Beside the mast was a large iron bell—the Angel of the Lord bell—which was rung so those in the fields knew the time for the *Angelus* prayer and meals. Outside of those three daily times, it warned of emergencies.

Josef thought of how the bell had rung twice without him that day. The late twilight of the summer solstice was now upon them, so most of his children were already in bed. Only the older boys would still be awake. Every night, they listened to a radio drama while Dorothea heard the same as she prepared the kitchen for the next morning's breakfast.

As he entered the foyer, he softened his footsteps. Actors' voices from the radio drifted from the living room. If this had been a night when he had been waylaid by a late meeting or a broken carriage wheel, Josef would have ventured into the kitchen. Dorothea would prepare a late meal for him and join him at the kitchen table—as might the boys to hear his stories.

That night Josef went straight to the stairs, but as he put a foot on the first step, Dorothea's voice rose from the distance.

"Josef?"

He looked over his shoulder and saw her standing in the dining room. Josef was a tall, intelligent, handsome man, and his wife was an intelligent and handsome woman. Dorothea was pretty enough, with dark brown hair contrasted by light blue eyes, but it was her wit and regal air that made her noteworthy. Carrying herself as if she were a head taller, she spoke in a manner certain she was a cut above most of the world.

Anger and happiness were emotions she displayed easily and publicly. Love, worry, and sadness were ones she kept to herself—often even with her children. Only Josef could see those feelings evident upon her. She stood with her hands clasped against her poplin work dress, still pressed and clean from the protection of a large apron. Her hair was piled tidily on her head, but her brow was furrowed. Most telling was her lack of smile, and the tremor in her voice.

"I'm tired," he replied. He glanced up the stairs and then

returned his eyes to hers, conveying she should follow as soon as she could.

As he took a step, another voice rose behind him.

"Papa? Did something happen?"

Josef looked over his shoulder to see Paul. A black forelock of hair fell into his dark eyes, which were too wise for his seventeen years. Paul knew the answer to his question. Something bad had happened.

"Good night," said Josef, before climbing the stairs.

Decorated with Dorothea's own paintings, the master bedroom had always been a refuge away from the children. After removing his watch and emptying his pockets on the dresser, Josef changed into his pajamas. Instead of brushing his suit so it could be worn another day, he placed it on a chair. With the smell and stains of jail, it would need a cleaning before he could face wearing it again.

When he exited the bathroom, he saw Dorothea standing with the same anxious expression and clasped hands. Now in the privacy of their bedroom, she rushed over and threw her arms around him.

"*Gott sei Dank,*" she whispered.

"Yes." He placed his arms around her. "Thank God."

"I could tell Margarete was hiding something," she said, pulling away. "What happened?"

Josef held her hands and nodded toward the bed. "Once we sit down."

Dorothea changed while he prepared the bed. It was actually two twin oak beds pushed together, and every day Margarete and Sophia were tasked to make it. They first placed the duvet on top —filled with thick down for winter or thin for summer—and then added two down pillows, a meter square. A sky-blue satin bedspread followed, topped by a white lace cover. Josef thought of the girls' handiwork every night when he removed the coverings. That night, he closed his eyes as he folded the lace thinking how he might not have seen his little girls ever again.

He climbed into the bed and opened a book, staring at but not reading the page. The enormity of his situation made concentrating on anything else impossible. Even though he had lived it, retelling his day seemed ridiculous. How could this have happened to him?

Clad in her long white nightgown, Dorothea soon arrived and snuggled next to him. "Now tell me."

There was no way to lessen the delivery or impact of the news, so he stated the fact, "I was arrested by the Gestapo."

"No!" she gasped and jolted upright. "What happened?"

"When we arrived in town, I saw Aaron Katz sweeping the street, and I asked him why."

Dorothea cocked her head. "Herr Katz sweeping the street? And on his sabbath?"

He held up his hands in self-evident agreement.

"He didn't answer me, which I should've known was a warning, but I asked again. Two Gestapo officers appeared and told me to go to headquarters. I was interrogated by the SS and jailed for questioning why a Jew was being punished."

"What? Don't they know who you are?"

"No. They planned to send me to Sachsenhausen tonight."

While he was speaking, Dorothea covered her mouth in shock. Her hand shook as she removed it. "Good God. How did you get out?"

"Thanks to Otto, Renkel arrived along with an SS major—Kablau, whom I'd met before. The major released me."

"Otto? Bertha's son?"

"Otto has taken a Gestapo job. I owe him my life for contacting Renkel."

"Otto is an angel."

"He is, but now the major wants me to be the Ortsbauern-führer for the town."

"What on earth? You've turned down that position before." Her look of disapproval turned to a sneer. "Renkel. This is his doing."

"Exactly."

She threw her arms around him again and closed her eyes. "But thank God you're home."

"Yes. It could be so much worse."

For the next half hour, Dorothea asked for every detail, sometimes in panicky tears, terrified for what this meant for her husband and family. She often repeated her questions, never quite comprehending his answers. The underlying motivations of the Nazis were foreign to her.

In Dorothea's mind, the world was right and just. God's laws were obeyed, children were dutiful, and beds were perfectly made. Hitler preached a vision of a German community, *Volksgemeinschaft*, where class and religion didn't matter. Beyond her family, Dorothea's religion and place in society meant everything to her. The Nazi philosophy of a classless society was a notion so antithetical to her worldview that an unladylike snort escaped her whenever someone mentioned it. Just as the Haupt family disregarded the Reich's disparagement of Catholicism, she told her children egalitarianism was propaganda to appease the masses. It wasn't to be publicly challenged, but it was to be privately ignored.

"What is this world coming to?" she asked. "Aaron is a good man, and his family has done much for this town. All the Jews are generous. Everyone in Guttstadt knows that."

"The Gestapo doesn't care if Aaron is generous. And many in Guttstadt no longer care when the government spews hatred against Jews. People are just happy it's not directed at them." Josef pursed his lips in bitterness. "Aaron's sons fought in the Great War with me. They're as German as we are."

"Naturally."

"Levi Weisman isn't allowed to treat our livestock anymore—as if a Jewish veterinarian is lower than our animals. He's leaving for England after he pays the Reich."

"I fear others are as well. The last time I was in Allenstein, I took my ring into the jeweler to have the prongs tightened on the diamonds. Rosa Katz and Barbara Stern were leaving as I arrived. We said hello, and after they left, the jeweler remarked that he was doing them a favor by buying a Jew's jewelry."

"Probably paying them a fraction of what the jewels were worth, and now Aaron must pay that money to the government so he can have the privilege of exiling his children to America."

There was a silence between them. Josef often felt the problems in their world were too large for words. He thought Dorothea's mind must also be burdened with the same worries until she pushed away from him.

"But the Ortsbauernführer? You?" she exclaimed with a disdainful wave of her hand. "Renkel knows that's a job for someone else. Someone who must do it to survive. Really... what will people think of us?"

He imagined the gossip when people heard the news that Josef Haupt, the successful farmer and Zentrum leader, was now the local Ortsbauernführer. Would they be shocked, or would they say they weren't surprised? His fellow Zentrum faithful would deem him a self-serving, weak collaborator, or they might speculate that the Reich had discovered something so unsavory about him that he was blackmailed. He had lived a life above reproach, yet now friends, family, and church would think him a lesser man.

He peered at her through the side of his eyes. "I think the question is what will I think of myself."

"Could you reason with these people? You have so much work here already. What about your service for the church and the hospital? You can't take on another position."

"There's no reasoning with the SS. I can't put our family at such risk."

"But... but..." Her blue eyes went wide in fear. "You don't think they might hurt us?"

"Dorothea," he said, holding his hands out in exasperation. "I was in prison this afternoon. I might not have been released for months, maybe years, and maybe if I'd irritated the wrong guard or said the wrong word, I might never have come home again. No one is safe anymore."

She sat still, her eyes searching his as she envisioned a life without him. Tears welled as she blubbered, "I'm sorry. I just can't believe how everything has changed."

"I know," he said, reaching out for her hand. "It's unbelievable."

The words came out of his mouth automatically because he said them all the time. In his family and sphere, dismayed conversations about their society and government ended with passive, incredulous remarks before reverting to normal day-to-day concerns. Josef now saw how irresponsible it was to say the world around him couldn't be believed. Continuing to act as if nothing had changed had landed him in jail.

Thinking aloud, he mumbled, "We must learn to survive. The children also…"

Alerted to a new threat, Dorothea raised her head. She was a parent who saw her children as an extension of herself. In her mind, she had already overachieved at motherhood. She had borne eight healthy, intelligent children. They went to church, had perfect table manners, performed their chores, and for the most part did well in school. The Haupt children were both an extraordinary work in progress and her life's achievement.

Blinking away her tears, she was ready to pounce on any danger. "We must protect the children."

He closed his eyes in worry. "That's all I can think of."

Each Sunday, the Haupt family climbed into their best carriages and traveled in style to church. Everyone dressed in their finest clothes. As soon as the weather allowed, Dorothea donned her fox stole until it became so cold that she needed her otter coat. The older boys wore suits, while the younger children dressed in woolen sailor shirts over their pants and skirts. Dorothea used

church as an occasion to wear her nicest jewelry, including the
piece Josef had given her when Albert was born—a ring with
three diamonds encircled in a modern gold setting.

Inside the church, ample morning light shone through the
windows and brightened the red brick interior. Against the white
plastered ceiling, intricate beams and supports looked like wooden
constellations in the church's heavens. As usual, Josef led his
family down the aisle to the front of the church to sit in the
Haupts' pew. Like other wealthy parishioners, he had contributed
to fund one of the black pews on the altar's sides. The pews were
new, but they were guarded by fourteenth-century lion statues.
The seats gave the family a prime view of the service and the
congregation a prime view of the Haupts.

Though his favorite priest, Father Schmidt, climbed the
ornate steps of the baroque pulpit to deliver the sermon that day,
Josef ignored his message. With his head bowed, Josef begged God
for a sign that his decision would be the right one. It wasn't
obvious to him. Rejecting the Ortsbauernführer role would keep
his conscience clear but put his family and him in danger.
Accepting the position offered his family protection, but it put
him in league with evil.

At the end of the service, the congregation mingled in front of
the church and chatted with the priests. Josef pulled Paul aside.

"I'll be coming home later," he declared. "Your mother
already knows. I need to speak with Father Schmidt and attend to
another matter."

"So that's why you rode your own horse," Paul said, as if he
were solving a puzzle. "This has to do with why you were so late
last night."

"Yes, it does. I may have to accept a position with the Reich."

"What? Why?"

"Say nothing to anyone. I'll know more later today."

"You're joining the party?" Paul reared in revulsion. "You hate
them."

"It's only a low-level ministerial position with the agricultural agency."

"I thought our family didn't get involved in politics. You don't even fly the flag since they took over. And now you've joined the party?"

"I'm not joining the party. I would just be helping the farmers here as the local Ortsbauernführer."

"That sounds like a Nazi to me," Paul said in icy judgment. "At school, they were once poor nobodies who are now double-crossing assholes in a uniform. I don't have anything to do with them. They're dangerous. Whatever it is, I mind my own business and stay out of it, but now people are going to expect—"

Josef's ire at being scolded by his son boiled over. "Maybe if you had gotten your high school diploma rather than going to trade school there would be a higher caliber of people."

"This again? I'm sorry if I don't care about Ovid. And I'm in an engineering program, not vacuum cleaner repair." Paul frowned at his father. "And I'm not the one working for the Reich."

Realizing he was causing an unnecessary fight, Josef tried reason. "Paul, you've always been more intelligent than intellectual. You know I don't want to do this."

"I know you don't. I'm sorry," mumbled Paul, before he stared at the ground in thought. "Something really bad must have happened yesterday for you to even consider this. The SS must be patting themselves on the back for catching you."

Josef gave his son a grim nod for his accurate assessment. "Now go to your mother."

A half hour later, Father Schmidt led Josef on a walk away from the Dom and toward the river. Josef relayed the events from the day before with little emotion or commentary because nothing more was needed. Father Schmidt lived in the same world as his parishioners; he knew the consequences.

When Josef finished, they had reached the banks of the Kleine

Alle. "Those are my troubles. I'm sorry for burdening you, but other than my wife, there is no one else I can trust."

"I understand," Father Schmidt said with a smile, though it soon turned down with regret. "It's an impossible choice. And one that people all over this country are reckoning, though the ramifications of their decision may not be as acute as yours."

"It would be easier if I didn't have a family."

"Perhaps," said the priest with a shrug. "Though your own conscience would be tested regardless. Priests face these questions without a family. Some have acted against the Nazi government, ending in their deaths. They're true martyrs, while most priests are not. There is a time to be outspoken and reject evil, but our primary job is to bring people closer to God. A priest can't do that from the grave."

"We do need some of you here," Josef said with sympathy.

"Bishop Kaller is designing the new prayer book to have the cross and crown on the cover as a symbol of Christ as the world's rightful ruler. Even if it's symbolic, people must be reminded to put their trust in God and not Hitler's propaganda."

"I was told that I don't have to join the party, but they'll continue to pressure me."

"I expect they will. What does Dorothea think?"

"She's horrified. Nazi anti-Catholic propaganda... imprisoning priests and nuns... that wounds her deeply, as does their treatment of people she respects, like Herr Katz." A genuine smile formed on Josef's lips as he added, "And she'd spit in Hitler's eye before she agreed all classes were equal."

Laughing, Father Schmidt touched Josef's shoulder with a pat. "Not many men could handle such a woman as their wife."

"Ja. I know."

"She will help you, whatever you decide."

Josef hung his head. "Do I have a choice?"

"Don't you?"

"Imprisonment? Ostracism? Losing my farm? Those are all

possibilities." Frustration erupted in Josef with an almost desperate whine. "What should I do?"

"I don't know. The decision is yours, but the Church will be here for you whatever you decide." A wry smile appeared on Father Schmidt's lips. "You're a good man and a good Catholic, Josef. You wouldn't make a very good Nazi."

Josef stared at the flowing river, always moving forward. Even a dam couldn't divert the water forever. Without taking his eyes from the rippling water, he said, "There's no way to take this position with a clean conscience."

Father Schmidt didn't reply, so Josef turned to him with a silent request for his thoughts.

The priest looked toward the river. "No, there isn't."

CHAPTER FIVE

MARGARETE

Two days later, Margarete plotted her path as she walked to the electrical transformer. Puddles from a morning shower dotted the way, and unlike her companion, she had to avoid them. Senta walked in a straight line without regard to the muddy water splattering on her white paws, while Margarete placed each step just so. Her new shoes still smelled of fresh leather, and her mother had warned her to take care.

None of Dorothea's children were safe from her demands on behavior, appearance, and grades, but none were scrutinized like Margarete. It was one of the reasons Margarete enjoyed chores that took her outside. Even her mother's eagle eye didn't extend as far as the edge of the Haupt property.

As they neared the top of the last steep hill before the transformer came into sight, Senta raised her nose from the ground to the air. Gone was her panting smile. She sniffed in a semicircle, while her floppy ears lifted from their usual droop.

"Was ist los, Senta?" asked Margarete.

A low growl answered from Senta's throat. As the hair rose on the ridge of her back, Senta lowered her shoulders as she did when stalking an unwitting rabbit. The growl grew deeper and louder as they approached the hill's peak. Right before they could see the other side, Senta barked a vicious warning.

Margarete stopped so quickly that dust rose around her, but Senta ran forward, her bark becoming more ferocious with every step. Following her protector, Margarete topped the hill and saw a truck and two soldiers.

As Senta barreled down the slope, the shorter of the soldiers shouted, "Get control of your dog!"

"Senta, stop!" she yelled with desperate fear. Her long braids bounced, and her dress flew in the wind as she ran to catch the dog.

Senta ignored her, heading straight for the soldiers. The short one dropped the tool he had been holding and drew his gun, aiming for Senta and Margarete.

At once, the taller soldier blocked him with his arm. "Good God, man. What is wrong with you?"

The short one lowered his gun. "Our orders are to shoot when attacked."

"By a little girl and a Saint Bernard?"

The tall soldier crouched down, extended an upward palm, and spoke to Senta like she was his own. "Hello. Who's a good dog?"

Margarete reached Senta and grabbed the ruff of fur around her neck. "Nein, Senta."

Senta reluctantly stopped her attack, though a low growl continued as she stared at the soldiers. Margarete noticed the SS insignia on the men's uniforms. From the murmurs and asides she overheard from adults, the SS weren't average German soldiers. They were worse than the Gestapo.

Still squatting, the tall soldier smiled. "Senta is a good watchdog."

Margarete's eyes traveled cautiously between the two men. "I'm sorry."

"Don't be. She's just doing her job."

"As were we," said the short one. He picked up the screw-driver from the dirt. "Let's go."

"In a minute." The tall soldier moved closer to Senta. "Maybe she'll let me pet her."

Senta walked to the soldier and extended her skeptical snout to smell his offered hand.

"Aw, she's a sweet one," said the soldier. "I miss having a dog."

While Senta allowed herself to be petted, the other man tapped his finger on his gun. He seemed more uneasy than bored. Margarete almost smiled because soldiers weren't supposed to be afraid of anything, but that one was afraid of dogs.

She wondered aloud, "The SS has dogs. Don't you see them?"

"We do," the tall man said, impressed with her observation. "But they have big jobs, so I can't bother them while they're working."

"Speaking of working," muttered the short soldier.

"Ja, ja," said the tall one over his shoulder. He turned back to Margarete. "What is your name?"

"Margarete Haupt." The tall man was nice, but he was an SS soldier, and she wanted to be away from him. She pointed to the building. "I was going to get the transformer's account books. May I? My mother is expecting me."

"Of course." The tall one rose to his feet and motioned behind him. "We were placing this sign for your father, Herr Haupt. Come see it."

Margarete took wary steps around the building to the side facing the main road. What had been a blank wooden wall now held an enamel white metal sign with black lettering. In an elaborate font, the word *Reichsnährstand* curved in an arch at the top, and the word *Ortsbauernführer* extended across the bottom. The black German eagle and the words *Blut und Boden* were in the middle. There was also a swastika, different from the usual one. This had a shaft of wheat and sword on top of it. Margarete didn't understand the meaning of the sign, but it didn't matter because the swastika took all of her attention. That was the Nazi government's symbol.

She took a step back from the sign, though her eyes remained on the swastika. Why had the SS now put a swastika on the Haupt farm with the ominous words *blood and soil*? What had her family done wrong?

"She's only a child," the short soldier said dismissively. "She doesn't understand."

"I think she understands more than you think." The tall one gave her an encouraging smile. "Don't worry. It's a good thing. It's a gift from the Führer. You should be proud."

"Danke," said Margarete, having no idea if it was the right thing to say. She was confident her father didn't want any gifts from Adolf Hitler.

"It's time to go," said the short soldier.

The tall soldier petted Senta one last time. "Guten Tag, *Fräulein* Haupt."

"Guten Tag," replied Margarete.

After the tall soldier gave her a final wave, the truck rumbled down the road. She grabbed the accounting book from its home on the ledge, but closing the door behind her, she saw Senta had disappeared. She found the dog resting in a patch of cool grass in the building's shade. Panting from the excitement and summer heat, Senta tapped her tail as if to ask if they could stay a little longer.

"Oh, all right..." Margarete sat beside Senta and stroked her shaggy fur. "I really don't want to go home either."

It was never good to be the messenger of bad news to Dorothea, and informing her that the family's property was marked with a swastika was too daunting to even contemplate. Margarete decided to show it to Albert or Stefan first. Then they could face Dorothea's wrath.

Safe with Senta, she contemplated the sign. Two symbols were ubiquitous in her life—the cross and the swastika. The cross symbolized Christ and the church. Every day she learned about the goodness of God at her Catholic school, and church was a safe, if boring, place.

The swastika symbolized the Nazi government, which was confusing and scary. When she was little, her parents talked about politics all the time. Her father was often at political meetings, and she remembered lively conversations at the dinner table between her parents and older brothers. But no one talked about politics anymore. Even though she knew her father was concerned about the country, he sometimes turned off the radio if Adolf Hitler was speaking. If the family refused to fly the Nazi flag, why would they want a swastika on their building?

After a few minutes, Senta rose to her four legs and raised her discerning snout to the air. This time there was no growl, just a tail wag as the clip-clop of hooves confirmed for Margarete it was her father.

All the Haupt children admired their father for his wisdom, humor, and kindness, and they knew others admired him for those same things. But to Margarete he was more than a great man. He was her refuge. While Dorothea noticed each of her shortcomings, Josef ignored them and saw her talents. He soothed her when life was confusing or harsh, putting any situation in perspective and resting her fears. He was the person who could explain that awful sign.

She waved to her father, who sat high in the wagon. In work clothes and hat, he had spent the morning helping a neighbor train an ornery horse. He smiled and raised a hand from the reins to say hello. When the sign on the transformer building caught his eye, he leaned forward to read it. He stopped smiling.

As the carriage slowed, all the thoughts in Margarete's head rushed out one after the other. "Papa, Papa. SS soldiers were here. Senta was upset. One of the soldiers took out a gun to kill her, but the other one was nice and made him stop. And they put up this sign. I don't know what it means. They said we should be proud and it's a gift from the Führer, but I think *Mutti* won't like it. It has a swastika. Can we take it down before Mutti sees it?"

"It's all right, Margarete," he said, tying the reins to the little hitch on the dash. "Calm down."

Feeling silly at what must have been her overreaction, she lowered her head as her father descended from the carriage.

When Josef approached her, though, he put his arm around her. "Don't feel bad. I also would've been frightened if a soldier aimed a gun at Senta."

"I was so scared." Tears she didn't know she'd been holding back escaped and rolled down her cheeks.

"Of course." Patting her shoulder, he muttered, "Endangering my child on my own property. I'm going to have a word with them."

She pointed to the sign and opened her hand in a plea. "But, Papa, what does it mean?"

Josef stared at the sign before removing his hat and rubbing his eyes. When he looked up, he took Margarete's hand. "Let's rest for a bit."

Taking a seat by the dog, Josef extended his legs as he leaned forward with his hands in prayer on his thighs. Margarete sat beside him, remembering to tuck her legs under her skirt like a lady. She waited for an explanation, and his continued silence told her the sign was a problem.

Eventually, he said, "Reichsnährstand is the department in the German government that regulates agriculture. It decides what we plant, where we sell our crops, and at what price."

"What does 'blood and soil' mean?"

"It's a saying..." Josef trailed off as he stared at the sign. "It's a motto that ties Germans to the land."

Margarete tilted her head. The blood reference still didn't make sense to her. She grasped for what her father might not want to say aloud. "All Germans? There are all those signs forbidding Jews everywhere. Brigitte Weber says it's because Jews aren't real Germans."

"That's not true. German Jews are German. Polish Jews are Polish. Polish Catholics are Polish. It's no different."

"Brigitte says if a gentile has a baby with a Jew, it's like when a horse and donkey mate. They'll have a mule, and it should be drowned like a two-headed kitten."

"*Ach du lieber Himmel*," mused Josef, appealing to the love of God as he cast a side glance. "What did you say to that?"

"I told her I don't like talking about such things," she replied with a frown. "And I don't. But is she right?"

"I can't have you thinking ridiculous things like that. One day you'll be the mistress of a farm like ours—even larger if your mother has her way. Your farm will breed and raise hundreds of animals. Brigitte is wrong."

"What happens then?"

"Horses and donkeys are different species of animals. When they mate, they create a mule." Josef smiled. "Jews and Gentiles are both humans. We're the same species."

"Then where do deformed babies come from?"

"Deformities occur all the time in nature in plants and animals. It has nothing to do with religion. In fact, deformities happen in animals when they become inbred because they're too closely related. It's better to expand your breeding stock. Look at our beautiful Trakehner horses. They're a combination of Thoroughbreds and Arabians."

Margarete smiled, now feeling silly for bringing any of it up. She glanced at the sign again and realized she had one more question. "Why does the sign say Ortsbauernführer?"

"Because," he said, taking a steadying breath. "I've taken on the position for the government. I'll be working with the Reichsnährstand and helping the local farmers with their crops."

"You would work for the government? I thought you didn't like—"

"Sometimes we must do things we otherwise would not."

Feeling the sting from being cut off by her father, Margarete withdrew and stared at the tiny yellow flowers woven into the fabric of her summer dress.

Josef lifted her chin and spoke with an apology in his voice.

"Sadly, under this government, we have limited choices." She nodded, and he turned away, picked up a pebble, and tossed it to the side. "Maybe I can do some good where there would otherwise be none."

Hoping to make her father feel better, she said, "I think Brigitte will be impressed. Does it mean anything for the family?"

"Nothing really," he answered with a shrug. "Though the boys do need to attend the Hitler Youth meetings more regularly, and you'll need to join the *Bund Deutscher Mädel* next year."

She thought of the older girls who were members of the Hitler Youth's female counterpart, the BDM. They marched through town in their uniforms with a superiority that she didn't think they deserved, but they were intimidating nonetheless.

"Those girls are bad. I've seen them throw rocks at Jewish kids. And they say mean things—things if I said, you would punish me."

"You and your sisters will always behave like ladies and your brothers like gentlemen. You'll go to the meetings, but your mother and I don't want you doing or saying things you would be ashamed of."

The two sat silently staring at the sign. After a moment, he declared, "It's best now if you no longer speak to anyone who is Jewish, whether they be a child or an adult, unless it's absolutely necessary. This includes people like the Katz or Stern family. Don't even wish them a good day. Only walk by."

Margarete's jaw dropped once again. Josef had taught his children that all people should be treated alike, whether neighbor, friend, or worker. The children were scolded if they entered a room or stable without greeting everyone present, including laborers. On the other hand, her mother often ignored people she thought unworthy. Dorothea wouldn't even let the German sharecropper children ride in the same wagon with the Haupt children to school. While Catholic Poles shared the same religions as the Haupts, she still thought of them simply as Slavs and little better than Russian serfs. Yet Dorothea always paid her respects to the well-to-do Jewish families in Guttstadt.

"Why, Papa? Why should we ignore them?"

"It's just the way things are now." He grimaced at the sign. "Hopefully, they understand."

Margarete looked at the sign and back at her father, thinking of what it would be like to publicly ignore Frau Katz or Herr Stern or even the tinker and his son. She would be embarrassed to be so rude. She hoped they would understand because she did not.

CHAPTER SIX

JOSEF

N o one warned Josef that a sign branding him a part of the Nazi government would be placed on his property. Major Kablau only had said he would receive a letter with further instructions from Kreisbauernführer Fink, the district's head of the Reichsnährstand. The sign arrived before the letter.

Of course, Josef thought. *If the sign is posted, I can't change my mind.*

Margarete had been right. There was nothing to be proud of, and Dorothea was angry.

"But we're not Nazis," fumed Dorothea. She had resigned herself to his new role but not to a sign advertising it at her home. "And it makes us look common!"

Franz, Stefan, and Albert were so dumbfounded that Josef would willingly take on a position in the Reich that he felt the need to tell them of the arrest as well. They understood the family's predicament, but they weren't comfortable with the outcome. And they certainly didn't like the idea of attending more Hitler Youth meetings.

Josef called on his brother Bruno, the titular head of the

Haupt family. Close to a mirror image of Josef but with more gray, Bruno had always taken the role of big brother seriously. That day, Bruno acted as if their father's full authority had been passed to him.

Bruno spat, "What is wrong with you, Josef? How dare you associate our family with these ludicrous Nazis! You should've consulted me."

Decades of sibling history—both bad and good—welled inside Josef. He glared at his older brother, realizing that Bruno would never be able to grasp his situation. Josef was the youngest and a second son. His father had gifted him a small farm, which he and Dorothea had grown in size. Bruno and his wife, Helga, had been blessed with the inheritance of the family farm but no children. They lived a life of entitled privilege, insulated from entanglements, compromise, and the responsibility of child-rearing. While Josef often saw blurred lines, Bruno saw only black and white.

Bruno continued ranting that Josef had failed his family and his faith. If a man like Josef didn't object to the Nazi government, then everyone was doomed. His speech both resonated with Josef and annoyed him.

Under attack by his brother and his own conscience, Josef broke in. "Bruno, please let me explain. I was arrested by the Gestapo."

The many lines on Bruno's face deepened with the gravity of the situation. "My God," he whispered. "Why?"

Josef told his story for what he hoped would be the last time. His brother asked few questions, walking slowly with his hands clasped behind his back. When Josef finished, Bruno assumed another duty of the family patriarch. He tried to console Josef by placing a hand on his shoulder. "I'm so sorry for you and your family."

"Danke," said Josef, exhaling in relief. "Now do you see why I agreed to become Ortsbauernführer?"

"Nein."

"Nein?" Josef's eyes narrowed in frustrated anger.

"I see your reasoning, but I don't agree with it. We could have gotten you out of Sachsenhausen eventually. We would've helped Dorothea and the children until you returned. Your resistance would've been an example to all. You would've been able to hold your head high as our family always has. Instead, you bow down to these fools."

"That's easy for you to say. You don't have children."

"One might say I have more to lose." Bruno glowered at him. "Helga and I are alone in the world."

Bruno had a point, but his moral superiority didn't sway Josef. They were of equal intelligence, but while Bruno enjoyed literature, Josef preferred the newspaper. Josef saw the politics of a situation, and Bruno the ethics. Josef realized that they would never agree because he would always choose physical safety over morality.

His voice was soft as he declared, "I've always only gambled for small stakes. You know that. I couldn't risk such a thing with my family."

"I understand your reasoning. I don't agree with you, but I understand."

"Our world has changed, Bruno. No one is safe." Josef looked off into the undulating farmland across the horizon. He turned to his brother and said aloud for the first time what he only said to himself. "At times, my being the Ortsbauernführer will help us."

"Possibly," Bruno replied, with little sincerity. "But there will always be a time where it hurts us."

A week after the sign was erected, Josef arrived at the *Rathaus* in Allenstein. The city hall's sandy-colored brick sprouted a spire with a belfry topped by multiple cupolas, each receding in size as they reached toward the sky. The romantic building had been transformed from a seat of the regional government to a regional seat of the Nazi government. Through a series of SS checkpoints, Josef made his way to the third floor and the door with *Kreis-bauernführer Gustave Fink* painted on the glass.

An unfriendly secretary led him into another office, grand in size, with a leather sofa and a marble fireplace. Photographs covered a wall—each with a man in an SS uniform posing with other officers and politicians. It was the display of a man convinced he was living a destiny. Josef assumed the man didn't plan on being the Kreisbauernführer in Allenstein for very long.

Fink stood at a window looking out onto the street. From the photos, Josef knew his appearance before he faced him. His body was short, but his face was long with narrow eyes and thin lips. For an SS officer, he didn't look particularly German or busy.

In a flash, Fink spun around and raised his arm. "Heil Hitler!"

Josef did the same, hoping his salute didn't appear as awkward as it felt. When Fink lowered his arm, Josef followed and waited for the man to say something.

"You're more civilized than I expected," Fink said. "Your kind in Baden were little better than vassals."

Josef gently fingered his hat, thinking the man was an idiot if he didn't realize that Allenstein was a promotion for him. "East Prussian farms are larger than those in Baden."

"Why is that?"

"Well, historically—"

"Never mind." Fink raised his hand to stop him. "I'm not interested."

Josef kept his face impassive, though he wasn't impressed that local agriculture would now be dictated by a man so uninterested in it.

Fink pointed to the desk that stood between Josef and him. The lacquered desktop held two file folders. "The large folder is for you."

"Danke." Josef assumed the smaller file was his own. He wondered what it included from his arrest.

As Josef took the folder, Fink spoke at a rapid-fire pace.

"There is a handbook detailing your responsibilities and a list of the other Ortsbauernführer in other regions. Go to them if you have a question. All reports will be filed by their deadlines, and there are many of them, so be prepared."

"I will."

"Based on your reports, Berlin will set production goals in March and prices in July. There is no need for grain merchants anymore. That role is now solely an administrative position. Former grain merchants may be appointed to these administrative roles." Fink raised a finger to make a point. "Unless, of course, they're Jews."

Josef's mind leapt to Aaron Katz. There were few occupations left for Jews now. How would they survive?

Fink must have seen his mind at work because he answered. "Until we place someone, the Jew will do the administrative work. Naturally without pay, including your friend Aaron Katz."

Josef's eyes drifted to what had to be his file on Fink's desk. What did this man know of him?

When Josef looked up again, Fink said, "My secretary, Frau Gunia, will be your contact for anything else. That is all."

While Josef wanted to leave the room, he saw an opportunity. If he was going to take on the Ortsbauernführer role, he needed to be able to do some good. He held up his hand. "Pardon, Kreisbauernführer Fink, but might I place a request from the farmers of Guttstadt? You have the ability to help with the situation."

"Certainly," said Fink, straightening his spine as he assumed his authority. "What is it?"

"We need a new veterinarian."

"Ach," Fink grunted, before he waved his hand in disgusted disappointment. "Talk to Frau Gunia."

Josef had directed his family to ignore anyone Jewish in Guttstadt. It was easy to give the direction; it was harder for him to perform it. Withdrawing a hat tip to a Jewish acquaintance felt out of character, but it eventually became routine. His business partners and former political colleagues were the difficult encounters. These were hands he normally shook and backs he patted, but now he ignored people he knew well. Dispensing with all etiquette, he also was ungentlemanly to their wives, even women his own wife aspired to be like.

But Josef's worst experience occurred walking by the synagogue. Approaching its wooden doors, one swung out and Rabbi Rosen stepped onto the sidewalk. A squat man with sparkling blue eyes, cheery cheeks, and white hair and beard, Rabbi Rosen could have played Saint Nicholas at any Christmas celebration. They had worked together on the hospital board, and Josef had seen the rabbi on occasion visiting Father Schmidt at the Dom.

Rabbi Rosen beamed at Josef. "Guten Tag, Herr Haupt. How are you on this warm day?"

Instincts and urges clashed in Josef as he looked into the rabbi's bright eyes. Here was a man of God—a good man, a learned man, a friend to Josef's own favorite priest.

Josef's respect and natural warmth toward such a man required him to stop and reply, "Guten Tag, Rabbi Rosen. I'm doing well. How are you?" An exchange of happy small talk would occur, and Josef would walk on feeling better for having seen the rabbi that day.

But fear also demanded Josef's attention. What if he was seen not only speaking to a rabbi but also in front of a synagogue? Would he be brought in for questioning again?

Unable to commit to ignoring the rabbi or paying him proper respect, Josef pressed his fingers to the rim of his hat for a brief second and gave the rabbi a furtive glance before quickening his pace away from the synagogue. The minimal acknowledgment was so fast that he didn't catch the rabbi's reaction. As he continued down the street, relief spread through him, knowing he had escaped a dangerous situation, but it was quickly followed by shame. The relief was short lived, but the embarrassment lasted like he had been rude to a Catholic priest.

While the incident was de minimis on the spectrum of sin, it gnawed at him in the weeks before his next confession. His conscience begged to confess his cowardice. He wanted to be told it was all right—that he could do better in the future. But he realized it was a childish desire. If necessary, Josef was prepared to ignore, even disavow Rabbi Rosen, just as he would any Jewish person in town. It was preposterous to confess a sin that you had every intention of committing again.

When he asked Dorothea what she felt ignoring Rosa Katz, she shrugged.

"Nothing. She's ignoring me as well. It's as if we have a pact, and eventually, this will all be over. One day, things will go back to the way they always were."

Josef searched his wife's eyes, not believing she was serious. "It's been five years now. Do you really think that?"

Dorothea met his gaze, deadly serious, before she stood and walked toward a door. With her back to her husband, she ended the conversation.

"I do believe it. I have to."

Over the next month, Josef did his best to ignore the nips at his conscience as he performed his job as Ortsbauernführer. He made his rounds to the local farms, checking on their needs and production. If the conversation was entirely about farming, all was well.

His troubles started when farmers whom he had always considered like-minded Christian men displayed their Nazi sympathies. Had they always held these beliefs, he wondered. Or had they adopted them now in order to get ahead in the world?

Bruno's words haunted him because his brother had been proven right. The Haupts were a respected family. By becoming the Ortsbauernführer, Josef had signaled to others that he believed resistance was futile and the Nazi government was permanent.

Josef greeted every neighbor as he always had, but several now led with "Heil Hitler!" No one had ever greeted him like that before even if they were a member of the Nazi Party. Now Josef had to reply in kind.

Yet he still considered the greeting as foolish today as he did when he was arrested. For all those who saluted him who he knew weren't party members, he took it as an opportunity to signal he wasn't a member either.

He waved his hand, dismissing the salute. "Come now. There's no need for that." He then added the lie, "Nothing has changed."

For twenty years, Josef had met with Aaron Katz in July to negotiate a price for his crops before the harvest. Even though the price was now predetermined by Berlin, he thought he should visit Aaron as usual.

The sidewalks bustled around him as he stood in front of the Katz family's building. A large window looked out the second floor with *Katz & Co.* painted in gold lettering. The base of the red brick building held two storefronts. Dorothea's preferred tailor for the children's clothes operated out of one, and the other housed Josef's preferred tobacco shop for his evening cigars or pipe. Graffiti reading *Kauft nicht bei Juden* covered the stores' windows, warning gentiles not to buy from Jews.

Dorothea had since changed to a gentile tailor, and Josef had heard her muttering about the poor quality of his pick stitches. As for his tobacco, Josef soured just thinking of the hassle and impersonal experience of buying his tobacco in Allenstein rather than two feet in front of him from the jolly Herr Zimmerman.

No lights appeared in the office above, but he climbed the

steps anyway. As he normally would, he entered without knocking, but inside he found a changed room and man.

In its previous state, the large room housed multiple staff members hard at work at their desks. To the side of the picture window facing the street, Aaron would sit in his leather chair behind an ornate desk with neatly stacked papers and a cut-glass lamp.

Now, only a card table, two wooden chairs, and a metal desk lamp remained. Aaron sat at one end of the table, and the other end awaited visitors. Josef guessed those were infrequent.

"Guten Tag, Aaron," he said, removing his hat as he closed the door.

Aaron rose from his seat and began to lift his arm in the Hitler salute. Immediately, Josef waved his hand. "Come now. We're old friends. There's no need for that."

Aaron lowered his hand as if he were unsure of Josef's sincerity. "Guten Tag, Ortsbauernführer Haupt."

Josef startled at the formality from a man he had known for most his life. "Josef, bitte."

"As you wish." Aaron gestured to the empty chair. "Please have a seat."

Walking over to the table, Josef noticed that Aaron had lost weight. He had always been a portly man with his vest tight and suitcoat unbuttoned. Now his clothes hung on him—most likely because the family economized on food. Wanting the conversation to return to better days, Josef went to the interest they shared most in the world.

"I drove Mond into town this morning. He's an exceptional horse and so handsome. He seems to enjoy the attention he gets from strangers."

Aaron had bred a fine line of Trakehners, and Josef had bought Mond from him as a colt a few years before. Aaron's eyes lit up for a second, but it was a dim flicker compared to his usual response to anything related to horses.

"That's nice to hear, but I know you didn't come to discuss horses."

Josef kicked himself for bringing up the topic. Aaron was out of the horse business and probably missed it terribly.

"I understand things have been difficult for you and your family."

"Yes... difficult," remarked Aaron, unamused by Josef's understatement.

"Aaron... I—" Feeling like a chastened schoolboy, Josef fumbled for a paper in his suit pocket. "I have my production numbers, but I also thought you might want the yields from the other Guttstadt farms. That may be helpful to you."

"Danke, but I'm to receive the form from Allenstein once they approve it."

"Ah, yes, but I thought you might want a preview."

"It makes no difference to me."

As the two continued to converse, Josef began having a flashback to his best friend in the army, Andreas, who died from combat wounds. When Josef first visited Andreas as he lay in the medical tent, Josef would try to joke about the army or talk about their friends' antics. He soon learned those topics were as painful for his dying friend as his lost arm. He would never experience either of them again.

While Aaron wasn't experiencing a physical death, his professional life had ended. This man, who had been a vital part of the civic and commercial community in Guttstadt, had been banished from it.

Josef tried to carry on the one-sided conversation, but Aaron mercifully cut it short.

"Thank you for the information. No doubt, you'll receive word of the prices before I do. When the farmers come, I'll review their production numbers against the form from Allenstein and report any inconsistencies back to the Reichsnährstand." He raised an eyebrow. "Neither of us are involved at that point."

Josef understood exactly what he meant. The two of them

were merely cogs in the Reich bureaucracy. Enforcement was left to the SS.

The silence grew between the men as Josef realized his old colleague wanted him gone. He rose from his seat and extended his hand. "I wish you a good day then, Aaron."

"And to you."

As their handshake ended, Josef automatically said, "Please give my regards to Frau Katz." But this time his stomach plummeted because he remembered he had just ignored the woman on the street the day before. Flushed with shame for such an offense, he fumbled to find some explanation for himself. "If you see me on the street and I—"

"Ja." Aaron withdrew his hand and added in an acid tone, "I understand, Ortsbauernführer Haupt."

Josef deepened his gaze, hoping it might convey his sincere apologies, but Aaron returned a grim smile. Offering a silent, humbled bow, Josef left the office. As he walked down the stairs, he knew Aaron Katz did indeed understand him, but he no longer respected him. Josef had to agree—he no longer deserved the man's respect.

Chapter Seven

Margarete

Margarete's eyes crossed as she stared at her English homework. While her parents sat in the dining room enjoying a cup of tea, Margarete sat at the kitchen table finishing her schoolwork. It was hard to concentrate on a foreign language with a conversation going in the next room.

Trying to focus, she began to recite aloud, "Catch, caught. Bring, brought. Teach, taught."

As she spoke, the screen door opened, and her brother's voice announced, "*Bring*, not *brink*. You need to work on your accent."

She looked up as Franz strode into the room. Being older and living away at boarding schools, her eldest brothers fascinated her —especially Franz. He was the blond golden boy of the family. She was sure that there was nothing he couldn't do well. He was brilliant in school and as capable on a horse as her father. He could even press his own pants and cook potatoes. Everything came easily to him.

"I know," she said with a discouraged sigh.

Franz flashed his charming smile. "It will come." As he walked past her and into the dining room, he tugged at one of her braids and added a cheeky, "Eventually."

Franz's excited voice came from the dining room.

"Papa, I just saw some friends down the road. I don't get to see them very often," said Franz. "There's a Hitler Youth meeting in town later this evening. I'd like to take a horse into town."

Margarete expected her father would agree at once, and when he didn't answer she knew something was serious. The more sober and quiet her father became, the more important the topic. She looked over her shoulder to see Franz with his hands on his hips, unhappy with whatever their father didn't say.

"Why not?" Franz asked.

Taking a deep breath, Margarete waited for the answer. Her older brothers often pushed the limits their parents set upon them. Even when she became sixteen like Franz, she doubted she would ever raise her voice to her parents.

Before Josef spoke he caught Margarete's eye, addressing her as well. "I want the family to remain at home tonight."

"Papa, everyone is going, and I'd like to spend some time with my friends."

"No, not everyone is going," said Josef. "Our family and friends won't be there."

"What's going on? Why don't you want me to go?"

"I'm not sure. It's some sort of Nazi activity."

"But you're the Ortsbauernführer," answered Franz. "Shouldn't you be there?"

"I'm not a member of the party. I don't need to go."

"Don't you think it would be good for me? If I were involved in the party, maybe it might be helpful for my application to officer candidate school?"

"Nonsense," said Josef. "You'll receive an appointment as an officer based on your schooling and abilities. Our government may have changed, but the standards of the German military have not."

"But—"

"My answer is final. No."

Margarete watched Franz's unhappy surrender as he slouched out of the room and stomped up the stairs to the second floor. When her eyes drifted back to her parents, Dorothea pointed at her. "Back to work."

But it was impossible for Margarete to concentrate when her parents were talking about something like a secret event in town. She kept her eyes on the English grammar book while she listened to her parents in the dining room.

In the softest voice, Dorothea asked, "Do you think it will be dangerous tonight?"

"Potentially," answered Josef. "The party doesn't fully trust me, so I hear very little. But we should avoid whatever is being organized. I worry for the Jewish families."

"Will it be happening everywhere? Is Paul in danger in Insterberg?"

"Paul? Our eldest, aimless child? Our selfish child? Paul would never put himself in harm's way for a cause."

"He lacks ambition, but he's not aimless."

"True. And his lack of ambition will protect him. It's Franz whom I worry about."

"Franz will obey you, but do you think the Jewish families know what's going on?"

"Someone should warn them. That would be the decent thing to do," answered Josef. "But it can't be me."

Her father moved the conversation to something about selling a cow, but Margarete had already stopped listening. She saw how the authorities and some in town treated Jews. The taunting, the stoning, and the beatings were inhumane and against everything she had been taught. Yet she was also taught to turn a blind eye like everyone else on the street. She didn't understand why Franz cared more about his ambitions than avoiding trouble.

Early the following morning, Margarete stirred in her sleep. The sounds of the house and farm were out of order. Usually, her parents' day began at four in the morning. She would hear her father move about the hallways, with her mother following close behind. Josef was always the first in the stables in the morning, starting the morning chores of caring for the animals, and the workers would join him soon after. Meanwhile, the clink and clank of pots and plates rose from the kitchen where Dorothea and her maids started breakfast for the family and workers. Margarete and her brothers joined everyone an hour later to help with the work.

That morning, not long after four, she heard a single horse galloping from the barn area. Bracing the chilly morning air, she ran to the window in her bare feet. Despite the sound of horse hooves proving someone was out there, she saw only darkness.

Wanting answers, but not wanting to wake Sophia, she tiptoed around the dark room as she readied for the day. She made her bed and donned a school dress. Even without light or a mirror, her fingers could braid her thick hair into two plaits. Curls would escape the braids over the course of the day, leaving her disheveled by the time of abendbrot. She wished she had Sophia's smooth blond hair which behaved itself all day.

After a detour to the bathroom, she continued to tiptoe as she made her way down the stairs. When she entered the kitchen, her mother and the maids were busy readying breakfast.

"*Guten Morgen*," Margarete murmured as she closed the door.

Dorothea eyed her. "Guten Morgen. But why are you awake so early? Are you sick?"

"No. I couldn't sleep."

Her mother pointed to a stack of plates. "Then you can set the table for the workers."

The family dined in the dining room, while the workers had their own room off the side of the kitchen. As Margarete went about setting the table with plates, cups, and flatware, she peered out the window, hoping she might see someone who could give her answers. She knew better than to ask her mother with the maids nearby. She wished her brothers would wake. They would learn what happened long before her.

Just as she began to turn away, she saw a familiar outline. The figure tied a horse to a hitching post. When the moon shone against the body's blond hair, she quietly slipped outside to the stable.

"Franz," she called in a loud whisper.

She didn't need to call him because he had already spotted her before she spoke. When he was close enough, he smiled, his white teeth visible in the night. "You're awake early."

"So are you," she quipped. "Who left the house so early?"

"It's nothing to worry about."

"Then what is it? Please tell me."

He stared at her for a moment before he lowered his voice. "There may have been some trouble in town last night. Papa went to see."

"What kind of trouble?"

Franz patted the horse's rump. "I can only guess. We'll know soon."

A half hour later, Margarete sat at the kitchen table grinding barley for the morning coffee. Coffee beans were a rarity now. It was something to do with international trade and the Reich, which she didn't understand except that her father didn't like the added barley. As she spun the handle on the grinder, she heard the gallop of a horse grow from faint to loud with every second.

Testing her patience, she kept grinding and waited for the story to unfold. When her father came through the kitchen door, he asked her mother to go into his office. Margarete shifted her eyes to the maids, who gave each other knowing looks. Everyone seemed to have some idea but her.

It was only near the end of breakfast that her father announced to the family, "I think it best that the children stay home from school today." He glanced at Franz. "No one in the family will go into town."

"Why, Papa?" asked Albert.

Dorothea looked down the table. "Margarete, please take the girls into the kitchen."

"No," Josef said, holding up his hand to halt her. "Margarete is old enough to stay."

After Sophia, Katharina, and Martha had happily left the boring adult discussion, he said, "It's no use hiding these unpleasant things from you. When you go back to school tomorrow, you'll see the town is changed. It may be frightening, but you need to remember that you're safe."

"What's happened?" asked Stefan.

"The SS has called for the destruction of synagogues and Jewish businesses throughout Germany. They began late last night, and it's still going on. When I went into town, the synagogue was burning. I spoke with a fireman who has orders to make sure no Aryan buildings catch fire, but the synagogue is to burn to the ground. Windows on Jewish stores have been broken. There's glass everywhere and shameful looting."

Stefan spoke slowly, "It's a pogrom."

"It's horrific." Josef made the sign of the cross, and the family followed. When he looked up, he added, "But we'll keep that opinion to ourselves."

Margarete looked around at her family as everyone considered the information. Dorothea's expression was grave as she looked down. Albert looked frightened.

Stefan was as serious as his mother, while Franz was contemplative. He spoke first. "What if this is actually a good thing, Papa?"

"Franz!" Dorothea exclaimed. "How dare you say that? These are innocent people being persecuted for no reason."

"Well, of course," said Franz carefully. "And it will only get worse for them. It's in the Jews' best interest to leave Germany on their own. If they're smart, they'll all go now. Then there may be peace again."

Josef stared at his son, eventually saying, "You're partially correct. Things are getting worse for Jewish people in Germany. Those who are able may be smart to leave, but that doesn't make this right. We always knew there would be no peace under Adolf Hitler. Everyone has less freedom today than we did before the Nazis came into power."

"And what of those who can't leave?" Dorothea asked, looking straight at Franz. "What about people without the money or health to leave? What about the elderly? Germany is their homeland."

"It is," said Franz. He glanced around at his family, trying to explain himself. "I'm just trying to be practical given the circumstances."

Always a listener before a speaker, Stefan said, "I know some families helping Jewish people go into hiding. Is that something we might do?"

Franz sneered at his younger brother. "You're supposed to inherit this farm. You would risk your birthright for some strangers?"

"They're not strangers," said Stefan. "We've known these people our whole lives."

"In these times," said Franz. "Anyone who doesn't live in this house is a stranger."

Albert piped up, "The Bible says we must welcome the stranger."

Margarete nodded at Albert to thank him for speaking what she was too afraid to say herself. She tilted forward for a closer look at Franz to see his response to what she thought was a good point.

"The Bible doesn't apply to the Reich," quipped Franz.

"Ach du lieber Himmel!" exclaimed Dorothea. "Where did you hear that?"

"Hitler Youth." Franz waved his hands across the table. "We

all hear it, even Margarete will in the BDM. Mutti, you know the Nazis teach atheism."

"That doesn't mean that you should accept it." She looked at him with scorn. "You know better, Franz."

Franz shrugged. "I just wanted to point out that the Reich's laws aren't based in the Bible."

"Now that is true. Both the Reich and the Pope would agree on that," said Josef bitterly. He scanned the table, looking squarely for a moment in everyone's eyes. "We will always welcome the stranger who comes to this house looking for food."

"No one hungry leaves our doorstep empty-handed," said Dorothea.

"But they can't stay," said Josef with finality. "Not even in the barn for an hour at night. It's too dangerous."

Margarete thought of the tired and hungry who came to the kitchen side door. Usually, they were weary travelers from far away. Some would ask if they could sleep in the hayloft. Her mother always allowed families with children, as long as they left in the morning. She imagined Dorothea saying no to a request by a Guttstadt Jewish family. It seemed impossible for her parents to be so unchristian on the Haupt doorstep.

Remembering everything her father had just described, she assumed many of those families would now try to flee or go into hiding. She imagined them on foot at night walking on the side of the road and turning onto the Haupt property. The scenario abruptly ended there in her mind. After last night, no Jewish person would come to them. Even if they trusted her father before, they wouldn't now—not with the swastika sign in front of their farm. The Haupt family didn't welcome the stranger after all.

Unless it was a blizzardy day, the children walked or rode bicycles the five kilometers into town. Despite the fair weather, the following day was different. Josef and Franz drove Katharina, Sophia, Margarete, Albert, and Stefan into town to make sure the children arrived safely at school.

Soon after the Dom's great tower could be seen in the distance, the smell of fire burned through Margarete's nostrils as she breathed.

Katharina wrinkled her freckled nose. "Why does it smell so bad?"

"A fire," said Josef.

The children looked at one other wondering if he would expand on his statement, but he was quiet. Margarete guessed he thought less information was better for the little girls.

Josef parked the carriage outside of town, which caused Albert to whine, "Why must we park so far away?"

"He doesn't want the horses stepping on the broken glass," Stefan answered with the seniority of an older brother.

While Josef delivered Katharina and Sophia to the lower school, Franz was put in charge of Stefan, Albert, and Margarete. Stefan didn't believe he needed supervision from a brother only a year older than him, so he ran ahead with Albert following close behind.

Franz shrugged as his younger brothers ran off and turned to Margarete. "Do you want to go with them?"

"No. I want to stay with you."

She wanted her family to see her as more mature, but she felt very much the little girl at that moment. Other than her father, Margarete felt safest around Franz and Paul. They both had a confidence about themselves that was reassuring.

"Come then," he said and held out his hand.

They began walking toward the school, and in only a block, the change in Guttstadt was obvious. Glass and papers spread over the ground. Jewish storefronts only had jagged shards framing what had been windows.

While Margarete scanned high and low observing the destruction, almost everyone else on the street walked with their heads down. Even more than usual, no one wanted to call attention to themselves. Margarete glanced up at Franz. He, too, seemed to be taking in the situation. He faced straight ahead but allowed his eyes to shift all around.

Margarete tugged on his sleeve and whispered, "Can we go by the synagogue?"

As they turned the corner, Margarete's eyes went wide. The formerly small but dignified synagogue was now a burnt carcass. Ash fluttered in the wind like deceptive blossoms. She stared at the pitiful remains, unable to believe her eyes yet sensing she was witness to something momentous. A building of God had been intentionally destroyed as if God himself was of no consequence.

Beneath the horror lay another feeling that clawed its way past the shock. It was terror. Her father was right. There would be no peace. All of this was happening to the Jews, but it was left as a warning to everyone.

She looked up at Franz, whose eyes had moved on from the building to the nearby Jewish butcher shop. As they walked by, only a portion of the windowpane remained on the butcher's window, and the burnt smell in the air had a nauseating undertone of rotting meat. Through the gaping hole, she saw that all the equipment and most of the goods were gone. Birds picked at animal innards strewn about the floor. She was repulsed, but turning away offered her no relief. In the distance, she saw two SS soldiers pushing a man down the street with the butts of their rifles.

"Let's turn around," said Franz, guiding her with his arm. "Don't look back. Don't talk."

They sped toward the school, her mind still swarming with images. She looked up again at Franz, desperate for some guidance. "What does it mean?"

"What does it mean?" he asked with a dark laugh. He glanced around them, and seeing no one nearby, he whispered, "Papa is right. It's horrific—an atrocity."

"That's what I thought." She gazed up at her older brother. "After this, do you still want to join the army?"

"Oh, yes." He looked up at the street and shook his head at the tragedy. "Other than our farm, the Wehrmacht is likely the safest place to be."

Chapter Eight

JOSEF

It was to have been another short trip into town. Guttstadt was a place to attend church or school or quickly shop, but it was no longer a place to linger. The streets still bore the scars of the last November. The synagogue's charred corpse had been razed, but the building's blackened foundation remained. It served Hitler's purpose to warn everyone—Jew, gentile, or atheist —of the Reich's power.

As Josef neared the train station, a whistle alerted another departure. The platform was always busy. Unseen but felt in the cold air was the chill of impending war. The nonaggression pact between Hitler and Poland was an obvious fiction. People without land left for cities with factories to outfit the Wehrmacht. Josef had lost both of his sharecropping German families, and the farmhands he could scrounge up never stayed for long.

Scanning the station, he noticed some passengers who stood out despite their small stature. Every few days, these special travelers waited on the platform for the *Kindertransport* to rescue them. The good people of England recognized that Nazi Germany had become so hostile to Jews that they should save some of the children. Priority was given to orphans, the poor, or children with a parent in a concentration camp. After last November, there were hundreds of thousands of Jewish children who fell into at least one of those categories.

That day, he noticed Rabbi Rosen standing on the platform next to his granddaughter. Josef believed her name was Sara. To the side stood Sara's mother, the rabbi's daughter-in-law. In one hand, she held a handkerchief with which she dabbed her eyes. In the other, she held the hand of her little son, Joshua. Their father —the rabbi's son—Saul, was gone. Like every other able-bodied Jewish man of a reasonable age, he had been arrested during *Kristallnacht*. While the Jewish men awaited their sentencing, Bürgermeister Renkel came to the prison with his thugs to beat them. The Nazis were drunk, so it was just for fun.

As with almost everything under the Reich, Saul's fate had been decided by luck rather than facts or merit. A friend of Josef's, Judge Bleissem, released the men who came before him, saying they had done nothing wrong. Although Saul was equally innocent, he drew the wrong judge. The Nazi loyalist summarily sentenced him indefinitely to Sachsenhausen.

Rabbi Rosen bowed to look Sara in the eye. With a hand on her shoulder, he appeared to be giving her words of wisdom. Sara reminded Josef of Margarete. Around the same age, both now had shed their braids of little girlhood and wore their dark blond hair bobbed, with a clip holding it out of their face. Sara gave her grandfather a stoic nod, appearing to understand the desperate situation. Josef was impressed with her composure. He imagined sending Margarete to a foreign land with no knowledge of whether they might see each other again. He hoped that she would be as strong as Sara.

A voice jolted Josef out of his imagination and into reality. "Guten Tag, Josef."

Josef turned to see Renkel coming toward him with an expectant look in his eye. He was the last person Josef wanted to see at that moment. Hiding his irritation with silence, Josef gave him the expected reply. "Heil Hitler."

The Guttstadt Nazi leader smiled broadly and returned the greeting. Afterward he pointed to the train station and laughed. "Are you enjoying seeing the Jews leaving?"

"Just observing." Annoyed by his glee, Josef added, "I think you have to agree that the children are brave."

"I suppose so. I didn't know that you had such a soft spot for children."

Josef arched a brow. "I do have eight of them."

"Ah, yes." He raised a finger. "Shall we go for a walk? We haven't spoken in a while."

As the two walked down the side of the railroad tracks away from town, Renkel said, "I wanted to ask you about joining the party. You've put it off for far too long."

Josef never said anything aloud that might put him at odds with the Nazi Party. He faithfully performed his duties as Ortsbauernführer. He was quick with a "Heil Hitler" when called for. But the emotional scene at the train station had filled him with regret and shame. He needed to rebel, even if it was feeble.

"I don't understand why my joining the party is necessary."

"Ah, you don't give yourself enough credit, Josef. You've been a successful Ortsbauernführer because people respect you."

"Danke," he said with a wary eye.

"You should return that respect to the Führer." Renkel leaned closer to Josef. "You're an astute man. You know we'll be at war soon—first with Poland and then with Britain and France. We must show solidarity to our enemies."

Josef did know, but his blood still chilled at the thought of another world war. "I believe that giving my four sons to fight for Germany is a great sign of respect and solidarity."

"They will be drafted, so it isn't a sign of respect. It's merely compliance with the law."

Josef pursed his lips, stopping himself from saying something he would most definitely regret.

Renkel continued, "If you support the Reich, why won't you fly its flag? In case of war, that makes me question your loyalty."

"I support the Reich. Have I not worked diligently for the Reichsnährstand?"

"Of course, and it would be a shame for you to lose that role."

Josef was silent, glaring at the Nazi. He actually would prefer only to mind his own farm, but losing the Ortsbauernführer position would cast a cloud of suspicion around his family.

Having made his point, Renkel changed his tone. It was almost seductive. "And if you joined the party, the Reich could support you more as well. You're facing a labor shortage like the rest of the farmers. The Reich is relocating workers to East Prussia for the war effort. Party members will be the first to benefit."

Renkel placed a hand on Josef's arm, startling him. He glanced down at the man's gloved hand, and there was no doubt he felt claimed.

"It's time to place you on the party rolls," said Renkel.

"I would like time to think about it," said Josef, grasping for a reason. "I've enjoyed being out of politics."

"You haven't been out of politics since you became the Ortsbauernführer." Renkel smiled and patted his arm. "I'll send some men by with a flag to raise over your estate. You can pay them for it. I'm sure it will look grand."

Josef felt his dignity leave him once again as he acquiesced to something he once thought unthinkable—him, a proud Zentrum member, hoisting the Nazi flag. It was just like the Nazis to coerce him to join and then make him purchase a flag. Selling his soul wasn't enough; he had to pay for it as well.

"And don't worry about your sons," said Renkel. Ignoring Josef's sour expression, he smiled. "Herr Hitler is the greatest leader in history. The war will be short. Your sons may not even have to serve."

Nine months later, Dorothea waited for Josef to shut their bedroom door before she asked a rhetorical question. "So, the war is over?"

"Only with Poland." Josef smiled and kissed the top of her head. "Conquering England and France will take much longer."

As she brushed her hair with her boar-bristle brush, she looked at him in the mirror. "And in the meantime, my daughters will be turned into common field hands."

Untying his tie, he sighed. "Dorothea..."

Pointing the brush at him like a judge issuing a ruling, she said, "You know I'm no stranger to hard work. But every day Margarete and Sophia take the cows to the meadow like they're shepherdesses with only Senta to help them. They should be focusing on their studies."

"I'm sorry," he replied testily as he removed his watch and pocket change. "But what would you have me do? We're short-handed. We were lucky to have the boys home this summer. Now they only come home on the weekends, yet the cows must eat every day."

"But you said the Reich was getting us help. What good is it being the Ortsbauernführer if we don't even get workers to run our own farm?"

"The Reichsnährstand has said the help is coming. I can't push them to move any faster." Taking off his jacket, he added, "Remember these people are coming from Poland and White Russia. They're immigrants, and this is a journey for them."

"I don't understand why it's taking them so long. Look at where they come from. They've probably never even seen indoor plumbing or electricity."

"I doubt they have," said Josef, too tired to put up an adequate defense of poor souls he didn't even know. "But it may be difficult to leave their homeland and families and friends."

"Humph," said Dorothea, unimpressed by his answer.

"Will you be happy if I tell you that the girls won't need to take the cows out tomorrow?"

"Yes."

"Well, good. Because tomorrow they must harvest potatoes."

Row after row, the Haupt daughters harvested potatoes. Moving in pairs on their knees, they followed a plow that Josef pushed himself to soften the earth so they could dig. It was backbreaking work for both him and the girls. When he turned to see his daughters scrambling in the cold dirt, he silently damned the Reich. Dorothea was right. This wasn't the life for which they were born.

The girls were chipper until they couldn't bear it any longer. "Might we have a break, Papa?" asked Margarete.

There was still much work to be done. Josef would never have agreed to stop had one of his farmworkers asked, but those men weren't his young daughters.

Using the discarded potato stalks, Josef built a small fire in the field, where they could rest with some comfort. The girls extended their hands to the fire, warming their hands as they rubbed off dirt. Josef searched for something that might elevate an unhappy situation. How could he make their work have some meaning? A poem from his school days came to him—Friedrich Schiller's *The Song of the Bell*. Schiller describes casting a bell and the labors associated with it:

> *From the heated brow*
> *Sweat must freely flow,*
> *That the work may praise the Master,*
> *Though the blessing comes from higher.*

When he began to recite the poem, the girls giggled at their father pretending as if he were in school. Their spirits rose, but Josef stopped when Senta's bark rose off in the distance followed by a truck's rumble climbing a hill. Josef rounded up the girls, and they hurried toward the house.

Nearing the courtyard, Josef first saw Dorothea walk toward Senta to calm her down. The truck then appeared, distinctly black with a swastika on the side. The SS had arrived.

As Dorothea took Senta by the collar, two SS officers jumped out of the truck. One approached Dorothea while the other went to the back. Out popped three men, all dressed alike in what looked to be military uniforms, which Josef didn't recognize from afar. With a few more steps, Josef realized they were Polish infantry.

"What on earth?" said Josef under his breath. "Why are they here?"

"Was ist los, Papa?" asked Margarete, her eyes full of fear.

"Nothing to worry about."

As Josef and the girls entered the courtyard, the commanding SS officer turned to acknowledge him. Dorothea met Josef's eye with confused alarm and said, "Rottenführer Dost, this is my husband, Herr Haupt."

After Josef and the sergeant exchanged Hitler salutes, the sergeant smiled. "The lovely Frau Haupt has introduced herself to me. And who are these sweet Fräulein?"

Rather than dressed in fresh dresses with bows in their hair, the Haupt girls stood disheveled from working in the potato fields. Their aprons were so covered in dirt that the dresses beneath them couldn't have been spared. Their look of peasant girls was complete with kerchiefs on their heads and grime embedded in their hands and fingernails.

Yet Josef introduced them as if they were ready for church. "These are my four daughters, Margarete, Sophia, Katharina, and Martha. My four boys are away at school."

"*Guten Abend*," said the sergeant with a bow to the girls.

The girls responded with a curtsy, varying in depth and ability according to their ages. "Guten Abend," they mumbled together.

Dorothea announced she was taking the girls inside, and when the girls were safely indoors, Josef turned to the sergeant.

"What may I help you with?"

"The Reichsnährstand has issued these men to work on your farm." The sergeant pulled out a letter from his uniform's pocket. "You have a meeting tomorrow with Kreisbauernführer Fink."

Josef scanned the letter, which mentioned the Ostarbeiter program, and glanced at the three Poles again. Standing at attention, their chests protruded from their clothes, but it wasn't from their stance. They were undernourished.

Josef pointed to the corner of the house. "Might I speak to you privately for a moment, Rottenführer?"

When they were far enough away, he asked, "Could you tell me more about these men? They're Polish soldiers."

"They're prisoners of war."

"But Poland has been annexed by Germany. Why are these men still prisoners?"

"I only know that they're part of the *Ostarbeiter* program." The sergeant lifted his hands as if he couldn't be expected to have any more information. "I do deliveries."

Josef stared in silent bewilderment at the idea that he was being given human cargo like from the slave ships of long ago.

"They shouldn't be any trouble at all, and they'll work hard," continued the officer. "They know that this is an opportunity."

"An opportunity?"

"Oh, yes. This is work outside in the country. They came from an armament factory in Dresden where they lived in a prison."

Josef opened his mouth and quickly closed it, thinking better than to point out the Reich was violating the Geneva convention. POWs could work in agriculture but not making arms to defeat their own country.

"I hope they enjoy the fresh air," said Josef as an understatement.

"We'll come by once a month to check on them, but there

shouldn't be any problems. You'll be getting more of them as well."

"More POWs?"

"I suppose and others." The sergeant looked at his watch. "I must be on my way to Heilsberg. The Ortsbauernführer there is also getting the first shipment."

As they went back to the truck, the sergeant continued, "They should sleep in your stables, and they're not supposed to get the same food as your family. Remember that."

"In my stables? Our worker housing is empty."

The sergeant answered with a shrug. "Those are the rules."

As quickly as they came, the two stormtroopers jumped in the truck and drove away, leaving Josef with three hungry men who stared at him with blank eyes of fear. Otherwise, there was silence until the Nazi flag slapped against itself in the wind. Josef thought back to when he was a soldier during the Great War. How would he have felt if he had been taken prisoner by the French? These men had committed no crime except to fight for their country. Yet here they stood, imprisoned with him as their jailer. As the Nazi flag whipped in the wind, it validated all of their feelings.

After stilted introductions in a mixture of German and Polish, he situated the prisoners in the fields before finding Dorothea in the kitchen making bread.

"Where are the girls?" he asked, sitting down at the kitchen table.

"Upstairs taking baths. Who are those men?"

"Polish prisoners of war. They're our new field hands."

"What?" she exclaimed, throwing dough onto the board. "The SS has placed Polish criminals at our home?"

"No. Polish infantry who had the bad luck of being captured. They're farm boys. The SS had them working in a factory, so they seem genuinely happy to be back on a farm." He nodded to the bread dough. "Especially after I mentioned abendbrot."

"I don't understand. I thought we were getting families who wanted to move to Germany." She put her floured hands on her hips, so angry she forgot to wipe them. "This is a farm. Not a prison."

"It's not the Poles' fault that they're prisoners. They're innocent, but this happens in war."

"But I thought the war with Poland is over."

"For some reason, the Reich hasn't released these men yet. Fink has called me to a meeting tomorrow. The sergeant said we'll be getting more workers soon. I presume these men will be released when the others arrive."

Dorothea looked to the ceiling for some assistance in her thoughts. "It's a relief that they're not criminals, but if these men are innocent, I don't like the idea of confining them here. They'll resent us."

"The officer said they should sleep in the stables." Josef rolled his eyes in scorn. "Ridiculous."

"In the cold stables? After they spend all day working? They'll be filthy and get sick." Wiping her hands, she joined him at the table. "The girls will set the table in the workers' dining room for them. They need food. I'll find some old clothes as well. Their uniforms need washing as much as they do."

"Danke," he said with a relieved smile that quickly became chagrined. "I believe the Reich doesn't want them to eat as well as we do, so we should serve them something else."

"What do they want them eating? Bread and water? How will they have enough energy to work?"

"Maybe you could make them a simple stew?"

"No, I will not." She wagged her finger at her husband. "And you can tell the SS that those men will eat what we eat. I'm not running a restaurant."

The following day Frau Gunia deposited Josef in Fink's office to wait for him. He wandered to the window to see the view onto the Allenstein *Platz*. The last few autumn leaves tumbled through the square. In the distance, he saw an old man with a pointed stick chasing after them. Only a year before, the sight would have gone unnoticed by him. He was just another pensioner who made extra reichsmarks by tidying the streets. Now he saw the man and knew he was Jewish, one of the few left. Either he was too old or sick or poor or with too many dependents to have fled the country into freedom, or he was too old or sick to be taken to a labor camp. Instead, he spent his days chasing litter and leaves with a stick, knowing his life might depend upon him skewering them in midflight. In Guttstadt, Aaron Katz was this man.

Fink broke Josef's thoughts with a loud clearing of his throat followed by a Hitler salute. Josef returned the greeting in a daze, and Fink offered him a seat, announcing, "This meeting is to discuss the Ostarbeiter program."

"I was surprised to have the Polish POWs arrive on my doorstep yesterday," said Josef as he sat. "We've been so short-handed, so they're a great help."

"You're welcome," said Fink as if the prisoners were a personal gift from him.

"I presume they won't be with us for long, though."

"Why is that?"

"Because the war with Poland is over. The Reich will release them."

Fink answered with a dark chuckle. "Whatever for?"

"Because they're POWs, not prisoners."

"They're Poles. They're here to work."

"But—"

"But they're Poles. They're Slavs—slaves, really. That's what they do." Fink's eyes narrowed. "Since when does a former Zentrum party member care about Poles? Haven't Poles been making you Prussians rich for centuries?"

Fink wasn't wrong. The Zentrum had always maligned the Poles, but Josef shrugged. "We didn't force them to work in servitude."

"The Ostarbeiter program is how the Reich will fulfill its agricultural needs during the war."

"I thought the Reich was relocating families from the East who wanted to live in Germany."

Fink smiled at his recitation of Reich propaganda like he was a good little boy who had learned his school lesson. "Indeed, we're finding strong Slavs and sending them to Germany for the war effort, but there aren't enough of them."

"How are you finding them?" Josef regretted asking, thinking he didn't want to know.

"Everywhere." Fink tossed his hand toward the window behind him. "We find them at their work, or the cinema, or church."

"You take them from church?"

"Why not? Poles are like a herd of sheep going to church, so it's easy to round them up and choose the best ones."

The idea was a strike to Josef's own heart. He imagined the end of Mass at the Guttstadt Dom. Germans and Poles both emerged from the church with a cheerful, peaceful ease brought on by their community and faith. It was a feeling only to be found after Mass. Now he envisioned a fellow parishioner grabbed by an SS soldier. He briefly closed his eyes, unable to fathom the affront to his faith.

When he said nothing, Fink snorted. "I see you don't approve."

Josef mustered up a statement that said nothing. "It's not how I've recruited farmhands in the past."

"We're at war. I understand that your young daughters are even out in the fields."

Recognizing that the SS officer had reported back on their visit to the Haupt farm, he anxiously gripped his hat. "Will every farmer in Guttstadt receive Ostarbeiter?"

"Eventually." Fink picked up a paper on his desk. "You should familiarize yourself with the rules for these workers."

"Will I have to enforce these rules with the Guttstadt farmers?"

"You? Good God, no," said Fink, derisively. "Nothing would ever get done. That's for the SS."

Josef noted the insult, though he took it as a compliment.

Fink glanced at the paper and rattled off the rules. "The Ostarbeiter don't have the right to complain. There is a strict curfew. They may not attend church, though if they need a clergyman because they're dying, you can provide one."

Pointing his finger directly at him, Fink announced, "If you're given women, sexual relations are strictly prohibited, and if it happens, it must be reported. You and your boys should stay away. There will be no mixing of the German and Polish races."

For the first time, Josef showed the disgust he felt for Fink as his lip curled in a sneer. "That won't be a problem."

"Maybe not," replied Fink flippantly before he looked again at the list. "You can work the Ostarbeiter as hard and as long as you want. Corporal punishment is fine. You should let the Reich know if there's a bigger disciplinary issue."

Fed up with the conversation, Josef said, "I have worker housing standing empty, so I've let them sleep there. I don't want people in my stables who might cause a fire."

"Fine, but you're spoiling them," Fink said in exasperation. "Don't let them steal your potatoes because that's stealing from the Reich, as you know."

Josef nodded, deciding not to mention the food Dorothea would provide the prisoners. If the alternative was working in an armament factory, living in crowded barracks, and starving on meager rations, he doubted the POWs would reveal Frau Haupt fed them the same menu as her family.

Fink held up an accusatory finger. "And you should know, there is severe punishment if you haven't maintained the necessary distance from the Ostarbeiter. Once a month an SS officer will come by to see that everything is in order."

"Of course," murmured Josef. His farm was going to be a prison, and the Ostarbeiter would be his prisoners. He would stand guard, but he shouldn't forget that he was an inmate as well.

CHAPTER NINE

MARGARETE

"Sometimes I wonder if this summer will ever end." Albert ran the brush through the draft horse's feathered hoof hair, proclaiming, "At school, I can relax."

"I wish I could go off to boarding school." Margarete held the bridle and stared into the mare's darkest brown eyes, which blinked as if she understood Margarete's plight. Albert had followed in the footsteps of Franz and their father at a prep school for his high school diploma. Paul had attended an engineering trade school in Gumbinnen, while Stefan took special courses in agriculture in Allenstein. Margarete eventually would have to attend high school in Guttstadt and work on the farm. "I have chores all the time."

Albert rose from his knees and looked down at her with an examining expression like he was taking stock of her. Had he not noticed she wasn't a little girl anymore? He would always be taller, but at twelve, she was growing so fast she would soon surpass her mother's height. She'd already lost interest in playing with toys with the younger girls. But because of the war and farm work, their parents didn't like the children spending time off the estate with friends.

Albert cocked his head in sympathy. "After you finish high school, you get to go to finishing school. I'll be jealous because you'll live in the big city..." His voice changed to a chortle. "In Königsberg!"

"I can't even imagine it." Margarete laughed, and her dancing eyes looked to the heavens as she wondered what life away from the farm might be like.

A rustling rose around the corner of the barn followed by a loud thump of something heavy hitting the ground. Margarete couldn't see who it might be, but seconds later an unmistakable noise started. With four brothers, she was well aware of male biology, and she raised her eyebrows.

Albert scowled and whispered something he wouldn't have said to a little girl, "Who's taking a piss out here?"

At a loss for whom it might be, Margarete shrugged. No one in the family would do such a thing, and it wasn't like the Poles. Boys and men would relieve themselves in the fields but never near the house or barns. The Poles were decent men and always used the toilet in their houses.

"Well, I'm not going to be blamed when Papa sees it." Albert dropped the curry brush and stomped around the corner.

Margarete waited for Albert to bark at the man, but the sound of streaming, splattering urine only got louder. She heard the voice of their eldest brother, Paul, greet Albert with a sunny, "*Wie geht's?*"

"What are you doing?" asked Albert in an incredulous voice.

"My boots are still stiff, even after basic training. The piss helps soften the leather," Paul answered as the urine sound petered out. "When they're dry, I'll work on them again."

"Margarete and I are grooming a horse around the corner," said Albert.

"Oh," said Paul, sounding like he didn't know one of his sisters was nearby. "Um, I'm done now."

Margarete smiled as she imagined Paul's surprised face. Her usually unflappable brother was home for a week's leave before he started weapons training and then his deployment. Now a full adult at twenty, Paul had become both an idol and a curiosity to his younger siblings.

"Do you want some saddle soap?" she called out, holding back a giggle.

"Later," Paul replied with a chuckle. "Danke."

Paul joined Albert working in the stable, while Margarete lingered with the animals. She was avoiding work in the kitchen and hoping to hear Paul's stories. The night Paul arrived home, he sat in the parlor with Martha on his knee, Sophia and Katharina on either side, and Margarete standing over his shoulder. With the big atlas open on the coffee table, Paul walked them through all the countries the army might send him. The war seemed like a great adventure, but Margarete knew it was everyone's gravest concern.

Outside of the family, conversations about the war were risky, but they also were uncomfortable even within the family. At the dinner table, Josef would monitor the discussion to avoid upsetting Dorothea or his daughters. Margarete had a hunch that he also wanted to spare the boys more unease about what might lie ahead for them. Franz was wary yet eager for his military career to start, but Stefan always went quiet when someone mentioned the draft.

Margarete volunteered to mix the horse feed, which was stored in an anteroom, and she pricked up her ears to catch her brothers' conversation. Paul strode by her carrying a twenty-five-kilo bale of hay like it was an empty box.

Albert made the comment that she had been thinking; "I can't believe you can lift that so easily now. Is everyone that strong after basic training?"

"Hardly," said Paul, as the bale of hay hit the ground with a thud. "You wouldn't believe some of these guys. There was one in my class who was a real *Sitzspinkler*."

The idea of a man who sat to urinate like a girl made Margarete smile.

Albert asked, "Will they be stationed at a desk?"

"I hope so. I don't want them in my *Panzer*."

"What made you want to join a Panzer division? Aren't you worried about claustrophobia?"

Margarete nodded as she mixed the oats for the older horses with a special feed. Paul was such a big man. How could he fit in a tank?

"I'm not worried about claustrophobia. I may not even be inside a Panzer. I'm just worried about dying."

Margarete tensed. Paul had obviously forgotten she was listening. Talk of her brother's death in battle was something she had never heard before.

The sound of a pitchfork scratching through hay broke the silence until Paul spoke again. "Do yourself a favor. Get your high school diploma like Franz so you can apply to be an officer. We're from a good East Prussian family—not aristocracy but good enough. You'll be picked."

"I don't even want to be in the Wehrmacht."

"You may not have a choice, so trust me. You want to be an officer."

Margarete didn't understand why Paul was telling Albert this. He was only sixteen, and the draft age was twenty. The war would be over by the time he could be drafted.

"I was going to finish high school anyway so I can be an architect," said Albert. "But why is it so important to be an officer?"

"You're a little less likely to die."

Margarete's eyes went wide; it was the second time Paul had brought up death. She wondered what Albert thought of that.

Albert's voice seemed to wobble. "I thought you didn't want to be an officer, though."

"That was before I was drafted." Horse stall doors squeaked, and Paul's voice carried over the horses' whinnies. "Maybe I'll be promoted and become a noncommissioned officer like Papa in the Great War. It's better than being a grunt."

Margarete sat on a nearby saddle box and considered what Paul had said. Often to his detriment, he wasn't one to tell a white lie to make someone feel better. Paul spoke the truth or remained silent. If he painted a grim picture of being in the army, she had to believe it. This was war. People died. She already knew of neighbors who had been killed in battle.

"So, being in a Panzer division is a good thing?" asked Albert as a stall door slammed shut.

"I like machines, and the Brits don't have the guns yet to stop our Panzers." After he muttered some loving words to a horse, Paul added, "Who knows? I could end up in the artillery."

"But maybe you won't even see combat. The war won't last much longer."

Paul snorted. "Who told you that?"

"That's what people say. Countries are surrendering quickly. Holland, Norway, and even France. England will be next, and then the war will be over."

Margarete nodded. That's exactly what she had heard as well.

"So that's what they say on the radio?"

"Yes," said Albert, though he didn't sound certain any longer. "They do say things are difficult, but the Reich will be victorious."

No one spoke, so Margarete leaned forward, hoping she wasn't missing Paul's response.

"Use your head," Paul said.

He must have stopped working and moved closer to Albert because his voice faded and he began to speak at length. "The Reich is calling up millions of men. England is strong, and Hitler isn't going to stop until he holds all of Europe and anything else he can get his hands on. This is going to go on for years, and God help us if the Americans join the fight."

"Does everyone in the army know this?" asked Albert.

"If you're smart—not that we talk about it much."

"Where do you think you'll be deployed?"

"I'm not sure. It could be anywhere. Belgium. Bohemia. I've also heard they may create an *Afrika Korps*."

"Africa? That's so far away. How long will you be gone? A year?"

"A year?" Paul snickered. "I'm in the Wehrmacht, not the French army. I won't be discharged until I'm crippled, dead, or the war is over—whichever comes first."

Margarete's mouth gaped, and she had to guess Albert's did as well.

"But you just said that you thought it was going to go on for years," Albert said.

"I did. But I was born the wrong year. I've been drafted at the beginning of this mess. I have to stay alive until the end."

"Oh, Paul," murmured Albert.

With her hand on her heart, Margarete wanted to say more than that. She was crushed for Paul. She had no idea, yet she assumed her mother and father knew. How could they know the danger Paul was in and still go about their day?

"Papa and Mutti won't want you to hear this, but the war might last long enough for you to be drafted. That's why I said you should make sure you finish high school."

"But I won't be eligible to be drafted for another four years."

"They might lower the draft age."

"No!" Margarete whispered to herself in despair.

It was surprising information to Albert as well because he replied with a tremorous squeak. "Really?"

"I could be wrong. It wouldn't be the first time."

Margarete frowned. Paul never thought himself wrong.

Born with a sixth sense, Paul lowered his voice. "Is Margarete still here?"

Margarete placed the pails of feed by the doorway, slipped

through the barn doors, and turned the corner so they couldn't see her escape. Blatant eavesdropping was unforgivable. Even if they suspected she had heard part of the conversation, it would be easier for everyone to pretend that she didn't know what lay ahead for her brothers.

Only sixteen months later, Margarete knew much more about the war. All was silent that Christmas Eve, except for the crunch of boots as Margarete and Albert forged their way to the coal shed. The falling mercury sent them to refill the ovens with coal for the long winter's night.

Margarete tightened the scarf around her neck and declared, "This Christmas feels a little less like Christmas."

"I agree," said Albert, as he swung the coal hods in each hand like they were baskets for a summer berry-picking expedition. "Papa is drilling me in Latin every day."

Margarete laughed, though she shouldn't have. Albert had received poor marks in Latin during the last term, and unfortunately for Josef's children, Latin was something their father considered important. "I wouldn't like that either, but I meant that everyone seems more serious."

"I was joking because you're right." Albert opened the door to the shed and held it wide. "Everyone is more serious."

"It's bad that we're at war with America now, isn't it?" asked Margarete, as she walked inside. "Papa doesn't like to talk about it."

Every night she saw her father twist the radio dial until it caught the BBC's scratchy broadcast in German. British news offered information that the Reich was adamant Germans shouldn't have, and listening could land someone in prison. The Reich jammed the broadcasts, but the BBC broadcasted so frequently, the Reich couldn't thwart them all. Her brothers and parents would all listen in silence when she was in the room. When she left, she heard the conversations begin.

"Papa is worried. It's bad that we're at war with the world again." Albert tugged on the chain hanging below the shed's solitary light bulb. "This is probably the last holiday we'll have most of the family together for a long time."

Margarete thought of the one family member who wasn't home. It was difficult to imagine what Paul's Christmas might be like in the desert and in battle. Both were so foreign to her. "What do you think Paul is doing tonight?"

"Wishing he was here."

After they brought the coal into the house, they went from room to room replenishing the ovens. In each room, except for the kitchen, a large oven stood from floor to ceiling, providing warmth better than any fireplace. Constructed with brick, ceramic tiles covered the ovens, and in the parlor and dining room, hand-painted flowers decorated them. Sealed heat from the fire box radiated throughout every tile and into the room.

As Margarete approached Martha and Katharina's room, she heard the murmur of their voices from the ajar door. The rule in the house was that before anyone could look at their presents under the Christmas tree, they must recite a poem of their choosing. She entered to see Sophia, Martha, and Katharina standing in front of the tiled oven with their focus straight ahead at the blank tiles as they practiced their Christmas poems. The girls wore their Sunday best, and red ribbons tied their braids to mark the holiday.

Margarete stayed upstairs reviewing her own poem and waiting for Saint Nicholas to ring the bell that signaled his departure. On Christmas Eve, he brought a decorated tree, presents, and treats. Everyone knew that actually her parents trimmed the tree with silver baubles and straw stars. Josef finished it by lighting dozens of tiny candles on the tree, and Dorothea set presents underneath.

When the bell rang, a stampede began of fourteen feet—some

small steps, some midsize, and some giant stomps. As the girls entered the living room, multiple voices cooed "ah" and "ooh" upon seeing the beautiful tree.

Margarete took a deep breath. "It smells lovely!"

"Sit, sit," said Dorothea, pointing them to the carpet in front of the oven.

While the little girls sat on the floor and stools, Margarete and the boys took to chairs and the sofa. Dorothea and Josef sat in their favorite wingback armchairs. Both chairs had been moved to a prominent position where they could properly judge the Christmas recital. As Margarete took in the holiday scene around her, she still thought Christmas didn't feel quite right, but it still felt special. Looking at her family, you wouldn't know there was a world war raging. Christmas made the world seem civil again.

The eldest always was first, so Franz took his place in front of the tree. On leave from officer training school, he wore the dress uniform of an army ensign. The green-gray wool was smart, with jodhpurs and a belted jacket. On the jacket's deep green collar, embroidered emblems with double bars designated him an officer candidate, a *Fähnrich*. As Franz began a long stanza of Goethe, their parents beamed with pride.

Josef smoked his pipe with an appraising smile. His strapping son stood before a Christmas tree in an officer's uniform reciting Goethe. Margarete doubted that even the Reich's propaganda newsreels could create such a vision of Germany.

Margarete suspected Dorothea believed Franz's appointment as an officer was a sign that the Haupts were now a step closer to the aristocratic class and thus a step further away from simple upper-middle-class farmers. The following day she would sit in church with even more pride with Franz in uniform at her side. And when he returned to the army, she would spend the morning in her room, crying and praying that his life be spared.

After he finished, Franz bowed to a round of applause. In chronological order, the children went one after another. Stefan recited in halting English what he could remember of Mark

Antony's monologue in Shakespeare's *Julius Caesar*. Albert used the opportunity to practice his Latin and recited Ovid, and Margarete recited Schiller. Only after little Martha took her curtsy could they see their presents of toys, scarves, watches, and books, all varying according to age. Beside each set of presents, everyone received their own colorful Christmas plate with special cookies, *Königsberger* marzipan, nuts, and one orange, a rarity during war. Margarete had delivered similar plates filled with treats to the Polish workers earlier that day.

Afterward, the whole family played cards, as they often did in winter. *Segen* was a favorite game because the younger children could win pennies, making them feel rich. At one end of the dining room table, Dorothea and Josef led the little girls through the game, expressing great dismay when they lost money to them. At the other end, Franz, Stefan, Albert, and Margarete played whist, where they gambled with matchsticks.

Everyone was in a festive mood with much teasing. When Franz made fun of Albert for a particularly bad play, Albert fought back.

"Klara Hennig asked about you the other day. Maybe you should pay her a visit tomorrow."

Franz rolled his eyes. Everyone knew he wouldn't be interested in Klara, who was as tall as Paul. "I can't. I'm busy."

"He's too short and too busy," said Stefan, laughing and sorting the cards in his hand. "Fähnrich Haupt is due at Christmas Mass tomorrow morning, so all the girls in town can admire him in his uniform."

Margarete tried to join in. "Franz, you always get a lot of attention from the girls. If you wear your uniform tomorrow, you're going to be swarmed."

"I have to wear my uniform." Franz smirked. "It's my duty."

"You see, Margarete," said Stefan. "It's our dear brother's solemn duty to wear his uniform to entertain the womenfolk during the war."

Stefan laid down his cards, sure that he had won the teasing and the card game. Franz inspected the hand and laid down his own cards with even more assurance. "It appears that I've won again."

Stefan punched Franz in the arm for good measure, and Albert tossed his hand on the table, announcing, "I'm out."

Still holding her cards, Margarete counted them one more time. With bright eyes, she laid them down. "I think I won!"

"You did!" said Stefan. "Good job beating us, especially Franz."

Franz grumbled, "You need to practice before February, Stefan. You're going to be eaten alive in the army."

The four siblings stopped what they were doing in unison, as Franz's words hung in the air. Margarete stared at Stefan with pleading eyes, begging him to tell her she misheard. "You haven't been drafted, have you?"

"No one was supposed to know yet," whispered Stefan. His eyes were as sad as hers until he glared at Franz.

It was so uncharacteristic of Franz to make a mistake. He pleaded to Stefan, "Forgive me. I'm so sorry. I don't know how I let that slip. I think I was just so happy being here." In a sign of his disgust with himself, Franz rubbed his forehead and ignored the fact that he was in his parents' home with children around. He cursed under his breath, "*Scheiße.*"

"Does anyone else know?" asked Albert in an uneasy, quiet voice.

"Only Papa," said a resigned Stefan.

Margarete looked to the end of the table at her parents, happy with her sisters. There was no hint that their third son would soon also be sent to defend the Reich with his life. The little girls giggled as they counted their pennies, not knowing anything more about the army than the drawings of camels that Paul sent home from Africa.

Franz implored Albert and Margarete, "Please don't tell anyone else, especially Mutti. Don't ruin her Christmas."

As Albert and Margarete nodded with fallen faces, Stefan

attempted to salvage the evening. He held up his hands and gave them his half smile. "Don't be so glum. My number was called up. We knew it would happen eventually."

Albert and Margarete found matching half-hearted smiles. Margarete had thought there was a chance Stefan would be drafted, but shouldn't the army have waited until he was at least nineteen?

Stefan continued still with a soft voice, "I won't be an officer like Franz, but I'm good with horses. I'll join the cavalry like Papa."

Finding his usual confident footing, Franz put his hand on Stefan's shoulder. "It doesn't matter. You'll ace the entrance exam, and you'll be on track to be a noncommissioned officer." He smiled reassuringly at Albert and Margarete. "He'll be Corporal Haupt soon enough."

"You think so?" asked Stefan, surprised he could rise to the rank of corporal so quickly.

"I'm certain of it," said Franz. "You'll stand out in the infantry. Even among the commissioned officers, there aren't many who can recite Shakespeare."

As Franz and Stefan continued talking about the army in hushed voices, Albert glanced at Margarete, who shared his heart-broken expression. Stefan was everyone's favorite brother. In an ambitious family, he was the easygoing happy one—hard to anger and the first to quell an argument. Animals loved him as much as his family did.

When Paul and Franz left for basic training, there was still an optimism about the war. Saying goodbye to Stefan wrenched Margarete's heart, and she squinted to dam the welling tears before anyone noticed.

Wanting assurance that everything would be fine, she turned to Albert, but his attention was focused on the wall across the room. He looked lost in the wallpaper's pattern. Margarete wondered if he was considering what Stefan's departure meant for him. The draft age was getting younger and younger. Paul had been drafted at age twenty in 1940. Franz was drafted at age nineteen in early 1941. Stefan was now drafted at age eighteen in late 1941. Albert had only turned seventeen, and he would graduate from high school in June. At the current rate of the Reich's draft, he could be drafted in six months.

Chapter Ten

Josef

Many families had already left. Relatives deposited their son or nephew or grandson at the train station as if he were going off to school. Goodbyes were punctuated with a kiss or hug or maybe only a wave before people turned their backs.

Josef wondered how those families felt. Were their emotions so shallow that they had already moved on to thinking about their midday meal? Or was their sadness mixed with relief that there was one less mouth to feed with limited rations? Or maybe their emotional core was so shaken they feared making a scene that might raise the Gestapo's ire? Regardless, while the relatives went on with their normal lives, the boy—not yet a man and not yet a soldier—remained on the platform. His feelings were also unknown, masked either by a cigarette or book or backslapping with school friends.

Josef chose to stay with Stefan until the train whistle. Because they were in the middle of an event too consequential to discuss, he didn't want a moment of uncomfortable silence, so they spoke of small things. When there was a lull in their conversation, he remembered something. He patted his chest pocket and smiled.

"I almost forgot. I have something for you."

"No more food, please." Stefan held up his hands to stop him. "Mutti has already packed too much. I'll be giving it away on the train."

"Don't give it away. You're in the army now. You barter. Trade the sandwiches for something good. Which is why I've bought these for you."

As he pulled out two packs of cigarettes from his pocket, Stefan smiled. "Danke, Papa. I hadn't thought to buy any. This was a good idea."

"One more thing," said Josef, searching deeper in his coat's inner pocket. "These are as important."

A small metal container appeared, causing Stefan's smile to deepen. "Matches."

"In a box where they will stay dry."

Placing the cigarettes in Stefan's pocket, Josef tipped his head in curiosity when he felt a lump. "What do you have there?"

With no comment or expression, Stefan showed him a pocket-sized prayer book with the cross and crown on its cover.

Touched and proud, Josef turned his lips upward in a smile. "Paul and Franz took theirs as well."

"They did?"

"I think Franz believes that a proper East Prussian officer from the Ermland would be civilized and carry his prayers into battle." Josef's smile became mischievous. "I think Paul sees it as insurance."

"I'm no better. I'm carrying mine because it reminds me of home."

"I think that's a fine reason," said Josef, silently warning himself not to choke up.

When the time came to say goodbye, he hugged his third boy, saying in his ear, "Everything will be waiting for you here. Remember that."

"I will, Papa."

The draftees boarded the train, and more relatives left, but Josef stayed. Until the train was out of sight, he believed his son was still with him. As he adjusted his collar and scarf against the winter wind, he heard a voice say, "Guten Tag, Josef."

Josef looked up and smiled at an old friend. "Guten Tag, Walter. What are you doing here?"

"I stop by on days like this. I want to wish my former students well."

"That's kind of you."

Josef was impressed, but it was no surprise that Walter Neuwald would know a draftee's train time. Since he had retired from teaching, Walter had joined the party and become a postman. Guttstadt still had its old postman, but the Reich had added a new position in charge of reading everyone's mail. Walter was now a friend who could no longer be trusted.

"Most of the boys are glad to see me," said Walter. His big belly began to shake with laughter even before he cracked his own joke. "Some would rather go to war."

"My boys always said you were their favorite teacher."

"The Haupt boys were always good boys. I was able to say hello to Stefan before he boarded. So mature. You should be proud."

"He's still a boy," mused Josef.

Walter touched his arm. "Don't worry. He'll be fine. He's able and smart."

"Danke."

"And that's far more than I can say for some of those boys on that train." Walter's eyes widened. He leaned closer to Josef and whispered, "Honestly, sending some of those boys to war is sending the proverbial lamb to slaughter."

Josef peered disapprovingly at Walter from the side of his eyes. Like many teachers, Walter had a way with words, but Josef couldn't understand why he had chosen those on such a day. All the boys on that train were lambs, as were the Russians, Americans, and British they would meet on the battlefield. The whole world had plotted against its young men and sent them all to slaughter.

Walter tilted his head in sympathy. "I see that wasn't the right thing to say. My apologies."

"It's all right," said Josef, not wanting to argue. "Stefan will be fine. He's bright and a hard worker, but he's my boy least suited for war. All he's ever wanted to do was to take over the farm."

"And he will!" said Walter, as if enthusiasm would make it so. "Of course, he will."

"Herr Neuwald, Herr Haupt," said a voice from behind them.

They both turned to see Guttstadt's new Bürgermeister. The Reich considered Bürgermeister Renkel such a success that they had promoted him to a larger city. Now Bürgermeister Helmut Krüger had come to Guttstadt. Hoping also to advance, he ruled the town with an even crueler hand than his predecessor.

Josef and Walter jumped to attention and threw their arms into the air. "Heil Hitler!"

Bürgermeister Krüger answered the same, and when his arm came down, the serious expression on his face changed to a grin. "I only have a moment, but I wanted to make sure to tell you the good news." Sticking his chest out with pride, he announced, "Guttstadt is officially free of Jews."

"Is that so?" said Walter.

Josef noticed that his friend didn't match Krüger's enthusiasm, but he managed a response. Josef couldn't. He had to concentrate to hide the shatter he felt inside.

The Jewish community in Guttstadt had already been destroyed. Once Soldau was just another town, but its name had now become synonymous with its concentration camp. The Reich first sent Polish intelligentsia and Catholic Church officials to Soldau; soon it became their destination of choice for the Ermland's Jews. Father Schmidt had told him that Rabbi Rosen had been sent there with his daughter-in-law. Josef stopped himself from imagining what it might be like for a man and woman who deserved nothing but reverence and respect enduring the hell of a concentration camp. It only made him feel guilty. He prayed young Sara and Joshua Rosen would have a good life in Britain. He doubted they would ever see their family again.

Only two Jews had been left in Guttstadt, Aaron Katz and his wife. Despite the endless anti-Semitic edicts from Berlin, Aaron and Rosa quietly survived in Guttstadt. They cleaned the street and otherwise stayed out of sight. They weren't allowed many places, but Josef assumed it was also by choice. Who would want to be amid such hatred?

Josef was ashamed when he saw Aaron on the street, bent over and chasing leaves and trash, his tattered coat emblazoned with a yellow star. But over the years, he also grew to feel an odd reassurance when he saw Aaron. Aaron's presence in town was a sign that the world had not completely changed. Someone was left from the old Guttstadt, the old Germany.

Now German society had regressed into pure evil. Josef imagined Aaron and Rosa Katz, old, frail, and frightened, being shoved on a train going to an unknown hell. Josef knew those trains. They traveled at night, but on occasion he saw one during the day. While he had to wait at the Radau's train crossing, he saw desperate human cargo. Faces pressed against the windows, gasping for air. He wondered how Herr Radau could sleep hearing their cries at night.

Aaron and Rosa were the true lambs sent to slaughter. Unlike the boys on the train, there was no hope they might survive. Wherever Aaron and his wife had been sent, they would die an early death or be murdered. Evil would kill two more innocent souls, and Guttstadt, as Josef had known it since birth, would die with them.

Every subconscious and conscious reflex in Josef needed him to make the sign of the cross, but he clenched his gloved hand to stop himself. Guilt washed through him followed by disgust. He was too terrified, too selfish to bless an old friend and too much of a coward to practice his religion. And if put in a similar situation the next day, he would act no differently. He survived and kept his family alive by living in a state of sin.

"We shipped off those two old ones last night." Krüger pretended to wipe his hands clean. "You won't see them again."

Josef watched Krüger and thought of Pontius Pilate, only the Nazi leader wasn't Pilate. Pilate had at least advocated for Christ before he left him to the mob demanding his death. Krüger was the leader of the mob, but Josef knew he couldn't stand in judgment. His hands weren't clean either.

"Congratulations," said Walter.

"Danke," Krüger said, slapping his arm. "I must go spread the news."

Without saying goodbye, Krüger moved on to a group across the platform. Walter shrugged and sighed. "So that's that."

Josef thought it a cynical sentiment, but he wouldn't correct Walter's characterization of the tragedy. It was futile to object to what had happened to the Jews, and he needed Walter as a friend.

Walter cleared his throat before lowering his voice. "If it makes you feel better, Herr Katz's family who left the country are all doing well."

"What have you heard?"

"There hasn't been much international mail since America entered the war, but before that, Aaron received mail from his children overseas. A letter arrived in November from his son in America. He works in a factory. The work seems hard, but he's been promoted. He and his wife have friends, and their children are healthy. The little ones already speak English with an American accent." Walter lowered his voice to a whisper. "It will be a better life than they would've had in Germany—maybe even before the Reich."

"Maybe so," Josef lied. Most families would prefer to be alive and together in their homeland than dead and scattered to the ends of the earth.

Walter stared at him, his eyes calculating. Josef began to worry that his lack of enthusiasm for Krüger's news was a problem. Walter had been a friend for many years, but in these times, you couldn't trust friends.

As he stood there silently, Walter's expression softened. "I'm sorry. This is a difficult day for you, sending your third son to war."

"Danke. It's been a hard day. I was wondering if you could do me a favor. If you see a letter or something from the army, could you hold it for me? Please don't give it to anyone else in the family."

Walter slowly nodded. "I understand. You want to tell Dorothea any bad news yourself, but you should know that any casualty, or God forbid a death notice, doesn't come via regular post. The party handles that directly. Krüger would deliver a notice to your home."

Josef shuddered at the thought of having that black-hearted man informing him of such news. "I'm speaking of anything regarding Albert's draft."

Finally, the troubling talk of the day impacted Walter. His shoulders slumped, as a sadness passed over his face. "It seems like Albert was just in my class, but yes, it makes sense that he could be drafted soon. I'm sorry."

"Danke. It will be hard on the family, particularly my wife."

"I'll set aside any letter from the army for you." Walter extended his hand. "It's the least I can do for such an old friend."

"You're very kind." Josef shook his hand with sincere appreciation.

"You know the Vaterland is grateful for the sacrifices of your family."

Walter's words were so false, but Josef mumbled "Danke" as he held back a dark chuckle.

The Vaterland showed no gratitude for anything. The Reich only took lives and livelihoods, children and futures. It never gave anything as precious in return.

CHAPTER ELEVEN

MARGARETE

Margarete swatted Albert's hand. "*Finger weg!*" But she wasn't quick enough as he grabbed another roll. He was happily defiant. "Ha!"

"Go back to the fields and make yourself useful."

"I can't be useful if I'm hungry," said Albert, taking a bite of the roll.

"We just ate." Margarete picked up an empty cheese plate as their sisters worked around them like elves clearing the table. "Why are you always hungry?"

Katharina walked near him with plates in both hands, and Albert helped himself to a pickle as it passed by. "I'm a growing boy."

"Why is being a boy always a defense for bad behavior?" grumbled Margarete. "No girl ever gets to say that."

"There's no reason to because you're too busy being good."

He tried to sneak a slice of cheese off the tray she held, but she moved the tray in time, saying, "Go away."

"I am." He chuckled. "On June sixth."

She didn't respond because draft dates were nothing to laugh at, but Albert continued to smile. Maybe it felt less frightening if he joked about it. Maybe he wanted things to be normal, so she said, "Sometimes I look forward to the day, but then I remember that I'll have to start feeding the pigs."

Before Albert could volley back, Senta's bark started and grew furious. When her bark rattled the windowpanes, Albert and Margarete stared into each other's eyes, trying to discern her warning.

When a truck rumbled, Albert whispered, "SS."

"But they were just here last week to see about the workers."

"Get Papa."

"I'm here," announced Josef from the doorway, having interrupted his midday nap. With one hand he straightened his suspenders, while the other hand buttoned his collar. "Albert, come with me outside. Margarete, stay with your mother and the girls in the kitchen."

During the monthly SS visits, everyone went about their normal day. On a special visit, everyone pretended to go on with their normal day. Dorothea put her daughters back to work on the strawberry jamming project they already had underway. During the morning, everyone chatted as they chopped, stewed, and jarred the berries. With the SS outside, the kitchen was quiet. Margarete raised her head every time Dorothea peered through the window.

As the notches in her mother's brow deepened, Margarete asked, "What is it, Mutti?"

Dorothea's expression was nonplussed. "I believe the Ostarbeiter from the East have arrived. There are two families with two children."

"How old are they?"

Dorothea stretched her neck for a better view out the window. "The boy looks to be Katharina's age, and the girl looks like she's a little younger than Martha."

"Can we play with them?" asked Martha as her head popped up from picking through a bucket of berries. Her apple cheeks shone at the prospect of new playmates.

Margarete stirred the strawberries simmering in their juice and tried not to smile as she wondered what Dorothea would say. Before the war, the Haupt children had always played with the German workers' children while on the farm. Off the farm, Dorothea wouldn't allow her children to be seen with them.

"Perhaps," announced Dorothea without Martha's enthusiasm. "First, they need a bath."

A hinge squeaked as the kitchen door opened and Albert stepped halfway inside, "Mutti, Papa asked that you and Margarete come outside."

As Margarete followed Albert and her mother, she stayed to the side so she had a view. Beside the SS truck, two stormtroopers stood guard with guns flanking the new Ostarbeiter. Two women, two men, and a boy and a girl were bedraggled with a foreign look. Margarete was accustomed only to seeing kerchiefs on women if they were performing manual labor. The men also wore strange hats. Their clothes were tattered, and all looked hungry.

The SS officer gave Dorothea a polite bow and greeting, which Dorothea returned with a skeptical smile.

"These are our new farmhands," Josef said to Dorothea and Margarete in a quiet voice. "They're White Russians. One family is a husband and wife. The other has two children, ages nine and twelve."

Josef was stone-faced, but Margarete guessed he was even more unhappy than when the Polish POWs had appeared. The propaganda had said the Ostarbeiter would be willing foreigners coming to Germany to make a better life. With the stormtroopers' hands on their guns, the families looked like they had been forced to work in Germany.

Dorothea wore a fixed pleasant expression as her eyes traveled slowly along the six strangers in front of her. Keeping her thoughts to herself, she smiled at the workers. "Welcome."

"Margarete, could you introduce the children to Senta?" asked Josef.

Surprised to hear her name, Margarete called Senta to her and with a bright smile, beckoned the children to join her. The children looked to their parents for permission, and their parents nodded. Still fearful, they slowly walked toward Margarete and what they thought was a vicious animal.

While Margarete and Senta played with the children, she kept an eye on her parents, who spoke with the Ostarbeiter. Each of them wore a blue badge with *OST* in white lettering. When an SS officer pointed to the badge on one of the men, the man flinched, not appreciating the brand on his body like he was livestock. These families weren't like the Polish POWs, sadly caught in the hazards of war. They were forced laborers. Yet, Margarete mused that soon all of her brothers would be off at war. The farm needed more help.

After the SS left, introductions were made, but there was little communication beyond names because none of the Ostarbeiter knew German and only Josef knew a few words of Russian. While Josef took the men on a tour of the stables and fields, Margarete and her mother led the women and children to the workers' dining room, the kitchen, the laundry, and the worker housing. Dorothea pointed out items, and Margarete pantomimed what wasn't self-evident.

After the tours ended, the Ostarbeiter families remained in the worker housing, while the Haupts regrouped in the kitchen.

As Josef and Albert sank into seats at the table, Dorothea made coffee and Margarete sliced a fruit cake.

After he placed his hat on the table, Josef rubbed his eyes before muttering, "Ach du lieber Himmel."

"Pitiful." Dorothea shook her head. "What has happened to them? Why are they in such a condition? Starving, with scabies and lice."

Margarete waited for a derogatory comment about Slavs from her mother, but none came. It may have only been *noblesse oblige*, but she seemed truly concerned for the White Russians.

"The army conquers a territory, and the SS rounds up the healthy and sends them in cattle cars to work for the Reich," said Josef matter-of-factly.

"If the Reich intends for them to work, why aren't they better taken care of?"

"In the Reich's eyes, they're dispensable."

"Ridiculous. I won't have them die at our home," said Dorothea. "They need food, but I fear we need to give it to them slowly. It's been so long since they've eaten."

"I agree. They need to regain their strength before they can work."

"What about school for the children?" asked Albert.

"The Reich won't let them go to school," answered Josef.

"Those children..." said Dorothea as if she couldn't get them out of her mind. She turned to Josef and pointed out the window. "How long are we to all live like this? We're dependent upon strangers—strangers who are imprisoned on our land."

"The Ostarbeiter will be here until the war is over," said Josef, not bothering with her larger commentary on the situation. "We need the help."

Dorothea poured the boiling water into the teapot and clanked the kettle on the stove. Margarete knew being noisy in the kitchen was an expression of her disapproval with their plight under the Reich. Her primary method was to maintain a civilized life as best she could. That always involved barking orders.

She turned and enlisted her junior officer, Margarete. Katharina and Martha were to pick chamomile flowers to make tea for the workers' weak stomachs. Sophia was to find the lice combs, delousing powder, and old clothes for the children. Margarete was to find clothes for the women and then light the stove and fill the cauldron in the laundry room. Lastly, she told Albert he was to go through his brothers' clothing to find something for the men and then help Margarete with the laundry.

"But what about the OST badge they must wear?" asked Margarete.

"Their clothes are full of lice and mites. They need to be boiled. Typhus could spread." Dorothea clanked another pot on the stove in disgust. "They can go without the OST badge for a time. The Reich is going to have to trust us."

A week later, Margarete walked to the stables after the midday meal. The Poles and White Russian men had already returned to the fields, while the women cleaned the dining rooms and kitchen. Everyone had settled into their roles and living arrangements, though no one was happy with the situation. As Margarete fed her horse a carrot, she heard Senta's bark. She stilled, waiting to hear Senta's further warning, but there was none.

After a moment, Paul's voice rose on the farm for the first time in two years. "You silly dog!"

Margarete raced to where she had a view of the drive. Senta had run far past her usual station at the flagpole to meet Paul as he walked toward the house. Well over one hundred pounds, Senta rarely stood on her hind legs, but Paul's return home was an exception. The giant Saint Bernard stood with her paws on his shoulders. Despite her size, Paul still towered over her. They would have looked like sweethearts if Senta wasn't licking his neck with her long tongue. Her white globs of slobber were visible against Paul's tan Afrika Corps uniform.

Sophia's voice came from the kitchen door. "Paul!"

In a flash, Sophia ran to him, followed by Martha and Katharina, their skirts flapping as they ran, while Margarete came from the opposite direction. Paul pushed Senta off him and squatted down, his arms open and a grin on his face. One by one, he grabbed his sisters as they hurtled toward him, gasping and laughing with surprised joy.

Dorothea and Josef hurried out of the house as well but stopped a few feet from the steps. Josef smiled with pride, while Dorothea covered her smile with both hands in shock. She looked to the heavens as if a prayer had been answered.

It wasn't a hero's welcome because no one cared about his deeds, good or bad. They only cared he was alive and home. It was the welcome of a loving family, fractured for too long.

As the family walked back to the house, Albert came running from the hay meadow, having heard the commotion. After the two brothers hugged, Paul asked, "Do we get to celebrate your graduation while I'm here?"

"We do," said Albert. "But I leave the next day."

"Where to?" asked Paul.

Margarete caught Albert's speaking glance at Paul, which looked like a warning that the conversation should probably stop in their current company. "I report to basic training on June sixth."

Only a second of hesitation betrayed Paul's dismay that his seventeen-year-old brother had already been called up. His smile remained as he said, "You'll ace it."

The following day, Margarete learned what Paul actually thought of Albert's draft. She'd been sent by Dorothea to retrieve more eggs for a special cake she was making for Paul. As she went to leave the chicken house with two eggs in one hand and another two in her apron, she heard a deep belch.

"It's a good thing you did that with me and not Mutti." Albert's voice came from outside.

She peered through a crack in the wooden door and saw Paul put his hand to his mouth in embarrassment. "Sorry. I've been in the army too long, and I haven't eaten this well in... I can't even remember."

Her two brothers stood with cigarettes in their hands with the smoke drifting above their heads. Since coming home, Paul chain-smoked four, sometimes six, an hour. He would stamp out a half-smoked cigarette only to pull another out of a pack a minute later. Margarete had never seen Albert with a cigarette before. Watching him with Paul, he seemed to have aged overnight.

"Mutti is planning on cooking you a goose tomorrow after church," Albert said.

"Goose on Sunday. I forgot," Paul said, shaking his head. "I think there are some things I forget because I'd miss them too much if I remembered."

"Ha! You think we still have goose every Sunday?" Albert looked at him askance. "I've almost forgotten about it myself. We haven't had it since Easter."

"Rations." Paul cringed.

"Rations for most but not all. I suspect most of our geese end up on the family dinner table of the Bürgermeister." Taking a drag, Albert shrugged. "We shouldn't complain. We have the farm. We don't rely only on rations like most."

"We're lucky. From what I've seen, it's much better here than in the cities."

"The goose tomorrow isn't one from her flock destined for the Reich or the two she's saving for Christmas dinner," said Albert with a smile slipping onto his lips. "It's even more special."

"How so?"

"Mutti has picked out new wallpaper for the parlor," Albert answered, breaking into a laugh. "Papa says it's an extravagance during a war and doesn't want to pay for it, so she's raising extra goslings to sell on the black market to get the money to buy it."

"*Mein Gott*," said Paul, stamping out his cigarette. "Why is Papa letting her do this? We're in the middle of a war."

Margarete had heard her parents speaking about the wallpaper, but she hadn't thought twice about it. In retrospect, what was her mother doing worrying about wallpaper?

"He lets her pretend that everything is normal. We still have a landscaper, by the way." A giggle escaped Albert as he added,

"Because it's important to have a properly designed garden while your sons are in battle."

Paul shared in the laughter, but Margarete looked down at the eggs in her hand. Life was so different from a few years ago, yet so much was the same on the farm. There was plenty of food, and her mother kept a home worthy of sophisticated company dropping by with no warning. Yet all four of her brothers would be in battle soon.

Paul pulled out his cigarette pack. "That's the thing. You get in the army, and you meet people from different places and families, and you realize how good we have it here. Until I left, I didn't know how special this place is."

"The farm?"

"And the Ermland. It's boring and provincial, but it's a wonderful place to be from."

"Where are you friends from?"

"All over—Swabia, Dortmund, Ulm. We're very different," said Paul, speaking as he lit a cigarette. "The funny thing is I miss them. I wonder how they're doing."

"How is the war going?"

"All right in Africa. The Tommies call Rommel the Desert Fox," said Paul, using the German nickname for the British.

Margarete waited for more information, but Paul wasn't forthcoming. Whatever Paul had been experiencing, he didn't want to say it aloud—even without his mother and sisters in the room.

After a minute of silence, Paul announced, "Papa said that Franz is in an artillery company somewhere on the Eastern Front. Stefan will be going there, too, in another artillery company."

"What do you think of those posts?"

"It's hard for me to say." Paul exhaled and kicked the dirt. "I can't imagine war without sand."

Margarete waited for more, but her brothers stood in silence. Paul was avoiding what everyone only spoke as hushed gossip.

Even Margarete knew no one wanted to be sent to the Eastern Front, and now both Franz and Stefan would be there.

"Where do you think they'll send me?" asked Albert in a cool voice.

"You?" Paul smiled, placing his large hand on Albert's shoulder. "Hopefully, nowhere. The war should be over by the time you're done with basic training."

Albert flinched like a little brother, knowing he wasn't being taken seriously. "Paul, I want to know the truth."

Paul withdrew his hand and stamped out his cigarette before he declared with finality, "The East. Where, I don't know."

"Danke. That's all I wanted to know."

Margarete's heart sank because Albert's tone was one of acceptance. Inside she protested that anyone so young could be sent to the Eastern Front. Yet, hearing Paul talk, she, too, thought it inevitable.

"Enough of this talk," said Paul. "How about we finish in the barn and go into town tonight? I need to go to one of these dances I hear about. The ones with the lonely women waiting for men like me to show up."

As her brothers walked toward the barn, Margarete stared again at the eggs while her heart felt like it was collapsing into her lungs. She peeled off the downy feathers still clinging to the brown shells and held back her tears. All of her brothers would soon be in the worst of danger. No one had told her. No one had ever planned to tell her. No wonder her mother was focused on wallpaper.

CHAPTER TWELVE

JOSEF

S leigh bells rang in the distance as Josef stepped out the front door to greet the guest. Tightening his scarf, he calmed Senta while fine draft horses pulled a sleek sleigh into the Haupts' drive. A young man chauffeured Bürgermeister Krüger, who sat in the back under bear furs.

Josef felt as tense as the dog, whose hair stood on her back. Krüger was never a welcome sight. Josef had yet to have a positive conversation with the man, and a visit by Krüger on a frigid Saturday meant something was wrong.

When the sleigh stopped, Krüger hopped out while the chauffeur stayed under the warmth of the furs.

"Heil Hitler!" said Krüger, flinging his arm in the air.

"Heil Hitler!" As Josef lowered his arm, he said, "Guten Tag, Herr Krüger. What brings you out here today?"

Ignoring the greeting and question, Krüger said, "I won't be long. Might we go inside for a moment?"

Immediately, terror struck Josef's heart, but he managed to

lead Krüger inside, wishing the man was here for another reason. As soon as Josef closed the parlor door, Krüger pulled an envelope from his pocket.

"I'm very sorry to have to bring you this news."

Josef reached for the letter, wanting both to read it at once and never to read it all.

Partial copy. Osten, January 22, 1943.

Dear Haupt family,

It is with great sadness that I write to inform you that your son, Stefan, was reported missing in action on January 15, 1943. His unit was under heavy fire from the Russians in Stalingrad. Stefan has fought heroically for the Führer, Volk, and Vaterland.

K. Hahn,

Oberleutnant

The correctness of the copy is confirmed. Bürgermeister Helmut Krüger.

Josef stared at the page as visions of Stefan floated in his mind. Stefan on the train platform one year ago. Stefan petting the forelock of his favorite mare as she gave birth. A younger Stefan taking his rabbits to sell at the market. And Stefan the toddler sitting on his grandfather Haupt's lap. More than any of his sons, Stefan was Josef's heir—heir to his estate, heir of his personality, and heir to his love of the land and animals. Josef loved all his sons, but with Stefan, he shared a kinship.

Josef read the letter again and then again, searching for information that wasn't there. He was a veteran. He knew the term *missing in action* downplayed the chaos of war. A man's body could have been obliterated beyond recognition. Or in retreat, the army had to abandon their dead and casualties. Or a soldier could be a prisoner of the enemy—in this case an enemy as merciless as the Reich.

Was Stefan dead or alive? Each Sunday in church, more names of local boys who had perished were read from the pulpit. Josef watched as families reacted to their beloved children's fate in stoic silence or uncontrolled crying. He always knew it was a possibility they could join those families one day.

Josef focused on Krüger's signature at the bottom. It did not confirm the correctness of the copy. It confirmed that Krüger had made sure the letter was sanitized of information that the Reich didn't want known.

Josef raised his head, his eyes narrowing as they met Krüger's. He said nothing, but Krüger knew what he was asking.

"I don't know anything else," said the Bürgermeister.

Josef closed his eyes, not accepting the lie. "Surely, you have something else you can tell me. My son, Franz, has been fighting in Stalingrad as well."

"I know nothing about Franz. I have no more information about Stefan either. I will only tell you what you already must know. You're not the only parent to receive such a letter today."

So much was ready to spill from Josef's mouth. He wanted to scream in pain for Stefan. He wanted to whisper prayers for the dead and suffering. He wanted to offer condolences to the families. He wanted to comment on the great loss of young men in their prime—a loss both to Guttstadt and Germany. And on the tip of his tongue, he wanted to say aloud what he had only ever said to Dorothea. Why were his sons risking their lives in these godforsaken places?

"Danke," Josef said instead. "I appreciate you coming to tell me in person and so quickly. I must now tell my wife."

"I understand," Krüger said with a slight bow of his head.

Josef led him to the front door and showed him out, wishing him a good evening. When Krüger turned to face him, he expected a polite farewell. Instead, Krüger pointed to the notice still in his hands.

"Your son was performing his duty for the Vaterland. I must remind you that you are an Ortsbauernführer and have a particular responsibility to the Reich. You and your family are expected to be resolute in your support of the war and the Führer, even now."

Josef glared at the man. Krüger didn't have the decency to let him grieve in peace. The sacrifice of a dear son was to be ignored. Blind loyalty to the Reich had to be maintained.

Josef mustered a bitter response. "I understand."

Krüger lifted his arm with a click of his heels. "Heil Hitler."

Every conversation with Krüger ended with the salute, but this time it felt different. Krüger was forcing Josef to display his commitment to the party, despite his son's likely death. Never before had Josef wanted more to keep his arm at his side and turn his back to him. It would be a small defiance with major consequences.

Josef raised his arm once again, albeit unenthusiastically. "Heil Hitler."

After locating Dorothea, he led her to the parlor. The office was Josef's private room, but the parlor with its fine rugs and embroidered draperies was Dorothea's domain. When he closed the parlor door, she took a seat on the sofa. Though she was in a work dress with a large apron and sturdy shoes, she still fit into her ornate room. Her posture and hair perfect, she sat with her legs to the side and crossed at the ankle.

"Why are we meeting in here?" she asked. "Why not your study?"

"Because I thought you might want to be comfortable."

"It's about the Bürgermeister's visit." She looked around guiltily at the wallpaper she wanted to change. "Do they know about my geese? Is that why he came?"

Josef wished the visit was only about three extra geese on the property. He took the envelope out of his pocket and handed it to her. In a steady voice, he announced, "Stefan is missing in action."

Dorothea gasped and covered her mouth. "Nein."

Josef sat beside her, placing his arm around her as she opened the envelope. He watched as she read. Her eyes were wide, and her breathing increased as she underlined the words with her finger, as if she was decoding each one.

When she said nothing, he said, "May God be with him."

As she raised her head with a crestfallen expression, her tone was determined as she declared, "Stefan is dead."

Josef stared at his wife, unsure how to respond to this moment of clarity. He always believed that she knew she lived in a state of denial. She was well aware her family was in the middle of a horrible war, living under an authoritarian regime, yet she required that her carefully crafted life not change too much. She may have been doing twice the work on the farm, but for everything under her control, she lived as if there was no war. She maintained a beautiful home and garden, and she even planned on sending Margarete to finishing school the next year. One would think her adult sons were off pursuing careers and higher education rather than deadly combat.

Despite her realism, Josef felt he must correct her for Stefan's sake. "But there is a chance that he's alive. He could be either captured or unaccounted for."

"No, he's dead. I know it." She stared at the notice still in her hand as tears started to roll down her cheeks. "My sweet boy."

His own throat choked as he agreed. "He is a wonderful son."

Her crying took an ugly turn, and her body shuddered as she waved the notice in the air. "I hate this war. I hate it. I hate what has happened to our lives, to our town. I don't want my son to die for Hitler. Hitler doesn't care about us, and my sons shouldn't die for a country that doesn't care about them."

"Dorothea, hush."

"I have to say it. I have to." She laid her head on his shoulder as she sobbed. "Our lives, our children's lives are being ruined."

They sat holding each other through their grief until Josef worried that they had been away for too long. "It will be hard, but we must tell the girls."

She kept her head against his shoulder, clutching the sleeve of his wool jacket. "What should we tell them?"

"Only what we've been told. Stefan is missing. We won't know more for some time."

"Could you tell them without me?"

He dreaded it, but he would. His wife was inconsolable and in no condition to see her young girls. "Go upstairs and lie down. I'll tell them you're not feeling well. They'll understand."

Never without a handkerchief, Dorothea dabbed her eyes, though the tears still flowed. "We'll say the rosary tonight as a family. I wish I could have a Mass said in his name, but I understand if we must only say that he's missing."

"Whatever has become of Stefan, he needs our prayers."

After she went to their room, Josef rounded up his daughters in the living room. As the girls sat unsure about a midday meeting, they fidgeted and gripped their skirts with anxious energy. He informed them as plainly as he had Dorothea. The younger girls cried in sadness and confusion. They loved their brothers, but sometimes the relationship felt more like an uncle and niece. The difference in ages between Stefan and Martha, Katharina, and Sophia ranged from seven to eleven years.

The sister who loved Stefan most sat in stunned silence with no tears. Extending a shaky hand, Margarete asked, "May I read it?"

She studied the document with determination before she raised her head and said, "It must be a mistake. Stefan has mentioned his commanding officers but never this Lieutenant Hahn. He's confused Stefan for someone else."

It was tempting to indulge her denial. Part of Josef wanted to believe it himself. Yet he couldn't. "I doubt it's a mistake."

"But, Papa—"

"Sophia, could you take your little sisters into the kitchen?" he said. "Maybe there is a piece of cake. We'll join you shortly."

As Sophia led Katharina and Martha away, Margarete's frown only deepened.

"There are many reasons why this lieutenant wrote to us," said Josef. "Stefan's commanding officer may also be missing or has died, and Oberleutnant Hahn now has assumed his duties."

She flashed a skeptical look before she read the page again. When she raised her head again, her voice was reasoning. "But how can Stefan be missing? It should be obvious where he is. He isn't a pilot lost in the sky or a sailor in a submarine lost in the ocean. Franz is also in Stalingrad. He'll be able to find him."

"Unlikely." Josef took in a breath of courage. Margarete desired answers that required a blunt explanation. Making her accept Stefan's plight forced him to accept it as well. "There are hundreds of thousands of soldiers in Stalingrad—as many as all the citizens of Königsberg. Battles can be confusing. Soldiers can be captured by the enemy, or the army needs to retreat and unfortunately some are left behind. The soldier can also die, but he hasn't been identified. Most likely the Wehrmacht itself doesn't know if Stefan has died or is a prisoner of war."

Overwhelmed by the blunt explanation, she took the words like a slap to her face and winced.

"I'm sorry," said Josef. "But this is the reality of the situation."

Bewildered tears slowly fell down her cheeks, and she said in a pleading voice, "But there's a good chance he hasn't died? He could just be a prisoner of war like the Polish ones working on the farm?"

Until that moment, Josef had failed to equate his own son's situation to the three Polish men who were imprisoned on his farm. For over three years, they had worked his land and cared for his animals as if they were their own. They had learned German and were always respectful of him and his family. Each day, Margarete or Sophia delivered them second breakfast in the fields to tide them over before lunch, and the men thanked them, treating them like the young ladies they were. It was as comfortable a coexistence as one could have between tragic prisoners and a reluctant warden and his family. Margarete hoped Stefan was in a similar situation.

She didn't know the Polish prisoners lived a life on the Haupt farm that most POWs in Germany would consider a holiday. If Stefan had been captured by the Russians, Josef couldn't bear to think of his fate.

He studied Margarete's blue eyes awash in tears. His heart breaking with hers, he took her hand. "Yes. Stefan might be a captive just like the Poles here. We should pray that is the case."

CHAPTER THIRTEEN

JOSEF

As Walter slowed his horse trotting down the Haupt drive, Josef raised a hand. "Guten Tag, Walter."

Walter greeted him with less enthusiasm. "I'm sorry to interrupt your day."

"It's not a problem at all." Josef motioned toward the house. "Shall we go inside?"

"It's better we stay outside." After easing himself off his horse, Walter reached into his coat pocket and handed an envelope to him. "I intercepted a letter from Albert today. I think you'll understand the problem with such a letter."

Josef took the letter but was unable to wait until he read it. "Is Albert all right?"

"Nothing has changed with his assignment or location. He's still a radio operator in Latvia." Walter raised a finger. "But if this letter had reached someone other than me, he could find himself on the front line in Ukraine."

With Paul fighting Americans in Italy, Franz fighting the

Soviets somewhere deep in Russia, and Stefan's whereabouts known only by God, it had been a small blessing to the family that one son didn't face death daily. Albert was safely tucked away in the small Latvian city of Dünaburg, or Daugavpils as the new Latvian Ostarbeiter maid called it.

Too young yet to be an officer and too educated to be wasted on the front lines, the army had placed Albert as a radio operator in a small command office. He spent his days receiving and distributing information, both mundane and classified. Because he was relatively nearby, mail was more reliable between him and the family. Josef was dismayed that Albert might jeopardize what he knew was a lucky situation.

Reading the letter, Josef searched for problematic content, but nothing stood out. The Haupt sons' letters all followed the same pattern. They wrote of the weather, new friends, questions and comments about events at home, and always a request for a care package. There was never a word about battles, geography, or even a whiff of politics. He searched for what might have sent Walter all the way out to the Haupt farm. His eyes then focused on one sentence inserted above Albert's request for a care package. It was a lyric from a well-known ballad, which Josef read aloud, "There were many rocks, but little bread."

"Exactly that." Walter's expression and voice were as stern as if Albert had added, "Long live our Soviet motherland."

Since the fall of Stalingrad a few months before, everything had become more difficult in the Reich. Resentment grew among families who had lost their sons and fathers. For most of the country, food was a constant worry. A quiet rebellion had begun with mutterings against the Reich and cheating on rations. Josef was the Ortsbauernführer, but first he was a father of sons in the line of fire. He shared the people's resentment. When a farmer held back food for himself from the quota he had produced for the Reich, Josef ignored it. He wasn't going to report an old friend for feeding his family.

The Reich heard the whispers of disenchantment. Mail was

under stricter control, and everyone's actions were under greater scrutiny. No one was even allowed to say out loud what was blatantly obvious—food was scarce.

"I see," said Josef.

"A statement like that could undermine military morale. Some would call it treason." Walter raised a brow. "It reflects poorly on your whole family."

Beginning to question their friendship, Josef chose his words with caution. "I'm very sorry. As you know, Albert is still a boy in many ways. He was careless. I'll speak to him when he comes home on leave."

"Good. I knew you would understand."

Walter extended his hand, and Josef reluctantly returned the letter. He didn't like the idea that there would be physical evidence against Albert and the Haupt family. He grasped for something to counter the evidence.

"This letter doesn't reflect my commitment to the Reich."

Walter held Josef's gaze. Whether he believed him or not, Walter replied, "I know."

After a moment of unfriendly silence, Walter's anger seemed to dissipate. A smile formed on his lips, and he sighed and tore the letter to pieces, destroying the evidence. "I'll admit that as Albert's former teacher, I did appreciate his use of a poem in the context. It was a nice literary touch."

A month later, Josef bowed his head as he finished the mealtime prayer. Dorothea and all four girls joined at the end, saying "*Im Namen des Vaters, des Sohnes und des Heiligen Geistes,*" as they made the sign of the cross.

He raised his head and waited for the complaints. Fasting from meat on Fridays during Lent always caused grumbles from the children, but the objections were loudest during the weeklong fast of Holy Week. The girls stared at the sparse fare on the table

—potatoes and salted herring. Josef bought the fish by the barrel to eat throughout Lent.

After years of complaints, Margarete and Sophia were resigned to the Lenten menu. Younger Katharina and Martha couldn't let the meal take place without comment.

Katharina curled her lip and groaned, "Again?"

"Nein," said Sophia, as she covered her giggles with her hand. "At lunch we ate herring with bread. Now we're eating herring with potatoes."

"Sophia," warned Dorothea.

"Isn't there another fish we could eat?" asked Martha. "Maybe one that isn't so fishy?"

"You'll eat what you're served," said Josef. "There are many who would think this meal was a feast, including your brothers."

The girls were silenced, knowing what he said was true. As they begrudgingly passed around the food, Senta's bark rose from outside. Josef took out his pocket watch, noting the late hour for a visitor, but when her bark quickly fell silent, he assumed only a wild animal had caught her eye. Normal family chatter resumed until there was a knock at the door.

No one spoke, but Josef rose from his seat. Still not out of his chair, the door creaked, followed by a clumsy thud and the scratch of paws on the floor. A voice called out, "Nein, Senta!"

Recognizing the voice, the girls cried out with joy, "Franz!" and scrambled out of their seats and headed straight to the door.

Josef looked at Dorothea, hoping to share in the moment. Instead of smiling at her husband and running toward her son, Dorothea sat with her eyes closed and hands clasped. He could imagine her silent prayer.

He whispered his own, "Gott sei Dank."

In the hallway, Franz laughed as his sisters clung to his dirty uniform with glee. Senta tapped her tail with a slow, guilty thump, acknowledging she was breaking a rule by being in the house, but she also wore a proud canine smile for finding Franz.

"Girls," he called. "Please take Senta before your mother throws her out."

Franz grinned at his father. "Forgive Senta, Papa. I shouldn't have let her get in."

"She's forgiven." Josef walked toward his son with his arms open. "She's as happy to see you as we are."

As the girls relinquished their hold on Franz, Josef saw that the stubble dotting his face couldn't hide the new wrinkles, aged by war, sun, and worry. Yet having lost weight, Franz's body seemed more boyish despite the bars on his collar and insignia on his epaulettes marking him a first lieutenant.

"It's so good to see you, Papa." Franz met him halfway and gave him a long hug.

Josef heard Dorothea's footsteps, and he released Franz. Turning to his wife, he said, "Look who we have here."

Dorothea had a hand to her heart, still in a state of shocked gratitude to God. She quickened her steps and grabbed Franz in a hug.

Chuckling at the strong display of affection by his otherwise stiff mother, Franz said, "It's good to be home."

Fighting tears with her eyes closed, she echoed Josef. "Gott sei Dank."

When he pulled away, Franz tried to keep his own emotions in check with a joke. He looked to the girls. "I hope I'm not late for abendbrot. I've been looking forward to herring for weeks."

"You can have mine," said Martha.

"Mine, too!" said Katharina and Sophia in unison.

"Wonderful. You're so generous." Franz placed his hand on his heart in mock gratitude. "Then tomorrow may I have your piece of *Gründonnerstagskringel*?"

Franz laughed, waiting for each girl to cry, "No!" because no one would ever relinquish their hard-fought share of the Gründonnerstagskringel. Maundy Thursday was a somber day when the family attended the solemn Mass before Good Friday. But the emotional load was lightened by the traditional pastry to commemorate the day. Dorothea baked a yeast cake with almonds, raisins, and icing in the shape of a ring. After so many days of fasting, it was a welcome treat and also a game. The family would each lay a hand on the ring, and the person who tore the biggest piece had the most luck in the coming year.

Instead of laughter and objections, the girls' smiles were replaced with silent, uncertain frowns. Margarete was the first to speak. "We're going to wait to have Gründonnerstagskringel again until after the war, when you're all home." Her voice quavered as she added, "Including Stefan."

Josef watched for Franz's reaction. He had written to him about Stefan but said nothing more than the facts in the notice. Whatever Franz thought of Margarete's statement, he kept it to himself. Tilting his head, he nodded. "Ah, yes. That's thoughtful of you."

The following night, Josef and Franz sat in the dining room drinking schnapps after the rest of the family had gone to bed.

Franz lit a cigarette and leaned back in his seat. "It's good to be home."

"Were you able to rest while we were at church?" asked Josef. He hadn't objected when Franz begged off Mass saying he was tired. After two years in the army, Franz had changed from boy to man.

"A little. When I woke, I walked around the farm to see how things were faring." Franz scratched the closely shorn back of his head in thought. "It's odd seeing all these foreigners here."

"You become accustomed to it," Josef said before he sighed. "And then you remember what life used to be like and you find it odd—to say the least. We now have three Polish POWs, two White Russian families, two Polish civilian men, one Polish civilian woman, and two Lithuanian women. They all work hard, but no one is happy with the situation. They would rather be in their homelands, and I would rather have my sons and old farmhands back."

Franz nodded and took a sip of the liquor. Though he hadn't taken a smoke from his cigarette, he exhaled as if he had to get something off his chest. "Papa, we should talk about Stefan."

Josef slowly leaned forward. "Do you know something?"

"I don't know anything specific, but I know the circumstances. The entire Sixth Army in Stalingrad was encircled by the Russians. I learned Stefan's artillery regiment was stuck in the *Kessel*. Have you heard of it?"

"No." Josef didn't understand why they would name a place after a kettle.

"It was the nickname for the pocket where the army was surrounded. The conditions were frightening there this winter for hundreds of thousands of men. Food and supplies had to be flown in, but it was never enough. The lucky ones ate the horses. Most soldiers starved. Stefan was reported missing the day the Soviets began shelling the Pitomnik airfield, one of the last places we could get in and out of. That was the beginning of the end of the battle."

"And where were you?"

"I was with the rest of the Fourth Army trying to break the Russian encirclement from the outside. My men and I shelled the Russians ruthlessly, but we couldn't break the bastards."

Josef felt a knowing that he had denied. He hadn't wanted to believe his wife. "Do you think Stefan has died? That's what your mother thinks."

"I don't know. I heard over ninety thousand men were captured by the Russians." Franz looked to the ceiling for guidance from above. When he met his father's gaze again, his shoulders hung in defeat. "In a way, I hope he died and is at peace after such a horrendous experience. I doubt he would survive being a POW, and if he did, I doubt it would be worth it."

Josef knitted his forehead, wondering what had become of his son. "You can't possibly wish your brother were dead. Even if he's in a Soviet prison, he's still alive. He has a chance for a future."

"Papa... you don't understand."

"I understand. I've been in a war."

Franz stared down his father. "Not like this one."

"War is hell. They all are."

"Fighting for the Kaiser and fighting for Hitler can't be the same." Franz put out his cigarette, watching his fingers grind it into the ashtray. "The cruelty of the Reich... it flows through everything."

"Indeed," said Josef more gently. "But what does that have to do with Stefan? Why would you rather him dead than imprisoned?"

"Because I know how we treat the Russians. The SS deals with them differently. They send the Americans and British to regular POW camps. It's a prison, but they do get Red Cross packages. But the Russians... they're sent to concentration camps where they're treated little better than the Jews."

The rumors about the concentration camps defied humanity, though Josef avoided those conversations. He did learn enough to know that someone was lucky if they stayed alive long enough to be worked to death. "Do the Russians know what conditions their soldiers are in?"

"I imagine they have some idea. They have spies. Prisoners escape." Franz took another cigarette from his pack. "More importantly, they know what the German army has done to their civilians. Given the opportunity, the Russians will have no mercy on any German—Wehrmacht or civilian. I hear friends all the time say they'll commit suicide before they'll be captured."

Josef looked down, taking in everything his son had said. His eyes focused on the table—the linen tablecloth, the crystal glasses, the stone ashtray. Outside of the farm, the civilized world was disintegrating, but it was a distant event. The Haupt family was safe, but now, the monstrous war didn't seem so far away from them. When Josef raised his head, he saw Franz was staring at the wall.

"If the situation was reversed, I can't say I would act any differently than the Russians are now," declared Franz, his eyes not moving from the wallpaper.

"I don't think so," said Josef, hoping he could look his son in the eye. "We raised you better than that."

Franz took a drag from his cigarette, while his focus remained on the wall. "I didn't go to Mass today because I don't want to go to confession. I've done things—unforgivable things. Sometimes I was ordered to do them. Sometimes not. I've seen others do unspeakable acts. Sometimes I stopped them. Sometimes I didn't. I don't know how to confess what I've done."

Franz's cool self-reflection was jarring. It was difficult for Josef to imagine his upstanding son having anything to do with unpardonable sins like a massacre or rape or torture. Yet he could easily see how the Reich could create a culture of war criminals even in the traditionally independent German army. Franz was an ambitious officer in that army, far away from the bucolic morality of Guttstadt. What might he do to succeed?

Josef treaded lightly in his reply. "Every sin can be forgiven."

Franz turned to once again look his father in the eye. With a weak smile, he said, "Let's hope so."

The solemnity of Good Friday passed with a long liturgy and then the prayerful Stations of the Cross around the columns of the church. To Josef's relief, Franz attended confession. When Holy Saturday arrived the next day, everyone was joyful. Breakfast was another simple meal, but fasting ended at midday. The children were excited for anything different on the table. Josef was so hungry that he stood at the clock in the living room, comparing the time to his pocket watch. He wanted the hour to be correct for the fast to end, but he also wanted it to occur as quickly as possible.

After the hearty meal of meaty cabbage rolls with a rich sauce and boiled potatoes, Josef and Franz rose to retire to the living room when they heard Senta's bark followed by the rumble of a truck. They locked eyes, both dissecting the sounds.

Dorothea wiped her hands on her apron as her voice filled with distrust. "Who would come here on Easter Eve?"

Margarete hurried from the kitchen. "It's the SS."

"Danke, Margarete," said Josef. "Could you see to Senta?"

As Margarete turned on her heel, Dorothea placed both hands on her hips. "I can't believe that they would interrupt a holy day."

"I can." Franz picked his jacket up off the back of his chair.

"Dorothea, I'll send Margarete inside. She'll let you know if I need you. This has to be about the Ostarbeiter." Josef held out his hand to halt Franz. "There's no need for you to come outside. They're general SS, not Waffen-SS. This isn't a military matter."

"General SS are even worse than the Waffen." Franz buttoned up his jacket, pausing on the red, black, and white ribbon around the middle button, designating his second-class Iron Cross for bravery. "They need a reminder that some of us are fighting for the Vaterland."

Before they stepped outside, Josef went into the parlor to peek at the visitors. Franz hovered over his shoulder and muttered, "God, I hate them."

"We all do, but why do you?"

"Waffen-SS are lazy, yet they have better equipment than my men. And they have no morals whatsoever. As they go up in rank, they become even more fanatical." Franz snorted. "But at least the Waffen fight; the general SS do nothing good for the German people."

Josef spied the first officer and the other as they jumped out of the truck. He leaned in closer. "I know one of these men. He interrogated me when I was arrested six years ago."

"Humph. Was he always this fat?"

"Unlike most Germans, the former Lieutenant Elsner has put on weight during the war," Josef said as he spied the braided epaulettes of a major. "He's also been promoted."

Once outside, Josef, Elsner, and a junior stormtrooper exchanged a Heil Hitler. Josef gave Franz a side glance, noticing he had skipped the salute. It wasn't required for him, but Josef thought he might participate for political reasons. Instead, Franz stood straight and proud, like a statue of a German lieutenant. He said nothing, but his statement was clear. Despite Elsner's rank and place in society, he thought them beneath any regular army officer.

"Guten Tag, Sturmbannführer Elsner. This is my son, Franz," said Josef. "He's home on leave from the Eastern Front."

Elsner turned his lips up into a half-smile. "Guten Tag, Herr Haupt, Lieutenant Haupt. We won't interrupt your visit for too long, but we need to exchange prisoners."

Josef kept his face impassive, but inside he was wary enough to bite his cheek. The Polish POWs had worked on his land for almost four years. None of them, nor the rest of the Ostarbeiter, had ever been exchanged. Workers had been added, but no one had been removed.

"Pardon, Sturmbannführer, but why? I have no complaints with these men."

"That's difficult to believe about any Pole," said Elsner.

"I've trained them well."

Elsner motioned to his junior officer. "No doubt you'll train this one just as easily."

The stormtrooper went to the back of the truck and opened the flap. Out jumped a man in a worn Polish army uniform. Nothing distinguished him except that he was freshly shaved and cleaner than any of the other Ostarbeiter when they arrived at the estate.

Elsner flicked his hand toward the barn area. "Now if you could bring us one of the others, we'll be on our way. You can pick which one."

Josef slowly clenched his fists at the monster before him. Elsner was forcing him to participate in their cruelty. It was up to him to change a man's fate. Given the range of awful outcomes for any Polish POW, Josef could be sending a man to his death.

Feeling a punch to his stomach, Josef said, "They've just finished eating. I'll return shortly."

With each step toward the workers' dining room, Josef debated which of the men to choose. At first he had known them all to be similar—young peasants, not yet with families of their own. Now he knew their personalities and work ethics. None of them deserved to be delivered back into the clutches of the SS.

In the end, he chose the orphan, Mikolaj, who had grown up alone with his grandparents. Josef decided if the man died, it would cause the least number of people grief. As he returned with Mikolaj, he explained the situation coolly, staring straight ahead. Before they reached Elsner, he looked at the man and whispered, "I'm sorry."

Mikolaj stared back and silently rejected his apology. They both knew wherever he was being sent it was worse than the Haupt farm. And despite the relative kindness of the Haupt family, Josef had turned out to be just another Nazi jailer.

Josef was too preoccupied with his stomach, sick from guilt, to pay much attention to the rest of the transaction. After the SS left, he brought the new Pole, Jan, to the workers' dining room for a meal. He knew a surprising amount of German.

Afterward Josef found Franz in the living room reading a book. When he met his son's eyes, he saw his son knew the moral dilemma he had just faced.

Josef muttered as he positioned a pillow for his nap. "Exchanging those men makes no sense."

"Watch that new prisoner."

"Why?"

"Something's not right." Franz went back to his book but muttered a random thought. "That Pole speaks German too well."

CHAPTER FOURTEEN

MARGARETE

"Is everything all right?" Margarete whispered as she wiped a plate dry.

Home on leave, Albert leaned against the kitchen counter in his uniform, looking more like a chagrined boy than a brave soldier. He stared at a cupboard and mumbled, "No. Yes. I don't know."

Margarete responded to his confusion by handing him the dried plate to place in the cabinet. Hoping her silence would encourage him to speak, she picked up another plate to dry.

"I made a mistake," he whispered. "I implied I was hungry in a letter home. Herr Neuwald brought it to Papa and told him it was treason."

"What?" gasped Margarete, almost dropping the plate. "Are you in trouble? Does the SS know? Is Papa in trouble?"

"No, but I need to watch myself. I don't want to lose my post and get transferred to Kursk like Paul."

Margarete's hand slipped on the plate again. With no more

news of Stefan, an unease had spread through the family. The Haupts were no longer immune to the tragedy of war, and all three boys were in danger. Paul's transfer to deep in Russia only worsened their fears. At least Albert was in Latvia. Another son far in the Eastern Front might send Dorothea to her bed until the end of the war.

"Please be careful," she said, gripping the plate.

A crooked smile crossed his lips. "Papa said I should come to town with him today and then visit some farmers. I think it's penance."

"Penance?" Margarete's brows turned downward. "I'd love to go. Mutti never lets us go anywhere anymore."

"Come with us, then." Albert flashed a smile. "I'll tell Papa."

Later that afternoon, Margarete sat in the middle between her father and Albert in the landau as they drove into Guttstadt. Upon seeing the city center, Albert said aloud what she had also noticed. "I don't recognize half of these people. And why are there so many of them?"

Margarete turned to her father, who briefly looked from side to side. In a low voice, he said, "City folk from western Germany. Life is hard there because of the bombings."

While the strangers ignored them, friends and acquaintances were overly friendly. They called from the sidewalks and gushed over Albert. Margarete had seen similar exchanges at church. With so many deaths, any son of Guttstadt, alive and in town was revered like he was a newborn.

As they drove through the middle of town, Albert craned his neck to get a better view. "It looks like they're repairing the street."

Margarete looked over the horses and onto the road. Two laborers with the distinctive OST patch ground arranging stones into the quaint puzzle that paved Guttstadt's streets.

"They've replaced the cobblestones with stones that don't match," grumbled Josef. "It doesn't look very good."

As they reached the construction, Margarete peered down to

examine the road. The stones were larger, irregular in shape, and flatter than a normal cobblestone. She turned to look ahead again but stopped halfway when she noticed the stones had writing. She leaned down, and her breath caught in her throat as the carriage wheels rolled over beautifully chiseled Hebrew letters and then onto the name *Max Stern*. A memory of a kindly old man who once ran the train station came to mind. He had given Margarete a lollipop when she traveled to Allenstein for the first time.

"Papa," she cried through a whisper. "The stones are—"

"I see," said Josef as he crossed himself.

Albert and Margarete crossed themselves as well, but Margarete continued to watch as the carriage landed on another stone with a Star of David and a birthdate. Ahead, an Ostarbeiter broke a headstone in two to fit into the cobblestone patchwork.

"I remember a few years ago some boys were rowdy after a Hitler Youth meeting and tipped over gravestones in the Jewish cemetery, but they were stopped," said Albert.

"This should have been stopped today," said Josef.

Desecrating any grave was a mortal sin. The only remaining Jews in town—the dead occupants of the Jewish cemetery—should have been protected throughout eternity by the sacred ground they inhabited.

"Bürgermeister Krüger is across the street," Josef said, switching the reins from his right to his left hand. He swerved the carriage to the first hitching post. "I'll say something."

Albert and Margarete stared at their father, remembering the last time he had publicly questioned the Reich. There was now even less freedom in 1943 than there had been in 1937. "Papa—" Albert said.

Josef snapped his head in reproach and at his children's stare. "I'll be tactful, but I must say something."

Other than one of the priests, Margarete knew few people in town who could raise the issue without being immediately arrested. While her father stepped down from the carriage,

Margarete looked at one of the Ostarbeiter, who split a gravestone with a hammer and chisel.

She surveyed the street to see if others were also outraged. Most people walked along with their focus straight ahead. Others noticed the activity but continued to walk as if it was only street repairs. Yet there were some who stopped and stared before making a furtive sign of the cross and scurrying away.

Krüger crossed the street, heading straight to the Haupt carriage. Before he reached them, he looked over at the Ostarbeiter, admiring their work on the road. Steps later he was in front of Josef, and they exchanged salutes.

"Herr Haupt, how do you like our street repairs?" Krüger extended his hand in pride toward the Ostarbeiter. "It doesn't quite match, but I think it will be a much smoother ride."

Josef pursed his lips before saying, "Thank you for your work, but forgive me, Herr Krüger. I know that you're trying to maintain the streets in an economical manner during a time of war, but I fear someone failed to alert you to something important."

"And what is that?"

"As you know, most of Guttstadt is Catholic," he said with complete calm. "We believe it is a mortal sin to desecrate a grave."

"And so?" Krüger curled his lip in annoyance. "You didn't do this. What do you care?"

"We must drive over them."

Krüger squared his shoulders. "So you must."

Margarete knew the expression on her father's face—the one that appeared when he was trying to control his temper.

Josef pressed his lips together in a smile. "I understand, Herr Krüger. As I said, you're doing a fine job in a difficult time. Perhaps they could be turned over so that the inscriptions aren't visible. The surface would be smoother for driving, and then no one would see the Hebrew, which I'm sure you also would rather not see."

Krüger looked at the gravestone pavement. The Ostarbeiter continued their work of configuring the pieces and breaking the stones when a new shape was needed. He turned back to Josef with a baffled expression.

"But I want the Jewish words visible. By driving over the words, we eradicate the Jews and their culture. Then there will be nothing left of them at all, and the German *Volk* can live in peace."

The same closed-mouth smile remained on Josef's face, as if Krüger had been speaking of the weather. "Danke, Bürgermeister Krüger, for taking care of our roads."

"Bitte," Krüger replied with no gratitude.

"Now, I wish you well because we must be off." He pointed across the street. "I'm taking Albert to the market to purchase things he can't find in Latvia."

"That must be a long list," said Krüger, mustering a smile. "Good luck to you, Albert." He nodded to Margarete, but his smile waned as he spoke to Josef. "Guten Tag."

Only when they left town did Josef declare, "Krüger did this now because the bishop is away in Frauenberg. If the bishop were here, we could have stopped them."

"Will he say something when he returns?" asked Albert.

"Yes, but by then it's done." Josef shook his head. "I couldn't say anything more to him."

"You tried, Papa," said Margarete.

Josef lowered his eyes, seeming defeated with regret and guilt. The three traveled in silence as Josef drove the carriage to Herr Konrad's small farm at the farthest outreaches of Guttstadt. He lived alone with his wife, Elsa. Their son, Hans, had died at the beginning of the war in Poland four years earlier. When they neared the home, Margarete noticed that the land around them had changed. The Ermland's summer horizonless fields of mani-cured crops had vanished. The fields either lay fallow or popu-lated equally with weeds and mangy crops.

"Is this Herr Konrad's land?" asked Albert, scanning the fields with disapproval.

"Ja, he has emphysema and can't work. Frau Konrad does what she can with laborers I send her, but as you can see, it isn't much." Josef pointed to a broken section of fence. "And that was supposed to be fixed by the new Polish prisoner, Jan. I won't send him next time. The Konrads need able help, not *Polnische Wirtschaft*."

Margarete's internal antennae raised. It wasn't like her father to use a derogatory term for the Polish prisoners.

Albert noticed the slip as well. "Is Jan a problem?"

"A problem? No. Just lazy compared to the rest of the Ostarbeiter. When I complained to the SS, they said we should be happy to have him at all."

"Why hasn't the SS placed Ostarbeiter with the Konrads if they need the help?" asked Albert.

"I've asked Kreisbauernführer Fink, but he's declined. I think they're waiting for Herr Konrad to die so they can confiscate the land for lack of production."

"What will happen to Frau Konrad?" asked Margarete.

"She'll be moved to town I suppose." His voice turned bitter. "And after sacrificing their only child for the Reich, her reward will be the loss of her farm."

When they arrived at the small cottage, Frau Konrad met them outside. A petite, birdlike woman, she had light gray eyes that lit up the world around her. She welcomed them with smiles and warm handshakes.

"Margarete, you're quite the young woman, now," she said with an approving nod.

As Margarete murmured her thanks, Frau Konrad turned to Albert and seemed unable to repress herself.

"Albert," she said, grasping his arms. As she pulled away, she touched the woolen cloth of his uniform in admiration. "You look so distinguished. You remind me of Hans."

Taken aback to be compared to her dead son, Albert took a moment before saying, "Danke."

"Please don't be offended. I know my son is at peace in

Heaven. You look well, and it makes me happy to remember him alive and strong."

Seeing the glow of life in Frau Konrad, Margarete thought her a remarkable person. Dorothea mourned Stefan with a fierce privacy that didn't make her any happier.

"Then it makes me happy as well," said Albert.

"We went to the market, so I picked up a few things for you while we were there," said Josef, presenting Frau Konrad with a brown bag.

"You are too kind, Herr Haupt." She put a hand to her heart. "May I give you some of my strawberry jam to give to Dorothea?"

"If you have some to spare, she would like that very much."

When they went inside, Herr Konrad stood at their kitchen table with one hand on the table and another on a cane. Margarete hadn't seen the man in years, and he seemed to have shrunk in that time.

"Guten Tag, Josef," he said with a wheeze. "It's so nice to see you today." He smiled brightly. "And you brought these two. We haven't had anyone young in this house for so long. Thank you for coming."

After everyone had enjoyed coffee and cake, Josef talked farming with Herr Konrad while he sent Albert and Margarete to help Frau Konrad with the chores. Neither of them minded the work because she was so pleasant and grateful.

When they returned from the barn, Margarete noticed that her father and Herr Konrad were doing more than chatting. There were documents on Reichsnährstand letterhead spread on the table. To Josef's right was a small black book that he took notes in as they worked.

While Josef and Herr Konrad completed the documents, Frau Konrad plied Albert and Margarete with more cake. She asked questions about his life in the army, Margarete's schooling, and the rest of the family. They were happy to talk with her, but as she spoke, Margarete found herself listening to her father and Herr

Konrad. She didn't understand the specifics, but something seemed uneasy about it.

After heartfelt goodbyes, they drove away. Albert looked over his shoulder, and Margarete did as well to see what he was looking at. The Konrads' door closed, and the old couple were safely inside.

"Papa," Albert said. "I couldn't help but hear your conversation with Herr Konrad."

"I expected that. I'm simply helping him." He snapped the reins, urging the horses onward. "I've planted a little more to compensate for his lack of production."

"But the Reich could say that extra production shouldn't be an offset to Herr Konrad's loss. It should just go to them," said Albert.

"They could, but they'll never know. Herr Konrad would never betray me. I'm one of his oldest friends."

Margarete saw Albert's eyes almost cross in confusion. Only hours before, Josef had chastised him for being careless in a letter. Now, his father was justifying his own egregious lawbreaking.

"I wouldn't worry about Herr Konrad, but someone else could implicate you—someone with a grudge against you or Herr Konrad," said Albert. "Think of Frau Wolf when she fired her farmhand and he told the Gestapo that she had slaughtered a pig for her husband's wake without permission. She was sent to prison, and that was after her son had died in Flanders."

"It was appalling," said Josef grimly. "Though she did return. They were making an example of her at the time."

Margarete piped up, thinking she could now add to the conversation, "Didn't a Berliner tell the Gestapo that Herr Becker was hoarding food? What happened to him?"

"Herr Becker has connections, so he only had to pay an exorbitant fine," said Josef, his mustache twitching ruefully.

"Could we afford such a fine?" asked Albert.

"It would be difficult." Josef clenched the reins tighter and turned to his children. "No one comes to visit the Konrads so far from town. The only people who have been here have been our Ostarbeiter. I wouldn't take such a risk for anyone except Herr Konrad. While I've prospered under the Reich, he and his family have declined. Helping him is the decent thing to do."

Albert took a deep breath and nodded in silence. Margarete was quiet as well. Her father was right, but it was dangerous all the same.

Snapping the reins again, Josef gave his final statement on the subject. "I, too, have lost a son. The Reich has taken far more from us than they've given."

CHAPTER FIFTEEN

MARGARETE

The letters came within weeks of each other. Each time, Margarete watched from the parlor window as her father stood with Senta to greet Bürgermeister Krüger while her mother would slip upstairs to her bedroom, saying she was going to pray. Margarete believed she was praying, but she was also listening from her window.

Outside, Josef stood at attention ready to hear his sons' fate. Rather than immediately telling Josef if one of his sons had died, the Bürgermeister forced him to respond to a "Heil Hitler!" salute.

Only then would the Bürgermeister hold his palm up to calm Josef. "It's only an injury. He's alive."

Josef would close his eyes in relief, and Margarete would make the sign of the cross. Upstairs a clatter sounded as Dorothea ran back down for more information now that she knew her remaining sons were still alive.

East, February 16, 1944.

Dear Family Haupt,

I regret to have to inform you that your son, Paul, was wounded in Korsun-Shevchenkivskyi, Ukraine on January 3. He was airlifted to Leipzig where he will recover in the hospital. Paul has fought heroically for the Führer, Volk, and Vaterland.

F. Jäger
Oberleutnant

The accuracy of the transcript extracts is certified. Bürgermeister Helmut Krüger.

East, February 28, 1944.

Dear Family Haupt,

I regret to inform you that your son, Franz, was wounded in battle outside of Orsha, Weißrussland on February 19. He was airlifted to the hospital in Nuremberg where he will recover. Franz has fought heroically for the Führer, Volk, and Vaterland.

```
L. Prümm
Major
-------
The accuracy of the transcript extracts
is certified. Bürgermeister Helmut
Krüger.
```

After each letter Dorothea's mood improved as the emotional burden of one son's safety was lifted. Margarete knew how she felt. Although Franz and Paul would return to battle once they recovered, she was still happy. Every minute they were away from the front was one less minute their lives were in danger.

At night, Margarete would sit with her parents to listen to the BBC. Dorothea sat in her chair by the radio, knitting woolens to send to her sons. To her side, Josef puffed on his cigar as he concentrated on the broadcast. Margarete sat with a book, her ears also pinned to the scratchy broadcast, trying to parse the German through a British accent. By spring 1944, the news was more bad than good for Germany, so Dorothea would retire early to pray.

At the end of the broadcast, Josef turned off the radio and often left the house in weighty silence. After Franz's casualty notification arrived, Margarete waited until Dorothea went to bed before she questioned her father. He stood at the mantel, staring at one of Dorothea's old paintings as he contemplated the night's news.

"What do you think, Papa?"

"The war isn't going well." Josef tapped a cigar into the crystal ashtray on the mantel.

She had heard about Germany's struggles. Hushed voices at gatherings mentioned the possibility of Russia arriving on East Prussia's doorstep. It was the nightmare from the First World War that no one wanted to relive.

"Will this be like the last war? Will the Russians invade East Prussia? Will we need to leave the farm?"

"Possibly."

Margarete's eyes widened as she imagined the impossible. Leave the farm? It would be like abandoning a part of one's body. She didn't know another life than the fields, the house, Senta, and all the other animals. How could you leave yourself?

Josef placed a hand on her shoulder. "But if that were to happen, it would be like the last war. We would leave for safety and return in a few weeks. Just as the visiting people in town from the cities in the West have done. This has happened for generations across Europe. You mustn't worry. There are hundreds of thousands of German soldiers between East Prussia and the Russians."

Margarete nodded, but she wasn't convinced. The people in town relocated from the West had been there for months—some even years.

"Margarete, I know this is upsetting, but you're sixteen now and old enough to know these things."

"Yes, Papa," she whispered.

"After all, you'll be going off to school next month. You'll be living alone in Königsberg."

She blinked at the abrupt change in conversation. A moment ago, they were discussing a losing war. Now the topic was her step into adulthood. Attending a posh school in the big city, she would learn everything to become a lady like her mother. She brightened a little.

"I'm excited."

He smiled and gave her another pat on the arm. "We'll be so proud of your accomplishments."

A month later, Margarete and her mother swayed in their seats as the streetcar rumbled across one of Königsberg's seven bridges and onto Cathedral Island. The conversation and clanging of the crowded trolley swirled around them. Dorothea sat tall in a fine gray suit with a fox stole and a jaunty burgundy hat, while her gloved hands rested atop a patent leather handbag. Urbane citizens of Königsberg who took notice might have pegged her as a hausfrau from the countryside putting on silly airs in the middle of a dire war. Meanwhile Dorothea sat with her eyes cast low in judgment, deciding who might be refined enough to be worthy of her society. She traveled to the East Prussian capital to shop and to visit her nephew, a dentist in the city, but she saw no reason to stay.

Meanwhile Margarete gazed out the window, enthralled by the sights of Königsberg. She had visited before, but now that she would live there by herself, the city looked new and more exciting. At the next trolley stop, she had a full view of the beautiful cathedral with its fairy-tale turret. It was as old as the basilica in Guttstadt, but the cathedral had become a Lutheran church during the Reformation.

She turned to her mother. "While I'm here, I'd like to go to the cathedral. It's so beautiful, and I've always wanted to visit Immanuel Kant's grave."

"You will go to Mass with your cousins."

Margarete grumbled. "I didn't mean I would attend a service there."

Her parents were gifting her freedom and responsibility to live on her own there, but there were limits in a city where the population was 95 percent Lutheran. It was one of the reasons she was living in a rented room with friends of her cousins rather than in the dormitories with the other girls. Margarete might attend a fancy finishing school and live alone in the big city, but she wasn't to forget her own kind.

The streetcar left the island, crossing the Pregel River, before arriving back on the mainland, where the Königsberg castle came into view. Its squat turrets connected long buildings that enclosed a grand courtyard. An imposing tower oversaw the castle and the city.

Margarete declared, "I'll visit the castle as well."

"You will study first. That's why you're here—not for sightseeing." Dorothea lowered her voice. "This is how you'll find a husband one day."

Not wanting to hear anything more about husbands, Margarete returned to her sightseeing. Amid the medieval buildings, historic squares, and busy streets, there were signs of war. There were fewer people on the trolley and streets than Margarete remembered from her past trips. Outside stores, people stood in line with ration coupons, hoping for their daily bread. Their eyes glazed with boredom, the shoppers stared at street posters vilifying Jews, Russia, Britain, and America. The cinema marquees, which once proudly advertised Marlene Dietrich's Hollywood movies, now announced Reich-approved films.

The neighborhood became greener as the road left the center of town. Signs pointed to the zoo, which Margarete was excited to be living nearby. The flat she would be staying in was close enough that she wondered if she could hear the elephants and monkeys at night. She wouldn't know until later that day because first she had to attend orientation.

When they exited the streetcar at the giant Adolf Hitler Platz, Dorothea strode with an entitled purpose and her focus squarely in front of her while Margarete was enthralled with the sights of her new home. The school was situated on a lovely city block connecting the streets, Beethoven Strasse, Brahms Strasse, Strauss Strasse, and Schubert Strasse. She had sung Johannes Brahms' *Ein Deutsches Requiem* in her old school's choir, and her favorite composer, Händel, had a street named for him only a block away. She considered this an auspicious sign.

When the school building came into view, she gawked because it was unlike any school she had ever seen. It was a massive example of Bauhaus architecture with stark lines of connecting brick, steel cubes, and hundreds of windows. It may have been a finishing school, but it was a modern and sophisticated one. Margarete wasn't aware that a local nickname for the school was the "Girls Aquarium" because of the fishbowl effect of the windows. Another nickname came from the curriculum at the school, the *Klopsakademie*—named after Königsberg's renowned meatball dish.

On every sidewalk, girls like her followed their mothers. They funneled into the school's entrance, where the mothers checked them into the registrar before they were sent upstairs to the auditorium. The elegant room was long and narrow, filled with dark-blue velvet seats and lit by Art Deco chandeliers and sconces on the sky-blue walls.

After they sat down, Dorothea started conversing with a mother from Elbing, so Margarete smiled at the daughter, who had bright red hair. There was little time for chitchat, though, as the headmistress began her presentation. A stern, silver-haired woman dressed in black, she stood on the stage and commanded the room with a voice larger than her slight body.

Margarete tried not to fidget as the woman droned on about the school's educational philosophy and how the girls were the future mothers of the Reich. Margarete looked at her list for the term: conversational French, Cooking, Etiquette, Piano, Needlepoint, and Garden Design. She liked anything to do with music and the outdoors, but she could do without cooking, sewing, and manners. Speaking French was an improvement from the Latin and English grammar lessons she had endured for years.

Maybe she knew her audience was wilting under the weight of information because the headmistress announced a demonstration of the school's bell schedule. The ring was loud like a fire alarm but short.

The bell then rang five times and repeated itself. Annoyed mothers touched their ears, and daughters clapped their hands over theirs.

The headmistress announced, "If the bell rings five times, there is an air raid. The teachers will lead the students to the shelter across the street."

Margarete froze. Even the Reich news now admitted to the terrible bombings of western German cities by the British and the Americans. Bombs dropped nightly, but she had always thought Königsberg was like the rest of East Prussia—isolated and safe. Margarete shifted her eyes to her mother.

Outwardly, Dorothea seemed unfazed by the information. Only someone who knew her would notice she had pursed her lips in worry. Still staring straight at the headmistress, she briefly lifted her gloved hand as a sign to her daughter to be calm.

The headmistress continued, "I know that many of you are from the countryside and are unfamiliar with bomb shelters. They're only precautions. The Russians have tried bombing Königsberg, but they can't even fly an airplane correctly, and the British and the Americans are too far away. They will never reach Königsberg."

Dorothea looked at Margarete and gave her a nod, telling her that she accepted the headmistress's explanation. Margarete smiled weakly. She wanted to believe the headmistress and her mother, but she was still nervous.

Later that afternoon, she learned her mother was worried as well. After a fancy luncheon with the other mothers and students in the cafeteria, it was time to say goodbye. When Margarete told her mother that she already looked forward to her first letter from home, Dorothea's lips set into an anxious line. She knew her mother felt as sad and uncomfortable as she did. Dorothea liked to have children under her roof. Her boys were all in danger and scattered over the earth, and now she was leaving her eldest daughter to live on her own.

"What is it, Mutti?" Margarete asked.

"Nothing." As if she realized she had been caught off guard, Dorothea muttered a distraction. "Maybe you can take this time to improve your figure and lose a little weight."

"Yes, Mutti," said Margarete, souring on her mother. Now she couldn't wait to be rid of her. "Have a good trip home."

Margarete lived with the Fischer family, who had no sons or near relatives in the Wehrmacht and weren't members of the party. Despite his young age, Herr Fischer had avoided military service because of a weak heart. With no military or party supplements to his income, Herr Fischer needed to take in boarders. A watchmaker, he had fallen on hard times due to the dwindling number of people left in the city who could afford a fine timepiece.

Unlike the Haupts, Herr Fischer and his wife, Agatha, weren't critical of the Reich or the war. Margarete never heard anything like Dorothea's resentful mutterings or even her father's unspoken yet visible disdain. In fact, she never heard talk of the war at all in the Fischer house. The couple were busy with their infant twins, and even late at night when they listened to the radio, they never searched for a BBC broadcast.

Margarete guessed they had less freedom living in the city than on a farm in the country. In Königsberg, there were always nosy people in close proximity who could witness the slightest insubordination to the Reich. Everyone was a potential spy.

Given the vitriol and severity of the Reich in Königsberg, Margaret saw the merit in the Fischer family's worry-free oblivion. She too could forget about the dark world. At school, she ate better meals in her cooking classes than those in the Fischer home, where the menu was limited by their ration coupons and income. She also could lose herself in music lessons and explore the natural world in her gardening classes. On the streetcar home, she admired the city's historic architecture and beautiful parks. In the evenings, she did her schoolwork, joined the Fischers for abendbrot, and helped with the twins before heading to bed. Weekends in Königsberg were full of adventure with her friends, exploring the lush parks, boating in the many lakes, enjoying the wonderful public art and museums, or visiting the shops and cafés of Steindamm.

The war would only reappear before bed when she knelt to

say her prayers for her brothers. The room was darker than at home with no moonlight streaming because it was forbidden to open the shades at night. At twilight, the whole city went from room to room drawing the curtains to hide their lights in case of an air raid.

CHAPTER SIXTEEN

MARGARETE

I n Königsberg, for the first time, Margarete had to regularly attend meetings of the Bund Deutscher Mädel. In Guttstadt, she went to BDM meetings occasionally, but Dorothea kept her under her wing on the farm. The meetings she did attend always started with an emphatic Nazi salute and an overview of Reich propaganda before the girls performed helpful tasks like rolling bandages, hiking to collect medicinal herbs, or singing in the hospital to wounded men.

The BDM was a different organization in Königsberg. She watched the BDM leaders from afar in the cafeteria and heard snippets of their conversations in the hallways. Brash and rebellious, the leaders snuck into bars and smoked cigarettes. They spent their summers at Hitler Youth camps for boys and girls that were known for their outdoor adventuring, Nazi indoctrination, and promiscuity. Naturally prone to unwitting comments and hearing gossip, the youth often used information heard from one another and adults in order to get themselves or their families ahead in life. Margarete knew to tread carefully around them. Being neither competitive, experienced, nor devoted to the Reich, she felt like an outlier.

When she walked into the school's auditorium for her first BDM meeting, she wore the same uniform as everyone else—a blue skirt, white blouse, and matching blue neck kerchief. The other girls' shirts were adorned with patches and medals showing their service and rank. Many had been faithful participants for years with awards and leadership positions to show for it. Margarete's uniform was one of the few that was otherwise blank, save for a swastika and triangle badge identifying her as part of the East Prussian region.

Before Margarete took her seat, she felt a tug on her shirt. She turned to see an upperclassman, older in appearance yet shorter than her. She looked into the girl's steely blue eyes, accentuated by the bushy white blond eyebrows fixed into a straight line of concern. A red lanyard hung from the girl's neck, signifying her high rank. In a paramilitary organization, it wouldn't do to address the girl without acknowledging her importance.

Margarete guessed and murmured, "*Mädelscharführerin.*"

"Don't you know your ranks?" The girl's upper lip flinched in offense. "*Mädelgruppenführerin* Ida von Fittkau. What is your name?"

"Margarete Haupt."

"Where you from?" The girl crossed her arms like a parent waiting to hear a child's story she had already prejudged not to believe.

"Guttstadt. In the Ermland." In only a week, Margarete had learned that many at her school knew little of the Ermland, while others familiar with the region thought it a backwater.

"Why don't you have any badges? You're too old to have achieved nothing in the BDM."

"The BDM was small at my old school. It was a religious

school." Margarete gripped her hands, regretting she had added the last part.

Ida rolled her eyes. "I bet it was a Catholic one at that. If you pay attention here, you'll learn that the Reich is the only religion you need." She nodded to the seats. "Go sit down. You need to catch up."

Margarete ducked her head in embarrassment and slid into the nearest seat. The girl to her right had her back turned, so Margarete stared straight ahead, thankful no one seemed to have noticed she had been singled out.

A whisper dashed her hopes. "What did Ida say to you?"

Margarete turned to see Helene Wichert staring at her with her hazel eyes in their usual state of mischief. In only a week, Margarete had learned this was a girl to avoid. The daughter of the head Lutheran pastor at the Königsberg cathedral, Helene was well known throughout the school. She ran with a crowd of local Königsberg girls who ignored Margarete, many of them BDM leaders.

Already once that week, Helen had teased Margarete. In their cooking class, the girls' first lesson was to learn the city's signature dish, Königsberger Klopse. Margarete focused on forming perfect meatballs, knowing she could do well in this class. She doubted the teacher's standards would be tougher than Dorothea's.

Others in her class were less interested in culinary perfection. They chatted and joked about the small meatballs in their hands, likening them to boys they knew. As Margarete's ears burned, she lowered her head farther to concentrate on her work.

One girl's voice rose to her left. "Helene, which one is more like Max, this one or this one?"

"I couldn't say," Helene answered in a coy voice, already raspy from too many cigarettes in her short life.

"I bet you could," said the other girl. "I saw you leave the café with him Saturday night. I was surprised to see you in church the next morning."

Too curious for her own good, Margarete gave a sideways

glance to see Helene's response. The girl wore her shiny black hair in a blunt bob like a fashionable woman in a Mercedes advertisement. With her hand on her aproned hip, she waved a knife as she spoke. "Have you ever even seen me late to church? I'm always at church and on time. I'm a pastor's kid."

"It's true," said another girl's voice from behind Margarete. "And Helene can always recite all of her Bible verses in Sunday school."

Just as Margarete was turning her attention back to her cooking, Helene spied her sneaking gaze. Helene's smile remained unchanged as she said, "Unlike a Catholic, I can hold my liquor, and I actually know the Bible."

Margarete blanched at the comment, which seemed directed at her for eavesdropping. She looked away at once, wishing she were anywhere else. While she vowed never to sit near these girls again, she heard Helene say, "Come now, Margarete Haupt. I was joking. I don't care if you're a papist. You know all that Latin, which is more useful than a bunch of Bible verses."

Margarete looked up to see Helene smiling, but she couldn't determine if Helene was joking to make her feel better or drawing her into an argument. "So far Latin hasn't been very useful," she replied.

The other girls changed the subject before Helene could respond. Margarete focused again on her meatballs, uncertain what to make of Helene. She had never met a girl before who was irreverent and wild while still being devout.

Now at the BDM meeting, Helene waited for an answer to her question, and Margarete was baffled. Why was she asking? She noticed the array of medals and badges on Helene's blouse, so she sheepishly touched her own shirt.

"The Mädelgruppenführerin reprimanded me for not having been more involved in the BDM."

"That's what she said? Ha!" Helene leaned back in her chair and crossed her legs. "I say good for you. The BDM is a bunch of nonsense. You're lucky to have avoided it."

Margarete stared, unsure what to say. Helene was friendly enough with the Mädelgruppenführerin to call her by her first name. She might be disparaging the BDM because she was an informant and wanted information to use against Margarete. Remembering how her father handled questions about his children's irregular Hitler Youth attendance, Margarete relied on his excuse with some added humor, "I don't know how lucky I've been. I had to work on the farm."

"What's that like?" Helene reared her head in fright.

"Boring. Dirty."

"Don't you have Ostarbeiter?"

"Yes, but it's a large farm, and our German farmhands and my brothers were all drafted. There's still so much work to be done."

"How many brothers do you have?"

"I have four older brothers and three younger sisters."

Helene looked dazed as if Margarete was telling a fantasy. "I can't imagine that big of a family. I'm an only child. What is it like to have so many brothers and sisters?"

As much as Margarete enjoyed Königsberg, she missed her family. She answered with a small sigh. "It's wonderful but sometimes annoying. You don't have much privacy."

"So, you must be happy to have your brothers gone and fewer people in the house."

"The house is quieter, but I miss them."

"Where are they stationed?"

"Paul and Franz were both on the Eastern Front, but they were wounded. They're in the hospital right now. Albert is in Latvia. Stefan is missing in action." She raised her head to see Helene's reaction, which was full of concern. A gut feeling urged her to show Helene, who seemed to be untouched by the war, what it had cost others.

"Stefan was at Stalingrad. It's been well over a year since he went missing. We fear he was killed."

"I'm so sorry," said Helene, her voice quieting with contrition. "That was stupid of me to ask. I've been to enough funerals at my church for parishioners whose sons have died. I shouldn't have assumed that your brothers were safe."

Their conversation stopped because the sound of a gavel banging resounded through the auditorium. The blue curtains around the stage framed a scene of four BDM leaders all standing at attention while Ida hit a gavel against a wooden table. Needing no direction, every girl in the auditorium rose from their seats.

Margarete startled when she heard Helene whisper, "You know, for Prussian nobility she looks much more Nordic than German."

Feeling like she was being tested again, Margarete kept her focus directly on the stage. She studied the leader's icy white coloring and replied with only a factual statement. "She's very blond."

Helene leaned in so close that Margarete could feel the girl's breath on her cheek as she said, "The product of a Viking invasion."

Margarete couldn't repress a smile. "Aren't you two friends?"

"Not really. We've always gone to the same schools."

From the stage, Ida threw up her arm, exclaiming "Heil Hitler!"

Margarete joined the hundred other girls in the room and mimicked Ida in the salute and then in a round of oaths of loyalty to the Reich and love of Adolf Hitler. At the end of the oaths, the chords of *Deutschland, Deutschland Über Alles* filled the room. As a girl played the school's grand piano, the rest of the auditorium belted out the German national anthem. The ritual finished as the girls chanted the BDM motto, "Be Faithful, Be Pure, Be German!"

When they were given leave to sit, Helene whispered, "I can tell you that not a single girl up there is pure in the biblical sense."

Margarete's ears burned once again. How was she supposed to reply to such a statement? Busying herself so that Helene might stop talking to her, she smoothed her skirt and whispered,

"Luckily for them, the Reich is only concerned about racial purity."

The meeting began with another BDM leader announcing upcoming events. Margarete decided she would join the group of girls knitting scarves and gloves for the soldiers. She also made a mental note to remember the BDM march through the city scheduled for that weekend to show their loyalty to Herr Hitler. That might also put her in good stead, and she could sightsee.

At the end of the announcements, Ida took the podium again. "I would like for us now to welcome all of the new girls to our group."

Margarete was surprised as several girls seated in her vicinity turned to greet her. When she was done shaking hands, Helene tapped her shoulder and offered her hand.

"Thank you for making this meeting bearable."

Margarete couldn't help but laugh, which made Helene's smile wider.

When the greetings stopped in the room, Ida cleared her throat and started again. "Unfortunately, some of our new classmates have been remiss in their expected BDM service. Some of you have nothing to show for your involvement in this most important organization to the future of the Reich."

Girls who had just warmly received Margarete now turned to her with suspicion. Her cheeks flamed as she felt the girls judge her for a lack of loyalty to the Reich. Unable to withstand the shame, she lowered her head, vowing to do whatever she could with the BDM to no longer stand out.

With her eyes on the floor, Margarete listened as Ida continued her speech by saying that she felt the need to offer some remedial lessons. She began an impromptu lecture on Nazism and the superiority of Aryans and the subhuman nature of Jews, Africans, Asians, and Slavs in order of degree. It was nothing that she hadn't heard or read a thousand times, and she let a small sigh of boredom escape.

Helene took the sigh as an opportunity for comment. She

whispered in Margarete's ear, "I have no idea why they continue to talk about Jews after they've sent them all away. The only ones left are the half-blood *Mischlinge*, and even they're being deported now—like my neighbor. His family has always attended the cathedral. My father says he's a devout Christian, but he was sent to a camp."

"There haven't been any Jews in Guttstadt in years," said Margarete, thinking of the respected families who had disappeared from the earth.

"None? Not even a half-blood or a laborer for the Reich?"

"None. There weren't too many to begin with."

The loss of the small but vibrant Jewish community was a gaping hole in the fabric of Guttstadt. Margarete knew her parents mourned how the town had changed under the Reich, but they rarely spoke of the missing Jews, no doubt from guilt and fear. She looked for Helene's reaction, which appeared genuinely glum, with a resigned frown and sad eyes.

Margarete's ears perked up when Ida declared that Christianity was old-fashioned and wouldn't be a part of Germany in the future.

"Not this again," grumbled Helene. "My father says it will never happen. She's trying to show off to the adult BDM leaders in the room. The Reich always sends a spy."

Ida then announced, "The end of Christianity in Germany will start with ending the Catholic Church. The papists have always been hostile to the Reich. I don't know why we even allow them in this school."

Margarete was used to hearing Nazi dogma, but this felt like a personal attack on her. As Ida continued her criticisms of the Catholic Church, Margarete looked at friends she knew were Catholic. Their faces all held the same tense expression of hurt and terror that they might be called out.

She felt Helene lean close to her. "Ignore her. She doesn't know what she's talking about. Many people in Königsberg have never even met a Catholic. They don't know that it's different in other parts of Germany."

"Have you met a Catholic then?"

"Of course. My father is friends with a priest." A smile crept across Helene's lips. "And now I've met you."

Ida finished her rant by saying, "Good Catholics cannot be good Germans. You can't follow a man in Rome wearing a silly hat and be faithful to the Führer."

Margarete sank farther in defeat in her seat, hoping this would be the end of the speech. Out of the corner of her eye, she saw Helene raise her hand and speak without being called on.

"Ida...oh, excuse me." Helene smirked as she corrected what had to have been an intentional insubordination. "I mean Mädelgruppenführerin von Fittkau."

"Helene?" the leader replied, fully annoyed.

"There are Catholics valiantly serving in the Wehrmacht."

Ida sniffed like an angry bull. "What is your point?"

Helene lifted her right palm as if what she was saying was self-evident. "Just that you can be a good Catholic and a good German."

Some girls nodded in agreement with Helene. Given her father's position, Helene was seen as an authority on religious matters. Other girls shook their heads and murmured no, safely siding with the BDM leader. Some stifled their amusement that Helene was rebelling once again. Most of the room reacted like Margarete—with eyes wide in disbelief that Helene had the temerity to debate a BDM leader.

Margarete's conscience also panged with guilt. Helene had taken a risk by speaking up, while Margarete wasn't brave enough to defend herself or her religion. She gazed in awe at Helene.

"Danke."

Helene waved her hand as if she had done nothing of importance. "It's always fun to annoy Ida."

Leaning closer to the podium, Ida gripped its side with one hand while her other pointed at Helene. "Fräulein Wichert, you may take yourself and your blasphemy against the Reich outside and lie down in the gutter for the rest of this meeting."

Helene looked out the windows at the pouring rain. "Really?" she asked with an incredulous laugh. "I was only stating a fact."

"Absolutely," said Ida. "That's the appropriate place for someone who questions the Reich."

The room stilled in flabbergasted silence so only the rain could be heard. No one would even want to walk in the storm. The thought of lying in a dirty gutter was unimaginable. Meanwhile, Margarete's heart beat triple-time as she blamed herself for Helene's predicament.

True to form, Helene rolled her eyes at Ida before she gave her a grumpy smile. "Fine." She jumped from her seat as if she had won a prize. The whole room watched as she strode out of the auditorium followed by a BDM leader tapped by Ida to watch her.

The rest of the meeting was uneventful. Margarete would have enjoyed it as they practiced folksongs for the march the following weekend. Instead, she wallowed in guilt. When the meeting ended, she bolted out of the room to find Helene.

Once outside, Margarete saw Helene had risen from the gutter. She stood on the sidewalk, using the rain to wipe mud from her arms and legs. Her white shirt and socks were now brown, while her soaked skirt clung to her legs.

Under the building's awning, Margarete popped open her umbrella and walked toward her. "Helene!"

Helene grinned as if the sun shone and nothing was amiss. "Wie geht's?"

"I'm so sorry. Can I help you inside?"

Ignoring her apology, Helene continued to clean her skin with the raindrops like she was in a shower. "No, but could you get my book satchel for me?"

"Is it in the dormitory?"

"No. The auditorium. I live with my parents." She bent down

and cleaned the back of her calves. "My family can't afford for me to board."

"I'll get your satchel and see you home."

"No. You don't have to do that."

"I want to. It's the least I can do." Margarete's throat tightened as she added, "You were very brave. Danke."

"You don't need to thank me."

"But I do. Will you be in trouble at home?"

"My father will be impressed." Helene deepened her voice, pretending she was a man. "We must always speak when others can't. Proverbs chapter thirty-one, verse eight."

Margarete laughed. "Well, you're very courageous."

"Or stupid," Helene countered with a smile. "My mother is going to kill me when she sees what I've done to this blouse."

Chapter Seventeen

JOSEF

Turning the corner from the barn, Josef saw the approaching wagon. High on the driver's bench sat Walter and Paul.

"Gott sei Dank," he declared, briefly closing his eyes, before he jogged to the wagon as it stopped.

"Paul!" Dorothea cried from outside the laundry room.

As Josef reached the wagon, Paul wore a reluctant smile, and Herr Neuwald announced with pride, "Look who I spotted at the train station this morning—Sergeant Haupt!"

"Danke, Walter," said Josef with a grin before he turned to his son. "You didn't tell us you were coming home."

"I didn't know it myself until yesterday," said Paul.

"Oh, Paul," said Dorothea, rushing toward the wagon. "Thank God, you're home."

"I suppose he had something to do with it," said Paul, his smile fading.

"Indeed," said Josef, as he eyed the ribbons and medals that had sprouted on Paul's uniform since he had last seen him two years before. He wore the Panzer troop's short black jacket, adorned with a Panzer badge and its lapels with the Panzer troop's Totenkopf—the German military's traditional skull and cross-bones. A silver wound badge, a first-class Iron Cross medal, and a Wehrmacht long service blue ribbon with a silver eagle hung from the jacket. The medals were similar to the ones Josef knew from the First World War, though the Kaiser's crown had been replaced with a swastika.

The Iron Cross was the most distinct, but Josef focused on another award off to the side of the others. Above Paul's left chest pocket, there was the close combat medal with sheaves, oak leaves, a bayonet, and a grenade. My God, he thought, as he thought of the number of times his son had fought hand to hand to receive the distinction.

"Come down," said Dorothea with a wave of her hand. "You must have traveled all night. You have to be tired and hungry."

Walter's smile flattened as he offered Paul his hand. "May I help?"

"Danke," said Paul, his expression even grimmer.

"Of course," said Josef, regretting that he had forgotten his son's wounded leg. He hastened to the other side of the wagon, where Paul braced himself against Walter's extended arm. Paul used his hand to lift his right thigh as he turned in his seat. After his right leg landed, it was completely still while he reached his left leg down onto the wagon's step.

When Paul again used his hand to ease his right leg onto the step, Josef's heart began to break for his son as he comprehended the situation. Paul's right leg had been amputated. As he rushed to help him down, Dorothea circled around to greet him.

She recognized Paul's plight at once. Her hand went to her heart as she whispered, "My poor boy."

Paul took Josef's hand. He eased one leg at a time onto the ground. "Not quite the same," he muttered as he took a cane from Walter.

"Yes, you are," snapped Dorothea. Her voice was thick, determined to hold back tears. "And you're home, which is the most important thing."

Senta rushed to Paul, her tail wagging at top speed. He leaned down to pet her, and she basked in his attention. After a moment, she sniffed his right leg, investigating the foreign object attached to her old friend. As a lesson to them all, she tired of it and lifted her head again to greet him with her wet Saint Bernard smile.

Josef took the cues of the females and ignored Paul's injury. "Welcome home," he said, patting his back.

After Josef, Dorothea, and Paul all conveyed their thanks and well wishes, Walter urged his horses on. While the wagon left the drive, Dorothea hugged Paul like he was still her little boy. She tempered her unusual enthusiasm by declaring that both he and his uniform needed a good cleaning.

When it was Josef's turn, he put his arm around Paul's back, offering his support. "I'm so glad you're home."

"I almost didn't make it," Paul said, finding a pack of cigarettes in his pocket. "Yesterday morning they told me I was assigned to an academy to train recruits."

"Ach du lieber Himmel!" said Dorothea, placing her hands on her cheeks in disbelief.

"I said something like that." Paul took a cigarette from the pack using only his lips and spoke with the unlit cigarette hanging from his mouth. "Then I told them they could go to hell. When they brought me to the major to be disciplined, I said I'd rather be executed than help send any more German boys out there."

Dorothea's face fell, and Josef swallowed hard.

"Sorry," mumbled Paul. It wasn't clear if he was apologizing for contemplating suicide or swearing in front of his mother.

"What did they say?" asked Josef.

"The major ordered the others to leave. When we were alone, he told me if he were me, he would say the same thing. He signed discharge papers, and a few hours later, I was on a train."

Dorothea made the sign of the cross in thanks, to which Josef couldn't have agreed more.

There wasn't much conversation while Dorothea stuffed Paul with all the food he could stomach. Paul smoked throughout the meal and spoke only when asked a question. His responses were jaded mumbles with enough curse words to make Josef thankful that the girls were at school.

It wasn't long before Josef realized that Paul's silence wasn't only because he was eating. Something was wrong. Josef stared at the medals on his chest, and Franz's words came back to him. *I've done things—unforgivable things. Sometimes I was ordered to do them. Sometimes not. I've seen others do unspeakable acts. Sometimes I stopped them. Sometimes I didn't.* After four years in the Wehrmacht, no one received those awards without sacrificing his humanity along the way. Paul was home in body, but his spirit had been left behind.

Yet Paul didn't have Franz's philosophical side. Paul had always been a proud, tough boy, both physically and mentally. Surviving a brutal war would be easier for him than others.

Accepting a new life as a cripple would not.

When Paul said he couldn't eat another bite, Dorothea pushed him. "Are you sure? I have cake."

"I'm not hungry anymore," he said, taking out another cigarette.

"All right." Dorothea wrung her hands before smoothing her apron in silence. Josef knew those movements as some of her anxious tics. Like Josef, she wanted to ease things for her son, but she didn't know how. Without another word, she began to clean the kitchen.

Josef asked, "Do you need help with a bath?"

Paul replied with a twisted frown, which Josef took as a yes.

Josef left to draw the water, while Paul made his way to the second floor. As he leaned over the filled tub to turn off the faucets, he heard the thumps of Paul walking down the hall.

"Danke," said Paul as he entered and closed the door.

"What do you need help with?"

Already unbuttoning his uniform, Paul examined the layout

of the bathroom. "I'll sit on the toilet and take off my leg. Then I'll need help to get to the tub."

As he undressed, Josef took his clothes and removed the medals so the clothes could be washed. Unclasping the close combat medal, he felt there was something in the pocket below. He withdrew a small black prayer book. It warmed his heart that his son had carried his prayer book with him into battle for four years.

With his chest bare, Josef could see what the awards had cost his son. His chest and arms were dotted with scars. Most were small, though there was gash on his arm that Josef recognized as a bayonet wound. It was a garish rosy mark with a gruesome story Paul might not be able to tell.

Paul lowered his pants, revealing his underwear covered in a crisscross of leather straps and buckles that held the prosthetic leg to his body. Only five inches of his right leg remained, which explained why Paul had such difficulty keeping his balance.

As he sat down, Paul raised his head, sensing his father's examination. "There's not much left."

"How did it happen?"

"Our Panzer was hit while I was riding outside. A Russki shot me when I hit the ground."

Josef was silent for a moment as he imagined the scene. It was horrific, and Paul needed to put it behind him. "Life will be more difficult, but what matters is you're home."

"Neither of which is true for the Ivan who shot me. I made sure of that. His comrade, too."

Josef noticed the impressive workmanship of the wood and leather, woven and bound together, allowing a disabled person to walk again. "At least they gave you a decent prosthetic."

"Who? The Wehrmacht?" Paul snorted, as he lifted each leg out of his pants and unbuckled the remaining bindings of the prosthesis. "The Wehrmacht would never produce anything this fine."

"Where did it come from then?"

"This is a gift from the Reich, which they stole for me," Paul answered with the same acidic affect that laced so much of what he said. He removed the prosthetic leg and handed it to Josef. "Read the inside."

Josef took the leg, noticing it was heavier than he expected. One needed to be strong to walk with such a contraption attached to you. He peered inside and read the fine engraving in the wood.

"David Levi." Josef looked up. "Who is David Levi?"

"A dead Jew. The SS makes the Jews remove their prostheses before they kill them. Every soldier in my hospital ward who lost a limb got a used prosthetic to replace it. Most weren't this fancy."

Realizing he was holding a murdered man's property, Josef felt a reverence for it. His hands lightened, wanting to treat the leg with respect, but he also had the urge to make the sign of the cross.

Paul took the leg and stared at it, also lost in his thoughts about the dead man. "David Levi was a big man like me. I wonder about him. Where he was from. What he did for a living." His voice turned dark again. "I owe him my thanks."

"May he rest in peace."

"I'd rather he be alive with this prosthesis and I have my leg back." Paul met Josef's eyes. "The Reich has been exterminating the Jews in every country we invaded. Just like the German ones. The lucky ones are shot in the head. The SS loads the rest on trains to death camps."

"There have been rumors," said Josef, repeating the cowardly denial gentiles told themselves.

"Ha! If a rumor is about the Reich doing something despicable, then it's true. You should only be skeptical of the ones where the Reich is kind."

Devoid of all modesty after the army and hospital stays, Paul stripped off his underwear and threw it on the floor. "Those should be burned. I don't ever want to wear military underwear again."

"Some of your old ones must still be in your room, and your

mother will buy more for you," he said, though his attention was on the short stump of Paul's right leg. The stitches had healed, but the skin was raw from the prosthesis. "You should let her take a look at that."

Paul pulled his head back with his old teenage expression of annoyance. He had some modesty left in him when it came to nudity and his mother.

"She changed your diapers for years." Josef chuckled. "She'll make sure you have new underwear first."

In the beginning, Josef forgave Paul for his slow adjustment to life on the farm, but his mood and behavior only worsened over time. His leg stopped him from doing many chores, and he sometimes lost his balance on the uneven ground, unleashing a tirade of curses to cover for his embarrassment.

When Paul fell in front of the Ostarbeiter, the Pole, Jan, snickered so loudly that Paul heard. Josef gave the man a disapproving look, which chastened the other Ostarbeiter, but Jan shrugged.

A dirty look from his father wasn't enough for Paul to reclaim his dignity. He returned to his feet and faced Jan with a sneer. As he began walking toward him, Jan stepped backward. When Paul didn't stop, Josef noticed Paul had moved his cane from his right to his left hand, and now his right hand was free and clenched. Paul was going to hit Jan.

While Dorothea disliked Jan and thought he was the stereotype of a lazy Pole, Josef despised him—though not for his ethnicity. Only the day before, Josef caught him whipping one of the draft horses. The Reich allowed those who managed the Ostarbeiter to discipline them at will, but Josef thought that beneath his family. He couldn't let Paul hurt Jan, even if he deserved a good smack.

"Paul, I believe your mother needs you to fix the stove."

Paul halted and glared at Jan before spitting at his feet. He turned to his father, unhappy at being stopped, but he left for the kitchen without a word.

Only the females on the farm received true smiles from Paul. Dorothea pleased him with endless meals and medicine for his leg's stump. Sophia, Katharina, and Martha made him laugh and hung on every word of his stories and every photo from his travels. Senta understood all his troubles.

Sometimes a woman at church might catch Paul's eye, and after the service, he would chat her up. And he was always eager to discuss the war with Josef. Otherwise, he was sullen and moody. Regular conversations with him were short, with gruff responses as he chain-smoked. He helped around the farm but not much. Throughout the day and night, he visited the liquor cabinet. Josef didn't complain about Paul's drinking because he knew it helped ease the pain, both physical and emotional.

Paul often slept during the day and stayed up late into the night listening to the BBC. While listening to the BBC, he would take out the atlas and study the locations of battles and bombings. On June sixth, he began a vigil at the radio. The British and Americans had invaded France, and even the Reich reported on it. When Josef walked down the stairs at four in the morning on June seventh, Paul was in the living room, still in his clothes from the day before.

"Guten Morgen," Josef said coldly, unable to contain his disapproval.

Paul acknowledged him with a nod but no greeting. He turned down the volume. "Papa, I've waited to bring this up, but it's time."

"What is it time for?"

"It's time we plan to leave the farm. Trust me. I've fought against all of these armies. We want to surrender to the British or the Americans. They'll be humane."

Josef took a deep breath. He knew there might come a time for this discussion, but it wasn't that day. The war was hundreds of miles away from them. "It's time to feed the animals. You could join me."

"No, it's time to plan."

"The Reich has issued an edict that the citizens of East Prussia must stay. We can't flee to western Germany." Josef placed his cap on his head, ready for the day's work. "We're civilians, and it's time to take care of the farm. You can help with that."

Paul shook his head in derision and turned up the volume on the radio.

Later that summer, Josef drove his carriage up and down the hills toward his home. He had been called to Allenstein by Fink to discuss production numbers. Only someone who didn't care about agricultural production would summon a farmer off his land during a harvest. Because of Fink's summons, Josef had to task Sophia with the job of driving the harvested rye from the field to the barn. Paul was still of little help, and Margarete's summer vacation had yet to begin. The Ostarbeiter had to harvest the grain. Although driving the wagon didn't require a man's strength, he worried about Sophia in a loaded wagon.

As Josef neared the farm, he spotted Katharina running into the road from the fields. Tall for her thirteen years, with auburn hair, she was even more noticeable as she waved her hands and sprinted toward him.

"Papa, Papa!"

"Was ist los?"

Catching her breath, she stopped in the road so quickly that dust flew in the air. She cupped her hands and yelled, "The wagon tipped over while Sophia was driving it! She's hurt!"

By that evening, all was set right again. Sophia went to bed early, scratched and bruised but with no broken bones. The Ostarbeiter picked up every sheaf of fallen rye, and Josef delivered the load to the granary.

When Paul settled down to listen to the BBC, Josef confronted him. With a drink and cigar at his side, he declared, "I spoke with Sophia and investigated the wagon. I believe Jan deliberately loaded the rye so it wasn't balanced. Your sister could have died today."

In silence, Paul took a cigarette from the pack on the side table. He lit it, inhaled deeply, and exhaled. After he flicked off the ash, he said, "I'll take care of Jan."

"How so?"

"Because of how I was discharged, I didn't go through the normal procedures. No one ever asked me for my sidearm, so I kept my P38." He took a quick puff and added, "Unless you would prefer an accident. I could use a hunting rifle."

Josef's chest tightened as he grasped that Paul was offering to murder the Pole, but it seemed silly to lecture him on morality after what he had been through the last four years.

Instead, he answered, "While we're allowed to discipline the Ostarbeiter, I don't think it would be wise to kill someone the Reich views as its property."

"Perhaps not," said Paul, his lips turned with some disappointment. "But Jan is a problem. I'm not sure whose side he's on—probably no one's but his own."

"He's a problem, but we're stuck with him. You could have driven the wagon today, and you're capable on a horse. I need you to work and keep an eye on Jan. The other Ostarbeiter are terrified of you." Josef squinted with suspicion. "With good reason it seems."

Paul slowly nodded as if he, too. realized that he couldn't spend the rest of his days smoking and drinking inside the house.

"I'll have one of them saddle a horse for you tomorrow morning," said Josef in relief.

"Nein," said Paul with distrust in his voice. "I'll saddle my own mount."

Chapter Eighteen

JOSEF

As the morning sun topped overhead, Josef adjusted his horse's saddle, biding his time for Paul, who was always slower getting out of the house. The harvest would have to wait as well.

Senta's bark broke the morning quiet followed by the noise of a truck. After a farewell pat for the mare on her rump, Josef corralled Senta, whose bark increased as an SS truck came over the hill. Maybe she, too, knew this was an unplanned visit.

The kitchen's screen door creaked, and he saw Paul peer out the door before shutting it again. Josef looked away in disappointment. Paul considered SS visits an opportunity for a drink and nap. Josef didn't need his sons to handle the SS, but he preferred Franz's offer of help rather than Paul's disappearance.

The truck stopped and four SS stormtroopers jumped out of the cab. Josef stiffened as he saw that his old antagonist, Elsner, was back. Senta commented with a low growl at the unfriendly strangers, making him whisper to himself and the dog, "It's all right. Everything will be all right."

After they exchanged their salutes to Hitler, Elsner nodded toward the barn. Two stormtroopers took it as a signal and ran inside it.

Josef caught his breath with fright at the SS wandering his property freely, but he kept his voice steady. "Guten Tag, Sturmbannführer Elsner. May I help you?"

Elsner's mouth twitched. "That won't be necessary."

"Are you looking for any of the Ostarbeiter in particular?"

When Elsner said nothing more, Josef told himself he shouldn't worry. He alone knew what was tucked away in that barn behind Albert's life savings in the sugar tin, so he told himself he shouldn't worry. Yet Elsner's silence didn't bode well. Josef's eyes drifted to the junior officer. The boy, no older than eighteen, stared at him, his hands on a machine gun.

Josef began to fear the worst, realizing this was a visit about him—not the Ostarbeiter.

The kitchen screen door creaked and then slammed behind him, and he kept calm as he turned to tell Dorothea to go back inside. Instead, he saw Paul heading toward him, causing him to do a double take. Paul wore his uniform and medals, which he now only wore to church on Sundays to impress the ladies. Somehow, he had donned it in a flash, which would have required Dorothea's help.

Although Paul was dressed for a visit of Reich officials, he seemed to be in no hurry to meet them. He didn't walk at his normal pace. There was a saunter to his hobble. As Josef watched Paul make his way across the yard, he noticed the sidearm in its leather pouch attached to his belt. That was something Paul didn't bring to church.

When Paul was near, Josef said, "Please meet my son Paul, Sergeant Haupt."

"Guten Tag," said Elsner to Paul before lifting his arm again. "Heil Hitler!"

Paul couldn't muster either a hello or a salute. He exuded contempt without concern. He glared at the two SS officers as he placed a cigarette in his mouth, lit it, and exhaled. "Was ist los?"

Josef was sure he was having a nightmare, but the tingle of terror running through him was real. Paul was deliberately antagonizing the SS.

Elsner froze for a moment. Since he'd first put on an SS uniform, he most likely had never been treated so rudely. To his side, the junior officer was frozen. His hand still rested on his machine gun, while his eyes focused on Paul's intimidating chest of medals.

While Paul leisurely smoked, Elsner also stared at his medals, his eyes dipping for a moment to the leg that was no more. Josef watched as their eyes met. Elsner and Paul were near the same age. While one had spent the last four years away fighting for the German people, one had spent the last four years at home fighting the German people.

Elsner seemed to know he came up short, and he cleared his throat. "We only needed to check on something."

Paul snorted before taking a drag.

Out of the corner of his eye, Josef saw movement. The two stormtroopers walked back from the barn, and Josef's heart began to thump. He saw that one officer held papers and Josef's own black notebook, in which he took notes from his meetings with the farmers. At Albert's suggestion, he had moved the documents to his hiding place in the barn. Panic gripped him. If someone read the papers and interrogated Herr Konrad, a case could be made against both of them.

He turned his head farther because a man's shadow covered the ground in the bright sun. It was odd that any Ostarbeiter would lurk around when the SS was present.

"It seems we've found what we were looking for," said Elsner with a smug smile.

"Is that so?" asked Paul, as he stamped out his cigarette.

Josef held his breath, not knowing what Paul was doing. No

one had less respect for human life than the SS, but Paul seemed to have lost that basic humanity as well.

Elsner clicked his heels together and lifted his arm. "Heil Hitler!"

Josef and the junior officers repeated the action, while Paul leaned on his cane, looking annoyed.

Without another word, the SS climbed back in the truck and left. Before Josef spoke to Paul, he looked to see if the shadow was still there, but it had disappeared.

"Let's go to the garden. By Stefan's rabbit hutches," said Paul.

As they walked to the weathered cages that memorialized Stefan, Josef asked, "Why are you in uniform? And why were you so antagonistic?"

"I've had to deal with those bastards for the last four years. They only respond to strength." Paul sneered. "I despise them."

"I do too, but I don't let them know that."

"It doesn't matter. No matter how dutiful you are to them, they'll still come after you."

When they reached the hutches, Paul pulled out a cigarette. "So what did they take?"

"Reichsnährstand papers and my journal where I kept notes on the farmers." Josef shook his head. "If they comb through those papers and speak to Herr Konrad, I'll be in trouble. I covered for his lack of production."

"You did what?" asked Paul, raising his voice in incredulous dismay.

"He's a dear friend and very ill. It seemed small compared to the corruption I see in the Reich. I thought my position might afford me some leeway." He sighed, ashamed of himself. "It was wishful thinking. They've always been suspicious of me."

Silence ensued, while Paul looked down at the rabbit hutches. Eventually, he let out an exasperated exhale. "You were reckless, but I understand wanting to help a friend in trouble. What do you think they'll do?"

"It depends on their whim and how much they value me. I

could face a fine. We could lose the farm. They might even imprison me. Or they might file it away to blackmail me later."

"Who knew about this?"

"Only Herr Konrad and Albert." He lifted his hands helplessly. "But who knows? Maybe someone visited Herr Konrad and saw how little work was being done on his farm. Someone with a vendetta against him."

"That doesn't make sense. Everyone thinks Herr Konrad is a *mensch*."

Josef racked his brain for some other answer, and when it came to him, he knew it to be true, but something was off. "I took Jan to Herr Konrad's to help him a few times."

"Ahh. So that's why he was near the barn when I walked out of the house."

"I thought there was a shadow there..." Josef looked to the ground as he considered the situation. "Though if he was spying for the SS, why has he been such a problem? He's actively sabotaging our farm, even risking Sophia's life."

"Because he's looking out for himself and spying for the Reich, but he's still a Polish partisan." Paul exhaled a puff of smoke. "You know what I offered before..."

"That's an even worse idea now," he said, scowling at his son's itchy trigger finger.

"Too bad," Paul grumbled. "Now we can never let him out of our sight."

The next week was hell for Josef. Anxious and guilt-ridden, he jumped any time the phone rang or Senta barked. No one came to the farm again, but when he saw the SS or Gestapo in town, he took a detour. On the farm, he and Paul took turns monitoring Jan and his taunting looks. Jan seemed both pleased with what he'd done and confident that they could do nothing about it.

After church the following Sunday, Josef took his turn to

greet the priests. "Guten Tag, Father Schmidt," he said, shaking the priest's hand. "That was a lovely sermon today."

"Thank you very much." Father Schmidt smiled at Josef's family, following him in the reception line. "And all is well with your family."

Josef cringed inside, wanting so much to tell him his troubles on the spot, but he held it back. This wasn't the time, and his guilty feelings were too raw. "Everyone is well."

Father Schmidt turned to the next Haupt family member in line. "It's good to see you, Fräulein Margarete. Are you on summer holiday?"

"Guten Tag," said Margarete. "I'm home for the month."

"And how is your life in Königsberg?"

Margarete beamed. "It's wonderful. I love school, and I love the city."

As the rest of his family said hello to the priests, Josef waited outside the church, where he spotted Krüger on the street corner. Krüger nodded at Josef and motioned for him. Josef walked at a normal pace, but his legs felt like lead. He thought of the Nazis abducting Poles after church because it was the easiest place to find them. Now, he was facing their same fate.

Proximity to the church and the end of Mass meant nothing to Krüger. He threw his arm up in the air, saying, "Heil Hitler!"

Josef did the same, hoping to impress.

Unmoved by Josef's display, Krüger didn't even greet him. "I'm here to inform you that you're required to join the *Volkssturm.*"

"What is that?" The "people's storm" meant nothing to Josef.

"The Führer has created a new militia. The Volkssturm will be a new line of defense against the enemies of the Reich. All able men will be required to join. You're one of the first, and we'll announce it to others in the next days."

"But I've just turned sixty years old. Surely, you don't want me to fight."

"All able men ages sixteen through sixty will join." Krüger's lips turned into a sneer. "And you, of all people, should see this as an opportunity to support the Reich after what the SS found. Kreisbauernführer Fink wanted you imprisoned, but the SS thought you would be more useful digging trenches. You're lucky."

Josef swallowed hard. "What must I do?"

"Report to the train station on Wednesday at nine in the morning. You'll be part of the Ermland battalion of a few hundred men sent to Lithuania. You may be gone for a month, so pack accordingly. You need a rucksack, a blanket, and a shovel."

Comprehending the orders, Josef was speechless. The shock wasn't only because he was asked to dig ditches and bring his own supplies and equipment to aid the army. Nor was it because the Russians were so close that East Prussia was sure to be invaded. Rather, if the Reich was ordering boys and old men to war, then the war was lost, and the Reich would fall.

He glanced to the steps of the church where his family in their Sunday finest stood watching him. The girls had no inkling of what his conversation with Krüger was about. They were fidgety and bored waiting for him. But Dorothea and Paul stood with grave faces, thinking the worst.

Until the end of the war when his other sons could be accounted for, this was his family—a wife, a crippled adult son, and four daughters, ranging from ten years to sixteen. He had to protect them all in the coming months, but how could he if he were sent away? His older brother, Bruno, had died of a heart attack that spring. Paul couldn't take care of the farm alone. Maybe Paul should start a journey westward now, and he would catch up later.

Reading his mind, Krüger said, "A revised edict has also been issued. East Prussians fleeing west or making preparations to leave will now be executed. We must defend the Vaterland." Krüger raised his arm again. "Heil Hitler!"

CHAPTER NINETEEN

MARGARETE

Two days after Josef departed, Krüger delivered another letter, but he slinked off before it was opened. Paul read the letter aloud, and Dorothea fled to her room for the rest of the day. Albert was missing in action.

Her mother's sobs came from upstairs, but Margarete felt as if they came from her own heart. First her favorite brother had been lost to the war, and now her closest brother was gone. Tears brimmed as she whispered to Paul, "Is this like Stefan?"

Paul stared at the letter, his face awash in despair at the loss of his baby brother. "I don't know, but the situation in Latvia isn't as dire as Stalingrad."

At night, Margarete sat with Paul at the radio as he tried to piece together what might have happened to Albert. When he pulled out his maps to show her the position of Albert's unit, she studied the geography and armies like it was a jigsaw puzzle.

"But look." She pointed with the surety she had found the

puzzle's missing piece. "They weren't entirely surrounded. There's the Baltic Sea. Maybe Albert escaped."

"It's true. They could have fallen back to Riga and been evacuated by our navy. Germany controls those waters." Paul lifted his prosthesis to adjust his leg before leaning back in his chair. After a drag from his cigarette, he declared, "But it's not likely."

His warning expression told her not to get her hopes up. She hung her head, her focus on the map, but she wasn't actually seeing it.

"Is there any way he might be alive?"

Paul pinned his eyes on her, his cigarette wafting a gray smoke, stark against the colorful glass of the Tiffany lamp. "It's been over a year and a half, and we've heard nothing else about Stefan. If he was captured, they would've told us something by now. The Reich doesn't want to admit he's dead. We have to wait to see if more information arrives about Albert."

Margarete slowly shook her head as her lip quivered. "Albert can't also be dead. He can't."

"Margarete..." Paul's voice trailed with a brotherly love as he crushed his cigarette into the heavy crystal ashtray. Leaning over her, he placed an arm around her shoulder. "I want to believe the same, but I've found it best to assume the worst in this war."

On the last Saturday in August, Margarete happily left Guttstadt on the eight o'clock train, and by noon, she was out with Helene and friends at a café. When the unnerving air raid sirens blared through the streets that evening, she was scared but assumed it was just another drill. When she came out of the bomb shelter a few hours later that night, the street looked the same as it had when she walked in.

The next day, rumors flew that the Reich's enemies had failed bombing the city once again, though for the first time it was the British rather than the Russians who tried. Like the Russians, they couldn't hit a proper target. East Prussia's capital would never be defeated, people said. In the back of her mind, she could hear Paul muttering it was only a matter of time before the enemy found its way inside the city gates. She wanted to believe that the locals knew more than her pessimistic brother.

Three days later, Margarete entered her room before bed, but as she took out her nightgown from the drawer, the wail of the air raid siren crashed through the windows. The sound was a whirling blast that escalated into a repeating shriek. A fearful chill struck her chest, but she told herself it was another drill that would be over soon.

She pulled open the side of the curtain an inch so she could peer at the sky. Nothing seemed different in the darkness, setting her further at ease. As she pulled the cord on her lamp, a voice from a bullhorn bellowed from the street, "Raus!"

Startled by the air raid protection police, she opened the curtain wide this time and looked down on the dark street. The streetlights were off, and in quick succession curtained lights in every window blinked into blackness as well. People banged on doors and shouted into the night air, their words drowned out by the sirens and bullhorns. Every building had an assigned air raid shelter, which often was the building basement or the cellar of a nearby restaurant or pub. The Fischers' building had been assigned to a proper bomb shelter, which was safer but required a longer walk to reach it.

A knock rattled her door followed by Herr Fischer's voice, "Bitte, Margarete, we must leave for the shelter now."

As she moved toward the door, she spied the amber bracelet her godmother had given her for Christmas that year. She had left it in her room during the last air raid. Something told her this one might last longer. What if a thief entered the flat while she was in a bomb shelter? She nabbed the bracelet and placed it in her pocketbook.

In the foyer, Herr and Frau Fischer waited for her. Each held a fussing baby on a hip, unhappy to have been woken from their sleep. Despite their groggy toddlers, the parents were calm and in good humor.

Herr Fischer gave her a reassuring smile. "It's a drill. No one would attempt a bombing again so soon after the last. We'll go to the shelter for bit."

Herr Fischer opened the front door of the flat to the scene of neighbors in the four-story building walking briskly down the steps in a resigned silence. The sirens blared from outside, reverberating throughout the hollow stairwell. Margarete noticed a few neighbors carried small suitcases.

She turned to Herr Fischer. "Should we bring a bag?"

"Nein, it's not necessary. We only brought some things for the twins. There's nothing to worry about." He readjusted the satchel on his shoulder and ushered her out the door. "The *Luftwaffe* will protect us."

Margarete merged into the flow of people descending the stairs. She noticed the people with bags were serious and quicker than others. Unlike Herr Fischer, these people thought there was something to worry about.

Once outside in the pandemonium of the streets, she was sure Herr Fischer was wrong. Outside of the city, the Luftwaffe's giant anti-aircraft cannons started to fire flak, creating another noise that crowded into the siren screams. The city was dark until a boom to the west brightened the sky like a full moon. A thunderous round of flak replied.

With each round of flak and sirens, Margarete's heart beat faster. She wished she were safe with her family in Guttstadt. Bombs would never drop on the Haupt family farm, and unlike Herr Fischer, Paul and her father would know what was going on. They would have a plan to protect the family. Even if the men were gone, her mother would provide safety. Dorothea would strike a bargain with Lucifer himself rather than allow anyone to harm her children or home.

Margarete followed the rest of her building's residents to the stairs in the nearby park. From the street, it looked like a nondescript railing, but at the bottom of the stairs you left the verdant city and entered a concrete bunker. Soldiers stood at the top of the stairs and forced people to relinquish large bags, saying they needed space for more people.

Margarete took a step down the stairs and heard a loud "Nein!" behind her. She stopped to see an older man carrying a cello case. Even in the limited light, she could see his chest heave in exhaustion from carrying the instrument.

"Bitte," the man pleaded. "I'm the first cellist in the Königsberg opera. We have a performance tomorrow."

A police officer grabbed the case handle. "It's too big. It stays outside."

Despite being over three times his age and three-quarters his size, the cellist stood his ground. "This cello is my life, my family."

Margarete settled her eyes on the two hands—one old, one young—both vying for the cello. Jackboots and a gloved hand then appeared between those of the officer and the cellist.

A young army lieutenant came into view, saying, "Let him have it. Just keep everyone moving quickly."

The cellist gazed at the lieutenant with relief. "Danke."

"Go on." The lieutenant nodded down the stairs. "Pray that we'll still need cellists tomorrow."

Inside the bunker, the air raid police stood guard, urging people inside while answering no questions. With the summer heat and crush of bodies, Margarete embraced the cool underground air. Other than natural air conditioning from being below ground, the shelter had no other charms to offer. Wire-caged light bulbs lit the bare concrete walls, and a red *Toilette* sign marked a door in the back. The air smelled of must and paint. While the shelter muffled the sound of the wailing sirens, she didn't feel safe, only enclosed from the unknown.

Long benches spanned the room, and the Fischers sat on one near the toilet. Margarete gave up her seat to an old woman, so she found a spot on the floor near the door. The cello case was tucked in the corner.

She watched as the police enforced order in a situation that could descend into bedlam. Anxious people streamed in single file —scared women with crying infants, teetering elderly, children holding a special toy, and only a few younger men. Most of those were veterans, often missing limbs or sight. The former soldiers wore a hardened expression like Paul's resigned disgust. Knowing what Paul might say if he were there, she assumed they were cursing in their minds. After everything they had already lost in the war, they were now in a bomb shelter.

As her mind wandered to thoughts of home, she jumped when she heard a girl's voice. "Margarete?"

Looking up, Margarete found a familiar smile in the unlikeliest of settings. "Helene? What are you doing here?"

"I'm with my mother and grandparents." Helene nodded to a matronly woman and an aged couple finding seats on a nearby bench. "After last weekend, my father wanted us to be in a safer shelter than our basement, so he sent us here."

"Where is your father?"

"He's in the parsonage basement at the cathedral. People will come to church when this is over." Helene glanced at her family, who were eyeing Margarete. "I'll tell my mother I want to sit with you."

If Margarete couldn't be with her family, there was no person she would rather be with than Helene. Given the number of strangers around them, Helene modulated her usual irreverence, but she could still joke and make Margarete smile. Helene even tried to flirt with the better-looking police officer, though he was too focused on packing people into the shelter to pay attention to her.

Most people kept quiet as the sirens, bombs, and flak continued outside the shelter. Close to the door, Margarete and Helene heard what was happening right above them. Soon the police from outside the shelter yelled to their comrades below to close the door. In response, the police began shoving the straggler civilians from the steps into the shelter.

Shouts of "*Schnell, schnell!*" drifted from above, and the police used all their body weight to move the giant metal door into place. As they slipped the iron bar into its slot to secure the door, the earth shook and rumbled all around them. The concrete floor vibrated through Margarete's thin summer dress. Babies led the cries of fright in the room. Margarete and Helene simultaneously sought each other's hands, as Helene whispered, "Mein Gott."

Cacophony rang from above—sirens, airplanes, flak, whizzing bombs, and then the explosions. Land that knew nothing of earthquakes shuddered. Unable to bear the terror in everyone's eyes, Margarete and Helene both chose to close theirs as they held hands. Margarete leaned against the wall for only a moment because the tremors jolted her head. Trying to temper her fright, she repeated her prayers.

After an hour of unending bombardment, Margarete sensed a trickle down her back. She placed her hand on the annoying sensation and felt that her dress was damp. She had been so frightened that she didn't realize she had become hot. Airing out the sweat behind her knees, she extended her legs. Her feet were immediately hot. She raised her head to see that the police had moved away from the iron door, though their eyes were steady on it. She studied the expanse of metal and saw it was bowed in the middle. Something was so hot on the other side of the door that it had caused the iron to expand. The smell in the air answered the mystery of the heat.

She turned to Helene and whispered, "Something is burning outside."

Helene nodded. "My grandfather is a retired professor of chemistry at the university. He's calculated the amount of carbon dioxide in the shelter. He says we can only be here for a few hours."

Margarete looked over to Helene's family. Her mother sat with her eyes closed, while her grandmother read what looked to be a silk-covered Bible just like Dorothea's. Helene's grandfather sat hunched over as he scribbled onto a scrap of paper.

Helene grimaced and lowered her head and clasped her hands in prayer. Margarete glanced around her, and not caring that she and the Fischers might be the only Catholics in the shelter, she did what would most comfort her. It was what her family would have done in a time of trouble. She reached into her pocketbook, took out her rosary, and prayed to Mary to intercede for them.

Hours later, the screeches and bellows of war dissipated from above. Helene's mother and grandparents moved near the door alongside Margarete and Helene. After Helene introduced her to them, the family made plans to go to the cathedral to reunite with her father.

More people came to the door, also wanting to be the first outside. When the Fischers arrived, Herr Fischer said to Margarete, "The twins are so tired. We must get them to cribs."

Using wet towels, the police slid the scalding hot metal bar from its place. When the door opened, Margarete could see there were more police officers waiting outside the door with stacks of blankets.

A policeman called into the shelter, "Everyone must take a blanket as you leave the shelter! Put it over your head."

Margarete and Helen shared befuddled looks as a woman nearby asked their question. "Why?"

"The city is on fire," said the police officer.

The room silenced as they all imagined what that might look like, but in dutiful Prussian fashion, they walked single file to the door. The police let the Fischers and their toddlers exit first, helping them with the blanket as a tarp over themselves and their babies. Helene's family followed with the cellist and his instrument next in line. All required help with the heavy, wet blankets.

Water dripped on her as she climbed the stairs, and she wondered about the time. It couldn't be daytime, yet the night was oddly bright. When she reached the top, she saw the reason. The city had turned into an urban hellscape.

Margarete joined the group of people who had collected outside, standing speechless. The city's stately buildings, tidy streets, and green parks were all aflame. Sparks and cinders exploded, shooting from buildings. Smoke moved through the city before ascending to the sky. The smell was unlike any she had inhaled before. The underlying feel and scent of gritty charcoal was overlaid with a pungent, chemical odor. Firemen and their trucks filled the streets, but even gushing water looked like a child's attempt against the inferno.

As people huddled together, their blankets created a makeshift tent above them. Taking in the loss of their city, Helene spoke for everyone, "Mein Gott."

Margarete made the sign of the cross.

Helene's grandfather turned to the nearest policeman. "Are any streetcars running? Or do we need to walk to the cathedral?"

The officer shook his head. "There is no more cathedral."

Onlookers overheard the officer and protested with gasps of disbelief. Murmurs of outrage and despair came from all around.

"They didn't!"

"Heathens."

"It's stood since the fourteenth century!"

"But Kant's grave!"

Helene's grandparents demanded more information from the officer, while her mother covered her mouth, her body convulsing in sobs. Margarete extended her hand to touch Helene, but she ignored her.

Helene dropped her blanket on the ground and cried out in pain, "Papa!" as if he might hear if she called out to him.

When the officer heard how they were connected to the cathedral, he encouraged Helene's grandfather to investigate the situation himself. "Pastor Wichert may be fine. Sometimes a building is burning but the people in the cellar survive. Don't give up hope yet."

"Pardon, officer," asked the cellist, who had draped a blanket over his cello rather than himself. "What of the new symphony hall?"

"Burning." The policeman shook his head at the cello like it was an orphan that had lost its home. "The enemy has destroyed everything we loved. The cathedral, the castle, the gates, the theater. Everything."

More gasps and cries came from all around. Realizing he had created unrest when he should have been calming people, the officer raised hands to dampen the crowd's fervor.

"You all must move from here if you can. If you have a place to stay outside the city, you should leave. You'll get a free ticket at the train station. The city isn't safe, and the streets must be empty to clean once the fires are out. If you can't leave the city and you have no home, go back inside the shelter for now."

As everyone turned to their immediate family and friends, Margarete stepped over to the Fischers. They bounced their toddlers while they conferred, nodding at each other in agreement.

Herr Fischer saw Margarete and announced, "We think you should go home to Guttstadt, Margarete."

She watched a ball of fire burst from a building into the night sky and wished she was already home. "I think so, too."

"We must stay here to see about the flat and my shop, but then we'll leave for my parents' home in Heilsberg." He raised his saddened eyes to the gray blanket above him. "If the flat has survived, we'll make sure your things arrive in Guttstadt."

Her goodbyes with the Fischers were hurried. Herr Fischer left to check on their properties, while Frau Fischer fled back inside the shelter with the twins. Margarete looked over to Helene, who stood with her mother and grandmother as her grandfather walked to Cathedral Island.

Wanting to help their family, she went back to Helene's side and spoke to her mother. "Pardon, Frau Wichert, I'm going home to Guttstadt. I know that my family would be honored to have you all stay with us. With my brothers gone, we have plenty of room. It will be safer for you."

The words were out of her mouth before she could consider

them. It was a kind but bold proposition. She was just a girl, making a generous offer without her parents' knowledge.

Helene's mother smiled beneath her blanket. "Danke. That is very kind of you, but we must stay here for now. We'll wait in the shelter for Helene's father and grandfather."

Helene reached over and gave her a hug. With a tight squeeze, she said, "We'll see each other in school soon."

Margarete cringed inside hearing Helene say something so unrealistic and overly optimistic. It wasn't like her at all. Helene must have been in a state of true fright.

Her throat tightened as she hugged Helene tighter. "Please write and let me know that you and your family are all right."

After the two said their farewell, Margarete joined the growing mass of people making haste down the middle of the street. With their blankets held over their heads, they looked like insects on parade, marching forward out of duty and instinct without regard for their circumstances and surroundings. Following hundreds of strangers, Margarete prayed she would make it out of the city alive to see her family again.

The authorities crammed the trains full before they headed out of the decimated city. Few people had any luggage, and all were covered in soot as if they had been cleaning a coal hamper. Tears for loved ones who had perished streaked sooty faces. Others cried in desperation for the loss of their homes and livelihoods. While Margarete was mournful for the city's loss and Helene's uncertainty, relief took over the farther the train traveled from Königsberg.

Right after dawn, the train arrived at the Guttstadt station, where Margarete was the only passenger stepping onto the empty platform. No one was there to meet the unscheduled train. The early morning streets in town were equally empty. She wondered if anyone in Guttstadt knew that the capital of East Prussia was destroyed.

Though she was exhausted, she walked as fast as she could to the safety of the farm. Before the hill, she heard Senta's bark, which filled her heart. Senta proved that some things were still normal and good in the world. Though Senta was also changing, the aging dog found a skip in her step for Margarete.

"Oh, Senta, I'm so happy to see you," she said as she reached to pet her lifelong friend.

Senta smiled but recoiled when she smelled Margarete's burnt stench.

The two reached the top of the hill together as her sisters and Dorothea ran out of the house. From Senta's barks, they guessed correctly that a family member had arrived, but they were wrong about the person.

Martha cried, "Papa!"

It was a strike to Margarete's heart because everyone would be disappointed their father wasn't there. She was disappointed as well. After what she had endured, she also wanted her father safely home.

Katharina was the first to see her. With a confused expression, she declared, "It's not, Papa. It's Margarete, I think."

Saying "hello" or "good morning" felt impossible for Margarete in her state of shock. She waited to speak until she was closer.

As Margarete's sisters continued rushing toward her, Dorothea stopped cold once she was able to fully see her daughter. She covered her mouth and gasped. "Margarete, what has happened to you?"

CHAPTER TWENTY

ALBERT

Albert's head lolled with the sway of the boxcar. He fought for sleep because it released him from reality, but each time he dozed off, there was always a reminder of his plight. He might smell the human waste and gangrene in the train, or pain might flare in his loose teeth where he had been pistol whipped by his own sidearm.

By the time he was captured in July, he was on foot with a ragtag crew of thirty men following a lieutenant one rank above him. The command post had been destroyed, and after a day of outmanned combat, Albert had retreated with the remnants of his battalion. Their numbers continued to decline as the Soviets hunted them. Knowing they were surrounded, he had watched in horror as five men, including his commanding officer, had committed the mortal sin of suicide rather than face Soviet imprisonment.

Albert's position and rank had given him relative safety

during the war, but they were now his downfall. As an officer radio operator in a command post, the Russians considered him a valuable prisoner, and Albert had failed his interrogation. He refused to give Wehrmacht information that wasn't commonly known. By that time, Franz would have returned to the front, fighting to hold back the Russian Army from marching into East Prussia where the rest of the Haupt family remained defenseless. Albert would do nothing to endanger his family. Nor would he reject his religion. The Catholic Church condemned the anti-Christian dogma of Bolshevism. Albert would never support communism.

Disgusted by his obstinacy, the Soviets had beaten him and demanded to know how many Russian women he had raped. They didn't care that he had never been near Russia or that Albert couldn't remember the last time he'd even danced with a woman. Soviet officers didn't abide by the historic military etiquette of treating captive enemy officers with respect as mutual leaders. To them, Albert was just an especially evil German.

The Wehrmacht was trained to immediately form new units if their leadership was lost. Like a starfish losing a leg, a unit regrew into a whole. Albert had been a lowly second lieutenant in Latvia; now on a prisoner train, he was the leader of forty men. Sometimes a random infantryman tugged his sleeve, asking for forgiveness for waking Lieutenant Haupt, but hoping he might have some information. Albert did not.

Albert woke when his friend, Hugo, leaned against him. Hugo warned Albert that sleep was the only way to survive. He was already a veteran prisoner of war, having been captured by the Americans when he was an infantryman in Italy. Once he had escaped, the Reich gave him the reward of a promotion to sergeant and a trip to the Eastern Front.

Hugo understood he wouldn't be escaping this time. Before they boarded the train, the Russians summarily executed scores of prisoners, and Albert and his men were forced to dig their graves.

The remaining men were given a stale piece of bread, but no water as they waited for their transport.

Hugo leaned over and murmured, "This is nothing like being an American prisoner."

"They never killed anyone?" whispered Albert as he tucked away half of his bread. He told his men to save some of it, but most had already devoured it. Despite not having eaten for three days, Hugo took a small bite and hid the rest inside his jacket.

"Oh, the Yanks killed one or two of us occasionally when a hothead GI snapped. Otherwise they were civilized. They're like us. They're not Slavs." Hugo glanced up at the Russian guards passing a bottle of vodka between them. "Russians...they're barbarians. They know we think they're nothing, and they hate us for it."

Albert had heard enough of the Wehrmacht and SS's atrocities to know that Germans could be just as barbaric as Russians. Speaking his thoughts aloud, he asked, "Which do you think came first? Them hating us, or us hating them?"

Hugo looked at him askance. He wasn't one for philosophy. "Who cares?"

Hugo reminded Albert of Paul, but when he thought of his family, guilt would also keep him awake. Having been a prisoner for a month now, he no longer worried for himself. Only luck and God would see him through it. His family's fate was another matter.

He had last sent them a letter a week before he was captured. Had the Reich informed them he was missing? Did his father know that the Russians were frighteningly close to East Prussia? Albert hoped that the family had sense enough to move westward, and he hated himself for not telling them to do so earlier. Now he couldn't help them at all.

So Albert's head would roll back and forth, and he would battle for slumber by setting the guilt aside. He tried to put himself to sleep by remembering the smallest details of the farm — the smell of the land, the hooves of the animals, and the structure of the buildings. He would think of his parents whom he admired, his brothers whom he looked up to, and his little sisters whom he adored. He hoped that if he could remember details, his memory wouldn't fade. Those people and that life would remain alive and real—if not for him, for them.

A few more days of dehydrated delirium passed on the train. Albert sensed that they were no longer traveling due east, but now north-by-northeast. The train slowed as it climbed steep inclines and descents, and his memory of geography told him they had crossed the Ural Mountains.

One day, the train lurched to what sounded like a permanent halt. The men waited in silent anticipation for whatever cruelty might come next. When the boxcar door opened, Albert and the others shielded their eyes from the blinding sunlight. Two Russian soldiers stood on either side of the door.

"Willkommen," said one in exaggerated German. He wore a menacing grin and pushed them out with his rifle. "Raus!"

"Ja, ja." The other Russian laughed and joined in the joke, speaking in German and Russian. "This is your new home. Siberia."

CHAPTER TWENTY-ONE

MARGARETE

The door thwacked, breaking the kitchen's early morning silence. Margarete shifted her eyes from the pot of simmering eggs to her mother's reaction. Dorothea glared at Paul, who had entered, and her lips parted to speak before she shut them again.

Without Josef at home, there was no buffer between Paul and Dorothea, and she received the brunt of his bitter worries. Margarete watched as her mother silently accepted his slights. If she did engage, Paul always steered the conversation to the ominous direction of the war. She ignored that like a horse with blinders. Months later, Dorothea still spoke of Josef's absence as if he was on a business trip to Königsberg rather than digging trenches for the Reich's last stand.

That morning, Paul was already in a bad mood. His eyes were bloodshot from another night's vigil at the radio, straining to hear every word from the BBC. Rather than returning her "Guten

Morgen," he declared without emotion, "Aachen has fallen to the Americans."

"Impossible," whispered Margarete.

Dueling images floated in her mind. In one scene, faceless enemies shot at German soldiers who looked like her brothers. In another, handsome American men—like those she had seen at the cinema before the war—strolled in front of the famous Aachen cathedral. It was the home of the gold-and-silver-encrusted tomb of Charlemagne, the first emperor of the Holy Roman Empire. How could Germany have surrendered the city of its first emperor? It was inconceivable.

As flatly as he was announcing the weather, Paul declared, "The Reich can't maintain a war on two fronts, and now it's losing both."

Ignoring the topic altogether, Dorothea announced, "Paul, you must go find Rasa. None of the Ostarbeiter say they know where she is, or they won't tell me because they don't want to feed the pigs. Also, I need one of them to harvest my turnips from the kitchen garden."

"The Ostarbeiter have more important things to do on the farm than pull your turnips," grumbled Paul. "Get one of the girls to do it."

"The girls are busy. When they arrive home from school today, they'll join Margarete planting bulbs in the front garden." Dorothea smiled as she kneaded the day's bread. "I have some new bearded irises that will look lovely against my tulips in the spring."

Paul answered with a dismissive grunt before turning to the door. He mocked Dorothea under his breath, "Tulips in the spring."

When he returned twenty minutes later with another door slam, he leaned against the door to support himself and hooked his cane atop the kitchen counter. With the heels of his palms, he rubbed his weary eyes. "What a mess."

"How so?" asked Dorothea as she looked up from writing her daily agenda.

"I spoke with Karol. He thinks Rasa fled in the night to return to Lithuania." Paul withdrew his hands from his eyes and sighed. "It was only a matter of time. The Russians have taken most of the Baltics. Other farms have lost their Ostarbeiter in the last weeks. They're escaping back to their homes."

Dorothea went to the window and pulled aside a curtain to survey the yard as if she might be able to see Rasa walking away. "What about the other Ostarbeiter? Did you speak to them?"

"Only Karol will ever tell me anything." Paul shook his head. "Besides, I don't want to be in the middle of this. The SS can deal with them. It's their problem."

Margarete stopped peeling potatoes at his mention of the SS. Placing the knife in the bowl of potato peels, she stumbled over her words. "You're going to tell the SS?"

"I must, but I won't do it today. I'm busy."

"Busy?" Dorothea closed the curtain and tutted disapprovingly. "Go have a carriage hitched. Your father would go directly into town and tell them."

"Two years ago, he might have, but not now. The potato harvest is too important." Paul's expression turned cold, and the familiar hopeless edge returned to his voice. "What is the SS going to do anyway? Ignore the Russians on our doorstep and chase down a peasant girl running through the countryside?"

With her hands on her hips, Dorothea snapped into her most motherly high-handed voice. "I'm not worried about her. What about us? What might they do to us for not immediately informing them? The Reich considers the Ostarbeiter its property. You need to go to town at once."

"Everything will be fine. If the SS cared, they wouldn't come for you. They'd come for me."

"Don't you dare even suggest such a thing," said Dorothea beneath her breath.

"Forgive me," he mumbled before turning to Margarete. "You'll need to take over Rasa's work. Could you get started right now?"

Margarete replied yes without hesitation, but as the reality of the job set in, she regretted it. Rasa was older and stronger than her. Feeding the pigs required cooking potatoes, beets, and soy in a giant cauldron over a meter wide and deep. Once finished, cooled, and ladled, the hundreds of liters of heavy slop buckets had to be taken to the troughs. She had always done the job with Rasa, who was pleasant enough, though they worked in an awkward silence. Either Rasa didn't know German, or she chose not to speak it because she had no interest in befriending one of her captors. For her part, Margarete was always grateful for the help.

Dorothea spoke up for her. "Margarete isn't strong enough to do that job alone."

"Rasa performed it every day by herself while Margarete was in Königsberg," answered Paul.

"Rasa is used to that sort of labor. Margarete isn't." Dorothea found her authority again and issued an edict. "Another Ostarbeiter will help her."

"Absolutely not. The harvest is more important." Paul smoothed his voice like he was catching his mother in a trap. "Sophia could quit school and help on the farm."

"Never," said Dorothea. "Sophia must finish high school like the rest of the family."

Margarete stared at Paul, praying he would ignore his mother's jab at him, but his lungs filled his chest as he retorted, "Not everyone in this family attended high school. Some of us have done well with trade schools."

Dorothea took her seat again as if he had been silent, but she couldn't force herself to remain quiet. Without looking at him, she said, "If you had a high school diploma, you would understand the importance of education outside of a trade."

"This is a war!" Paul lurched forward as far as he could on his single steady leg, and he continued with a fury, "What does it matter? Stefan didn't have a diploma, and he's most likely dead in a mass grave in Russia. Albert finished high school, but he's probably dead as well if he's lucky. Your other two sons are casualties, and Franz is headed back to the front soon. Who knows what will happen to him! Keeping Sophia on the farm is the most sensible thing we can do."

Margarete sat motionless, now wishing she wasn't included in the conversation. As Paul had spoken, Dorothea flinched as the horrors of her beloved sons were hurled in her face. Margarete felt for her pain, but she also understood that Paul's tirade was motivated by the same emotions.

No one spoke. The only noise in the kitchen drifted from the windows as the Ostarbeiter went about their day's work. After a minute, Dorothea's eyes twitched as she found her resolve.

"Sophia will stay in school. Margarete will need to make do by herself." Dorothea turned to her and said ruefully, "Do the best that you can, Margarete. The pigs will eat whatever you give them."

Two weeks later, Margarete crossed her legs at the ankles as she settled into the straw to spend time with the mama pig and her piglets. Every day she watched the huge, dappled mother lie still while her children jockeyed for position in a frenzied feeding. The mother seemed weary and bored by the responsibility, occasionally grunting as if to say "Get on with it."

The mother paid no attention to which of her children ate or how much. The little gray runt of the litter was often crowded out, so Margarete always moved her to a better position to feed. She wanted to make sure that once a day, the runt received her fair share.

Once Paul had caught Margarete resting in the stall, and when she explained what she was doing, he lectured her. The runt should be culled, leaving only the strongest to survive. That was the natural order of life. She didn't argue with him, even though she had proof he was wrong.

A few days earlier, the family had received a letter from a soldier who had fought alongside Stefan in Russia. He wanted to share their story, and without explicitly stating it, he confirmed Stefan's death.

I was wounded and Haupt pulled me out of the combat area. The Russians started another artillery attack. When I called Haupt's name, he didn't answer. Because of Haupt saving me, I am alive today.

Dorothea immediately retreated upstairs after she read the letter. Though tears filled her own eyes for Stefan, Margarete was left to console her younger sisters, who also cried. Paul had left the room, and she looked down the hallway to see him at the liquor cabinet. He poured himself a glass and held it up in the air. With his eyes closed, he offered a private toast to his brother before tossing back the drink.

Within the hour, Dorothea and the rest of the family were back at work. The news was saddening but not unexpected. The letter had confirmed what everyone already knew—Stefan was dead. They all felt a closure, softened by the knowledge that Stefan died helping someone else. It was just like him.

To Margarete, Paul was wrong. The strongest didn't necessarily survive. Stefan was a hero. The strongest of people, who had sacrificed himself for others, had died.

Running her hand over the bristly hair of the mama pig's side, she heard Senta's bark in the distance. When she joined Paul and Dorothea in the courtyard, she saw the portly man in the carriage was Herr Neuwald. Both Dorothea and Paul were smiling, but as Margarete approached, she noticed Herr Neuwald reciprocated with barely an upturn of his lips. She looked to Paul, whose smile had disappeared as well.

After everyone had shared stilted greetings, Herr Neuwald declared, "I have a treasonous letter addressed to Herr Haupt that should have been intercepted when it was posted."

Terror took away Margarete's breath. How could her father be involved in treason? She looked to her brother and mother for guidance but found none in their expressionless silence.

"As you know, the Reich dictates we report any mail with sensitive information or treasonous sentiments." Herr Neuwald breathed in, thrusting his chest, which drew attention to the ever-present swastika on his lapel accompanied by Nazi Party medals. "No one can doubt my allegiance to the Reich."

"Never," murmured Dorothea with an uncharacteristic warmth that Margarete knew was fake. "You're a faithful servant to Adolf Hitler."

"Danke." He gave her an appreciative bow. When he raised his eyes, he continued, "But this job of reading my friends' mail is often hard. It's a dilemma for me. I delivered the letter from Stefan's comrade to you, but this letter crosses the line. I can only guess my counterpart on the other end is a friend of the sender and mercifully allowed its passage, praying I was a friend of your family. I have sympathy for everyone involved," he declared as he pulled the letter from his coat pocket. "And I owe it to him and to your family to ensure its delivery."

Herr Neuwald hesitated, glancing back and forth between Paul and Dorothea, debating who should receive the news. Normally, he would address Dorothea in such a situation, but at that moment, she clenched both arms against her chest. With fisted hands, her arms formed an *X*, physically barring anything dangerous to her heart. She simultaneously shook her head in warning.

Even with his unsteady leg, Paul stood solidly like the unflappable soldier he once had been. With a detached voice, he extended his hand. "I'll read it aloud."

Herr Neuwald removed the letter from its envelope so Paul could remain stable on his cane. Taking the letter in his hand, Paul cast his eyes down to read from the page. His voice remained cool as he progressed through the letter.

15 September, 1944

Liebe Family Haupt,

It is with a heavy heart that I write this letter. No doubt, you have received the official word by now. We give you our condolences for the death of your son Franz, who died with our son Horst. They died in an American air raid while walking into town to a dance the day before they were to travel back to the Eastern Front. After a funeral Mass, we buried Franz with Horst in our town's cemetery. Horst and Franz were great friends, and Horst told us Franz was a brave soldier and respected officer. In the time he stayed with our family, we found Franz to be a perfect gentleman. We would welcome your family into our home at any time should you wish to visit the grave.

Johann Shutz

As he read, Margarete's mind reeled in a frenzy of disbelief. Another brother—another part of her heart—had died. Like so many families in Guttstadt, the Haupt family was shrinking one by one.

She could barely hear the ending because a wail screeched through the yard. Confused, Margarete turned first to Senta and then to the barn, searching for the animal in pain. When the wail broke again, she realized it was her mother's strangled voice. Dorothea hid her face with her hands as her shrill screams carried through the wind like the slaughter of spring lambs.

The Ostarbeiter could be heard scurrying and calling from the barns and their houses to see what was the matter. Margarete knew her mother would be mortified to be seen in such a state. As she ran to shield her mother from their sight, Paul shouted at them in a voice that sent them away as quickly as they had appeared.

As soon as Margarete touched her, Dorothea jerked away from her. The rejection stung Margarete like a severe discipline, but Dorothea couldn't see her daughter's hurt. With gasping sobs, she cried, "My son."

Herr Neuwald's voice broke through Dorothea's display, saying, "I also have a letter from Josef. He hopes he'll be coming home next month."

"Did you hear that, Mutti?" asked Margarete, begging to connect with her mother. "Papa is coming home next month."

Dorothea raised her head in acknowledgment but continued to cry.

Despite his mother's demonstration, Paul maintained an emotional absence. He thanked Herr Neuwald for delivering the letter and invited him inside. Eager to leave, Herr Neuwald said his condolences and goodbyes with the fewest words and jumped in his wagon with a speed defying his weight.

As Dorothea slowed her sobs, her attention roused, and she looked at Margarete and Paul. Margarete could feel her mother assessing them, and she hoped Dorothea would remember her place and responsibilities. Dorothea was the only parent at home, and she should have given her living children consolation for their own grief.

Instead, as she stared at Paul and Margarete, Dorothea's expression turned for the worse. Rather than finding compassion for her eldest son and daughter, the sight of them caused her to cry anew. Hiding her anguish, she covered her mouth with her hand and ran into the house.

When Dorothea allowed the door to slam, Margarete jumped, but her gaze held on the door to the family home. She focused on the welcoming entrance, trying to sort through the differing feelings muddling her mind—pity, grief, rejection, and terror. The Haupt manor represented stability and graciousness, which didn't match any of her feelings or the reality of war outside the farm.

There was only one person left in the family to tell her everything would be fine. She turned to Paul, expecting his resolute stoicism. Instead, her giant brother hung his head. His lips were downturned with his eyelids clenched like they were forcing back tears. After a moment, he met her eyes, and Margarete recognized his despair.

Though seven Haupt children had followed after Paul, he had never felt completely in step with the family. More shrewd than intellectual, more rough than genteel, more skeptical than religious, Paul had always existed apart from the rest of the family. Dorothea had cried "my son" for Franz and reacted more intensely to his death than she had to any of her other sons' official notices of death or missing in action. Franz was the prized son of the family—not firstborn Paul. Given how Dorothea doted on Sophia, Margarete understood exactly how Paul felt.

Paul grieved for all his brothers, whom he loved, but he also regretted and resented being the last Haupt son alive.

For a moment, the siblings stood in silence, absorbed in their own thoughts and troubles. Paul eventually heaved in a deep breath and wiped his eyes with his sleeve. Without looking at Margarete, he turned to the house. The liquor cabinet was most likely his next stop.

As he hobbled in front of her, she started in the opposite direction toward the swine house, paying him no heed. His gravelly voice brushed by her. "Pray that Papa returns, or everything will fall on us."

CHAPTER TWENTY-TWO

JOSEF

After only a few hours of sleep, Josef jerked awake. As his eyes took in the inky darkness, his heart raced, panicking that he had been captured. He had to be in a prison. That was the only reason he could be in such a dark place. Seconds later the rest of his senses corrected him. The mattress was soft beneath him, the clean sheets smelled of sunshine, and he heard Dorothea's whispering breath at his side. He had forgotten he was home.

He remained upright while the misplaced terror subsided in him. The murmur of English-accented German came from below, where Paul sat as the family sentinel listening to the BBC. Though his morning chores wouldn't start yet, Josef dressed for his day's work. He left his wife and daughters in their innocent slumber and arrived in the living room to see Paul had been expecting him.

Paul gestured to the coffeepot and cup waiting for him. "Bitte."

"Danke," Josef said, heading toward his chair.

As he poured his coffee, Paul extended a bottle of brandy to him. "Perhaps you might want something more?"

Josef would drink with a meal or socially, but he wasn't the sort to drink in the middle of the night with his workday soon approaching. His eyes drifted to the papers spread across the coffee table. Annotated maps and worn pages of notes showed Paul's careful script. He was prepared for a serious discussion—one that would need a bracing drink. Josef lifted his hand in assent to the brandy before he pointed to the papers. "What do you have here?"

"I've been making plans for the family to leave," Paul said, pouring a splash of brandy into Josef's coffee.

He leveled a stare at his son. While he had been living like a hobo and digging trenches for the army, Paul had been committing treason. Dumbfounded, he declared a fact they both knew. "Gauleiter Koch has issued orders to the SS to shoot anyone on the spot who is caught planning to leave East Prussia. That is an order from the top of the Nazi Party."

"I spent the last four years in the army under the threat of summary execution if I disobeyed. I don't care."

"You should care." Anger welled deep inside Josef. "I left you in charge of the family and farm. You had your mother and four sisters to protect and our livelihood."

An annoyed rasp escaped from Paul's throat before he raised his voice. "And I've been doing exactly that!"

Josef reached for the needed drink, and his fingers touched one of Paul's papers. The document sprang backward because it had been folded several times like an accordion. The handwriting was legible, but the paper was worn with deep creases. These were treasonous documents, and Paul wasn't being careful with them.

Josef touched the paper. "Shouldn't you take better care of something like that?"

"I couldn't be taking better care," Paul said, withdrawing a cigarette from its pack. "That bastard, Jan, is one of the few Ostarbeiter we have left. Most of the others have fled, but the one we want to leave is still here. And he lurks everyplace he shouldn't. I put these papers in the safest place I know."

"Where is that?"

Paul's lips curved into a slight smile, and he knocked on his prosthesis. "My leg. David Levi was my height, but the leg doesn't fit me perfectly. There's empty space in the cavity."

"Good thinking."

Hearing his father's approval, Paul eased in his seat. "I've done this with the best of intentions. I'm ready to discuss everything with you, but first I want to hear how things are at the front."

"The front? Awful." After a drink, Josef continued, "It felt like we were pretending to be back in the army again. We marched. We took orders and dug trenches. We slept on the ground. We're veterans who want to protect our homes and families, but we're old men. We look ridiculous on the front lines, toting our shovels from home."

"I'm sure the army appreciated any help you could give."

"They did, though they also didn't like our presence. It reminded them that there aren't many reinforcements." Josef raised a brow.

"And what of our borders?"

"The Russians are well into East Prussia in the northeast, but we're holding our lines for the most part." Josef pointed to a spot on the map. "You heard what happened at Nemmersdorf? The Russians only occupied the town for a few days before we beat them back, but what they did..."

"It was in all the papers and newsreels. The Reich put up propaganda everywhere— photos of women raped and murdered by Russian soldiers."

"Did you discuss it with your mother?"

Paul exhaled deeply, sending his cigarette smoke far across the coffee table. "I tried, but I was told I wasn't allowed to speak of it on the farm. She didn't want the girls to know, though Margarete and Sophia must have heard. As the war has worsened, Mutti ignores the situation even more, and she refuses to have any conversation about my brothers. I can't even—"

"I know," Josef said with a raised hand. He no more wanted to face the reality of his wife's psychological state than she wanted to face the war.

"With the Ostarbeiter leaving, we've had a hell of a time with the harvest. The girls have helped as they can, but it hasn't been enough. I wager every farm in Germany is in the same situation as ours. There simply aren't enough men."

Josef stared at the brandy, still a dark swirl uncombined with his coffee. Everything he had expected about his life at home while he was away was proving to be true.

In the silence, Paul puffed on his cigarette before he added, "It's more important for the Reich to send German men to die than to let them stay at home and feed the German people."

What Josef had witnessed the last few months only proved Paul's point. He sipped his coffee, appreciating the brandy. "Though I doubt I'll be successful, tomorrow I'll go to Allenstein to ask the Reichsnährstand for help for the farmers. Maybe we can avoid sending all the local men to the Volkssturm after Christmas."

"Don't be surprised if no one is in the office in Allenstein. The powerful have all found convenient reasons to leave for the West with their families." Paul poured another shot of brandy into his coffee cup, forgoing any additional coffee to accompany it. "Of course, Mutti didn't tell you this about her sister and brother-in-law. Tante Gertrude's husband—that bastard—Uncle Hubert. He—"

"Don't call your uncle such names."

Paul's voice dripped with insolence. "Dear Uncle Hubert is a major in the SS, which automatically makes you a bastard. But if that's not enough for you, you should know that he snuck his money, Tante Gertrude, and their daughters to Stuttgart. Tante Gertrude told Mutti it was because of her poor health."

"Gertrude has never been in poor health," muttered Josef.

"They're all liars and cheats." Paul adjusted his prosthesis and leaned back in his chair. "Though I can't blame them. They just want to get out of here alive. You have to look out for yourself."

Josef glanced at the mantel above the fireplace with the array of family photos. The photo of his cousin's daughter's first Holy Communion stood out. Over fifty members of one branch of the Haupt family stood before his brother's house. The photo was only fifteen years old, but it looked like a different era. It was in the middle of the Depression, so there were economic troubles, but everyone was happy and healthy. The people and their country were at peace. They could go about each day enjoying and sharing their lives.

Turning back to Paul, he asked, "And what of the rest of the family? Have you spoken with any of them?"

"Uncle Bernard says he's going to have a reasoned conversation over vodka with whatever Russian officer shows up at his farm. He'll give the Russians whatever they want if they let him and Tante Ingrid live peacefully in their home."

"If anyone could make that work it would be Bernard."

"But anyone who still has children at home is considering leaving. They talk about it as if it will be like the last war. Prussia will evacuate westward, but everyone will return home after a few weeks when the war is over."

"But it won't be like the last war. Look at Nemmersdorf."

Paul crushed his cigarette into an ashtray. His voice entirely matter-of-fact. "I've seen what the German army has done to Russian civilians. I've been a part of it. The Russians will want revenge, and it's obvious I'm a veteran. They'll kill me."

Josef stared at his son, not wanting to confirm what they both knew was true.

"And the girls..." Paul's eyes widened, conveying what couldn't be said aloud.

Revulsion and panic swept over him. Josef couldn't bear to consider what might befall his daughters and wife. He held up his hand again. "That's enough. At the right time, we will leave."

"Good." Paul leaned over to his papers, pleased that he had been convincing. "Let me show you the potential routes west. I also have lists of supplies and preparations."

While Paul was eager, the papers repelled Josef. He imagined packing up his family and fleeing his farm; it was like planning his own torture.

Before Josef bought his train ticket the following day, he thought it best to visit Krüger. Josef felt he had paid his penance for falsifying the agricultural records, and a meeting with Krüger would signal his respect for the man's authority. He was also curious what he might glean from the man.

Krüger welcomed him inside his office with a salute and asked him the same questions as Paul about the front, but Josef's answers were now different. They held no emotion, reflection, or criticism—only patriotism, optimism, and fortitude.

"We will win this war," Krüger replied with a delusional confidence.

"This is why I plan on taking the train to Allenstein today. I want to speak with the Reichsnährstand about its plans for the spring planting."

"There's no need," Krüger said, raising his hands from his desk like he was refusing the offer of coffee. "It's a far better use of your few days here to spend time with your family and get some rest."

"Few days?" asked Josef with a tilt of his head. "I understood we wouldn't return to the front until after Christmas."

"Nein. The Volkssturm are now expected to leave for the front again on Monday. You'll receive some time off at Christmas."

Krüger scratched his neck, making the dire order seem like a trivial request, but Josef could find no words or oxygen. The Reich was in a dismal place if old men and young boys couldn't be spared even for a month. His chest thumped again as his panic returned. His family should have fled weeks ago.

"It's better this way," said Krüger. "Men need to be put to work. Some who have stayed in town have the impression they should flee rather than defend East Prussia from the barbarians."

"That's unfortunate," said Josef quickly, hoping he spoke without a hint of guilt.

"It's treason and has been dealt with accordingly." Krüger arched a brow. "Naturally, the local Ortsbauernführer and his family would never consider such a traitorous act, would they?"

Josef answered without lying, "I know my duty, of course."

CHAPTER TWENTY-THREE

JOSEF

Josef's hands stung from the icy cold, so he barely skimmed his fingertips over the holy water font. His hand trembled as he touched his heart. Alarmed at his own body, he halted for a moment. He was a steady man. His hands rarely shook from fear, labor, or cold, yet now he could blame any one of those things for his tremor. The weather was arctic, Russian artillery and German flak rang in his ears, and he was exhausted from the preparations for the flight.

The giant wooden doors creaked open behind him, and a blast of frigid air entered the church. He nodded to the old widows, Frau Bludau and Frau Bartsch, shuffling inside beneath the weight of their woolens caked with snow. Their carved faces both returned his silent greeting with the same forlorn expression —a stunned hopelessness. They never expected the end of their lives might be so horrible or so near.

In another time, the widows had seen Josef as a man of influence, a man who could help them. He might reason with a greedy landlord or send one of his sons to help with a heavy chore. Now, Josef was of little use. He had his own problems, and God was everyone's only hope.

The nine o'clock Sunday Mass had always been the best-attended service. Instead, only a dozen parishioners knelt in the silent church. No music bellowed from the imposing organ, and the choir pews were empty.

Josef grimly mused to himself that if Dorothea were with him, she would blame the heavy snow for the poor attendance rather than the Russian airstrike that had hit Guttstadt the previous day. The Russians had captured Allenstein, and every man and boy in Guttstadt had been called to join the army for the final defense of the town. Wives and children were alone at home or sent to relations out of town. It was the unsaid start of the trek westward to safety. Flight was inevitable now. It was only a matter of time, but that time was still forbidden.

Rather than joining the Volkssturm again, Josef had chosen to stay with his family. He was sure the Gestapo was aware. If asked, he and the other farmers making the same choice would say they must remain to ensure the food supply. While it was a straight-faced excuse, it was treasonous. Josef understood he could be shot. He reasoned he would be even more likely to die at the front, so it was better to stay home and protect his family as long as he could. The most important thing was for his family to stay together.

Two weeks before, Jan, the suspicious Ostarbeiter, had run away in the night with one of the remaining Polish women. Paul insisted the family flee at once. If a Gestapo spy had left his post, Guttstadt was a lost cause. Still fearful of a summary execution, Josef kept his family on their property until the bitter end—despite all the warning signs and Paul's haranguing.

Now, Josef took a chance by attending Mass, but he wanted to see Father Schmidt for a final goodbye. As he walked down the center aisle toward the pew he had donated decades ago, he grasped how silly he looked—how silly maybe he had always looked. The family pew, which had been a status symbol, meant nothing. Everyone was equal in God's eyes, and Guttstadt's gentry was in the same peril as its commoners.

Father Schmidt's sermon focused not on the prescribed reading for the day but on passages in the Bible about fortitude during struggles and journeys. After the Mass, Josef took a seat in the middle of the pews to wait his turn with Father Schmidt. Despite the small number of parishioners, the priests' receiving line was slow to move. The priests took time to offer comfort and assistance to everyone.

Once the doors closed on the last parishioner, the rest of the priests hurried toward the sacristy, while Father Schmidt joined him. With grim smiles, they greeted each other.

Josef pointed toward the sacristy. "Are they leaving?"

"Not yet but soon." Father Schmidt sat back in the pew and crossed his arms in resignation. "Now that the last Mass is over, we'll finish storing the church's valuables. The linens, vestments, crystal, and parish records are crated in the cellar. The gold and silver chalices, crosses, and candlesticks are hidden elsewhere, though no doubt the Russians will find them."

"We're doing the same. Dorothea has the girls packing and hiding everything. Katharina fell yesterday carrying a box of family silver to the cellar." Josef fidgeted with his hat. "I don't have the heart to tell Dorothea that a padlock won't stop an army."

"How is she doing?"

"She works hard so we may leave. She never complains, and she does a good job of keeping the girls calm. She tells them that this will be just like the last war, and we'll soon be back home." He grimaced and looked to Father Schmidt for guidance. "She's so convincing because she believes it herself, but this is nothing like the last war. It's maddening to talk with her unless it's about the next task at hand."

The priest gave him a sympathetic smile. "Dorothea is a strong person. Many who have lost sons or husbands are paralyzed with grief and fear. She appears to be doing everything she can to protect her children who are still alive. She's acting with faith and hope. What more can you ask of anyone in these times?"

"I supposed you're right." He glanced over his shoulder to make sure the church was truly empty. "What are your plans? Have you been given any direction from the Bürgermeister?"

Father Schmidt also shifted his eyes left and right in search of any threats. Sounds in the front of the church caused both men to turn to see a priest lifting one of the heavy silver candlesticks from the altar. As he heaved the candlestick toward the sacristy, Father Schmidt pointed to the priest.

"We're leaving slowly for Elbing. Vicar Weisselbaum and Kaplan Hahn accompanied the women and children in the most need of help. I've been told an order will come for us to ring the church bells as a final signal. Then, we'll shut the church and leave with any remaining civilians." Father Schmidt pinned Josef with a steady stare. "What have you heard?"

"Yesterday I heard from someone the signal might come to flee as early as tomorrow." Josef lowered his voice to a whisper. "Krüger is under orders to burn every document."

Father Schmidt slowly nodded, and the two men sat in silence for a moment watching the other priests dismantle the grand altar. With little time to spare, Josef said, "I must go."

"As must I," replied the priest, as they both rose.

Despite the emotions tormenting him, Josef offered him a solemn handshake. "Thank you for everything you've done for me and my family. I wish you a safe journey."

Father Schmidt clasped his palms around Josef's hand, countering his somberness with a smile. "May God be with you and your family. I look forward to seeing you soon. Hopefully, we will celebrate Easter together."

Josef felt his heart sink. Easter was so long away. "Hopefully."

Father Schmidt raised his head to admire the ancient basilica.

"I pray the building survives. There are those who say we Catholics treasure our buildings too much, that buildings are less important than the actual ministry to people. But churches bring us together. This is our community's home. It's my home."

Josef tilted his head upward and then toward the altar, taking in the grand building of God. After his farm, the Dom was the center of Josef's life—his marriage, his children's baptisms, and his sons' funerals had all taken place there. Guttstadt had received its name before construction on the Dom had commenced. The architect designed a structure that outsized the small town but lived up to its name. It was the right size for such a good town.

Josef smiled at his old friend. "It's my home as well."

***

As the wind whistled outside the horse barn the next morning, Josef's pace was slower as he moved from stall to stall. He had risen early to spend more time feeding the horses. Anyone could do such a task, but he felt a duty to say goodbye to his dear friends.

The family would only take six horses. Josef would drive the landau with the matched Trakehner pair because they were the most valuable. The mare was pregnant, which wasn't ideal for an arduous trek in deep snow, but a Trakehner foal was a future commodity. Paul would take two thoroughbreds for the buggy, the fastest vehicle they owned. Draft horses would pull a wagon with a makeshift roof covering their belongings and hay for the horses.

One of the Polish workers, Karol, would drive the wagon. While the other two remaining Ostarbeiter preferred to stay on the farm until the war ended, Karol decided his lot was better with the Haupts than the Russian army. He had heard of the mass deportation of Poles from Soviet-controlled Poland. He had already spent four years as a slave laborer on a German farm. He didn't want to go to a Siberian gulag next. For Karol, it was better to remain with the devil he knew than meet the devil he didn't.

As Josef fed his herd, he patted their sides and gently scratched under their forelocks. He said endearments in thanks for their service. The farm buildings and their less valuable belongings might survive an occupation, but any army would take all of the horses and livestock. Josef would never see them again.

As he moved along the stalls, Senta followed behind. Her waddling trot had aged to a plodding meander. She stayed asleep in the wee hours of the morning, but today she was at his side. A wise dog, she knew change was afoot on the farm. By the end of the line of stalls, Josef knew he must say something to her as well.

Bending on his knees, he looked into Senta's bloodshot brown eyes. The name Senta meant "female assistant," and the dog had always been true to her name. For the last decade, she had protected his property, offered him support, and given his family joy. She panted, grinning her canine smile with a curious wag of her tail.

"Senta, I must say goodbye. The family will be leaving this morning. The workers will take care of you while you take care of the farm."

Senta wagged her tail in agreement, while her gentle eyes seemed to want to reassure him.

Josef scratched behind her ears, concentrating on how much the family loved her rather than the sinking feeling this was a permanent goodbye. A dog wasn't safe in war. The workers cared for her, but he understood their own lives came first. If they abandoned her, he could only hope someone would take pity on the old girl.

A forgotten memory came back to him of twelve-year-old Stefan training Senta when she was a puppy. Franz and Paul stood off to the side, their arms crossed as they both admired and critiqued Stefan's methods. Albert knelt on the lawn, in awe of Stefan's ability to get a wiggly puppy to follow his command.

Josef shut his eyes just for a moment, feeling the loss of his three sons again. He knew they were dead and long gone from the mortal earth. Yet, leaving the farm felt like he was leaving his sons behind. His memories of them were tied to the farm—the buildings, the land, and the animals.

Feeling his throat tighten, he stifled his emotions before they overtook him. It would be a long day of hard work. Difficult goodbyes couldn't get in the way of the family's departure.

Focusing on better times, he patted Senta's velvety ears and repeated what Stefan had always said to her.

"You are the best of dogs."

Later that morning, Josef spoke again with the Pole most likely to remain on the land to the bitter end. Since coming to the farm as a young POW, Hirek had become a good farmer with an instinct for animals. He was now fluent in German and still knew some Russian. Each day for the last week, Josef had dictated to Hirek instructions for the spring planting. If the Russians left Hirek alone, Josef was sure he would take care of the estate as best he could.

Though Josef was outside, he heard Paul's shouts from the kitchen. He ventured into the house to see Paul towering over Dorothea. Unimpressed by her son's size or booming voice, Dorothea stood tall with one hand on her new electric stove and the other hand poking her finger into Paul's chest.

"I will not leave my stove for the Russians, and even if the Russians don't steal it, Hirek might break it. I know that Hirek and the other Pole will be prowling all over the house, but I want him out of my kitchen. The coal stoves in the workers' buildings are fine for them."

Turning to Josef, Paul's eyes bulged, as if his head might explode in frustration. "Papa..."

Josef held his tongue for a moment, his eyes shifting from his wife to his son and then to the stove. With no thought at all, he announced, "Fine. I'll ask Hirek and Karol to load the stove on the hay wagon."

As he turned on his heel and headed for the door, Dorothea called from behind, "You must tell them to be careful when they move it."

Paul's awkward footsteps followed him, faster than their usual pace. Josef held the door open for him, as Paul spoke through gritted teeth, "Have you gone mad as well?"

"Ignore her." He tucked his scarf tighter around his neck to avoid the increasing snowfall. "We need to depart. It's easier to put the stove in the wagon and leave it somewhere than to fight with her right now."

"But the weight of the stove will slow us down!"

"It will but not as much as arguing with your mother. She's remarkably calm today, and she's managed to keep the girls calm as well. I don't want to upset her."

"She's calm because she's not right in the head," said Paul, touching his bearskin hat. "She had Margarete pack her new wallpaper. She said the Russians might take it, and she won't find the pattern again."

Josef raised his eyebrows, taking in a sharp breath. Ever since he had spoken with Father Schmidt, he had worked to see the best in his wife, despite her eccentricities. Now he didn't have time to worry about her mental health. "This is a pointless discussion. We must leave within the hour."

A giant boom came from the southwest as if fate agreed with him. Paul swung his head toward the direction of the continuing booms. "Why are the bombs coming from the west? The Russians are south and east of us."

"Not bombs. Dynamite. I overheard in town the Wehrmacht is destroying the Tannenberg memorial."

Paul's expression went blank for a moment. He was slow to speak, coming to terms with the fact that the Reich was voluntarily eradicating a memorial to Germany's greatest military victory—and a victory over Russia at that. "Only Hitler himself could order the demolition of Tannenberg."

"And he would only destroy it if he was certain the Russians would capture that territory. This why we can't waste time squabbling."

———

Josef had another reason to force everyone to hurry that day. If everyone moved with haste, their emotions could be kept in better check. If they were slow, someone would linger saying goodbye to Senta or searching for a forgotten memento. Someone might become emotional, and tears would be contagious. If they focused on everything they were leaving behind, tears might cost them their lives.

At noon, the Haupt family caravan was finally ready to depart. The remaining two Poles stood in the snow to wish them a safe journey. Dorothea took the opportunity to babble instructions on which potatoes should be eaten first and a final plea not to sit in the parlor. Meanwhile the younger girls hurriedly climbed into the back of the landau under piles of bear furs. Dorothea would join them there, while Margarete would sit on the driver's bench with Josef.

There was an edge of excitement among the daughters. A frightening adventure awaited them, but in due time, they would return to their home, their school, and their lives. The future would be difficult until it slowly returned to the time before the war.

Josef and Paul didn't share in their excitement. Duty and survival fueled them forward, bidding quick goodbyes before taking the reins of their carriages. Karol waited atop the giant wagon, moving the reins back and forth in his hands. He was the only person eager to leave, wanting to be far away from his current prison and his potential new captors.

As the carriages and wagon neared the hill, they were at a

distance with a view of the whole farm. Josef kept his eyes on Paul. Would Paul look back at their home? No, Paul's focus was straight ahead, navigating his team through the snow. Four years in the Wehrmacht had deadened him to sentimentality and regrets. Josef looked at Margarete, now a young woman wearing a fur hat and muff like her mother. Bright eyed, with full confidence in her father and brother, she stared straight ahead, waiting for the future to unfold.

When the landau approached the rise, Josef couldn't deny the cry from his heart. He was leaving the life he had built for himself and his family. It was impossible for him to be as indifferent as his son or as confident as his daughter. He let his head drift over his shoulder for a last look at the barns, the stables, the workers' buildings, and his home. Pride and woe filled him seeing the physical manifestations of decades of hard work and dedication to his family. The Angel of the Lord bell was quiet, though there had never been a more dire emergency in his life.

In the center of the courtyard, Senta sat just as she always did when someone left—alert and watchful. She must have taken the sight of his face as a signal. Deciding that her master and family were safely on their way, she vanished from the snow into her doghouse.

With the snow continuing to fall, the terrain proved a challenge even for Josef's strongest horses. More than once, Margarete jumped off the carriage to help guide them to an easier route. Despite her furs and heavy coat, her woolen stockings became wet and she needed the hot water container made of zinc at her feet to stay warm. When they reached a wooded area with less snow, she announced hopefully, "It should be easier here."

He surveyed the wood ahead. "Yes, but we must stop for a moment."

"Why?"

Josef didn't answer her question or those of Dorothea or Karol coming from behind him. He handed the reins to Margarete and jumped down. Reaching beneath the seat, he grabbed the items he had stashed until he found the right time and place. Before walking to Paul's wagon, he glanced at Margarete. She and everyone else had their answer. She looked not at him but at the shovel and Nazi flag in his hands.

By the time Paul had maneuvered himself off the buggy, he had also seen the flag. In a voice low enough to keep the conversation between the two of them, he said, "So, you didn't want the Russians to see a party member lived on the farm?"

"I'm afraid of what they might do if they knew."

"I doubt Hirek or anyone else will mention it if they want to continue living there. They'll never have as nice of a place if they flee. But what about the Ortsbauernführer sign by the road? The Russians will see that first."

"I buried it near the river outside of town yesterday. It will be rusted beyond recognition by the end of the snowmelt." Josef handed Paul the flag. "It won't take long to dig a hole."

Paul held the flag like it was rotten meat. "I'd say we should burn it, but I wouldn't want to waste a match on it."

Josef walked to the side of the road and shoveled the snow aside. The frozen soil required more effort, so he only dug a shallow hole.

Paul came to his side and dropped the flag into the ready dirt. "Good riddance."

"I'm glad to see the end of the Reich... the end of the madness," said Josef, staring at the flag that had flown high over his farm for years. "But there was no alternative. It was better to be in the party than not. This flag has kept us safe and out of trouble."

He looked to his son, expecting his cunning nature to agree. Instead, Paul's expression was dubious, his voice mocking. "Oh, really?"

A furor of anger rose in Josef fueled by embarrassment from

his son's ridicule. As a father, he still commanded respect. "Now see here—"

Ignoring him altogether, Paul turned and shuffled toward his carriage. The slight drag of his prosthesis left awkward footprints in the snow. Josef raised his eyes to see his wife and four daughters surrounded by what might now be all their earthly goods. While his family waited for him, he turned and buried the flag.

CHAPTER TWENTY-FOUR

MARGARETE

"We can't stay here any longer," Paul said, handing her a clothespin.

Margarete took the wooden peg and secured her father's clean shirt to the laundry line. Despite the cold temperature, the sky was clear with bright sunshine. Now was the time to do the washing. The rest of the women were in the warm shed boiling and wringing laundry while Margarete hung clothes in the crisp air. Paul sat on the garden bench, smoking and distributing clothespins. As he fought more with Josef, he confided more in Margarete.

Olga and Wilhelm Volkmann had been kind to take in their distant Haupt cousins, who were weary from trekking fifty kilometers in freezing snow and sleeping in vacant farm buildings at night. With only one teenage daughter, Angela, the Volkmann house was snugly built for a small family—not an additional eight people.

Shaking out another shirt, she asked, "Why is that? Have we overstayed our welcome?"

"We're leaving together. The Volkmanns are coming with us." He surveyed the yard, looking to see who might be in earshot. "I spoke with some soldiers last night along the road. The Fourth Army can't hold back the Russians much longer. They're now in Wormditt. That's only twenty kilometers away. We'll leave tomorrow while the weather is still fair."

This wasn't what Margarete wanted to hear. Remembering sleepless nights in icy barns, makeshift dinners over an open fire, and bushes for a privy, Margarete mused, "I suppose we've enjoyed being in a warm house with hot food."

"We've been too complacent. We must join the others again."

The others. The people who moved in columns down every passable road that wasn't commandeered by the Wehrmacht. Lines of people trudged by, always heading in the same western direction. Depending on wealth and ability, some were in carriages, others wagons, and many on foot—pulling a handcart or pushing a pram stuffed with belongings. Some wore fine clothes and furs, others rags. All were covered in snow.

Paul had said "the others" like these people were friends or family, but they weren't. The East Prussian diaspora was made up of comrade and stranger. Their only connection was their race against the war's tide, which threatened them with drowning. There was a bond among them, but also none.

"At least the weather is better. Traveling won't be so hard," said Margarete, searching for hope.

"It will be harder." Paul flicked ashes on to the ground, leaving black and gray soot against the white snow. "The soldiers said Elbing will fall soon, so we can't travel directly west. We must cross the Frisches Haff and down the Strait of Baltiysk. With this warmer weather, though, the ice is breaking. It will be dangerous. The Russians are bombing—"

He checked himself for saying too much. He rested his eyes

on her, assessing whether he could say any more. "I told Papa this would happen, but he wouldn't listen to me."

When Margarete was at school, she had heard stories from her classmates about how wonderful the Frisches Haff was in the wintertime. The giant lagoon was an icy playground where people skated, fished, and even rode ice yachts. Over three hundred meters wide and five hundred meters long, the lagoon was separated from the Baltic Sea by the narrow spit. Margarete couldn't comprehend how all of the Haupt vehicles and horses could safely cross.

She grabbed another shirt, wanting to ease her focus from the dangers ahead. "Is that what you and Papa have been arguing about?"

The two men could often be seen on the far edge of the property in animated conversations. When they returned, they barely spoke to each other.

"Among other things."

"What would you have us do now?"

Paul looked up at her through his eyelashes, silently asking if Margarete truly wanted to know. When she didn't shrink from her question, he announced, "We would leave this minute. The family would all crowd into the landau, taking only a few bags, and head for one of the boats the navy has launched for civilians. That's the quickest way to get out of here alive, and it would work. I'm a crippled veteran. There's Mutti and four girls. That should put us at the head of the line. Even though he's a man who could fight, they might even let Papa on the boat. He's older and an Ortsbauernführer. Maybe he could talk his way on."

Margarete looked away from him and down at the basket of laundry, considering his delusional idea. It wasn't a scheme that either of her parents would agree to. Her parents would never separate, and her father wouldn't want to leave their belongings and horses. Margarete knew Josef would prefer not to be carrying an electric stove, but he had said that they needed the vehicles and horses both to survive now and to rebuild their lives once the war was over. The Russians would ransack their home, so there wouldn't be much left once they returned.

Paul outlined a plan that admitted defeat. Escaping East Prussia by boat was for city dwellers or the poor. It was a plan for people who didn't care if they returned to their homes—not for people whose wealth was rooted in their land.

Searching for a compromise, Margarete asked, "There has to be another route. Is crossing the Frisches Haff the only way?"

"It is now."

The following day, the Haupt and Volkmann caravan was indistinguishable from the thousands of vehicles in the convoy that stretched from horizon to horizon. The Trakehner horses were no different from the mules as they plodded ahead through the snow, slush, and mud. Other than the sounds of war behind them, the road was quiet with fear. With the number of animals, people, and vehicles, it should have been noisier.

It was less than a kilometer into their tortoise-paced race to the Frisches Haff that Margarete first saw a horrifying scene that she would see again and again. She spied a woman ahead shuffling and stumbling. The woman carried a child near her own size, which made progress on foot next to impossible.

Like many blessed with wagons, the Haupts often offered a seat to those on foot. Paul or Karol would let the crippled veteran, jettisoned grandparent, or penniless woman and child join them. Margarete stared at the woman ahead and wondered why no one had taken her yet. The child had to be sick. Some people avoided veterans or the elderly, who often carried a host of problems, but most people found mercy for women with children.

"Don't worry," said Josef, noticing her focus on the woman. "Paul will take her and the child."

Margarete watched as Paul slowed his carriage and spoke to the woman. She heard his voice but couldn't make out what he said. The woman didn't turn to acknowledge him.

Paul leaned over and spoke louder, though still mannerly. "Excuse me, Madam."

He craned to see her better before straightening at once in his seat. A split second later, he turned away from her and raised his left arm, pointing forward.

"He's saying we shouldn't bother her."

"But why not? We have plenty of room."

"She doesn't want our help."

Josef's clipped tone sounded a warning that Margarete should ignore the woman, but she couldn't. The woman continued to slog along, sometimes advancing only to stumble and retrace her steps.

When their carriage approached the woman, Josef peered at his daughter. "Keep your eyes on the road."

Margarete obeyed too slowly, recoiling at a glimpse of the child. He was dead, his skin gray and body straight and hardened by rigor mortis. His mouth and eyes remained wide open in a permanent last gasp.

Terrified, Margarete followed her father's instruction and focused on the road. After a moment, she whispered aloud, "Why hasn't she buried him?"

"Either she doesn't want to leave him behind, or she can't bury him in the frozen ground."

"But doesn't she know she can't carry him all the way to safety?"

"We don't know what has already befallen her." Josef turned to Margarete with soft eyes. "She already may be a war widow, and he is her only child. We should pray for them."

Prayer. Since Paul first went to war and then with each brother following him and then with each sad letter from the army, they had tried to find comfort in prayer even when they questioned how God could permit the cruelty of war, the deaths of the ones they loved. But there was no answer, so they tried to accept what was so hard to accept. They continued to pray, believing God stood at their side in suffering.

Margarete raised her scarf over her mouth. She kept to herself, wishing to God the nightmare would end soon.

From that point on, she mimicked her father staring straight ahead because the scenes around them only worsened. Lame people who had urged their families to go ahead. Lost children begging for parents and food, and more distraught parents carrying dead children. Soldiers passed going in the opposite direction. They headed eastward into battle, sometimes even shouting at the refugees for getting in the way—as if it was the civilians' fault they were in such a plight.

In the back of the carriage, Dorothea kept the younger girls distracted from the horrors. Katharina and Martha would play with dolls or read. Sometimes they napped or joined their mother in saying the rosary. Margarete had never seen anyone continuously pray the rosary for so long.

A kilometer away from the Frisches Haff, the speed of the convoy began to pick up. As the horses sensed the extra room, Josef clicked the reins to encourage them forward. With the lagoon now in the distance, the reason for the increased speed became evident. The convoy was dividing. The Wehrmacht had established a single route across the Frisches Haff, chosen for its short length and solid ice, but the sole path was the reason the wagon train had moved so slowly. Now the well-marked tracks on the ice were empty. Ahead, the majority of wagons and pedestrians veered to the right, heading north. A smaller trail of vehicles and people moved southward, while others pulled off to the side in indecision.

As they neared the junction, a man with a rucksack over his shoulder stood smoking a cigarette. He appeared to be debating his options.

"Was ist los?" called Paul.

"The army says it's unsafe to cross. We must choose another route," replied the man.

Paul tipped his hat in thanks before he turned around in his seat to consult Josef from afar. Josef motioned north and south, asking which way they should go. Paul signaled for them to pull aside so they could confer. Josef, Karol, and Herr Volkmann congregated around Paul's carriage for only a few minutes. When Josef returned, he climbed aboard the wagon, first looking at Margarete and then over to her mother. "We'll try to cross."

Stunned to hear they weren't following the rest north or south, Margarete peered over shoulder to see her mother's response. She paid no attention to the ramifications of the decisions made by her husband, but instead Dorothea repositioned a pillow underneath a sleeping Martha. Katharina and Sophia met Margarete's eyes before anxiously returning to their reading.

As the Haupt and Volkmann caravan struck out alone toward the Haff, Margarete had to ask, "Why aren't we following the others if the ice is unsafe?"

"It's unsafe for thousands of people and vehicles." Josef gave her a reassuring smile. "But it will be safe for just us."

Traveling closer, but still far from the lagoon, a group of soldiers could be seen near the entrance to the trail across the ice. An army *Kübelwagen* was parked horizontally and directly in the track's path. While it was an automobile, the military vehicle was as imposing as a tank. People had scattered to the winds rather than wasting time.

Giant piles of debris stood on each side of the entrance. It reminded her of the local dump outside of Guttstadt. The closer they came, Margarete could identify suitcases, bicycles, prams, shovels, rocking chairs, dishes—anything that one might find in a home and none of it junk.

"Why have people left these nice things?" she asked.

"They carried too much weight for the ice."

"Will we need to leave anything behind?"

Josef's mouth twitched, which she interpreted as a silent "yes." Because her mother could be listening, he spoke aloud a different answer, "Possibly, but don't worry. This ice is still solid until March."

Margarete stared ahead at the piles of possessions. Each item was once so important that it couldn't be left behind; now it was discarded. All value was lost once the owner's life took precedence. Out of the corner of her eye, she saw movement among the soldiers. Another Kübelwagen appeared, driving down the tracks of the ice and onto the land. All but one of the soldiers hopped into the two automobiles and drove northward.

She stole a look at her father, whose eyebrows had risen. The knot in her stomach eased as she realized they had come across a stroke of luck. Though the single soldier kept one hand on his machine gun, he sauntered across the entrance, smoking a cigarette.

The lucky feeling left just as quickly when the soldier noticed them. He dropped his cigarette in the snow and grabbed a bullhorn from the ground. His voice boomed, echoing into the white wilderness. "*Achtung!* The crossing is closed. Turn back now."

Josef raised his arm acknowledging the soldier, but the Haupt and Volkmann caravan kept moving forward as they had agreed. The soldier repeated his warnings, which were answered by the vehicles arriving at the entrance one after another.

Josef and Herr Volkmann stepped down to speak to the soldier, and as the soldier strode over to them, Margarete saw he was young, already with two medals on his chest. He raised his eyes first to her, then to her family behind her, and then to the Frau Volkmann and Angela. He returned his gaze to Margarete and frowned.

Josef raised his hand with a humble wave. "Guten Tag, Corporal."

"Guten Tag, mein Herr," the soldier replied testily though still giving Josef his due respect. "I'm afraid you and your family must turn around. This crossing is closed. You may be able to cross farther north or south, but it's too dangerous here."

"I just watched a Kübelwagen cross. It should be fine for another month."

The soldier looked to his side for a moment before he turned his head back with an incredulous smile. "Have you not heard the Russian planes and artillery?"

"We've come from north of Allenstein. We've heard these sounds for weeks. It's nothing new."

"The Russians are targeting refugees on the Haff. They gun them down." The soldier pointed to the ice. "You can see the wagons that have fallen into the ice because of the Russian attacks."

Everyone looked into the distance on the frozen lagoon where a wagon wheel bobbed in the broken ice.

After Josef and Mr. Volkmann had crossed themselves to honor the dead, Josef looked to the skies. "There are no Russian planes right now. It seems that we could cross."

"Mein Herr, please turn around. This is better for your families."

"The quickest way to get our families to safety is by this crossing. No one else is here. We can drop extra weight to make the trip even safer. It won't matter if you let us pass."

The soldier brought both hands to his rifle. "I'm under orders to shoot anyone who tries to cross. It's too dangerous for anyone but military personnel."

"Too dangerous for German civilians, Corporal? Is that what you said?" Paul's voice rose from behind. He walked toward the group of men with his uneven but determined gait. "Why is it so dangerous for German civilians? Because of the Russians? Or because of the Wehrmacht?"

Margarete's mouth dropped open in fear, her head snapping to see her father's reaction to Paul taunting the soldier. Josef's face was placid. Whether he agreed with his son's tactic or not, he didn't stop him.

The soldier straightened his stance. "As you know, I don't make the orders. I follow them. Only the Wehrmacht can cross the Haff."

"How old are you? Eighteen?" Paul asked with a quizzical brow. "You're prepared to gun down two families fleeing for their lives? You saw the innocents we have with us. Two mothers. Five girls. Do you want that on your conscience for the rest of your life?"

The soldier narrowed his eyes. "I must obey orders. I have no choice."

"I know. I was in the army for four and a half years. There are things on my conscience for eternity as well." With a slow turn of his head, he examined the terrain all around them. "But you see, I also have no choice. Somehow, I've survived this war for this long, and I refuse to die by Russian hands now. If we go north or south, I'll be killed. You know that."

The soldier's silence was confirmation.

Just as casually as he leaned on his cane, Paul drew his sidearm from his pocket and aimed the pistol squarely at the soldier. "Whereas you do have a choice. You can either let us cross and take your chances on the Wehrmacht ever finding out. Or you can try to shoot us, and I will kill you."

As the soldier jerked to aim his machine gun, Paul scoffed, "Really? I said I'll kill you." He tapped his cane. "Just like I did the Ivan who shot me."

Margarete froze the moment Paul had drawn his weapon, but her eyes now darted to see her father's reaction. He and Herr Volkmann were also stunned at Paul's readiness to commit murder. When she looked at the soldier again, she saw that he, too, seemed unable to believe his eyes.

After a moment, the soldier lowered his weapon, muttering, "You're insane." He waved to the lagoon. "Go. But don't blame me if you fall in the ice."

"Danke," said Paul with a smile.

Margarete allowed herself to take a deep breath, and Josef and

Herr Volkmann relaxed as well. Paul slipped his gun into his pocket, withdrew a pack of cigarettes, and offered them to the soldier. "For your trouble."

The soldier took the pack and shook his head in annoyance. As the soldier lit up a cigarette, Paul, Josef, and Herr Volkmann conferred in low voices. Minutes later Margarete watched as the Haupts' stove and farming equipment joined the other refugees' unnecessary possessions. She turned to see her mother's reaction, but Dorothea sat with her eyes closed. Margarete couldn't tell if she was praying or she simply couldn't witness what was happening.

When the caravan moved again, the soldier called out, "Stay on the tracks."

As Josef drove by, he tipped his hat to the soldier, who gave him only a somber nod. The soldier shifted his gaze to Margarete and added, "Good luck to you."

Paul was the first to enter the ice field, keeping the carriage slow and steady. His horses instinctively adapted to the perilous ground and kept their footing. The ruts from the previous thousands of vehicles helped create the friction to keep the carriage on track. When Margarete felt the solid ground give way to creaky ice, she tensed and gripped the bear fur on her lap.

Josef spoke over his shoulder to the women of his family as if there had been no drama at all at the checkpoint. "We will be fine. This is the shortest path across. It should only take two hours. You should sleep because I don't know when we'll stop once we get to land."

Margarete turned to look behind her. Dorothea still clutched her rosary as her eyes remained closed. Margarete's terrified sisters clung to each other, their eyes determinedly winced shut.

"It might be better if you joined them," said her father.

"I'm not tired. I'd rather be up here with you."

"Thank you for the company," he replied, with a genuine smile.

After only half a kilometer, the results of the Russian bombings came into focus. Blood splattered over the ice, while gaping holes could be seen ahead of them on either side of the track for as far as she could see. Wagons and carriages protruded from the little ponds. Before they reached the open waters, Margarete wrinkled her nose at the stench of death drifting from ahead. Covering her nose, she saw the corpse of a man only half-submerged and a horse's head floating beside him in reddish water.

She pointed to the gruesome sight. "Papa..."

"It's natural to be curious, but look straight ahead and pray for their souls."

Margarete nodded, suppressing tears for the tragedy all around them.

"We must pray for them," he said, crossing himself. "And thank God for sparing us."

Days after crossing the lagoon, Margarete sat on a stump watching the wagon train slowly plod by. It was an unfortunate stop for her family. Arduous travel through ice and snow had taken its toll on the pregnant mare. With an infected hoof, the horse needed a veterinarian and weeks of rest. The family couldn't provide her with either. Josef and Paul had taken her into the woods to end her misery.

If they were back at home, Margarete would have been in tears. The mare was a beautiful horse, just like her mated stallion, and their foal would have been extraordinary. Margarete had always loved the farm's baby animals. On the stump, she sat in a numb gratitude at the mare's death. She had seen enough dead animals and people recently that she was thankful if a suffering life found a quick end.

While the men dealt with the horse, Margarete was the first to reach the decrepit outhouse at the nearby derelict farm. Now she waited for the rest of the women to relieve themselves. Off in the distance, she noticed Karol sharing a cigarette with another refugee. She could hear them speaking in Polish.

Karol came to her and said, "Fräulein Margarete, you should stay away from the woods. Please tell the other women as well."

Margarete nodded, assuming he referred to the killing of the mare. As he walked away, two gunshots reverberated from the woods. Some refugees looked to see where the sound had come from. Most kept moving forward; gunshots were nothing new. She glanced at the forest and hoped her father and brother would return soon so the family could be on its way.

Out of the corner of her eye, she saw a familiar-looking red coat with large black buttons in a heap on the snow. Turning her attention back to the convoy, she searched her memory for where she had seen such a coat before. An image came to her of the red coat swishing ahead of her as she climbed the stairs at school in Königsberg. Immediately, she ran toward the coat, convinced that it had to be Helene Wichert's. She remembered someone asking Helene where she had purchased it in. Helene had given the name of the shop but said that her grandmother had added the more stylish oversize buttons. No one else had a coat like that.

When she reached the coat, she was positive it was Helene's. She looked all around, wondering why Helene would leave her coat. Sunshine broke through the clouds, hinting that spring was near, but the air was still cold. A coat was necessary.

Thinking Helene might have dropped the coat on her way to the outhouse, Margarete looked at the line to the privy, hoping she was there. What a blessing it would be to see her dear friend again; it would be a small joy during the worst of times. She turned to the woods in front of her in search of another clue. When her eyes drifted to the ground, she saw a woman's winter boot jutting out from behind a small bush.

After a few cautious steps, Margarete saw it was a row of women's feet splayed open. With one more step, she saw the three bodies and screamed in horror. There, in a line were Helene, her mother, and her grandmother, dead on the ground. The necks of all three were slit, and all were naked from the waist down with their legs spread where blood smeared over their genitals. Stockings, undergarments, coats, and scarves were strewn around them. Each woman's open, empty eyes stared out to the world, disbelieving what had befallen them.

Karol's voice came from behind her. "Fräulein Margarete!"

Margarete shook as she covered her mouth, unable to stop looking at the unfathomable display. How could Helene, her brave and kind friend, have met such an unspeakable death?

"This is why I told you not to go here," said Karol with sympathy, briefly touching her coat. "I heard the Russians raided this area yesterday."

"I knew her," she cried, turning to Karol. He had his back to the scene in respect for the naked women, but she still asked, "How could anyone do this?"

Karol only looked over his shoulder enough to meet her eyes. "We must get to Danzig. This area isn't safe."

Margarete couldn't think of future problems. She returned her gaze to the raped and murdered women; tears began to flow as her sight settled on Helene.

"She was my friend from school in Königsberg, and that is her mother and grandmother. Her father was a clergyman at the cathedral. He died in the bombing last August. The last I heard from her was his death announcement. They must have been traveling alone." She looked again at Karol, who still faced away from the women. In a determined, teary voice, she declared, "We should bury them."

"Pardon, Fräulein Margarete, but we don't have time and your father will never allow it. Please return to the carriage." To appease her and for his own faith, he made the sign of the cross. "May God grant them eternal rest."

Margarete reflexively responded by also making the sign of the cross. She knew he was right that they must leave. Arguing with her father would be futile. "Danke, Karol. Please give me a moment."

Karol walked back to the wagon, while Margarete knelt before the women. Whispering her own prayers for the dead, she closed their eyes and pulled down their skirts for dignity. She found clothes to cover Helene's mother and grandmother. Lastly, she picked up the red coat off the ground and draped it over her friend, sobbing a prayerful goodbye.

CHAPTER TWENTY-FIVE

MARGARETE

Despite having traveled two hundred kilometers from Guttstadt, the Haupts were no farther away from the Russians and the family's conditions continued to deteriorate. The German army fought around the convoy, protecting the civilians the best they could, but the Russians often permeated their defenses. German refugees were ripe for the taking. Horses, vehicles, and food were stolen; jewelry and watches were ripped off arms and necks before their owners faced rape, murder, or deportation to a gulag.

Helene's death remained with Margarete, but it wasn't the last time she saw such an inhuman scene. Other families told stories of finding themselves surrounded by Russian soldiers. While Dorothea distracted her younger daughters and shielded their eyes and ears from the horrors and rumors, Margarete was perched with her father atop the driver's bench, seeing and overhearing reality.

Sometimes she doubted her mother truly understood what was happening because she resolutely ignored all negative talk. That changed one evening when the family huddled in another empty farm building with two other families. One family were the sort of Germans Dorothea wouldn't have even allowed her children to play with; another family were of the aristocracy Dorothea aspired to join. Now they were all together—dirty, weary, hungry, and terrified.

Margarete overheard the blue-blooded matron tell Dorothea that she planned to bury her jewelry to keep it from the Russians. She was waiting until they crossed the Danzig Corridor and entered Pomerania. Her reasoning was that when the war was over Germany might have to return the Danzig Corridor to Poland. The good German soil of Pomerania would protect her jewels until the war's end when she could retrieve them on her return to East Prussia.

Dorothea nodded approvingly at the woman's plan. "That's very smart."

Later, she whispered in Margarete's ear, "Where is your bracelet?"

"In my bag." Without turning her head to see her mother, she added, "Why?"

"Did you hear what Frau von Berg said about burying her jewelry? I have a better plan."

Before they left that morning, Dorothea handed Paul a black velvet bag. He opened the bag and nodded at the jewelry and watches. With a magician's sleight of hand, Dorothea conjured into her palm a red leather ring box. She dropped the red box in the pouch, and Paul cinched the silk cords. Slipping it inside his pocket, he walked in the direction of the forest.

Margarete had only seen her mother part with the diamond ring for a visit to the jeweler to tighten its prongs and to hear his praise for such a fine piece. The ring was as much a part of Dorothea as the hand she wore it on. Only if she was in true danger of losing it would she ever willingly give the ring away.

When her father was near, she whispered, "Where is Paul going?"

Not giving any suspicion to his son's wandering off, Josef stared straight ahead and replied in a barely audible voice, "To hide the bag in his prosthesis."

The signs of a lost war continued to build. When they were deep in the Danzig Corridor, Karol fled the caravan one night, which forced the Haupts to leave the wagon and two draft horses. It was a loss of cargo space for possessions, food, and feed for the remaining horses. Taking care of the animals had been easier in East Prussia where farms still had provisions. The farther west they traveled, the worse the conditions became for human and animal.

"Why would Karol leave?" Margarete asked Paul as she picked through the family's second-best china. She kept only a place setting for each person.

Paul tossed an extra lantern onto a pile of now extraneous items. "I imagine he believes this land soon will be Poland again. He's off to find some countrymen."

Margarete had hoped when the family entered Pomerania that things would be better, believing there would be a feeling of security and maybe more food. She envisioned lively towns untouched by the war—like Guttstadt when she was in primary school. Instead, they entered a ghost countryside. Most of the inhabitants had long since fled west. The Wehrmacht had commandeered any remaining farm animals, so the only food to be found were forgotten potatoes in a root cellar. Beyond a drafty barn or workers' quarters, the few Pomeranians who had chosen to stay had little to share with the hundreds of refugees rolling past their homes each day.

When they arrived in Lauenberg, they planned to go to the town center to water the horses at the public trough. The town was similar to Guttstadt, with a medieval church and wall. As the central platz came into view, Paul stopped the carriage. He turned around to make eye contact with Josef and Herr Volkmann and pointed to the right.

"What's going on?" asked Margarete.

"I'm not sure," replied Josef. "I believe Paul thinks we should avoid the platz."

Josef guided the horses to follow Paul. As the carriage turned right, a view opened up onto the square. Margarete took in a sharp breath at the sight of two German soldiers hanging from makeshift gallows. She had seen so much death already, but a lynching was ominous. Execution by shooting was common for traitors under the Reich. Forced labor in a concentration camp was also a possibility. She had never seen anyone hanged like in medieval times.

The stiff corpses swayed in the wind like pendulums in a grandfather clock. Crows flew around their faces and bare feet while signs hung from their broken necks. One sign read, "I am hanging here because I didn't believe in the Führer." The other read, "I am a traitor."

Josef looked at her, and they both made the sign of the cross to pray for the dead. His eyes were regretful, as they often were when he had to explain something he would rather not. "I assume they're deserters. They were found by another unit of the army and executed. They don't even get to keep their boots."

"Why weren't they shot or sent to a camp?"

"The Reich wanted to make examples of them. It's a warning to any other soldier considering desertion rather than fighting to the end."

Margarete nodded, understanding that Paul wasn't alone. There were other soldiers who would rather be killed by a fellow German than fall into Russian hands.

A week later, Margarete sat on a bare mattress with Martha on the floor as she combed through her sister's dark bob. To her right, Sophia sat doing the same for Katharina's auburn curls. Dorothea quietly managed the hardships of the trek, but she wouldn't tolerate lice. Many women on the trek wore kerchiefs to hide their bald heads, a sign of surrender to pests. No daughter of Dorothea's would have her head shaved like a boy, so the older sisters were tasked with keeping the Haupt girls' hair lice free.

Darkness had fallen outside, and Margarete was happy they had found a more prosperous house to stay in that evening. Though they would be crowded under their own dirty blankets, the girls would sleep on a real bed for the first time in a week. As she finished smoothing Martha's hair, she heard Herr Volkmann's stern voice from the window behind her.

"They're in the woods!"

"Get the girls," Paul said from the living room.

Dorothea appeared in the doorway, commanding, "Girls. You must come now."

"Why?" asked Sophia, as the girls rose from their seats.

When Dorothea didn't answer her favorite daughter, Margarete assumed the worst. There were Russian soldiers near the house. The girls followed Dorothea into the living room where Josef stood by an opening in the floor that hadn't been there when they entered the house. The floor was now bare, with the carpet rolled halfway at Josef's feet.

"Climb down the ladder into the cellar, girls," said Herr Volkmann, entering the house. His big body heaved, as he fought for air, having run faster than he had in years. Despite his breathlessness, he added, "Bitte," using the same tone as if he asked them to sit down for dinner.

Margarete was confused because the adults seemed so calm, as if they had already planned for an encounter with Russians. Without another word, Frau Volkmann led her daughter, Angela, down the stairs, and Margarete followed with her sisters. Dorothea brought up the rear.

When Margarete landed on the cellar's dirt floor, she saw earthen walls fortified by boards with shelves holding forgotten jars of preserved vegetables. Maybe they could eat some for dinner. Crates that had once held potatoes, onions, and carrots were now empty and jumbled into a pile. Frau Volkmann took one from the top, set it on the ground, and motioned for Angela to sit. Wanting to be helpful, Margarete set down the other crates so everyone had a seat. After Dorothea stepped down, Josef handed her a lit lantern. He gave the women a grim smile and closed the trapdoor.

The lantern illuminated the cellar enough so everyone could find a seat. Clinging to each other in fear, they raised their eyes to the wooden floor above them. They stared and listened, waiting for fate to arrive.

Within ten minutes, Russian voices rose in the distance. Dorothea hugged her younger daughters closer, while Sophia and Margarete clung to each other and Frau Volkmann tightened her grip on Angela. Horses whinnied and neighed, and Margarete's heart sank, guessing the Russians were taking their horses. Now the family would have to walk westward.

Soon the door to the house slammed open, and heavy boots clomped on the floor, causing the ceiling to shake above the women's heads. Chaotic yelling began in Russian words that Margarete didn't understand but also Russian-accented German, which sounded wrong.

The Russians called out "Frau, come!" like they were calling a dog. The girls all looked to their mothers, knowing the Russians were out to find German girls, bound to be with their mothers.

When the boots entered the living room, Josef's voice could be heard in a broken Russian. His tone was calm, even welcoming, while the Russians continued yelling for Frau and Mutti. Others shouted *"Uhr! Uhr!"* demanding watches. Herr Volkmann's voice was unruffled as he replied in German that their watches and jewelry had already been taken by other Russians.

Margarete hoped the absence of women and watches would

send the Russians away, but instead a cacophony began above them. Furniture crashed on the floor, with more yelling. Within moments, the trapdoor opened above the women. They squinted into the lamplight, seeing Russian soldiers. The men's sinister smiles conveyed that they couldn't be deceived by the hide-in-the-cellar trick.

"Mutti, come!" they said.

Margarete looked at her mother, wondering if she would obey their command. Dorothea clutched her Katharina and Martha with her rosary wound around her right hand, but she stared at the soldiers with the visceral animalistic glare of a mother ready to kill for her young.

One of the soldier's smiles grew bigger, showing his jigsaw collection of teeth. He pointed a gun into the cellar. "Mutti, come."

Though there was a gun in her face, Dorothea didn't move. Margarete thought that maybe she was waiting for her husband or son to save her, but no Haupt man appeared as the yelling and banging continued above. For a moment, Dorothea looked like she was calculating fate. Should she put her trust in the Lord and get out of the cellar, or should she risk eternal purgatory by allowing her own murder and those of her daughters?

Dorothea whispered, "God be with us," and let go of her daughters. She glanced at Frau Volkmann, who motioned for all the girls to hold hands. They formed a human chain as they slowly climbed the steps, one hand on the ladder and one hand holding another's. Dorothea led the way, and Frau Volkmann came last.

As Margarete lifted her body onto the living room floor, she saw furniture strewn about the room. Soldiers pushed and probed her father and Herr Volkmann, searching their bodies for anything valuable while barking at them in Russian. Another set of soldiers ransacked the family's suitcases and crates.

When she first heard Dorothea cry out, Margarete guessed it was because some of the soldiers were stuffing the Haupt sterling silverware in their pockets. One looked ridiculous with a serving spoon, engraved with an elaborate *H* monogram, sticking out of his back pocket.

At Dorothea's second cry, she turned her head to see Paul splayed on the floor and backed into a corner. Two soldiers held him at gunpoint, ready to shoot, and even Margarete could identify one word of what they were yelling, "Stalingrad." The Russians assumed Paul had lost his leg killing other Russians, and his death would avenge their comrades.

Margarete had never seen her surly, bruiser brother so meek and humble. The Russians were small in comparison, but they held weapons ready to kill. Paul held up a hand in surrender, repeatedly saying, "*Nyet! Nyet!*" His other hand fumbled at his chest pocket before pulling out a photograph. She remembered Paul showing it to her years ago when he was home on leave. He stood in his Panzer uniform high in the middle of an ancient Roman amphitheater on Sicily with Mount Etna in the distance. He held out the photo to the soldiers. "Italy! Italy!"

One of the soldiers took the photo, stared at it, and showed it to his comrade. The comrade looked down at Paul's fake leg and shrugged. She couldn't believe they took Paul's photograph as proof that he had never fought in Russia. When they lowered their guns, she heard Dorothea whisper, "Gott sei Dank."

The soldiers turned their rifles upside down and began beating him. Their hatred for Paul gleamed in their eyes as they battered him with their rifle butts, kicking his remaining leg. Paul yowled and moaned in agony, which made Margarete wonder if a beating really was a mercy. Paul might die regardless.

Seconds later, Margarete felt someone grab her arm. She turned to see the Russian soldier with the spoon. His greasy blond hair was matted to his head, his face oily. Even from a foot away, she could smell the stench of someone who hadn't bathed in months.

Josef bellowed from the other side of the room, "Nein!"

With one jab of his rifle, a soldier threw Josef to the ground.

He turned the gun on him and motioned for Herr Volkmann to join him in the corner. Holding them back by gunpoint from defending their women, the soldiers sneered and taunted the emasculated men.

Margarete tried to jerk away, but the slimy Russian clamped his fingers into her arm. Out of the corner of her eye, she saw another soldier grab Sophia, who shouted, "Mutti!"

As both girls struggled to free themselves, Dorothea ran in front of them. "Nein!" Her scream was so shrill it drowned out the rest of the noisy room. With desperate, wild eyes, she furiously tapped her chest, trying to trade her own body for those of her daughters. "Me! Me!"

Rather than releasing her daughters, another soldier grabbed Dorothea as well. She fought with all her might. She thrashed, kicked, and shrieked, inciting Frau Volkmann and all the girls to do the same. None of the soldiers let go; some even seemed to enjoy the women's struggle. After a moment, the Russian holding Dorothea gave her an annoyed look and slapped her so hard her head snapped backward. He said something to another soldier, who grabbed Katharina and Martha. Dorothea cried even louder until she saw the soldier shove the younger girls at Josef and Herr Volkmann.

The soldier with his hand on Margarete began dragging her out of the house, and the other soldiers followed with their chosen women. All hostility left Margarete as she stumbled along. Tears of terror took hold over her, which seemed to anger the greasy soldier far more than her fighting. He stopped a few feet away from the building, lifted her quivering chin, punched her face, and flung her to the ground.

Scrambling backward like a crab, Margarete tried to get away, but the soldier pounced on her and pinned her arms over her head. This time he ignored her crying pleas as he ripped her undergarments. Seconds later, she clenched her eyes together in pain as she was sure her body was splitting in two. She told herself this had to be a nightmare. Hearing the screams of the other women and disgusting grunts of the men proved it was a reality.

Though the violation felt endless in the moment, when he climbed off of her, she felt a relief that it was over so quickly, that she was alive. Before she could even raise her head, though, the soldier who had grabbed Dorothea was before her, his pants at his knees.

"Fräulein," he said with a menacing grin.

After him there was another and another and another. Most were rough and cruel, ripping her clothing so she was all but naked. Some soldiers feigned sweetness, but it made no difference whether she wailed in pain or if she ignored them. They hit her at whim as if she wasn't properly fulfilling the lustful revenge they had envisioned.

Eventually the men tired, or maybe they were due elsewhere. They left the women, bloody and broken in the dirt. Walking away, the Russians slapped one another's backs and celebrated their sweet and swift revenge. Even when they were out of sight, the soldiers' sick laughter echoed through the woods.

Chapter Twenty-Six

Josef

Though he had done hardly an hour's work, Josef wiped the dirt off his hands and sat on a nearby stump. Only six months ago he had been able to work a full day on his farm and attend to his Ortsbauernführer duties. Now he was so hungry and weak that gardening required him to stop to catch his breath.

A glum pride filled him as he looked at his little rows of potatoes, carrots, and other vegetables. Thanks to a prescient moment, he had grabbed a few handfuls of seed before they fled the farm. Other than some clothes, blankets, photos, and seeds, the family owned almost nothing. Dorothea's jewelry and his watch miraculously survived hidden in Paul's leg, but their other belongings had long since been lost to marauding Russian soldiers. For months the family had run from them, only to be caught again. With no horses, there was no means of escape. The Haupts were stuck.

Removing his hat, he blotted his brow with a handkerchief as he scratched his chin and cheeks. Lice and scabies were rampant, causing everyone to scratch and rid themselves of unnecessary hair. The women and girls wore short hair, and the men shaved their heads in addition to their faces—just as Josef always had. But Josef had forgone his clean-shaven face and grown a long gray beard. When the Russians came looking for German men to send east, it was best to look as old and frail as possible. The younger and healthier disappeared.

The high-pitched squeal of metal rubbing against metal broke the silence around him. He turned to see Margarete filling two buckets of water. Though it was midday, she was getting water to bathe. Haltingly, he raised his hand with an awkward smile; he was never certain the best way to approach his daughters after they had been raped.

When the first assault had happened three months ago, he and Wilhelm Volkmann had run out to meet their women as they straggled back to the house. The men tried to calm and soothe their wives and daughters, all the while feeling shamefully pathetic themselves. Though they had been beaten, it was the rape of their womenfolk that humiliated them. Their manly pride had vanished as they'd listened by gunpoint to their wives and daughters being defiled.

The attacks were relentless. Regardless of what direction the family went or how many other refugees they banded with, they encountered Russians ready to claim their revenge. Paul, Margarete, and Sophia were their prime targets. Though Dorothea was a victim as well, she was often ignored by the soldiers, leaving her for her older daughters. The Russian soldiers weren't above raping young girls and boys, but Martha and Katharina mercifully had been spared. Malnutrition made them look years younger than eleven and fourteen.

Margarete gave Josef a reassuring wave and returned to filling the water buckets. In a fluid motion, she forced the pump handle up and down, causing the old well to find a burst of water.

Pumping and carrying water was an easier job for her than the rest of the family.

The frequent beatings had taken their toll on Paul, who moved even more slowly than usual. At only fifty years, Dorothea should have been stronger, but like Josef she was weak from often giving her share of food to her children. Dorothea had always praised Sophia's svelte figure and harped on Margarete for her shapelier one. Now, Sophia had the weakest constitution, easily succumbing to every cold and taking the longest to recover from the assaults. Margarete had physical and mental reserves that allowed her to toil on despite everything.

Later that afternoon, Josef knelt before Paul, tightening the leather straps and buckles of his prosthesis. Paul continued to lose weight, so his leg regularly needed refitting. The Volkmanns and the rest of the Haupt family had ventured to the creek behind the house to get some fresh air and to give Paul privacy, but Margarete remained. She had sewn a scrap of toweling into a sock that Paul could wear over the stump of his thigh to reduce the chafing.

Margarete tended the potatoes boiling for the day's meal and asked, "How does it fit?"

"Better," said Paul.

Josef adjusted the last buckle. "It should be easier to walk now."

"I doubt that it will be any easier," Paul grumbled before he took a few steps around the bare floor of the room. "But it may be better."

Josef noticed that he appeared to be steadier on his feet. Paul recognized the change as well. He nodded at Margarete. "Danke."

"Bitte," she said with a smile. "I hope—"

A knock at the door interrupted her, and they all froze in place. The person behind the door could just as easily be friend as foe. Josef rose from his knees, and Margarete turned to slink out the back door, but the front door swung open. A tall Russian soldier stepped inside. He wore the standard brown tunic and riding pants of the Soviet army, and the tunic bore the epaulettes and insignia of an officer.

Josef couldn't have imagined a worse situation for his two eldest children. His son, who had an outsized ego even for a Prussian, stood half-clad with his weakness exposed to his enemy. His traumatized daughter was trapped, ripe for the picking.

The officer scanned the room, first taking in Josef before moving on to Paul where he lingered on his prosthesis. When his attention arrived on Margarete, she shrank back. The officer removed his hat at once.

"Pardon, Fräulein." His German carried a heavy Russian accent, and he turned to Josef. "Guten Tag, mein Herr. My name is Lieutenant Aleksander Orlov."

Already taken aback by the officer's politeness and German, Josef was dumbfounded when the soldier offered Josef his hand.

"Guten Tag. I am Josef Haupt. These are my two children, Paul and Margarete. We have nothing of value anymore."

The lieutenant raised a calming hand. His gaze traveled among the three Haupts, landing on Margarete. As if he recognized what his countrymen had inflicted on the family, his expression became a sheepish grimace. "I'm sorry for your losses, but that's not why I'm here."

Paul grabbed his pants from the table and hobbled to a rickety chair. He began dressing, though he never took his eyes off the enemy in the room.

Josef explained, "We were adjusting Paul's prosthesis when you walked in."

"I see." The lieutenant focused on Paul's leg. "I don't mean to be rude, but may I take a look at it? I had started medical school before the war. I've never seen such a fine one."

Josef gave Paul a warning glance. They would have to allow the officer to see the leg, but they shouldn't cause any suspicion about the leg's cavity. Glaring at the enemy officer with distrust, Paul shrugged and allowed him to come near.

The lieutenant knelt before him, asking how the mechanisms

worked and inspecting the hinges and buckles. Paul's answers were informative but gruff. The officer never questioned where he had lost his leg. When asked if all amputated German soldiers received such an exceptional prosthetic, Paul kept a few seconds of silence.

Josef knew he was holding his tongue to keep his macabre humor in check. It wouldn't do to make one of his usual dark comments that he was the beneficiary of a murdered Jew's leg. Instead, he grunted, "I don't know. I suppose I'm lucky."

The Russian halted a moment recognizing Paul's sarcasm but continued admiring the leg. Worried he would ask Paul to remove it, Josef tried to distract him. "Thank you for speaking German. It's impressive and far better than my Russian."

"Danke. My father is a violinist. We lived in Berlin for a time when I was young." He stood and looked at Josef. "We have nothing like this in Russia. If I ever have a patient with such an injury, one day I hope I can provide him with something similar to ease his situation."

The officer was being unusually friendly, so Josef touched a chair. "Please have a seat."

The Russian glanced at the chair in the circle of stools and a piecemeal bench, built by Josef and Paul from scraps of wood. "Danke." He sat down on a stool instead.

Margarete softly padded over to the three men. She stopped in front of the lieutenant and asked, "May I get you some water?"

The Russian smiled, recognizing the small signal of hospitality. "Nein. Danke. I have a canteen."

"I'm sorry we can't offer anything else," said Josef.

"No one has anything to offer," said the officer with a wry expression. "But hopefully that will change soon."

"How so?"

"I came because I was out for a walk and remembered hearing there were displaced persons hiding away back here. You should know the war has ended."

"Gott sei Dank," Josef said, exhaling his relief.

"Germany has surrendered unconditionally." The lieutenant waved his hand toward the window. "This region will be under control of the Polish authorities, though we'll remain."

"Under the Polish government? But why?"

"I don't know." Holding up his hands in helplessness, the Russian said, "You do know Hitler is dead? There is no functioning German government."

"We know." Josef sighed. "Forgive me. As you can imagine, we're anxious to go home."

"Aren't we all?" chuckled the officer. "But who knows when that will be. We've been ordered to collect all the displaced persons. You need to travel to Birkow."

"What will happen there?" Paul asked with narrowed eyes.

"I don't know. You'll wait until things are more organized, I suppose." The officer pointed to the scabs on Josef's hands. Every member of the family had scabs and red marks. "There's a typhus epidemic. Many of my troops are ill. Are any of you sick?"

No one in his family felt perfectly well. There were a multitude of afflictions and ailments among them, but admitting such could be dangerous. Josef shook his head. "No. No one is sick."

"Good for you. I imagine it will take you a day to walk to Birkow." The officer looked down at Paul's legs, his prosthesis now covered by his pants. "I'm sorry about that."

Never wanting any pity—least of all from his enemy—Paul said nothing.

The lieutenant rose from his seat, placing his hat back on his head. He turned to Josef and extended his hand again. "And what will you do when all of this is over?"

"Return home," said Josef, shaking his hand. "I'm a farmer."

"Where are you from?"

"The Ermland of East Prussia. Our farm is outside of Guttstadt—not far from Allenstein."

The officer took a moment, trying to place the location in his mind. "Ah yes. I know where that is. We were near there. I suppose it's very beautiful there in the summer."

"It's very beautiful." Josef stood a little taller with pride for his homeland. "I hope we can return home soon."

"I hope we all can." The officer stood and stopped in front of the door. "Travel to Birkow next Monday, please. The Polish authorities have taken over, but Russian troops will be here indefinitely. It will be better if we don't have to come for you. Guten Tag."

In September, Josef, Wilhelm, and Paul sat outside the family's assigned house. They passed the days on the benches with other men, whittling scraps of wood and talking of better times. Though the discussions always centered on an idyllic life before the war, certain subjects were discussed with care. Missing sons were spoken of without mentioning their fate. It either ended in death or the unknown.

There was no discussion about their vanished Jewish friends and acquaintances. They knew of the death camps; they knew Jews across Europe had been mass murdered. Guilt and shame stopped them from speaking about the atrocities. And no one ever mentioned their own acts in support of Hitler and his Reich. After all, they, too, were suffering now they thought—as if somehow it was equivalent.

When other refugees passed by the house, they always shared information. There were stories of transports to Russia, rumors of a train to Berlin, and dreams of being told they could go home again. Josef prayed for the miracle that Guttstadt and his farm still stood waiting for him.

They didn't spend much time inside the house, other than to sleep on the floor. The Haupts and Volkmanns shared the cramped building with three other families. The quarters had already been tight, but now they had shrunk further as the typhus epidemic had reached them. Every family had at least one person who was afflicted. Two rooms of the four-room house were quarantined for the sick. Josef thought they were lucky that in his family of seven only Sophia was sick.

For Dorothea, the situation was heartbreaking. During the war, she had lost all but one son, but her daughters had remained with her. Now, her treasured Sophia was gravely ill, lying on straw among strangers. Chilled and burning with a high fever, she vacillated between agitation and listlessness. When she arrived at full consciousness again, she was confused, wondering why she wasn't in her bed and if she had finished her schoolwork. Dorothea risked her own health and nursed her daughter.

Margarete, Katharina, and Martha were directed to find chamomile and mint for tea to calm her and her stomach. Dorothea mashed her own daily potatoes into a weak soup, adding it to Sophia's ration. She wouldn't let the devil take another of her children.

That day, dust rose on the distant road, the first warning that someone was approaching. Josef craned his neck at once to get a better look and announced, "It's a truck."

All the men were surprised to see Polish nurses in their white uniforms step out of the truck driven by Russian soldiers. The flap in the back flipped open, and a man's head peeked out. Even from afar, Josef saw that the man's face and hands were covered in typhus spots.

With no greeting, one of the Polish nurses pointed to the truck and spoke in German, "All typhus cases must be quarantined in Słupsk."

Since the Polish government had assumed the administration of the region, more Poles had moved into the area. After the destruction of their nation by Germany, the Poles were pleased to preside over a German enclave. Some Poles took pity on the pathetic German refugees, but many taunted and harassed them, calling Germans filthy murderers and rapists. Even though he hadn't done the killing and raping himself, the words stung Josef with a truth he tried to ignore.

The Polish government had even begun claiming the region

for itself, changing the German names of towns to Polish ones, which galled the Germans. The signs all around the nearby town Birkow had been changed to Bierkowo.

Though the nurse had spoken in German, she referred to the Polish name for the town six kilometers away.

"Stolp," Paul corrected her.

"Słupsk," retorted the nurse.

Paul gave her a dismissive wave because it was a useless argument when the Germans were out of power and so outnumbered.

"Bring all the typhus patients to the truck," said the nurse, pointing to the vehicle. "They'll receive care in Słupsk."

By this time, the healthier of the other families had stepped outside to hear what was going on. They blanched at the command to hand over their flesh and blood to the Poles. Josef did as well, certain that the Poles and Russians were using the epidemic as a convenient excuse to rid the region of large groups of Germans in one fell swoop.

In a unison of objection, the refugees complained they couldn't leave their families.

"You have no choice," said the nurse with no patience for Germans. "Typhus could kill you all if we leave the sick among the healthy."

"I will not leave my daughter," declared Dorothea's voice from behind.

At first glance, Dorothea looked like a cross between a city bag lady and a peasant. Her tattered clothes were made of fine fabrics that hung from her gaunt frame. Her bespoke shoes were worn and held together by her own mending. Her tidy hair was covered with a worker's kerchief. Though she didn't have typhus, scabby bites covered her skin. Despite her appearance, she stood with a regality that defied her circumstances. Dorothea Haupt was starving and destitute, but she didn't waver in her belief that she was better than most.

She stared down the nurse. "I think you can understand a

mother wants to take care of her child." She added a modicum of civility. "Bitte."

Inured to haughty Prussians, the nurse rolled her eyes. "Fine, but you can't ride in the truck. You'll have to walk to Słupsk."

Dorothea never left Sophia's side as the girl was chased by death. A week later, Sophia succumbed to typhus just days shy of her sixteenth birthday.

Margarete had spent the week walking back and forth the many kilometers, keeping the family informed of Sophia's decline. After Sophia's death, she ran back until a kind Polish couple offered a ride. She hopped out of their wagon and informed Josef in the now common manner used to deliver bad news—short sentences, only the bare the facts. Dwelling on the words seemed to make the terrible events tear at their hearts even more.

Though their German was as limited as Josef's Polish, the Polish couple joined with Josef and the rest of the Haupts in a short prayer for Sophia. They even offered to take the family back to Stolp. It was a welcome invitation given Paul's leg. To spare Katharina and Martha from the epidemic and the difficult burial, Margarete stayed behind with them.

The small wagon swayed with the weight of the passengers, and the poor condition of the road slowed their speed. While Paul sat with his legs extended in the back of the wagon, the friendly Polish couple had invited Josef to sit on the driver's bench with them. They were also new to the area, having relocated from the East.

Josef spoke in a mixture of German and mangled Polish, and after thanking them profusely, he asked, "Is there a priest at the Catholic church?"

"Catholic?" The Polish farmer peered at him with pleasure, surprised that he had some connection to the family he was helping. Pomerania had always been a Protestant stronghold in Germany, so until more Poles moved in, there were few Catholics.

But the Pole's smile left him. "No Catholic church. The Russians burned the old town. Must go to the Protestant church."

For most of his life, it would have mortified Josef for anyone in his family not to have a proper Catholic burial. Now, he accepted it without much thought. Any man of the cloth would do.

The farmer's wife spoke quickly in Polish, and the farmer nodded. She turned to Josef and spread her arms wide, saying, "Box."

Josef stared at her. "A box?" Then it came to him. "Oh. A coffin."

The farmer motioned toward Josef's hands, informing him he would need to make the coffin. "We'll find wood. I give you nails."

"*Dziękuję*," Josef thanked him in Polish.

The wife nodded encouragingly before lifting up her hands again, gesturing something large and holding up ten fingers. She pointed downward with one hand and then lifted one finger before pretending to shovel.

Josef stared in confusion until she made the sign of the cross. Then he understood, and a wave of despair overcame him. The woman was telling him he must make a coffin for his daughter and bury her himself. Otherwise, she would be buried in a mass grave.

Stolp was known for its mass graves because hundreds of the city's German citizens had committed suicide in the spring rather than face the Russians. The townspeople had found cyanide at the nearby death camp and taken matters into their own hands. The Reich's cyanide, which had once been used by Aryans to kill Jews, had then been used by Aryans to kill themselves. There were so many dead that their burials took place *en masse*.

When they arrived at the cemetery, Josef thanked the Polish couple from the bottom of his heart, wishing them the best in life.

While Paul began constructing the coffin, Josef looked for Dorothea. The graveyard was full of people mourning and burying their dead. In the far corner, he spotted his wife.

Dorothea stood guard over their daughter, who lay behind her wrapped in a sheet. Josef wondered how long she had stood there. She looked out before her as if she saw everything and nothing at the same time. He understood the feeling of being alert but numb.

When he came within hearing distance, Dorothea announced, "We must hurry. They keep trying to put her on the truck to the graves. Look at them over there."

Josef turned to the direction she pointed. In the far reach of the cemetery, there was a hive of activity. Gravediggers shoveled dirt, either digging giant holes or filling them in. Beside them were piles of bodies—some shrouded and others not. Taking each corpse by head and feet, two gravediggers swung the body for momentum so it landed in the pit.

Josef made the sign of the cross for the strangers' souls. He glanced down at the covered body of his second daughter. The vital, sweet girl was now another corpse that needed to be disposed of. He drew nearer, wanting to see her face one more time, but Dorothea let out a shrill, "Josef!"

He looked to see Dorothea with her lips pursed with impatience. She had no time for her grief or anyone else's. If they didn't act quickly, her cherished daughter might spend eternity with a collection of unknowns. She pointed back to Paul working on the coffin. "Go on!"

Over the next hour, Josef orchestrated the barest of funerals. He buttonholed a Protestant minister walking through the cemetery, who agreed to say a few words at Sophia's graveside. He took over the building of the coffin from Paul, whom he sent to speak to the gravediggers. Paul was able to convince one of them to help dig a single hole for Sophia.

Dorothea lost all of her reserve as she wailed behind Josef when he brought Sophia to her makeshift coffin. With his wife's sobs a lullaby of agony, he carried Sophia in his arms with the same reverence as when she was newly born. But now there was no joy in her presence or pride in what Sophia might become. He kept his empty eyes ahead as he walked to the open grave, stunned by grief, followed closely by guilt for what he might have done to save his family had he not waited so long to flee. Half of his eight children were now dead.

Chapter Twenty-Seven

JOSEF

"Here she comes," grumbled Paul.

Josef looked up from his whittling to see the now familiar woman exiting the house. Under his breath, he asked, "What will she complain about today?"

Earlier in the month, Polish authorities had moved the refugees out of the house and into the barns. The town's new schoolteacher was not only given the house but also Margarete as her servant. While Margarete performed her duties in earnest, she wasn't prepared for the role.

The prim schoolteacher was always polite and spoke German well. "Guten Tag," she said as she approached the benches where Josef, Wilhelm, and Paul sat.

After the men responded in kind, she said, "Herr Haupt, I have a question for you. Might your wife help Margarete with the cooking? Margarete is very good at cleaning, but her cooking is still poor."

"I'm sorry, Frau Nowak, but my wife is weak. She can't stand for long." It was a convenient excuse for a request that was out of the question regardless of Dorothea's health. Unless her children's lives hung in the balance, Dorothea just might choose death over being a servant for a Pole. The fact that their own daughter was forced into such a role was shameful enough.

Josef smiled at the woman, hoping some charm might placate her. "Margarete's cooking will improve with time. She's still young."

"She seems only able to cook potatoes or make fancy dishes that no one has the rations for." The schoolteacher pushed her glasses up her nose. "After a long day of teaching school, I now must come home and teach Margarete as well. She told me she's seventeen, which seems old to be such a poor cook. Don't they teach girls to cook in East Prussia?"

Despite the slight, he chose not to directly answer the schoolteacher's question. It wouldn't do to tell her his daughter had been raised to be the sort of woman who hired servants, not to be one herself.

"My wife may have some suggestions for Margarete. There may be—"

The sound of multiple hoofbeats halted Josef's speech. His eyes slid to Herr Volkmann and Paul, who both bore looks of mutual concern. Russian soldiers were coming. He turned his attention back to the schoolteacher, who stood with her hands on her hips looking toward the road.

"What do they want now?" she spat. Disdain for the Russians was a bond she shared with the German refugees.

Two Russian officers came to an abrupt stop, causing the horses to whinny. After a nod to the Polish woman, the officers scanned the three men. Emaciated, Paul looked even more the wounded veteran. The Russians had given up on beating him because he looked like he might die on his own soon enough. With their gray beards, Josef and Wilhelm appeared a decade older than their years and just a touch of flu away from death.

The higher-ranking officer spoke to them in a brisk German. "All displaced Germans are to meet at the train station in Słupsk at ten in the morning. You may only bring eighteen kilos a person."

Josef felt a jolt to his heart at the mention of a train, sending his mind and nerves reeling. He stared down the officer and asked, "Where are we going?"

"I don't know."

"They can't leave," huffed the teacher as she pointed to Josef. "His daughter is my servant."

"Then you'll have to adjust," the officer replied in Polish with an insincere smile. "I doubt you had a servant before you came here."

The officer snapped his reins, and as their horses turned to leave, he called over his shoulder. "Tomorrow. Słupsk. Ten o'clock. There will be no exceptions."

As the Russians galloped away, the teacher looked at the three men. She understood the potential death sentence that had befallen them. Her own countrymen had been sent to the gulags never to be heard from again. With true sympathy, she said, "I'm very sorry."

When she left, Josef turned to Paul and Wilhelm. They had spoken of this day in the past, though not lately. Since Sophia's death and the decline of everyone's health, they had doubted the Russians would bother to send them anywhere.

Josef noticed Paul and Wilhelm appeared to be in the middle of a silent conversation, their eyebrows raised as they nodded to each other.

Wilhelm met Josef's questioning gaze and announced, "We can't travel as a group this time. You'll move more slowly because of the young ones. I must think of my own family. We can leave at the same time tonight, but we must go in different directions."

Josef leaned in closer to the man. "You can't mean you want to flee. You'll be caught."

"We may," conceded Wilhelm. "But we will be no worse off,

and if we're not caught, we'll be in a better place. There are enough Poles who dislike the Russians. We'll find some who will help us."

"But we don't even know where they're sending us." Josef threw his hands in the air. "They could be sending us back to East Prussia. We might be living under the Russians, but we'll be on our own land. We'll be home."

"They're not sending us home," said Paul, his voice soft. "I can promise you that."

"No, you can't," retorted Josef. "You can't promise that any more than you can promise we'll be sent to Siberia. Look at us. We're not workers."

"We're in poor shape, and we have no idea what's going on. But that will be the case as long as we're under the Russians," said Wilhelm. "I can't just wait here until we all die. I'm sorry, but this is where our families will part. I'm leaving with Olga and Angela after the moon rises tonight. I'll travel west by southwest toward Berlin. The Americans or the British are more likely to help us return home."

Josef stared at his cousin—once a distant poorer relation whom he'd had little contact with over the last sixty years of his life. In the last nine months, they had bonded like brothers. They shared in each other's distress, treated each other's wife with the utmost respect, and cared for each other's children as their own. Yet, each was his own man. Josef wouldn't dissuade Wilhelm. The man had made a choice that he might have taken as well if his circumstances had been different.

"I understand. I wish you Godspeed."

"Danke," said Wilhelm, extending his hand. "And I wish the same for you. I pray we meet once again in our *Heimat*."

Josef silently shook his hand, sharing in the prayer of seeing their Heimat—their homeland—once again. Surely, they had suffered enough by now and a return was imminent. God would answer their prayers.

As Wilhelm left to speak to his family, Paul let out a loud

exhale. "I'm not getting on a Russian train. I'll leave an hour after the Volkmanns. If I steal that mule from the old man down the road, I'll be able to keep up with them."

Josef whipped around to look his son in the eye. "The family will stay together and obey the authorities. We'll meet the train tomorrow morning."

"Nein!" Paul slammed his hand on the bench. "They'll kill me and put the rest of you in some sort of camp."

"Why would they imprison us when we're so weak?"

"Why not? They want every German dead." Paul's eyes bulged with rage. "Why did the Reich send every Jew no matter their age or health to the concentration camps?"

Josef glared at his son in fury, refusing to answer. Paul was only thinking of himself, not his mother and sisters. Josef couldn't believe his last son would turn his back on his family.

"Look how sick your sisters are. They can't run away. We must follow the orders." Josef narrowed his eyes in warning. "I don't want to hear another word about you leaving us. Your mother has already lost four of her children."

Paul's stare hardened, and Josef waited for an explosion of anger, but it never came. Paul broke his gaze and looked at the ground.

"All right. Never mind."

By half past nine the next morning, the roads and paths were full of German refugees descending upon Stolp. Some Poles taunted them; others stared with pity at the sorry collection of humanity. A kind Polish farmer let Dorothea, the girls, and their one battered suitcase ride in his hay cart, but he made Josef and Paul continue to walk. The farmer's sympathy stopped at German men.

Not far from Stolp, Paul's stride became shorter and slower. He grabbed Josef's arm, trying to steady himself. "I need to rest."

Josef glanced down at his son's missing leg. Paul had to fight for his balance every step of the several kilometers. The Polish farmer's voice called back from his wagon, saying he would continue on and the men could catch up with him.

"Let's sit here," said Josef, motioning to a patch of grass by the road.

"Nein." Paul's eyes were on the rolling wagon. "Go with Mutti and the girls. I'll meet you in Stolp."

"I don't think that's wise." Josef looked at the farmer's wagon as well. "We need to stay together. I'll get the women off the wagon."

"Even I walk faster than Martha and Katharina. They're lucky to be in the wagon. Let them stay there, or you won't make it to Stolp today. I need a few breaks. I'll be in Stolp just a half hour or so after you."

Josef assessed his son with a long glance. Paul leaned on his cane with his coat draped over his arm. Despite the amputation and months of hunger, he was still a strong man. After silently saying a quick prayer of safety for his son, Josef said, "Hurry."

In an unusual public display, Paul briefly touched his father's hand in assurance before he hobbled to the roadside. Josef watched him ease his body onto the ground, and seeing him safely settled, Josef turned to the road ahead and hurried toward the rest of his family.

When the family arrived in Stolp, Josef's chest was tight with anxiety as they moved with the herd of other refugees toward the rail station. Their destination was unknown, but he would have some idea the moment he saw the trains. Were they pointed east or west? He told himself that east wasn't necessarily a bad thing. Maybe the eastbound trains would drop refugees at their hometowns on the way back to Russia. If they were headed west, then the family would avoid Siberia but would have to wait longer to get back home.

Arriving at the railway, the trains were lined up on both tracks. Cattle cars appeared to be headed east, while coal wagons were going west. The family's future was still undecided.

In the middle of a street surrounded by rubble, the Russians collected and assessed the German refugees. Junior officers made snap judgments based on appearances and identity papers. Josef noticed they kept some families together but not all. Stronger-looking men and boys were parted from their families. Single, healthy women were also set aside. Any objections were met with the wave of a gun. The Russians seemed to process the very young and old with little regard, quickly moving them along. Life and death decisions were made, yet the soldiers seemed bored. Managing displaced persons was as interesting as factory work.

Dorothea clutched her three frightened daughters as if there was a fierce winter storm raging around the family. Like so many times since they had left Guttstadt, Dorothea's terror of what might come next was overshadowed by her determination to protect her children. Her girls were with her, but where was their only son? She eyed Josef, and he understood her direction. Find Paul.

Though age and starvation had diminished Josef's height, he still stood above most of those around him. He scanned the top of the crowds flowing into the holding area looking for his tall son, but Paul never appeared. He should have already arrived.

The girls stared up at him, fully aware he was searching for Paul. Josef tried to quell their angst with a smile.

"Paul will be here soon, and we'll be together. He'll know to tell the soldiers his family arrived earlier. They'll send him to us."

He wanted to believe it himself, but as the time wore on, he realized he might be wrong. Those would be the actions of a dutiful son—of Franz, Stefan, or Albert. They would never leave their family. They wouldn't care if they had to supplicate before a hated enemy to be reunited with their parents and sisters.

Yet Paul had never been a dutiful son and had argued with Josef his whole life. Since his time in the Wehrmacht, he had only become more self-centered. If Paul believed leaving the family would keep him alive, he could very well flee.

No, Josef told himself. Even Paul wouldn't abandon his family at its most dire hour. Paul may have been at odds with Josef and thought Dorothea mad, but he adored his little sisters. He had always put their protection first.

And Josef reminded himself that even if Paul had wanted to leave the family, he never would take his mother's ring and the family's other valuables with him. Outwardly, the Haupts appeared like the other refugees, carrying nothing but the clothes on their backs, family photos, and maybe a dirty blanket or broken toy. Unknown to everyone, the Haupts also carried a valuable insurance policy. Dorothea had offered to sell her diamond ring as soon as it was necessary.

A fine piece of jewelry could pay for a wagon and horses, some livestock, and seed. They could even hire farmhands to start a new harvest. If the family could reach a city with Americans or British soldiers—people who had money—the Haupts could return home and restart their lives.

Josef set the thought aside as he heard the request for their identity papers. He handed the cards to a young soldier, who gave a cursory glance to the papers and the family. With a dismissive wave, he pointed toward the large group of families.

Josef's sigh of relief abruptly stopped when the soldier touched Margarete's shoulder. Like her mother and sisters, her head had been bowed, not wanting to draw any attention. The soldier barked something in Russian, and Margarete raised her head, barely meeting his eye. Giving her a long once over, the soldier no longer looked bored.

Josef feared the Russian's intentions, and likewise Dorothea grabbed her daughter even closer, giving the soldier a murderous glare. The soldier's expression softened with a hint of a regretful smile. He appeared to recognize something in Margarete that had reminded him of a sister or a sweetheart. He dropped his hand and motioned them to move on.

Other families weren't so lucky, and they called in agony to their separated loved ones. The sounds of revving train engines added to the cacophony. Meanwhile, the organized groups made their way in their opposite directions.

They couldn't see what was happening to those heading east, but when they saw the trains west, murmurs spread across the crowd. Dorothea was the first to comment on a sight that no one could believe. The refugees were climbing the railcars and sitting atop the mountains of coal like street urchins.

"Nein..." she said.

Josef placed his hand on her shoulder. "We don't know what this means."

In minutes, they found themselves climbing onto the soot-covered railcars, helping their youngest girls heave their bodies up the ladder and onto the coals. Dorothea ignored the coal dust covering her and her children. Instead, she used the high vantage point to survey the crowds, desperately looking for her last remaining son. Josef did the same.

Soothing himself as well his family, he declared, "Paul will follow us. Don't worry."

Four hours later, with no food, water, or opportunity to relieve themselves, they arrived in another obliterated town—the largest one they had seen since Danzig. Signs that once identified it by its German name of Stettin now were covered with its new Polish name—Szczecin.

The refugees now looked like a herd of chimney sweeps as they followed orders toward a half-bombed hotel. The building had no electricity or nearly enough rooms for all the people, but the indoor plumbing was much appreciated. The soldiers told them there would be soup soon.

After they had used the facilities and washed up, Josef and Margarete searched for Paul or any news of him. Neither was found.

Margarete's shoulders slumped; her forehead furrowed with worry. Josef saw not only her sadness but also the increasing responsibility he and Dorothea had placed on their seventeen-year-old daughter.

"Should I tell Mutti?"

"Nein." Josef looked down the dark hallway and noticed a new soldier speaking to their guards, his medals and insignia signaling a higher rank. "I'll continue to inquire."

With his hat in hand, Josef approached the group of soldiers. He knew he was just as likely to be shooed away as received. The soldiers ignored him as he neared, so he spoke in a strong but polite voice, using the little Russian he knew.

"Good evening," he said.

The soldiers opened their small circle of conversation to see Josef. From their insignia, he saw there were two enlisted men and two officers. He guessed the rank of the most decorated and bowed his head a bit. "Major."

The major cast a glance of judgment over Josef. Deciding he was worthy of conversation, the major spoke in perfect German, "Guten Abend. What do you need?"

"I can't find my son, Paul Haupt. Maybe you have seen him. He's very tall with one leg." Josef gripped his hat and hoped for some sympathy as he added, "My wife and I are worried."

Looking at the three other soldiers for an answer, they all shook their heads. The major turned back to Josef and grimly said, "I'm sorry."

Josef felt a stab of pain strike at his heart, worse than a bayonet. The major hadn't apologized because he couldn't be of help; he had extended sympathy for a son who most likely wouldn't be seen again.

"Danke." He closed his eyes and acknowledged the officer's

humanity before he tried to find some hope. "Will there be more trains here from Stolp? Would he be placed on one?"

"I don't know if there will be more trains, but I doubt a straggler German veteran would be sent here."

Josef nodded in silence while a keening grief overtook his very soul. Paul—his infuriating yet adored firstborn—had rejected him for a foolhardy quest for freedom that would result in his death. Josef would have to tell Dorothea that Margarete, Katharina, and Martha were their only children now.

The officer's brutal honesty was painful to endure, but Josef realized he might now have an opportunity. He cleared his throat. "Pardon, but might you tell me when we will be sent home? I'm from Guttstadt in East Prussia."

The major raised an eyebrow. "You don't know?"

"Know what?"

"You won't be going back. There was a treaty of the victors. Germany has new borders. East Prussia no longer exists. It's been divided between the USSR and Poland." The officer watched as Josef's face fell, but continued, "Guttstadt is near Allenstein if I remember correctly?"

"Yes, but what do you mean we won't be going back?" asked Josef, his voice a rapid panic.

"That area belongs to Poland. Guttstadt is now Dobre Miasto." The major gestured down the hall. "All ethnic Germans are being expelled from the region. This is why you're here."

The officer had spoken German, but Josef couldn't grasp what was being said. "But... but... East Prussia has always been Germany, and I own that farm."

"Not anymore."

A tremor took over Josef as he began to understand the hand fate had dealt him. He couldn't react in words, and the major continued, "You'll be sent to Rügen tomorrow."

"Rügen? The island?" whispered Josef.

"I doubt that will be your final location, but you'll stay the winter there."

Unable to take in any more information, Josef turned. He almost forgot his manners before turning back and meeting the major's gaze. "Danke."

The major nodded with no expression. In a final show of sympathy, he said, "This must be difficult, but you should tell your wife that you're lucky. It could be worse."

Josef nodded and slowly walked down the hallway, barely advancing with each step. All four soldiers passed him without another word. German voices came from each doorway in confused and tearful conversations.

He focused on the officer's last words. *It could be worse.*

The officer was right. The remaining members of his family had escaped death multiple times. They weren't in Siberia. They were together and headed west. There was hope for them.

But there was no hope for him. Josef stopped and leaned against the wall, looking for any support that life might still give him. Even the wall wasn't enough. Like a marionette dropped by his puppeteer, he collapsed.

Despite being in public, tears overwhelmed him, and he cried sitting on the battered linoleum floor. Without East Prussia, Guttstadt, and his farm, he had no homeland, no identity, no livelihood. He would be a different person now in a different world—a person he didn't want to be in a world where he didn't want to live.

CHAPTER TWENTY-EIGHT

ALBERT

With the temperature dropping that evening, Albert rubbed his arms trying to create some friction for warmth. Freezing weather began early in the Urals, and he was wearing only the summer uniform of his capture the year before. Many of the men had lost their Wehrmacht boots long ago and either wore makeshift shoes or tortured their bare feet into human leather. After months without shoes, Albert's blackened bare feet could withstand most discomfort, but that night the icy ground burned through his soles, radiating cold throughout his body.

On a cold night in the camp's yard, a *proverka*—the nightly head count—seemed endless. He peered over the men lined in front of him, wondering why this proverka was taking so long. Albert usually didn't mind a head count because it broke up the monotony, though he did think it was inefficient.

He thought it would be simpler to subtract the number of

men who died each day from the last day's count. There was never a day without at least one death because the Soviets saw little reason to keep the enemy alive—even if the war was over. And escapees weren't really a problem so deep in Russia; if anyone did try to escape, they were always caught and killed. His friend Hugo was too smart to try, but he still died from a beating for insolence.

A lumber yard and plywood factory, Camp Number Two held one thousand men in two barracks with a small number of guards and fences. This was Albert's third camp, and the food was always the same—two cups of watery soup three times a day and up to three slices of bread, depending on whether the camp had flour.

As he shivered, Albert watched a set of guards enter the yard carrying giant bundles. Thank God, he thought. With the weather turning into the long winter, the guards handed out life-saving clothes—a sheepskin coat and hat and *valenki*, boiled wool that had been shaped and hardened into a boot.

As Albert stood quietly with the other ninety-nine men in his work brigade, the only sounds were the stilted conversations between the guards and prisoners receiving their clothing. When loud voices rose from outside the compound, everyone turned to the entrance. Using their guns, two guards herded in five new Germans, shouting to urge them along. They were new inmates to Camp Two, but not newly in custody. They were as dirty and scrawny as Albert's brigade. Though the epaulets designating rank had been removed from their uniforms, Albert guessed by their demeanor that two of the men were officers. Three hobbled with feeble movements, and he assumed their fate would follow that of so many prisoners he had known. They would survive the journey to the next camp only to die soon after their arrival.

After Albert received his winterwear from the guards, he stepped aside to put them on. Placing his foot in a Valenki, he moved slowly so he could watch the fates of the new inmates. The three weakest weren't given outerwear—just a shove toward the barracks.

The guards thrust bundles of clothes into the hands of the two remaining prisoners. One prisoner, who had a bit more weight on him, thanked the guards in Russian. He continued to speak to the guards, but Albert didn't know enough Russian to understand the conversation. The other prisoner gave the guard an insolent look and walked toward Albert with his gear.

Albert slowed his movements, wanting to speak to the newcomer. There was no welcoming of someone to a labor camp —only an empathetic greeting. Tall, but gaunt with sunken blue eyes, Albert guessed that at his full strength, he would be as imposing as Paul. The man gave Albert a blank glance, not seeming to trust even his own countryman. In a whisper, Albert said, "Albert Haupt, Lieutenant."

The man nodded as he donned his new coat until he halted and winced from unseen injuries. Feathered wrinkles remained on the man's face as it stayed in a painful scowl while he finished putting on the coat. When the pain appeared to subside, he replied, "Major Andreas von Lehmann."

Hearing he was in the presence of a major, Albert felt the urge to hop to attention and salute, but that could be deadly. Instead, he gave a reverential nod to the new commanding officer and German blueblood.

Major von Lehmann acknowledged the silent salute before he fixed his attention on the other new prisoner who was chatty with the guards.

Albert caught the major's eye and murmured, "Who is he?"

A slight huff escaped the major's throat. "Lieutenant Fritz Zimmerman, faithful member of the *Nationalkomitee Freies Deutschland*."

Albert leaned forward to get a better look at the man he now considered a backstabbing traitor. During the war, the Soviets had created the National Committee for a Free Germany to defeat Germany and indoctrinate Germans into communism. The German POWs who joined in the camps cared only about their own hide.

While Albert stared at Lieutenant Zimmerman, the major asked, "Are there any Communists among you?"

"A few. There's more food for them." Albert didn't want to elaborate until he knew more about the major. He baldly asked, "Are you?"

Major von Lehman lowered his eyes in offense. "No. Communists aren't sentenced to twenty-five years hard labor."

Albert frowned and remained quiet. Saying "I'm sorry" didn't convey his depth of feeling for someone likely destined to spend the rest of his life in a gulag.

While Albert searched for a response, the guards ordered the brigade to the barracks for the night. As the men filed in, Albert felt a touch to his shoulder. He turned his head to acknowledge the tap and heard the major's voice say, "Does this place have drinking water?"

Albert shook his head. "The only water is in the soup, three times day."

"Unbelievable," growled the major from behind. "There's no drinking water in a single damn prison in this country."

The next day, Albert went through the same motions as he had for months, but his attention followed the two new inmates. At breakfast, he watched as the guards handed Lieutenant Zimmerman a wooden spoon with his bowl of soup, while Major von Lehman received only soup. The major appeared nonplused at being denied a spoon. Albert saw him ask another inmate about the spoons. When the major rolled his eyes, Albert knew he had learned there was only one way to get a spoon besides being a Communist. You had to carve one yourself. Sipping soup from his own handmade spoon, Albert snickered thinking of how Major von Lehman would react when he learned he had to carve the handles on his axes and saws as well.

Another POW camp logged the forests higher in the mountains, and the timber floated down the river to Camp Two. Like Egyptian slaves, Albert's brigade hauled the giant logs from the river and sawed them into thirds. An inmate would begin rolling a log using a metal rod, and every ten meters a new inmate would take over the rolling until it reached the sawmill. The eight-hour work shifts ran almost continuously regardless of weather. The long winter nights were the worst with only one electric bulb to light the way.

After lunch, Albert moved from rolling logs to hauling them out of the water. It was the least desirable job, but everyone took their turn. When he went to fish the first log with the metal rod, Major von Lehman followed to be his partner.

After they had developed a rhythm to their work, the major pointed to the factory. "I presume factory work is better."

"It's inside, so you're protected from the elements, but there's no heater, so it only runs in the warmer months," Albert replied as they dragged the log together. "You do eat more."

"Even if you're not a Communist? The food amounts are set by law. Every camp is the same."

A sardonic half-smile formed on Albert's lips. "When it's not freezing, you can eat the glue they use for cabinetmaking."

"You're joking."

"The glue's base is a milk powder. You add baking soda and water to make the glue, but because the glue freezes, they don't build cabinets in the winter, so then there's nothing to eat."

"So men are eating glue, and rather than heating the factory to continue to make cabinets in the winter, the Soviets stop production entirely?" The major snorted. "Bolsheviks."

"I don't understand either."

"I hate them," declared Major von Lehman with his eyes on a guard smoking a cigarette. "But Stalin treats the Russian people only a little better than us."

"At my last prison, I was sent to help on a Bolshevik farm. I even looked forward to being back on a farm until I saw the

Russian farmworkers were starving. I felt sorry for them. I grew up on a farm, and our workers never starved."

"Where are you from in East Prussia?"

"You noticed my accent?" Albert tried to pick out an accent from the major's speech. "You don't sound like you're East Prussian."

"I'm not. I'm from Hamburg, but after years in the officer corps, I know an East Prussian accent. I also was captured near Bartenstein."

"You were?" Albert's heart jumped, and he put down his side of the log at once. "I'm from Guttstadt to the south, near Allenstein. Can you tell me anything?"

The major's expression softened with sympathy, and he also set down his side of the log. "Only that there was heavy fighting in the area. Most East Prussian civilians had fled west. What about your family?"

The excitement in Albert plummeted to the familiar feeling of helpless despair at the thought of his family as refugees. He had seen civilians fleeing for their lives in Latvia, and envisioning his own family in such distress felt almost like physical pain. It took a moment to find the words to answer.

"I don't know. I have no idea what's become of them."

"I'm sorry," said the major with heartfelt eyes. "From what I saw, the trek out of East Prussia was awful that winter. Even if they made it eastward, they still would be living under Russian occupation. Many have been sent to Russia to rebuild what the Wehrmacht destroyed."

"My father is strong and capable, and we have means, but I can't see my family moving quickly in those conditions. My brother is back home, but he lost his leg at the front. I have four younger sisters," said Albert, his voice lowering in sadness. "I hate to think of anything happening to them."

"I understand." Major von Lehman placed his hands on his hips and looked upstream. "I had been telling my wife for months to move out of Hamburg, but she was pregnant and her mother was in the hospital. They died in the bombing."

"I'm so sorry."

"My family is gone, and Hamburg is flattened, but it's still Germany." The major's voice was flat, as he met Albert's eye. "East Prussia is gone, but your family might be alive."

"What do you mean East Prussia is gone?"

"Ah...you may not have heard. A higher-up guard at my last camp told me. America and the rest of Europe never want Germany to rise again, and Stalin finally has a Baltic port. They've divided East Prussia between the Soviets and Poland. Königsberg is Kaliningrad now." The major spit in the river, displaying his spite. "It's appalling."

"Kaliningrad?" Albert leaned toward him in disbelief that Königsberg—the city as grand and as German as Berlin—was now Russian. His mind continued to reel. "Is Guttstadt in Poland or Russia now?"

"I'm not sure of the border. It doesn't matter. All the ethnic Germans who didn't flee have been expelled." The major sneered as looked around him. "Many to gulags probably like this."

Albert's voice was almost a childish wail. "Where will I go? How will I find my family once I'm released?"

A gunshot blasted behind them, and they turned to see the Russian guard with his rifle in the air. He screeched in Russian. "Stop talking! Get moving!"

Albert expected silence as they again hauled a log, but Major von Lehman spoke in a quiet, pedantic voice while they worked.

"During the war, the Reich separated Russians from the British and Americans in our POW camps. We allowed Red Cross packages for the Yanks and the Tommies. We starved Ivan and worked him to death." He looked Albert squarely in the eye. "Lieutenant, you seem intelligent. Do the Russians appear to have any interest in releasing us after what we've done to them?"

Albert couldn't bring himself to answer the rhetorical questions, so the major did. "We most likely will die here."

CHAPTER TWENTY-NINE

MARGARETE

Every morning was the same as Margarete waited for the daily soup. The Russian guards, the Germans, the quiet conversations—even the thin soup and slice of bread were all unchanged. Only the weather varied in its degrees of cold. That morning the icy wind thankfully howled at such a high pitch that it drowned out the murmuring around her. She didn't want to chat about Christmases past or joke about the feast the Russians had prepared that day. Crammed onto a former Luftwaffe airbase with hundreds of other refugees, she couldn't find any humor in the current day. Time was at a standstill. From such desperation, she couldn't imagine the future, and memories of home, just like those of her brothers, were too crushing to bear.

The news that East Prussia was no more had devastated her family and the other refugees. It boggled the mind that their own farm was no longer theirs and their entire homeland was gone— land where generations of their family had fulfilled their lives and rested in their graves. Life as they had known it was over, and no one seemed to take it harder than her father. He was still loving and reassuring to his wife and daughters, but his bright eyes for the rest of the world seemed to have permanently dimmed. He spent his days absorbed reading prayers in a missal he'd found stashed high on a shelf—likely left by a Luftwaffe pilot who never returned from his last mission.

Margarete fingered the stack of chipped cups, wondering about their past lives. Did a farm wife save her pennies for them? Or were they a gift from an annoying mother-in-law? The porcelain was cold as she studied the cracks and divots, but each cup would soon be warm with soup for her family. The watery broth with a tidbit of fat and vegetable for nutrition managed to keep her a few steps ahead of death. Yet the rest of her family had begun to fall behind. Her parents and sisters struggled to sit up to eat their ration, and her father often just passed his portion on to his wife and children. In a single year, Josef had shrunk from an imposing man of vigor and strength to a feeble skeleton. He was by far the worst off.

After breakfast, Margarete would join the rest of the healthy hauling seawater to the barracks. Over an open fire in the middle of the camp, they boiled the salt from the water to make it drinkable. Before the day turned to night, she would climb atop the burned-out carcasses of the once mighty Luftwaffe aircraft. The plastic from the planes provided fuel for a smoky, stinky fire that only added to the chest ailments of the sick, but the fires did provide light. Later, when the camp had gone quiet, she would sneak out to scavenge the kitchen garbage piles for potato peels or anything that might provide a little more food for her family. The morning started the cycle over again.

As usual that day, a group of Russian soldiers stood off to the side, smoking cigarettes and laughing. Not wanting to draw attention to herself, Margarete dared not raise her head. She kept her eyes on her cups, willing herself back into the safety of the barrack.

Movement ahead caused her to lift her gaze for a moment. A Russian officer walked down the soup line assessing each person. Margarete watched as he tapped a girl on the shoulder and spoke to her. He moved on without replying, an apparent rejection because the next girl was pulled aside after she spoke. When she saw he was creating a small group of teenage girls, she jerked her head down. She needed to get out of there quickly, but if she didn't stay, her whole family would lose their day's ration.

Just as she stepped to flee, the officer's boots appeared and his voice rose. "Fräulein."

She glanced up and murmured, "Guten Tag."

"Can you read and write?" he asked with a near perfect accent of someone who had learned German as their second language in Königsberg.

Margarete nodded, feeling some hope at the odd question and his accent.

"In English?"

"Yes."

"Excellent," the officer said without a smile. "Come with me. I have a job for you."

While his manner wasn't lascivious, Margarete froze at his request. Nothing was more dangerous than being alone with a Russian soldier.

"But the soup." She held out her cups as an excuse.

"If you succeed, I'll give you something better than soup."

"But I must bring my family their share."

"I'll tell the guards to save some for them. Follow me to the front."

Margarete joined the group of girls as he led them beyond the soup lines and toward a large building with broken windows that she had never seen anyone enter. She looked to the other girls with their fearful glances or blank expressions—as if their heart and soul had already made a full retreat. When the soldiers rounded up young women, there was no doubt what was next.

Wearing a wooden clog she had found in a ditch on one foot

and a cardboard improvised shoe on the other, Margarete avoided the glass shards around the building's steps by hopping as if she were crossing rocks in a stream. Once inside, the wind's howl dulled, and the place was otherwise silent. She had expected there to be other soldiers waiting for them, but there were none, and rather than going into the first empty room, the officer started up the stairs, motioning for the girls to follow.

Up three flights the girls trudged, trying to keep up with the officer, who had far more strength than them. On the third floor, he entered an office suite, and Margarete spied the title *General der Luftwaffe* on the door's obscured glass. As the officer led them through the anterooms and into the colonel's spacious quarters, they stepped over papers strewn everywhere. Documents spilled out of file cabinets and covered desks. Papers beneath the windows were wrinkled from rain and snow. Deep in her memory, she remembered a year before her father remarking to Paul that the Reichsnährstand had ordered the destruction of all its documents. The Reich had ordered it nationwide, yet this Luftwaffe office appeared not to have complied.

The officer gestured around the office. "I need you to organize these papers. Translate the English ones. Set aside all papers in Russian."

Margarete blinked in astonishment. Since she had fled Königsberg a year and half ago, no one had asked her to use her intellect, let alone her rudimentary English. In unison the girls nodded, accepting the task in relief.

The officer continued, "I'll be downstairs. Bring your work there when you're done."

Two hours later, Margarete and the other girls brought stacks of Russian and translated English papers to the officer. He sat in a far corner near a tiled oven for warmth, his eyes trained on the workings of the camp below him.

"Ah, you're finished." He stood to meet the girls and extended his hand. "Please let me see."

Margarete handed over a stack of English translations. There were many words that the collective knowledge of the girls couldn't understand. They had made notations of words they were sure were important but they didn't know.

As the officer examined the documents, a close-lipped smile crossed his face. When he raised his head, he looked at them with warm eyes, appreciating them as people. "Well done, Fräuleins. You all are very accomplished." His smile became contrite as he added, "Too accomplished for such a place as this."

He pulled loaves of bread from a desk drawer. Looking down at the bread, he shook his head. "This hardly seems a fair trade for the work you've done, but it's all I have."

Margarete and the rest of the girls stared at the bread loaves on the empty desk. Unlike their daily bit of bread, this smelled fresh. To their eyes and stomachs, it was a Christmas goose with all the trimmings.

With his combat knife, he sliced the loaf into hearty pieces and passed two pieces to each girl, muttering additional thanks. As he handed out the final piece, he looked around the group of young women each with raggedy clothes hanging off their rail-thin frames. His hardened demeanor returned.

"Eat the bread here. Don't take it back to your family. I don't know what lies ahead for you, but I wish you the best of luck."

When Margarete returned to her family with their cups of soup, she told her parents about the officer and the bread.

"Naturally, this was something you would be chosen for," said Dorothea before she wrinkled her nose. "Most of the families here are peasants or laborers. You have good breeding."

Josef fought for his words through difficult breathing. "Remember character and education are the most important things in life. They can never be taken away."

As the weeks went by and her family's health deteriorated more rapidly than hers, Margarete often looked back on the fresh bread.

She always had been the sturdiest of the sisters, but she had to believe that that extra bit of nutrition had staved off her decline. One morning as she gathered the cups to retrieve the family's daily meal, a soldier came into the crowded barracks, ordering everyone regardless of their physical ability to come into the yard. This was new. Usually, the sick remained inside rather than lining up to be counted.

The sound of coughing, congestion, and wondering conversations filled the air as the Haupts hobbled into the yard with hundreds of other weak and battered souls. Once they reached the center of the yard, the unhealthy collapsed on the ground in exhaustion. Nurses were already attending people who had fallen, while another set of nurses walked through the crowd assessing people. A Russian soldier's voice called to the crowd, "You're being relocated from this camp. Those who are too sick will be taken to the hospital."

Fear gripped the masses, as they suspected the soldier's words to be the worst of lies. No doubt, the sick would be left to die in the barracks, and the healthy would be sent east to Russia.

The soldier looked around at the shocked crowd as they gripped one another tighter. Realizing that no one believed him, he lifted his hands to calm the crowd. "You will be placed in houses. If your family is taken to the hospital, you may visit them."

Margarete looked to her family, sitting on the ground at her feet. Dorothea clung to Katharina and Martha, while a withered Josef sat alert. Despite his weakness, he still carried himself as the leader of the family.

He met Margarete's pleading gaze as she searched for guidance. "I think it will be all right," he said as he raised the collar of his coat to shield himself from the chill. "Those nurses are German."

Raising her head, Margarete looked more closely at the nurses. Indeed, they all spoke a native German, showing kindness to the refugees. Her intent examination caught the eye of one of the nurses, who started toward the Haupts. She appeared to be Dorothea's age, with the quick gait of someone with no time for niceties or nonsense.

"Guten Tag. My name is Luzia Gerlind," she said, nodding to Josef and Dorothea.

Though Josef introduced his family, the nurse directed her question to Dorothea. "May I assess your children?"

Dorothea nodded, having accepted the woman as one whom she could respect.

The nurse first turned to Margarete and declared, "You seem to be doing better than the rest of your family."

She nodded as the nurse stepped in front of Margarete, shielding the conversation from the rest of the family. "You've probably been through many troubles. Do you have any problems I can't see?"

Margarete was caught off guard by the simple but loaded question. The nurse was asking if she had been hurt when she was raped. Her expression was filled with sympathy, though it could have been empathy. Just because the nurse was in a position of authority and as old as her mother didn't mean that she wasn't prey.

Though Margarete had often bled after a rape, she had healed. Thankfully, she had never found herself pregnant like some. Those women were the saddest sight. Rather than joyful as they carried new life, they hung their heads in shame as if the baby they carried was a penance.

Margarete whispered, "I'm all right now."

"When was your last menstruation?"

"Last summer? Maybe spring?" Margarete exhaled an anxious breath and revealed, "When my period stopped, I thought I might be pregnant, but then nothing else changed. My mother said it was a blessing from God. Is something wrong with me?"

"Most likely not. You're not healthy enough to become pregnant, and your mother is right. Given your situation, it's a blessing."

The nurse pointed to an open wound on Margarete's neck. "You have scabies, though. I can see it's a mild case."

"My sisters and mother have them as well."

"I saw," answered the nurse grimly. "Their cases aren't mild."

After a quick examination of each family member, the nurse placed her hands on her hips and announced, "Herr Haupt, your heart is weak, and I fear you may have pneumonia. You must see a doctor." She turned to Dorothea. "You and your daughters all have scabies, but your youngest has the worst case. She should go to the hospital with Herr Haupt."

Josef spoke with a polite firmness. "My family must stay together. If we're all sick, we should all go to the hospital."

"We only have enough beds for the very sick."

Margarete watched as her father weighed the situation. Since they had left Guttstadt, the family had lost another daughter and the last remaining son. If he went with Martha, the family would be split further.

The nurse also saw Josef's indecision, and her voice softened, "You must see a doctor, Herr Haupt, as must your youngest. I promise it's a good hospital in Garz where you both will be treated well by German doctors."

Dorothea reached out and touched her husband's coat. "Please go with Frau Gerlind. You can watch over Martha."

As Josef remained quiet in thought, Margarete asked hopefully, "And may I visit them?"

"I suppose," said the nurse. "I believe you're being relocated to farms near Karnitz. It's ten kilometers away."

"That's so far," mumbled Margarete, trying to imagine such a trek. Even in the best of health, a twenty-kilometer round trip was a journey for her.

"You'll have more space, a private room for your family," the nurse continued. She looked around the courtyard of collapsed people. "It will be better than here."

When it was time for Josef and Martha to board the truck for the hospital, her parents appeared to have a conversation that went beyond the few words they exchanged. Their eyes held to each other so intensely that Margarete felt like an intruder. She couldn't know what was said, but she understood the significance of the moment. The family was dividing once again.

Over the course of the war and its aftermath, their family had been torn apart, but her parents had remained together like a nucleus of a smashed atom. Now, the war was taking husband from wife as well. Her frail father reached down and clasped her mother's skeletal hand. He gave Dorothea a reassuring smile—the same that Margarete had seen on his face her whole life whenever someone in the family was discouraged.

Yet, from the start of the war, when someone left the family, most likely they didn't return. Staring into her husband's eyes, Dorothea appeared to recognize her future. She had already lost five of her children, and now her husband and youngest were being taken away as well. Her expression became more distant. The thought of losing her husband seemed to make part of her own consciousness disappear.

Dorothea nodded and strained to return her husband's smile. This wasn't the arrogant, fearless gentlewoman and mother of eight, secure in her belief that she outranked almost everyone by both birth and merit. Instead, Dorothea was small and uncertain, daunted at the prospect of life without her husband.

Realizing she had seen too much, Margarete looked away and saw other families struggle through similar scenes. Those families faced their plights with more tears and drama than would ever befit a Haupt. When she turned again to her family, her father and mother continued silently communicating as they held hands.

Josef eventually said, "Martha and I will return healthy and sound."

"Of course," murmured Dorothea.

Of course, thought Margarete in silent agreement. She hadn't considered her father's declaration because questioning it was futile. Of course, he and Martha would return in good health. One had to believe it was so. Faith had fueled the family for years now and only grown in the last months. Any other alternative was unthinkable.

When she felt Josef's hand on her shoulder, Margarete raised her head. Her father's expression was somewhere between a frown and a smile. He seemed to want to reassure her, but he was too worried himself.

She choked on her words as she struggled to hold back tears. "I'll come visit you and Martha in the hospital as soon as we're settled."

"Danke." His half-smile disappeared, and his gaze became direct. "Trust in God, and take care of your mother and sister for me."

Josef's order was like those he had often given to Paul in the last year, but now Paul was gone. Given her mother's health and Paul's disappearance, family responsibilities would now all fall on her. She straightened her stance, not wanting to fail her father.

"I will, Papa. I will."

CHAPTER THIRTY

MARGARETE

Margarete struggled to keep her balance on the icy snow on her way to the hospital. Wearing two different shoes made for difficult walking in the best of circumstances; in the January snow, it was treacherous. The deeper patches provided surer footing, but the loose snow seeped into the wooden clog on her right foot. The hard driven areas were layered with ice, causing her left foot to slide around the better one of her father's old boots. Made by a fine bootmaker in Allenstein, the footwear was built to withstand an East Prussian winter, as was Josef's coat, which cloaked her from the elements.

Margarete had balked at taking her father's things, but the nurse at the hospital insisted. She relinquished, saying, "I'll give them back when he needs them again." The nurse replied with a skeptical nod.

When she arrived back at the farmhouse that they shared with two other families, Margarete presumed her mother would question what she was wearing. She walked inside their room and saw nothing had changed since she'd left in the morning. Dorothea lay on straw, clutching Katharina to her side as they huddled together near the tiled stove. Their coats and weathered blankets covered them.

For a moment, Dorothea's eyes quickened when she noticed her daughter wearing her husband's attire. Margarete hoped for accusatory questions as to why she would ever take something from her father. She would have welcomed a muttering by her mother about how only the lowliest of peasants wore wooden shoes. It would mean part of her old self was still alive.

Instead, Dorothea's alertness dissipated, and she asked her usual, assuming question, "He is doing better?"

"Yes, Mutti," Margarete answered as she rubbed her hands together over the fire. "Papa slept most of the day, and Martha is now strong enough to sit up."

Dorothea closed her eyes, accepting the information with no further questions.

The truth was Josef hadn't improved. From the moment he'd arrived at the hospital, the warm bed and clean sheets seemed to beckon him back to the past. He hadn't even acknowledged Margarete. With his eyes closed, he muttered beneath his breath, lost in his subconscious. He no longer existed as an invalid refugee in a hospital on an island seven hundred kilometers away from his homeland. He was in Guttstadt in the same robust form of his old life.

He spoke in snippets as if he were on the farm, seeing to his horses and crops and spending time with his family. In his dream state, everyone was still alive. He argued with Paul, talked crops with Stefan, corrected Albert's posture, chided Franz for his vanity, and coddled Margarete and her younger sisters. He spoke to Dorothea about mundane things with loving endearments that Margarete had never been privy to hear. He even called out to his old farmhands and petted Senta.

His conversations were so real that Margarete felt she was

there as well. On the lonely walk home, tears spilled down her cheeks as she worried for her poor father and grieved the life they had lost.

At times his dreams were of the war and the flight. His whole body tensed in agitation, thrashing about the bed. Margarete became frightened and tried to calm him, but he couldn't be brought out of his troubles. He whimpered for his dead children and cursed the Russians, Hitler, and the Nazi Party.

Once he called out "But I am the Ortsbauernführer!" Margarete's heart cringed with a desolate embarrassment, praying none of the nurses or doctors had heard his wail. She would always be proud of her father. He was the hero of her family, and in Guttstadt, people considered him the best of men. The Reich had recruited him to be the Ortsbauernführer because he was respected by the community. But after months of rape, starvation, and forced servitude, Margarete understood what her parents had known from the beginning—being a Nazi was nothing to be proud of. The Nazis had practiced a discriminatory hatred that once unleashed destroyed indiscriminately, including her family and homeland.

When Margarete arrived at the hospital that January morning, she began her visit as usual by checking in on Martha. The regular meals had nourished her sister and healed her wounds. Each day Martha was closer to her cheery normal self.

After they had exchanged greetings, Martha said, "I'm worried about Papa. I can usually hear him speaking, but I'm not sure if he's awoken at all today."

Margarete promised to report back after she saw him. She ventured down the antiseptic white hall, keeping her eyes straight ahead to avoid looking into the rooms. She wanted to give the other patients privacy, but she also didn't want to draw attention to herself. She was filthy compared to the clean hospital. When she walked on the streets, most people ignored her. She was just another of the millions of outcasts barely alive. The lack of attention made her plight easier. Inside the hospital, the diagnostic glare of the nurses was trained upon her; the humiliation was acute.

Margarete knocked as she crossed the threshold. "Papa?"

She entered the room that held nothing but a bed, a chair, and Josef. He lay on his back, prone and in a deep slumber. The only noise was the throaty air he took in and expelled through his mouth. At his sides, his arms rested with fists half-clenched on the thick wool blanket.

As she took a seat, the chair cracked and creaked, but Josef didn't stir. She stared at him, hoping that his eyes might flicker open and they might share some connection. His smile had always soothed her heart, assuring her things weren't so bad.

A half hour passed, and Margarete feared he may not wake and he wouldn't know she had visited that day. She clasped his hand with its cold, rough skin.

"Papa, it's Margarete. I've come to visit you."

Willing him to revive, she stared at his closed eyes and rubbed his hand. The friction between his aged, gaunt skin and her overworked palms brought a warmth to them both. After some time, his lips began to silently move.

"Are you saying something, Papa?"

"He said we're from a land that no longer exists," he whispered.

Margarete lurched forward, eager to grab any conversation she could from him. "Who said that?"

"The Russian major."

Dwelling on the loss of their homeland and family devolved into doom. It was a wretched way to spend the short time she had with him, and it couldn't be good for his health.

"Mutti and Katharina send their love," she said. "Martha is doing better."

His eyelids twitched and then sprang open, focusing like a beam into her own as he asked, "How can land not exist?"

"I don't know," she fumbled, trying to find some purchase for the question.

Based on the devastation they had seen in every town they traveled through, Guttstadt most likely didn't exist as it did in their memories. She prayed that the Poles who had remained on the farm were safe and had saved Senta. The buildings might stand. Then again, it was a Nazi's home. It could have been burned with every animal or person killed.

"But how?" Josef strained to ask. "How can land not exist? Land is God's, not man's."

Realizing she couldn't escape the conversation—especially when he spoke so rarely, Margarete resorted to simple facts. "Of course, Guttstadt still exists."

Iconic images of the Ermland came to mind, and she spoke aloud as she saw them. "The hills, the lakes, the trees are still there. Storks fly over the countryside and roost in the tower. They will always be there, even if we aren't."

Josef's eyes stayed steady on Margarete, while she held her breath unsure how he would react. Slowly, his eyes closed as he mumbled a prayer, ending with "Amen."

He fell asleep, looking peaceful, though his rattly breathing continued. After an hour of examining his still frame, she resigned herself to the fact that would be the end of their connection for the day. As she rose from the unstable chair, the wood creaked again.

Josef's head twitched at the noise, and Margarete regretted waking him. She didn't want him to become anxious again.

"You should rest, Papa," she said, touching his hand. "Goodbye."

His eyes lifted for a mere moment, not meeting hers or registering where he was. "I must see to the horses," he announced through another ragged breath.

She smiled while his eyes shut as he returned to another world.

Late the next morning, Margarete dragged two branches through the snow, leaving a ragged path in her wake. It was her job to collect the day's firewood, which was hard to come by. With so many people scavenging trees for fuel, she had to stand on her tiptoes to hack away at the higher limbs. The branches were too large to carry, so her only choice was to drag them.

When she rounded the corner of the house, she startled at the sight of a horse munching on a patch of grass peeking out of the snow and a man knocking on the front door.

"Frau Dorothea Haupt?" he shouted, as his knock changed to a bang against the wood.

While his voice was authoritative, he wore no uniform, and his short, well-fed body indicated a man who had avoided the worst of the war. His German carried the local accent. Margarete wasn't afraid of him, but his presence was ominous nonetheless.

Dropping the limb with a thud, her voice held a timbre of trepidation. "Dorothea Haupt is my mother. I'm Margarete Haupt. May I help you?"

The man turned to Margarete with eyes practiced in snap judgments about someone's honesty. Her ragamuffin appearance made a bad impression.

"I must deliver this to Frau Haupt herself."

As he withdrew an envelope from his coat pocket, Margarete's heart clenched. A lone man delivering a thin envelope was a messenger of death. Someone had died. At once, she knew it was her father, but she quickly lied to herself, declaring in her mind that it was news of Paul, Stefan, or Albert. The family assumed they had perished. This was just a letter about someone who was already dead to them.

A rustling came from the other side of the door, and it slowly drew open. Dorothea propped herself up by balancing between the doorknob and jamb. Despite her frailty, she found her imperious voice to inform this mere deliveryman that she didn't appreciate his banging.

"I am Dorothea Haupt. What is it?"

Extending the envelope to her, the man matched her clipped tone. "A letter from the hospital for you."

Dorothea's hand trembled as she took the letter, with the shaking becoming more pronounced as she opened it. Margarete held her breath, denying what she knew to be true. She wishfully hoped Dorothea would announce Martha was to be released and Margarete should fetch her at once.

But Dorothea stared at the page far too long for its short paragraph. The messenger had already mounted his horse and tipped his hat to Margarete, but Margarete dared not ask her mother what she was reading. The word "no" defiantly welled up inside Margarete, but she remained quiet, waiting for her mother to speak.

Dorothea didn't turn to her daughter. She lifted her eyes from the paper, only to stare straight ahead. Her voice broke as she whispered, "Your father has died."

"No!" shouted Margarete—as if she hadn't presumed the worst, as if she hadn't seen her father's decline. She was almost eighteen and had endured horrible times, but her father's death reduced her to a young child. She felt the agony as if she was ten years old. "No! Not Papa!"

Desperate for consolation, she rushed to her mother to hug her, crying, "Oh, Mutti, not Papa. Not Papa."

Dorothea raised a hand to hold her back. Margarete stopped, her hands falling to her side. Her mother wouldn't want a public display. Her mother never even liked private displays. Her father was the affectionate parent. Josef was the one who consoled and encouraged Margarete. He explained the world when it made no sense and smoothed things over when it was harsh. Dorothea's hand didn't touch her, but it was a slap in the face. The comfort of her father was forever gone in Margarete's life.

Still not looking directly at Margarete, Dorothea shifted her head to address her. Margarete could see the tears standing in her mother's eyes. She would shed them at some point but not then.

Dorothea spoke in a brittle whisper, "Go to the hospital. Find a priest."

"And I'll find someone to fetch you and Katharina."

"Nein."

"But Mutti..." Margarete gasped. "You're sick. The snow is deep in some places. You can't walk into town. I'll find a way to get you there."

Dorothea didn't answer. She stared ahead and blinked, trying to rid herself of her tears. After a moment, she met Margarete's pleading gaze with a cold, direct one. "We aren't well. We will pray here."

Margarete caught her breath as she recognized her mother was avoiding her father's funeral. Shouldn't she want to be at her husband's side when he was buried? Wasn't it her duty?

All her life, Margarete had seen her mother as an indomitable person. Despite her anguished loss, Dorothea stood resolutely at all the masses said for her dead sons. She made sure Sophia died with a dignity denied others. She repeatedly threw her own body to the Russian soldiers, trying to save Margarete from rape. Yet burying her husband proved to be the one tragedy Dorothea could not bear.

Margarete felt that the weight of the burden of burying her father now rested solely on her. She would have to bury and grieve her father for the entire family. The husband and father of eight would go to his grave with only a single child at his side.

Margarete didn't believe she could withstand it either. "I can't—"

"The priest will help you." Dorothea clutched her shawl more tightly and looked up to the gray sky. Without turning to Margarete, she declared, "You should go now. It may snow."

As Margarete stepped out of the hospital, the wind whipped around her, slicing through the barrier of her father's coat. She looked again at the little map a nurse had drawn for her. One X marked the old rectory where the sole Catholic priest in the area resided, and another X marked the cemetery where her father's body had already been taken.

Placing the map back in her right pocket, she withdrew the lump that another nurse had slipped into her left pocket. She unfolded a pair of worn woolen mittens and a hard roll. The kindness touched her to tears, but she stuffed her emotions inside. She had cried for most of the long walk into town, but after telling Martha of their heartbreak, she'd kept her grief at bay. She had to make sure her father was given a proper funeral.

When she arrived at the small house, she took a steadying breath and pulled out of her other pocket the prayerbook her father had found. This priest was her only hope because it was a Protestant town. Otherwise, she would have to read the prayers for the dead herself.

After her quick knock, a tall man appeared dressed in a priestly black suit with collar. His face was wizened with lines, and his shoulders stooped, indicating at his prime he had been even taller.

"Ja?" he said as his white wooly eyebrows fixed together upon fully seeing Margarete.

"Father Wagner?" she ventured.

"Ja?"

"Guten Tag, Father Wagner. My name is Margarete Haupt. My father, Josef Haupt, has died. I was told you might be able to come to his graveside."

Father Wagner studied her for a moment. She wasn't sure what he was seeing. The boot and wooden clog? The man's coat? The snow caked to her kerchief? Then she saw his eyes rest on the Catholic prayer book in her hand—the one her father had found at the displaced persons camp.

He opened the door wider with a gracious sweep of his hand. "Please come in."

"Danke," she said walking into the dark foyer.

As he closed the door behind her, he said, "My child, I'm very sorry. Where is your family from?"

"Guttstadt in East Prussia."

The priest's mouth set into a grim smile. Margarete didn't expect much more conversation. Most of the locals had no interest in poor refugees from the East crowding their towns, and they certainly didn't want to hear eastern tales of woe after they themselves had survived years of British and American bombing.

"And your father is your only family?" asked the priest.

"My youngest sister is still in the hospital. My mother is with my other sister. We've been placed in a room outside of Karnitz."

"That's not so far. I could arrange for someone to get them."

"They're too sick." Guilt and regret washed over her. She had just lied to a priest for the first time in her life, and the lie she perpetuated had come from her mother. It was a sin, but explaining the situation seemed impossible without exposing her mother to criticism.

"I'm sorry. These are hard times," he replied as his white brows softened. "But one day God will wipe every tear from your eyes."

Her voice choked, so she only nodded, willing herself not to shed the tears that were ready to spill.

Snow continued to fall as they made their way to the cemetery. Father Wagner asked questions about Josef—his full name, age, family, and occupation. He didn't pry too much about the lives they had left behind or the family members who were no longer with them. He did ask when they had left Guttstadt, which made Margarete realize that they had left exactly one year and two days before. A single year away from their old life had been enough for her father.

When they arrived at the cemetery, the gravediggers leaned on their shovels, sharing a cigarette. They were rough, dirty men back from the war and unhappy, now forced to dig graves in the frozen ground. To one side of them, an oblong hole opened in the ground; to the other side a large wooden trough sat full of straw.

It took a moment for Margarete to realize that the trough was a rudimentary coffin without a lid, and her father lay underneath the straw.

Father Wagner wasted no time and began the funeral rites as soon as they reached the empty grave. Margarete mumbled amen and blessed herself at the appropriate times, but her mind was focused on her father's coffin. This couldn't possibly be his burial.

There should have been a choral Mass with every pew filled with those who knew him well and those who only knew his good reputation. His coffin should have been finely polished, with brass fittings. Paul, Franz, Stefan, and Albert should have been his pallbearers, resting the coffin on their shoulders as they brought Josef's body into the Guttstadt Dom.

Instead, the gravediggers lifted the undignified trough and opened one end. Josef's corpse and its shroud of straw slid into the grave. After Father Wagner said more prayers to end the burial, Margarete stood motionless as the gravediggers filled the hole, finishing her father's life on earth.

She startled when he placed a hand on her shoulder. "Please give your mother my condolences. I'll see to it that a cross is placed on the grave."

"Danke."

She assumed that he would then say goodbye, but the priest lowered his head to see into her eyes. She steeled herself for his parting words.

"My child. I know this is difficult, but have faith. God has been with you on your journey here. Look how far you've come."

Margarete nodded. The family had lived off of faith and gratitude for the last year, but at that moment, they gave little sustenance. Josef always reminded them that God was with them. Even Paul with his dim view of the world would always say things could be worse. She thought of the torture that poor Helene endured—a dead father, a brutal rape, and her own death. That was worse. Now with her stalwart father gone, Margarete was sure she had entered her own worst of times.

Father Wagner smiled with encouragement. "Your father will rest in peace knowing he has such a brave daughter to take care of his family."

Margarete was sure he didn't understand her situation. She felt no confidence or triumphant spirit, only cowardice and shame.

"I don't think I'm very brave," she admitted.

"You may not feel it, but courage comes simply from taking another step forward—for yourself and for others—when times are difficult. Bravery is simply the choice to act."

Margarete nodded, though she still disagreed. She avoided considering her circumstances before she acted because the emotions were too much to bear. In every awful event that had befallen her, there was no choice but to endure it. Life was happening to her, around her, but she had no agency. Just as she was an observer of tragedy befalling others, she had become an observer of her own life. It was the only way to protect her soul and her mind. It was the only way to continue to live.

CHAPTER THIRTY-ONE

MARGARETE

After her father's death, Margarete stopped keeping track of the days. Since they had left Guttstadt, every day was a day further away from home and into increasing tragedies. Each seemed impossible to outdo, but losing her father felt like the beginning of the end of her own life. Time had moved beyond the possibility of happiness and lost all consequence.

She was growing accustomed to Josef's general absence, but her heart ached more missing his guidance and love. She felt closer to him when she visited his grave. Father Wagner had kept his promise and erected a marker at the head of the mound of dirt. The crude cross memorialized her father with lettering burned into the wood: "Here rests in God Josef Haupt." In the deep of winter, wildflowers weren't an option to brighten the plot, but she straightened the cross and kept it clear of ice and snow, so it wasn't lost in a blizzard.

Josef had kept the family together physically and emotionally, united by his love and strength. Even if Dorothea had been healthy, her husband's calming wisdom and affection weren't in her nature. In her current state—sick, starved, and distraught over the deaths of her husband and children, Dorothea was incapable of comfort. Margarete, Martha, and Katharina were left to grieve alone.

The date on the calendar was also irrelevant with death hounding them. Martha remained at the hospital, while Katharina continued to lie immobile on the floor. So starved, it was a chore for her to get to a chamber pot. As Margarete was still the healthiest, she fended for the family's survival. Every minute was a battle to keep the family alive.

In the morning, her muscles and bones ached from months of hunger and another poor night's sleep. A single room in a farmhouse was more humane than crowded Luftwaffe barracks, but with a broken window covered in cardboard, frigid air seeped inside. There was no furniture, and scattered hay was their only insulation from the cold floorboards.

After she found the day's firewood, Margarete remained on the floor with her mother and Katharina staring at the stove. Starvation had settled in, leaving her with no energy to spare. Unnecessary movements were impossible when her body ate itself in search of food. With her stick figure, men now left her alone, so she no longer feared being raped. She was just another living corpse people ignored as they lived with their own troubles.

As they lay staring at the tiled stove, there was scant conversation other than prayer. They prayed for the repose of the souls of their family and gratitude for their own lives. And they always thanked God for keeping them together.

During each long, dull day, Margarete stayed on edge. The war had taught her tragedy was a possibility at any point, and certain during a downward spiral. Her family was too cold, too sick, and with too little food to survive for long. Death had picked off the Haupts one by one, so Margarete was sure it lurked nearby. It was only a question of whom it might claim next.

When Martha returned from the hospital, Margarete realized how badly off they were. It was a joyous day when Martha was dropped off at their door. Their little sister was cheery and healthy, the sisters were reunited, and Dorothea had the remainder of her flock back together again. Martha had gained weight and strength while in the hospital. The nurses had even cut her curly black hair back into its bouncing bob, which set off her rosy cheeks.

While Martha looked like her old self, the rest of the family no longer resembled themselves. Margarete compared Martha's rounder cheeks to the dark hollows of Katharina's face, and it was clear the eleven-year-old now weighed more than Katharina, three years her senior. Margarete worried that Martha might relapse without the food from the hospital, but there was no extra food to offer her.

The Russian authorities distributed a weekly piddling ration to each of the families. Every Wednesday, Margarete joined other refugees and ventured out to pick up their families' small sack of flour and a mealy potato or two. As the winter wore on, the trips became increasingly hard for her. She could still walk, but exhaustion quickly chased her down. Knowing food was at the end of the trip kept her going.

She also enjoyed listening to the rumors she heard on the outings because without her father and Paul, she had lost all information. Dorothea hardly spoke to anyone, so Margarete only learned what she could glean from listening to others' conversations.

Near the time of Margarete's eighteenth birthday in early March, the hardship and monotony began to thaw. There were rumblings that the refugees would be moved from Rügen to elsewhere in Germany. Even if they would never return to their own home again, every refugee wanted off the tiny island so far removed from the rest of the country. On Rügen, they couldn't begin the impossible task of locating any missing loved ones who might be alive. Moreover, if they were moved to another part of

Germany, they could find a job in a city or an idle plot of land to work. They were still self-sufficient people, not institutionalized inmates, and they wanted to rule their own lives again.

With Germany divided among the Russians, British, French, and Americans, it was a roulette wheel of fortune where one might end up. After a year of rape, beatings, deportations, and death by their worst enemy, the refugees were desperate to land with the British or the Americans or even the French. Before the war, most Germans had immigrated to Great Britain and the United States. Only Communists ever risked immigrating to Russia and its eternal poverty. Relocation to the British or American zones meant they could rebuild their lives in Germany without the fear of deportation to a Siberian workcamp.

One day in the middle of March, Margarete walked back from the ration distribution with her neighbor, Herr Dargel. Originally from Allenstein, he was a grandfatherly man whose entire family had perished. Having heard Margarete was taking care of her mother and sisters, Herr Dargel tried to lessen her burdens. If he begged for a slice of bread at a farmer's house, he would always pass her half, and he entertained her with the stories and jokes of a sweet old man.

That day, everyone was in higher spirits because the Russians had distributed more food than usual. It was the third week in a row that each family received more potatoes and flour, and this time it was even more than the previous week. Having had so little food for so long, Margarete thought she was bringing home a feast.

She carried the food in a bag slung across her back, but the extra weight made walking even harder for her. Each exhausted footstep she placed in the spring mucky snow was harder to execute than the one before. She focused on watching first the wooden clog moving in front of her and then her father's boot taking her one step farther.

Herr Dargel offered to lighten Margarete's load, but she maintained she could go on. She tried to distract herself from her weariness by asking, "Herr Dargel, why do you think the Russians are giving us more food?"

"After months of starving us, it does seem odd."

"I was curious if there was a reason," she said, catching her breath. "They've never been generous before."

"I've been mulling that over, myself. Perhaps it has to do with the rumors about moving us to other parts of Germany. Russia is a poor country. Maybe they've received food from the British or the Americans."

"Do the British and the Americans care about German civilians?"

"More than the Russians," answered the old man. He looked over his shoulder as his breath vaporized into the cold air. His craggy face deepened with concern. "Margarete, are you well?"

"I'm fine," she answered, forcing the words out of her mouth because in truth she felt light headed. "But maybe we could stop for a moment?"

———

The sheets were clean but threadbare. The wool blankets were warm but moth eaten. The mattress was supportive but musty. The bed's metal springs sank in the middle, but sleeping off the floor made Margarete feel like a queen. Only someone on the cusp of death would take such pleasure in those bare comforts.

She arrived at the hospital on the back of a farmer's wagon, which Herr Dagel had waved down while she still lay in the mud. He didn't have the strength to prop her up. She remembered the farmer helping Herr Dagel push her onto the wagon's bed where she rolled onto her side, nestling into fresh hay. Alongside her, two cages of geese squawked at her as if they asked her to release them. Their squawks brought her back to semiconsciousness for a few moments, sending her thoughts back to home.

Geese honked as they flew over the lakes around the farm. A trussed goose stuffed with apples roasted in the oven. Paul's and

Albert's voices joked about Dorothea's special geese to pay for her new wallpaper. Josef tossed the coveted wallpaper onto the giant heap of discarded belongings before they crossed the Frisches Haff.

The dark vision of the Frisches Haff frightened her into consciousness, and she opened her eyes to blue sky directly above her. The scent of fresh hay reminded her of where she was, and she looked at the geese who had given up squawking at her. Thankfully, she was far away from the Frisches Haff, but the memories from that point to the present day were none she wanted to revisit. Fearing what she might remember next, she tried to keep her eyes open, but the rocking of the wagon sent her back into blackness.

At the hospital, Margarete woke again as they placed her on a stretcher, though she was still dazed. From her time visiting her father and sister, the nurses all knew her well, and they seemed disappointed to be seeing her. Yet they soon smiled and handled her like a life-size doll, depositing her in a room near those Martha and her father had occupied. After stripping her of her filthy clothes, they helped her into a hospital gown while they gave her a bed bath, checked her vital signs, and spoon-fed her a hearty broth.

When she leaned back onto the bed, she also succumbed to the same call of comfort that had transported Josef away from the hospital and into the ease of sleep. She flicked her eyes open for a moment to acknowledge the doctor who had arrived, but she fell back asleep because his poking and prodding was painful and the conversation was too confusing. He spoke with the nurses about rheumatic fever, an enlarged liver, and jaundice.

Who was this person they were talking about? It couldn't be her. She didn't have a fever. She wasn't even sure where her liver was, but she was sure she would feel it if it was larger than usual. And she couldn't be jaundiced. She remembered her grandfather's yellow skin when he was dying of liver cancer. She hadn't seen herself in a mirror in months, but someone would have told her if she looked yellow, wouldn't they?

So she slept, and like her father, it was far more comfortable to return to their happy life in their Heimat than the hopeless half-existence since they had left. She hated when the nurses turned her body or forced medicine and broth down her throat, but at least they were kind and encouraging and didn't judge her like the doctors. She sensed the doctors looming over her with disapproval just because she lay there—as if she represented everything that was wrong in the world.

The neverland of sleep was a much better place. There were no worries about her mother and sisters. There was no grief for her dead father and siblings. She could just exist without pain or fear. After a time, she thought she might like to stay there permanently.

Chapter Thirty-Two

Margarete

As the nurses and doctors seemed to fret over her more, Margarete responded with no reaction at all. Deep in the blackness, at first she failed to recognize a new presence in her room.

There was a familiar comfort to the presence, though, that reached her when no one else could. She thought she must be in church again in Guttstadt. She smelled holy oil on her forehead and heard prayers in Latin. Was she being confirmed again?

After the presence left, she returned to the deep sleep, but when it returned, her conscious stirred. Latin prayers set her at ease, and she began to feel that a man was holding her hand. His skin was papery and cold, but it was his laugh that brought her fully back to the present day.

A rough, distinguished voice spoke with a chuckle, "I see you know your Latin."

She fluttered open her eyes and first wondered why Father

Schmidt was sitting next to her and why he had grown so old.

"Guten Morgen," the grandfatherly priest said, rubbing her hand.

Even sitting in a chair, the man was tall, and after a few blinks, Margarete recognized him. "Father Wagner?"

"Ja. I'm so glad to see you again. I had some hope when you began to recite the prayers with me. Your Latin is very good."

"Danke," Margarete managed to say as she took in her surroundings. She was now back in her current life with all its pain and suffering, and she remembered one duty given to her by her father. Margarete must take care of her family, but she had not followed his instructions. She had abandoned them when her mother was incapable of caring for herself or children. She jumped to the logical, terrifying outcome and spoke in a rush.

"Is my mother alive? Are my sisters?"

"Of course, she's alive—as are your sisters. I'm here because of your mother." He raised a brow. "Would you like to hear her letter to me?"

First relief and then surprise came over Margarete. She stared at the man for a moment because she couldn't believe her mother still had the wits or physical ability to write a letter. She wasn't sure if she could bear hearing her mother's words when Dorothea was in such a diminished state.

"Don't worry." He smiled and took a folded piece of paper out of his pocket.

Though the paper was worn and the script was in pencil, Margarete saw it was in Dorothea's exacting penmanship.

He cleared his throat and spoke as if he was beginning a sermon.

Liebe Father Wagner,

Thank you for all of your help with the burial of my beloved husband, Josef Haupt, and for your kindness to our daughter, Margarete. Unfortunately, she is now in the hospital

and very ill. You must go visit her and perform the holy
sacrament of unction. I am sure God has a plan for her and
he wants her to live.
Another child of mine will not die from this cruel war.
Please inform me of how she is doing as soon as you see her.

Vielen Dank,
Dorothea Haupt

Margarete's throat began to close in tearful joy. At least part of
Dorothea was back to her old self. For the first time in her life,
Margarete considered her mother as a person. The family had
often thought Dorothea delusional to the point of stupid, but
there was a strength about her actions. And in her most dire
moment—she threw her own body to the Russians trying to
preserve her daughters' lives.

As her throat choked, Margarete felt a tear trickle down her
cheek at her mother's words. In Dorothea's somewhat selfish but
always all-seeing way, she had said she loved Margarete.

Father Wagner smiled and clutched her hand again. "I have to
say that after reading your mother's letter I felt like I had been
directed by God himself to see you."

Margarete found a weak smile and nodded. "She has that
effect on people."

"She must be a formidable mother." He squeezed her hand.
"But she loves you, and she's right. God does have a plan for you."

Unable to hold the kind man's gaze, Margarete cried in silence
and looked to the ceiling. A plan? What kind of heavenly plan
began with such cruelty and desperation? She didn't see any plan
at all.

A month later, the wagon wobbled Margarete as it rocked up and
down the muddy ruts of spring. The pockmarked roads made for

a boneshaking journey. Margarete thought she could make the trip herself on foot, but the nurses had paid a farmer chocolate to give her a ride back to her family. After a month in the hospital, she swayed in the back of the wagon, studying how spring had transformed the island. She had only seen a view of a road in town from the window in the hospital. In the countryside, green had begun to dot the branches of leafless trees, and wildflowers proclaimed the end of winter.

Only a kilometer away, she told the farmer she would walk the rest of the way. The happy flowers proved too tempting. They were the perfect gift, and the only one she could afford. She felt indebted to Herr Dargel for finding a transport for her to the hospital, and her mother loved flowers.

No one from the family had visited her while she was at the hospital. She asked the nurses if they knew how her family was doing. The nurses shrugged and said they had sent word to her mother of her condition, and if the family had problems, the nurses or Father Wagner would know of it. Margarete assumed that was true. Anyone sick enough would end up at the hospital with her, and she was sure Herr Dargel would help the family get their rations.

Yet, when she arrived back at the house with flowers in hand, she braced herself for the scene she would see. She assumed the door would open, and nothing would have changed. Her mother and sisters would still be lying on the floor, unable to move.

When she entered the room, her mouth dropped open before it melted into a smile. The room was the same spartan old farmhouse, but her family had changed. She first saw Martha hadn't lost her health since returning to the squalor of refugee life. She sat with her legs crossed, holding a bowl of soup, which she sipped with a smile blooming beneath her rosy cheeks. Remarkably, Katharina sat upright. While her legs were scarred and her body thin, renewed energy seemed to course through her as she whispered to Martha, seeming to share a joke.

Overseeing the two girls, Dorothea stood with her hands on

her hips. Her hair was tidier, and a ragged triangle of cloth fashioned an apron about her waist, keeping her dirty dress from getting any dirtier. She was still far too thin, but the wounds on her legs were closing. Without Margarete as a crutch, she appeared to have taken over her rightful role as leader of this new entirely female family.

Dorothea proved she was back to her old self, as she issued commands. "Katharina, eat your dinner. Remember your table manners. You'll eat again at a table one day, and you're too old to behave like a child at a meal. Martha, sit up straight. You look like a lazy farmhand."

Disbelieving what she saw, Margarete peeped from the door, "Mutti?"

"Margarete!" screeched the girls from the floor.

Dorothea snapped her head to the doorway. With a relieved smile, her hands went to her heart, and she exhaled with relief. "Margarete, you're home. Gott sei Dank."

"I'm home." Margarete extended one of her bouquets. "I brought these for you. I have another for Herr Dargel for seeing me to the hospital."

As her little sisters clamored over her and she returned their hugs, Dorothea stared at the bouquet now in her hands. When she raised her head, she whispered, "Danke, Margarete. Danke."

Margarete's eyes widened in wonder as she studied her mother's face. It held the same expression that had been reserved for her brothers when they had returned from war. Dorothea Haupt wasn't an imperial lady then; she was a mother, releasing months of worry and immersing herself in relief, gratitude, and pride. Margarete felt she was the joy in her mother's heart.

In April, Easter arrived. The previous Easter had been spent hiding from the cruelty of Russian soldiers, so they didn't attend church. In the displaced persons camp barracks, Christmas had been marked by only a few prayers and songs. A short time later, Josef had died. Yet, despite all the harrowing events since the flight, Easter in 1946 had a feeling of rebirth and renewal.

But nothing was like the Easters of the past. There was no Gründonnerstagskringel on Maundy Thursday, and there were no brothers to fight for a share of the cake. There were no new dresses for church on Easter Sunday or goose for Easter dinner. There was no carriage drive to the great Guttstadt Dom—just the quaint church of Saint Boniface, where they arrived by foot over many kilometers. Yet the resurrection of Christ was celebrated by the priest's gospel of hope and a thunderous organ, proving that God's word and music were eternal.

Margarete brought up the rear as her mother marched her line of three daughters out of the church. Dorothea was proud of her brood, as clean and pressed as their circumstances would allow. Their shabby clothes still hung from their thin frames, scabies scars remained all over their bodies and faces, but their short hair was brushed neatly. Dorothea led them out of the church with her usual air—admired by all, especially herself.

After Mass, the church had arranged for cake and lemonade for the children, and the adults were given coffee and tea. While her sisters enjoyed their treats with other girls their age, Margarete stayed with the adults. The talk among the churchgoers was the relocation plans for the refugees to other parts of Germany. Margarete overheard someone say that the authorities would send refugees to relatives if the family members lived within the new borders of Germany. If not, they would pick a location for you.

While others spoke of their relatives around Germany, Dorothea remained quiet. Margarete knew her mother had distant family in Dortmund, but she doubted Dorothea would ever leave the island with Josef's grave. Margarete couldn't even imagine asking such a question of her.

The following day on their visit to their father's grave, Katharina and Martha asked the question instead. Despite the modest cross, Josef's grave was as attractive as those nearby with ornate gravestones like the one that would have stood over his grave in Guttstadt. Dorothea laid weekly wildflowers and had even dug up bulbs and flowering plants and planted them around the site. If she couldn't erect a fine tombstone recognizing her husband's life, she would show the world in plants what a revered man he was.

That day, after they had gardened and said their prayers at the grave, they stared in silence at the cross with Josef's name. Katharina broke the quiet scene and turned to Dorothea.

"Mutti, when the other refugees leave, might we move to Garz so we can be closer to Papa?"

"Nein," Dorothea answered with a tilt of her head. "We'll be leaving Rügen as well."

"We will?" asked Martha. A panic rose in her voice. "But we can't leave Papa."

Margarete watched in a pleased silence as her sisters discovered all the answers.

Dorothea's expression hardened for a moment, and her voice was firm. "We will not leave Papa any more than we have left Sophia or your brothers." She made the sign of the cross before she continued, "They're in Heaven with God. They have eternal life and will always be with us wherever we are."

The three girls had wide eyes, and Margarete decided it was time for her to ask a question.

"Where will we go, Mutti?"

"Dortmund. My Teschner cousins live there. They're a big family. Some of them must have survived. We may even be able to live with them."

"We still have family?" asked Katharina incredulously. "I thought we were all alone."

A sigh escaped Dorothea, and her eyes softened. With an emotional voice she rarely displayed, she replied, "We still have family. We don't know whom. We don't know where they are. But we do have family living somewhere."

CHAPTER THIRTY-THREE

MARGARETE

As the family walked to the Samtens train station to leave the island, Margarete sensed something had changed within them and most in her mother. There were more smiles, fewer rebukes, and a sense of optimism—even eager excitement—feelings they had forgotten for the last two years. To an outsider, they had little to be optimistic about. They were four females facing the world alone except for the clothes on their backs and a crushed suitcase.

Margarete carried the suitcase the three miles to the train station. It wasn't heavy, but her palms sweated in the hot sun, so she switched hands often along the way. She didn't complain. They had been told that it would take an entire day before they reached the Friedland transit camp. There, they would first have to register, and doctors would make sure they were healthy enough to move on. Living again in close quarters with hundreds of people wasn't appealing, but the Friedland camp offered something they hadn't heard in months—new information.

The Red Cross had a search service to locate lost family. Other refugees had said that the Friedland camp brought together so many people that often you could hear news about loved ones or reports from your hometown.

Neither Dorothea nor Margarete expected to hear anything about Paul or Albert, and they had little hope for good news about Guttstadt or their farm. Still, it would be a joy to hear that distant family and friends from the Ermland had survived the war.

At the train station, long queues formed for tickets. The Red Cross workers sat at tables passing out papers that granted the refugees transport to their new location. Guarding the perimeter of the platz, Russian soldiers strolled along, bored as usual with their refugee duties. Even with all the pain she had endured from them, Margarete knew that many were like the kind ones they had met. She could imagine that they, too, wanted a train ticket off of Rügen. They had also lost family and towns; somewhere there was a new life for them as well.

While Katharina and Martha found girls their age to talk to, Margarete waited in line with Dorothea. She noticed that when some people left the tables with their papers they shook their heads or even argued with the authorities. She hoped Dorothea wouldn't cause a scene that might force them to stay on Rügen.

When their turn arrived, Dorothea marched up to the table, announced her name and those of her children, and declared, "We're registered to travel to Dortmund today."

The young man with the Red Cross armband trailed his finger down the page, looking for their names. As his head rose, he spoke in a Swiss German accent, "Actually, you'll be going to Friedland transit camp first and then to a town called Hannoversch-Münden. It's not far from Göttingen."

Margarete looked at her mother, whose annoyance was already apparent. Dorothea stood a fraction of a centimeter taller, and her hooded eyes lowered with disdain.

"I'm sorry, young man," said Dorothea, giving the worker a *pro forma* apology. "But we're traveling to Dortmund. I have cousins there."

"That may have been what you requested. My apologies, but that can't be accommodated," answered the Swiss in a voice of practiced firm compassion.

"Why not?" Dorothea replied as the woman she once was— one whose wishes were always met.

While Dorothea's anger was rising, the man became even calmer. He rested his arms on the table and leaned closer, his icy blue eyes matching his soothing voice. "Frau Haupt, I'm sorry, but Dortmund has had significant destruction. The authorities will only send a limited number into the area."

With narrowing eyes, Dorothea snapped, "My family should be part of that number. I overheard the gentleman before me being told that he was going to Essen, which isn't so far from Dortmund. Why is he allowed to go to his chosen destination and my family is not?"

"The authorities are also redistributing the population."

"What does that mean?" asked Dorothea, taking a step backward.

"They want to settle refugees around the country—not only in major cities. Also, Catholics are being sent to traditionally Protestant areas, while Protestants are being sent to Catholic regions."

"What on earth for?"

"To make society more homogenous. To learn to accept other people different from ourselves." The Swiss man's lips twitched, making Margarete think that he knew Dorothea had no interest in learning to accept others.

"Ach du lieber Himmel! That's ridiculous." Dorothea glanced around her and gestured to the people around her whom she had no interest in knowing. "Whoever would want that?"

"If you don't like Hannoversch-Münden, we could send you some place farther east. There's space there."

Margarete jerked in surprise as a male voice whispered in her ear, "Excuse me, Fräulein."

She turned to see an older man near Josef's age, tipping his hat to her.

"Don't let them send you to the East. You'll stay under the Russians there. Hannoversch-Münden is in the British zone like Dortmund."

"Danke," she said as the man walked away. Margarete looked up, saw a Russian soldier smoking a cigarette, and immediately tugged on her mother's sleeve.

"Mutti," she whispered in her ear. "Hannoversch-Münden is in the British zone like Dortmund. Some place east would be in the Russian zone."

"Fine," Dorothea snapped before she scowled at the kindly Swiss man. "We'll travel to Hannoversch-Münden and then move to Dortmund."

While her mother and sisters fell asleep on the long train ride, Margarete stayed awake. The towns and landscapes that sped by her window were all new to her. Cities she had only ever heard of like Hamburg and Hannover didn't live up to her past imagination due to the scars of war, but in the bright sunshine, black sarcophaguses of ruined buildings showed promise for a future. When they switched trains in Hannover, Margarete left her family to search for a shorter toilet line. She promised Dorothea she would make it to the right platform for their next train. Just in those few minutes as she easily navigated a big city train station, Margarete remembered the independent young woman she had been in Königsberg before the bombing, before they fled Guttstadt. Maybe she could be that person again, she thought.

But their first destination, the Friedland transit camp, was nothing like an exciting city. A sprawling compound of low-slung, long buildings and hut-like structures, the transit camp had been built in the fall of 1945 by the British army to process displaced persons. At first, Jewish people liberated from the hell of Nazi concentration camps, Ostarbeiter, and Russian POWs had been processed and sent on to their futures. By June 1946, millions of refugees from Germany's easternmost provinces had arrived at Friedland, followed by the first of the two million German POWs still alive in Russia.

The two days they spent at the camp were a blur of activity shrouded in a haze of DDT delousing powder. The barracks were laid out in a half circle on the ground. The bunk beds were an improvement from a hard floor; the food was simple but more plentiful than they'd had in over a year. The camp was staffed by British soldiers, the Red Cross, and British and German charities and volunteers. Despite the thousands of people and enormous operation, Margarete felt at ease there because no one spoke Russian or Polish, and she soon realized it was simply because she understood both languages being spoken. Her younger sisters had less schooling in English, and Dorothea knew almost none, so Margarete acted as an interpreter.

When they weren't standing in long lines for new identity cards, refugee cards, and food ration coupons, they were poked, prodded, and powdered as nurses made sure they were healthy. Delousing was frequent. The workers used a handheld pump to spray powder all over their hair and down the back and front of their dresses. After the first delousing, Margarete was handed a pair of shoes.

Tears pooled in Margarete's eyes as she looked at the sturdy shoes. The leather was creased and marked with wear, but they were a fine pair of ladies' oxfords. She hadn't worn a pair of matched shoes for a year. Looking up she first saw a large cross hanging on a silver chain around the woman's neck and over her black habit. When she met the woman's kind brown eyes, Margarete was sure she was an angel and not an elderly nun.

"Thank you, Sister," said Margarete in English. "The shoes are wonderful."

"You're welcome," the nun replied in a sunny voice. "Your English is good."

Margarete tilted her hand back and forth. "I know a little."

"That's wonderful. It will be helpful for you."

It was on the first round of visits to the nurse that Katharina was diagnosed with a mild case of tuberculosis. The nurses all said it was a miracle that the whole family didn't have it.

"She'll need to go to hospital immediately," said one British nurse. She turned and called over her shoulder, "Put this one on the bus to the sanatorium."

Before Margarete could even translate, the nurse called out, "Next patient."

Dorothea shot back in a fierce voice, "Nein."

Margarete looked at her mother glaring at the no-nonsense nurse and saw two women unused to having their authority questioned. Fearing an international incident, Margarete stepped closer to the nurse. "Pardon, but my mother would like the family to stay together. We're all she has now. Could my sister go to the hospital this afternoon when we travel to Hannoversch-Münden?"

"Fine." Not wanting to spend any more time on a single patient, the nurse turned away. "Next."

All around the camp were large official notices, titled *Deutsches Rote Kreuz Suchdienst*, with lists of names and sometimes photos of missing people. Not satisfied with the official Red Cross tracing system, refugees had created their own billboards plastered with photographs and names of loved ones they had lost during the war. Any inkling of information was appreciated. Margarete, Katharina, and Martha were drawn to the photographs. They knew none of the people, yet they all seemed familiar—like friends and family. Dorothea refused to look at the photographs. Margarete understood why. Many were handsome, uniformed young men in the prime of their lives, and none would be Paul, Franz, Stefan, or Albert.

Masses of people swirled around the camp, and Margarete was

intrigued by them all. There were city folk in once fine clothes and peasants—some even in traditional dress. Many people appeared to be in worse physical shape than the Haupts, while others seemed to have had better luck during the war. One little girl caught Margarete's eye. While the rest of her family dressed in drab grays and browns, no doubt shaded partly by dirt, the little girl wore a red, black, and white dress. The white was dingy now, but Margarete imagined it a stark white at one time. She couldn't understand why the dress was so familiar until she recognized it for what it once had been—a Nazi flag. No one would dare display a Nazi flag now, but Margarete guessed if your daughter had no clothes and you had no money for material, the flag of horror would have to do.

Empty buses continuously arrived at Friedland, while packed buses quickly departed. As Margarete boarded the bus with her family, excitement burst in her heart again as it had on the train to Friedland. They weren't returning home, but they were going to a home. Margarete wasn't going back to her old life, but she would be arriving into a new one.

The twenty-five-minute trip to Hannoversch-Münden wound through a dense forest, which seemed endless before it opened up to a beautiful valley with a confluence of rivers, the Fulda and the Werra, which merged and created the Weser. People in the camp said that the Hannoversch-Münden had been spared by bombs and battle. Even Dorothea was impressed with the medieval, timbered buildings set along the rushing rivers.

When they arrived in town and stepped onto the platz, Margarete was surprised to see a group of people waiting for the bus. Names were shouted from the crowd, and in the distance "Bitte, Frau Haupt!" could be heard.

Dorothea waved her hand, and a portly gentleman in a rumpled suit approached the family. After a quick bow, he introduced himself as Gerald Menzel, the local butcher.

"Willkommen to Hannoversch-Münden, or Münden as we

locals call it." He gestured behind him. "My family will be hosting yours in a room in our home until you get on your feet."

Dorothea thanked Herr Menzel and introduced him to Margarete and Martha, explaining that Katharina would arrive in a few weeks. While she spoke, a woman appeared before her.

"Excuse me, Madam," said the squat woman with cheery cheeks. "I'm Frau Bernard. I own a restaurant not far from here—"

"It's quite beautiful," interrupted Herr Menzel. "Up high on a hill with a view of the Fulda."

"Danke," said Frau Bernard, smiling at the man. She turned to Dorothea and motioned to Margarete. "I see you have a strong daughter. I need more help at the restaurant. I would provide food and board and a little pay. She would live in a room with three other girls her age."

Before Dorothea could say no, Margarete piped up, "I would like that a great deal, Frau Bernard."

Dorothea peered at Margarete, unamused by her forwardness, but Margarete met her gaze, holding her ground. She was eighteen now, and it was time for her independence. Dorothea considered her for a moment, and Margarete silently willed her mother to agree if only for the money she could bring to the family.

Dorothea turned to Frau Bernard. "Danke for the generous offer. I believe that will be a fine situation for Margarete, and this way, we will be less of a burden on Herr Menzel."

For the summer, Margarete worked for Frau Bernard. The restaurant was in a lovely spot with food that nourished her and interesting patrons from all over Germany. While the days were long with little free time and she missed her family, she hadn't felt closer to herself in years. The comradery with young women her own age reminded her of school in Königsberg, and the time away from her family gave her a reprieve from being the dutiful older sister. The shared room was cramped, but to Margarete a real mattress and indoor plumbing made it a palace.

In the autumn, Katharina returned healthy from the sanatorium, and the whole family came together again. Dorothea approached the city for more living space, and they received two rooms above a café along the Werra. Small and spare, the rooms were their own, and the family was reunited.

While Katharina and Martha were back in school, Dorothea found the only work she thought suitable for herself—taking in piecework sewing for a local lampshade business. This way she didn't have to mingle with others. Her belief was that she wouldn't have deigned to be friends with these people before the war, so why should she befriend them now?

Margarete sewed in the lampshade factory and did small jobs for bartered supplies like furniture and cookery. With precious pennies, they sometimes splurged on a real treat—a trip to the cinema to see a film.

The winter of 1946 was a hard, hungry time. When there was no coal for cooking, Margarete would follow the rest of the poor in town to the train station to steal from an unattended pile. Food was scarce, and Margarete and Katharina begged local farmers for scraps. When the café's endearing mascot, a German shepherd named Schatz, went missing, everyone knew she wasn't lost. She'd been stolen and eaten.

Yet, despite the hunger and poverty, it was obvious their situation had improved. The Catholic church in town was small, but the congregation was welcoming. To be able to attend a Christmas Mass and sing the old songs was a joy to their world. Life would never be the same, but it would be new.

CHAPTER THIRTY-FOUR

MARGARETE

The noise in the café below their rooms was a reliable alarm clock for Margarete. She had learned the schedule of the town by the activity beneath their floors. In the morning, as the voices below started to increase, it signaled that Münden had come alive.

"I know it's raining, Katharina, but you must go to the store before it gets too busy. We need butter," said Margarete, as she wiped dry the breakfast dishes. "Martha went the last time, and I have to work at the Kochs' house soon."

Fifteen-year-old Katharina slouched in a chair as she stared through the window at the pouring rain. "I'm going to wait just a little longer. I think it might stop."

Still moving in her rocking chair, Dorothea looked up from her lightning-fast knitting and spoke without dropping a purl. "Listen to your sister, Katharina."

"If you don't go now," said Martha with her attention on

washing dishes, "Margarete will take the umbrella, and you'll get wet."

"All right," groaned Katharina. Having only one umbrella annoyed them all, yet Katharina still didn't move from the window. "There's a man limping down the street in the rain. He doesn't have an umbrella either."

Margarete was ready to nag again, but Katharina sighed and took a step away from the window. Before she turned, she leaned toward the window as if she had seen something new.

"Really, Katharina," said Margarete, throwing the dishtowel over her shoulder. "The weather won't change, so—"

"No... yes," said Katharina one after the other under her breath. Her voice became shrill and quick. "Yes, it is! It's Paul!"

"What?!" called Martha.

Margarete looked at once to her mother, whose head jerked up from her knitting. When their eyes met, anxious hope flashed across Dorothea face before it disappeared into resignation.

"Katharina," Margarete said with hushed disapproval. "You don't joke about that."

"But it is!" Katharina ran to the door and swung it open. There was no one outside the door, but she still called out, "Paul!"

Even though the family had never heard any evidence about Paul's whereabouts, something struck Margarete at that moment. Her heart thumped with the surety that Paul was outside the door just as Katharina said. She glanced again at Dorothea, who was frozen in disbelief—not knitting, not moving—her eyes on the doorway.

As Margarete and Martha raced to the door, Paul's voice boomed from below. "Give me a minute, sister. These stairs are hard for a pegleg."

All three sisters crammed onto the tiny landing with only a small portico to shield them from the rain. They shouted his name, while Paul carefully made his way up the wet stairs, placing his prosthesis on each next step. Margarete noticed he had put on weight since they last saw each other on the road outside of Stolp.

He wasn't yet his burly old self, but he had fared better since he had left the family.

When he arrived on the landing, his sisters smothered him with hugs and left tears on his drenched raincoat. He would have lost his balance had they not all been propping him up. He kissed the tops of their heads and mussed their hair like they were puppies.

"I finally find you, and my little sisters have all become young women," said Paul, beaming at his siblings. "It's good that I'm back to beat away the boys."

"Don't worry. We have Mutti to scare away any boys," said Katharina.

Martha giggled. "Mutti scares away everyone!"

"Come in, come in," said Margarete. "Mutti is right here."

Noticing Katharina's comment, Paul looked Margarete in the eye and asked in a quiet voice, "And where is Papa? Did he make it here?"

Margarete's smile vanished. "No. Not Papa."

Paul nodded grimly. "That's what I thought."

Margarete took his hand and led him inside, telling him to watch his head as he entered the small room. All four children looked to Dorothea, who now stood near the dining table, her hands clasped in anticipation. She drifted her eyes in inspection from his hat to his shoes, confirming it was indeed her son. With one hand clenched around a handkerchief, she made the sign of the cross. "Gott sei Dank."

"Ja, Gott sei Dank," repeated Paul, as he took off his hat.

Dorothea moved in an uncharacteristic, undignified skip to clutch Paul's arms. "My Paul. My son. God has brought you back to me."

"God had must have played a part." Paul chuckled. "I couldn't have made it here on my own."

Margarete begged off work that day so she could spend time with her brother. The Koch family understood. Doorstep reunions with the dead were common in postwar Germany, but they were still miracles that needed to be properly honored. It wasn't every day that a family member came back to life.

Sitting in their motley collection of furniture, Paul told his tales of outrunning and outsmarting the Russian army. "I pretended to be almost dead, and it worked. Eventually, I made it to Dessau and into the American zone."

"What did you do then?" asked Martha, sitting at his feet on a stool and hanging on his every word.

"I moved deeper into the American zone. I ended up in Kassel where I met a locksmith at a pub. I told him I was good with locks, so he hired me. He pays me mostly with room and board, but as a disabled veteran I also get a stipend from the provisional government. There's an engineering school in Dortmund that I've heard of. I hope to go there in the autumn."

"You always were so handy with mechanical things," said Dorothea, still at a loss that her eldest son was before her.

When it was their turn to tell the family's story on Rügen, Margarete narrated an edited version for Paul. There was no reason to relive all the trauma at once. She soon learned Paul also wanted to limit the emotional toll of living with the past.

After a joyful but simple meal, the family took advantage of a break in the rain and stepped out to show Paul the town. Along the bridge, Paul walked even slower than usual, peering into the river as he motioned for Margarete to join him.

"I've waited to ask until we were alone," he said while leaning against the railing. "Has there been any word about my little brother?"

Margarete noticed how Paul couldn't bring himself to say Albert's name. With her own emotions brimming, she couldn't either.

"No." She turned to the river and looked at the green trees lining its banks. "Mutti recently had a mass said for him."

Paul made the sign of the cross as he stared at the river as well. "I always said it was foolish to think Albert was alive, but in my heart, I still hoped."

"We all did," Margarete said, her voice faltering at the end. She waited a moment to calm herself. "But Mutti said it was time."

"Mutti was right." After a moment, he touched Margarete's shoulder. As if he realized he might be turning maudlin, he gave her a cheeky smile, "It's not often I say that. It's a good thing our brothers aren't around to hear it."

Margarete wiped the tear that had started to roll down her cheek and smiled, wanting to join him in the humor. "Oh, they know. They're in heaven laughing at you right now."

After hours of conversation and another meal, Paul said he needed to return home but would visit tomorrow.

"But before I leave, I have something for you, Mutti."

"That is kind of you, Paul," said Dorothea. "But your presence here brings me more joy than any gift."

"It's not a gift," said Paul with a sly smile. He reached into his pocket and pulled out the black velvet bag that Margarete hadn't seen since that day in Pomerania. He opened it and removed a small red box. "I'm returning something that's yours."

Margarete noticed the gold lettering on the ring box and turned to her mother. Dorothea stared at the little box, her mouth open as if she had seen a second ghost that day.

"It's your ring from Papa, Mutti," said Martha, as if it needed explaining.

"I'm sorry I ended up taking the jewelry and watches with me," said Paul. "But you know it was safer in my leg than with you. Ivan would have found it anywhere else."

He handed the box to Dorothea, who remained speechless. Everyone watched her shaking fingers open the box to reveal the three-diamond ring that Josef had given her so long ago. Her hair was now mostly gray, but her expression was childlike, staring in wonder at the ring.

Margarete felt her throat tighten as tears threatened to spill from her eyes. She saw the ring as her mother did. Dorothea was now an impoverished widow of fifty-four with three daughters living in two rooms above a café. The ring was tangible proof of a previous, privileged life with a beloved husband who had worshiped her and their eight children.

Feeling all of her father's love, Margarete couldn't hold back her tears any longer. Her sisters started to cry as well. Before anyone could reach her with a hug, Dorothea tucked the box in a pocket and slipped into the bedroom without a word.

After the doorknob clicked, Paul let out a long sigh. "I know the ring is sentimental, but Papa was a practical man." He looked around the small room that was both kitchen, dining, living, and bedroom over the course of the day. "You could sell that ring and have a much easier time of it."

Margarete laughed softly through her tears. "Mutti will never sell her ring."

Paul shook his head with a smile. "No, she won't."

A few months later, Margarete gripped her secondhand pocketbook as she waited in the employment agency. She sat in a small office with stacks of files on every available space, though the walls were bare. Only a calendar partially covered a rectangle of brighter paint where a photo of Hitler once most likely hung. The secretary told her that Frau Frederica Peter would be with her shortly.

Paul had hectored her to get a real job from the day he arrived on their doorstep.

"Why are you sewing and cleaning toilets?" he would say. "You're educated. You shouldn't be a maid."

"But who would hire me? And to do what? I'm not that educated."

"I don't know, but someone would and the pay would have to be better."

A potential increase in pay made Margarete brave the employment office. Just in the few minutes she sat in Frau Peter's office, she had already decided it was a mistake. Observing the secretary,

Margarete could tell she wasn't qualified to do any of her work—from typing to shorthand to ordering people around.

When Frau Peter appeared, Margarete stood and greeted the stylish woman. She wore her blond hair in a pixie cut, and her red lipstick matched her red fingernails. Peering down her long nose at Margarete, she sighed. "Another one."

"Pardon?" Margarete looked down at her best dress, which wasn't fancy, but she looked respectable.

"Never mind. I'm always able to place people, no matter how unskilled," Frau Peter said with a wave of her hand as she sat at her desk. She peered at Margarete's application form. "So you've been a maid, a waitress, and a seamstress."

"Since we arrived here, and I've done only a little sewing. I wouldn't call myself a seamstress. In Königsberg, I—"

"I don't need to hear about Königsberg," Frau Peter replied with a roll of the eye. "Finding something for you won't be difficult. I can always place a domestic. You don't need to sew if you can cook." She shifted her eyes warily. "You do cook?"

"A little."

Frau Peter frowned. "Cooking is expected in better-paying domestic work."

Margarete shrugged, which caused Frau Peter's frown to deepen, as she continued, "Can't cook. Doesn't sew... Can you type?"

"No."

"You can read and write, can't you?" Frau Peter asked, tapping her pencil in further annoyance.

Margarete pointed to the paper in her hand. "I completed the application myself."

"Hmm," said Frau Peter, unimpressed.

Margarete felt her own frustration rise. Her father's belief in education and her mother's ingrained self-respect dwelled inside her as well. Frau Peter didn't know her character—how she was raised, what she had endured just to be sitting before her today. Who was this woman to assume so little of her? Channeling

Dorothea's disdainful pride, she spoke with her mother's cutting tone. "Obviously, I wasn't raised to be a servant. I graduated from high school, and I read and write three languages."

"Oh, really?" asked Frau Peter, leaning toward her as if she caught a glimpse of something worthy in her. "German and what else?"

"English and Latin. I also speak a little French."

"Now that changes everything. But you still can't type. That's too bad, but it's easy enough to learn for someone so literate." Frau Peter studied the ceiling as if she was combing through mental files. After a moment, she said, "Latin. English. The university. They might be able to use you."

Frau Peter reached over to a folder and rifled through the papers. After a minute, she raised a form and declared, "I think I have it, but first, how do you like the outdoors and nature?"

"I love it. In Guttstadt, I grew up on a large estate and we—"

"I don't need to hear any more. You'll do fine," Frau Peter said, holding up her hand. "It's a research technician apprenticeship in the Department of Entomology at the University of Göttingen. The position is with the forestry faculty here in Münden."

Margarete sat back, astounded at the suggestion. A soft giggle escaped, as she said, "Me? A scientist?"

"Why not?" Frau Peter raised her eyebrows. "You're not saying you're too good for it, are you?"

"No! Not at all. I simply never thought I would do anything like that."

"Well, what did you think you would do with your life?"

Frau Peter sat back in her chair, crossing her arms. This was a professional woman who expected other women to have considered their options in life as well. Yet, Margarete never had. Frau Peter repeatedly had said she didn't want to hear about East Prussia, but Margarete couldn't answer her question without reverting back to the only life she had known. It was the only life her mother, her grandmother, or any of her female ancestors going back to the dawn of time had ever known.

"In East Prussia, I would marry a farmer. We'd have a large family, and I'd help him manage the farm."

"Well, I suppose you could go find a local farmer here, but why? That life can be over for you. It's over for hundreds of millions of women around the world." The surly woman gave her a genuine grin. "Now, you can be a scientist."

With a file folder in hand, Margarete walked back to the apartment. Frau Peter instructed her to complete the paperwork before her first day at the university the following Monday. Margarete couldn't believe that she—a farmer's daughter— might have a career in science. She looked around the quaint, timbered buildings in town, reminding her of what a different life she now lived from how she had grown-up. The strife, loss, and struggles of the war would never be forgotten, but she realized that horrible, terrible war had brought her to this opportunity.

In the meantime, she would have to tell her mother just what sort of job she had been given. Dorothea hated that her daughters worked at all, but she might consider a job at a university too worldly for Margarete who was just nineteen—even if it did pay a bit better than being a nanny.

Both Katharina and Martha were still at school, so only Dorothea was at home when Margarete arrived. Elbows deep in suds, Dorothea stood at the sink working one of Martha's dresses over the washboard.

After Margarete said hello, Dorothea returned the greeting by asking, "Well, how was it?"

"Good," Margarete said, placing the file on the table. "They believe they've found a position for me."

Stopping the washing, Dorothea took the towel she had

thrown over her shoulder and dried her hands. "That's wonderful. What kind of family?"

"It's not with a family."

"If it's a café, I will want to meet the owners."

"No." Margarete took a seat in front of the file, and she remembered how pleased Frau Peter had been for her. She realized that she shouldn't feel awkward. She should be proud that her accomplishments allowed her to be considered for such a position. "It's an apprenticeship."

"An apprenticeship?" Dorothea's eyes widened before they narrowed with disdain. "It is one thing for my daughter to have to work odd jobs in order for us to survive, but you will not take on an apprenticeship to become a menial laborer like a baker for the rest of your life. It is entirely beneath your station."

Margarete had rarely questioned her mother or even raised her voice to her, but at that moment, Margarete would do the unthinkable and laugh at her. Giggles erupted as she looked around the tiny apartment. It wasn't even as spacious or nice as the workers' housing on the farm. "My station?" she exclaimed.

"Yes, your station." Dorothea's ire grew with veins bulging from her neck. "You will only meet poor, uneducated men, if you find any man at all."

Margarete couldn't stop her giggling which only irritated her mother more. "Margarete, this is serious," Dorothea decreed.

"I'm sorry, Mutti," Margarete said, clutching her chest to stop laughing. "I've given you the wrong impression."

"Well, then what do you mean?"

"It's an apprenticeship at the Department of Entomology at the University of Göttingen. I would be working as a laboratory technician with the forestry professors here in Münden."

The tension eased in Dorothea's expression as she took in what Margarete's explanation. When Dorothea spoke, her voice was cautious. "Entomology? You would be studying—"

"Insects...I suppose, but maybe trees? I don't know. I start on Monday."

"And you would be working with professors?"

"I believe so. I'm supposed to meet with Professor Schaefer at nine in the morning."

"Well, an apprenticeship at a university is entirely different. Why didn't you say so?"

"It's still just an apprenticeship, Mutti."

"Ah," Dorothea lifted her finger and smiled. "But this an apprenticeship at a university with educated, professional men. They might even be intellectual bluebloods who have land— that's why they're studying insects. You could find a good husband there."

Margarete looked to the ceiling, stopping herself from rolling her eyes. "I'm nineteen. I don't want a husband."

"Maybe not at the moment, but you will. And you'll have children."

"At the employment agency, Frau Peter said that life is over for women. Women can do anything now."

"Frau Peter has no idea what she's talking about." Dorothea tossed the towel back over her shoulder and went back to the sink. "And she probably can't find a husband, or she wouldn't be working at an employment agency."

Thinking of the chic Frau Peter, Margarete restrained herself from again laughing at her mother. She eagerly opened the file folder as a distraction, but she couldn't stop smiling. The world would change; Dorothea Haupt would not.

CHAPTER THIRTY-FIVE

ALBERT

"Raus!" Albert jerked awake, flinching to attention into an unknown world. He registered that he was on a train again and had been told to get out. While the order was given in German, it was missing a Russian accent. He turned to see who gave the order, still expecting to see a Soviet soldier. Instead, a train conductor's uniform sped down the aisle of the shiny refurbished car. The fresh lacquer's shine and odor reminded him of his surroundings. Since he had arrived in this new country, reconstruction was everywhere as Germans rebuilt their lives. Albert felt left behind.

Unaccustomed to electricity, he blinked into the bright lights and saw he was alone in the car. How could he have fallen asleep? He had planned to push his way to be the first to leave. He was home, or as close to it as he ever would be again. Home was far, far away; even farther was where he started his weeklong trip.

The first four days had been spent on the floor of a cattle car, rocked into an unconscious twilight between the refuge of sleep and the hell of wakefulness. Urine, vomit, feces, and sweat wafted throughout the train. Despite the human biology working around him, sometimes he forgot his own personhood—the man he was and the boy he had been. It was easier to be just another in a horde of foul humans, crammed into foul quarters. That train trip had been like so many he had taken in the last six years —the destination unknown. It didn't matter. It was always Siberia.

When the guards threw the daily bread into the car on the fourth day, he noticed they were all smiles and chatty with one another. More than once, he heard them say, "Moscow."

Rumors spread through his fellow prisoners, but they were conditioned for despair rather than hope. Yet Albert noticed inexplicable oddities. This journey wasn't a regular exchange of prisoners from camp to camp. At each stop, new inmates arrived, but none left. The strangest thing, though, was the train's direction. Albert was certain he hadn't been this far west in six years.

At a derelict train stop surrounded by a blank horizon of fallow farmland, the guards herded the prisoners from one train car to another. The men unfolded their bodies and stumbled out of the cars. Filthy and starved, they limped with battle and prison injuries. Like the others, Albert had begun his imprisonment as the healthiest, watching his wounded and sick comrades die in numbers too high to count and too heartbreaking to care. When releases began, the Soviets first sent home the weakest. Slave laborers who couldn't labor were worse than useless—they were a burden to be rid of.

Dazed by sunlight, the men found their orientation and fell into order. Caveman shoes of wood and cloth aided their hobbled gait. It was during those times of group movement that the men acted out their only defiance—the slow march. They formed perfect lines, their order of precedence decided by military rank for a country that no longer existed.

The Reich was defeated, Germany destroyed, and their pride vanquished, but centuries of military culture couldn't be eliminated. Whether they had once been a young Luftwaffe draftee, a career army officer, or an older veteran sent to the Volkssturm at the war's end, they were all German military men. They were nothing if not regimented and orderly.

The Soviet guards were lackadaisical, though they held no sympathy for their enemy. Their job was to control and herd the prisoners—not to keep them alive or show a whit of mercy. Germans had caused so many of their troubles.

A grisly Soviet waved them along toward the new cattle car. The rumpled tunic of his olive-brown uniform hung without its belt, and he leaned on the butt of his rifle. Bored by the whole production, he muttered, "Next stop for you, Warsaw, then Berlin —maybe West, maybe East."

Guards often played the cruelest jokes on the inmates, so the prisoners assumed they were being taunted. Returning to Germany had been a possibility, but Albert had learned early on that it wasn't worth hoping for. Death was a likelier outcome— just as it had befallen Major von Lehman. Unfazed by the guards, the prisoners continued walking in formation to the next train.

When the guard saw he was being ignored, he snorted. "It's true."

Wary from years of disappointment, few of the inmates would tempt a random beating for insolence and ask a question. Yet, Albert had seen the evidence that something about this trip was different. He glanced at the guard to acknowledge he had spoken.

"You're going home," the guard replied to Albert's silent question.

Still unable to believe his captor, he stole a look at the prisoner to his right. A rank above Albert, the first lieutenant's gaunt mouth gaped before it changed to a smile of disbelief.

Turning again to the guard, he saw the big Soviet glowering at the line of inmates as if he regretted being the bearer of good news to his enemy.

The guard met Albert's curious gaze and curled his lip into a sneer. "You don't deserve it."

When Albert arrived at the border between East and West Germany, he was sent across and processed at the Friedland transit center. There, hundreds of POWs looked as bad as him, many even worse. But now he was in a city train station, and a starved man in rags with cardboard shoes was an oddity. When he made eye contact with someone, they looked away at once. He hoped he wouldn't scare his mother as well, if indeed the Dorothea Haupt in Hannoversch-Münden was his mother. The Red Cross couldn't give him any other information. She might be the only living relative he had left, or she might be a stranger.

As he continued to walk through the town, he sensed it wasn't only his appearance or smell that made people shun him. The townspeople had all spent the last five years moving on from the war. Modern buildings were being built, and new, strange looking cars sped past him. Shops were stocked like when he was a child. While Germany tried to work away its shameful history, Albert was a ghostly reminder of the horrific past—like the war had never ended. For him it never had. He guessed it hadn't for them either, or they wouldn't be so reviled by him.

The Red Cross had given him a map and his mother's address. Walking through the streets, he saw the Catholic Church of Saint Michael. He hadn't been in a church in so long that he yearned to enter, but no. He didn't want to be a distraction to others during their prayers. He also needed to prepare himself for confession. It would take some time for him to have the strength to relieve himself of the weight on his soul.

From his estimation, he had another kilometer to reach Dorothea's flat. He admired the architecture and river as he continued to walk, but the frightened looks from strangers made him uneasy. He kept his head down until he stopped to check the map.

Confirming a street name, he saw out of the corner of his eye three women standing in front of a store window shopping. They registered with him because they were pretty and young, and until his arrival at Friedland, he hadn't seen many women in the last six years. As he placed the map back in his pocket, he heard a woman's laugh followed by a melodic voice.

Familiarity rang through him as he heard them all speak. It wasn't just the East Prussian accent that he hadn't heard in years; the voice itself was a forgotten sound. He raised his head again and stared at the women as they discussed the fashionable mannequins in the window. If only they would turn to him so he could see their faces.

Sensing she was watched, the woman with the voice looked over her shoulder, tilted her head in acknowledgment, and returned to her conversation with a confused expression.

"Margarete?" he mumbled, sure he was imagining her blue eyes and dark hair.

Her attention flashed straight at him. "Albert?"

As he nodded, she flew to him, and as she came closer, he realized he wasn't hallucinating. The grown woman running toward him was his little sister. His empty heart filled with the love for his family that had fueled him for years.

When she threw her arms around him, she almost toppled him over. "Oh, Albert, Albert. We thought—"

"I know." Tears overwhelmed him as he cried in her arms. "At times... I did, too."

ACKNOWLEDGMENTS

No one gets to choose their ancestors, but their family history still remains part of their identity. I couldn't have written this book without the help of my dear German cousin, Eva-Maria Will. Like me, she has worked to find some meaning to our family's experience. A theologian, art historian, writer, and explorer, her research, tracing of steps, and cultural insights have been invaluable. I thank her from the bottom of my heart for her contribution of work, conversation, and love.

This novel would really have told only one story of Guttstadt had I not found, David Lisbona, a descendent of one of the first Jewish families in Guttstadt and an armchair historian of Jews in East Prussia. David's mother left Guttstadt in the early 1930s before most of her friends and family were tortured and murdered in the Holocaust. Despite the betrayal of her German gentile neighbors, David recalls his mother always speaking fondly of her childhood in Guttstadt. My life is richer knowing David, and the book would be less authentic without him.

If you find yourself more interested in the history of the region, I suggest reading *The Death of East Prussia* by Peter B. Clark. Peter's meticulous work was a great assist, as was his encouragement.

So many people helped me bring *Good Town* to fruition. Thanks to you all because I'm sure I'll leave someone out. I'll start with: Anne Forlines, Carrie Engfer, Deena Metzger, Dominic Wakeford, Elizabeth De Vos, Laura Kellison, Laura Summa,

Laurie Wagner, Marion Gerlind, Martha Keely, Michael Ross, Susan Coventry, Theresa Lindburg, and the Wild Writing Family.

Finally, I'd like to acknowledge my family: my sisters, Jacque and Terry, who know my mother's story as well as me, and my beloved children, Nico and Anna. No Omi doted on her grandchildren more. To my husband and best friend, Drew Caputo, thank you for your love and support and for being a history nerd. My love for you goes to eleven.

ABOUT THE AUTHOR

Mary Louise Wells is a former environmental lawyer turned romance writer who for the last few years has focused on the research and writing of *Good Town*. Mary was born in the Midwest, raised in Texas, and now resides in northern California with her husband, two children, and their rescue dog.

Made in the USA
Monee, IL
23 July 2023

78b7d3d1-c73d-457e-a1fa-9fc450d2a30bR01